TASTE
AN EROTIC FANTASY SERIES

B. SHARISE MOORE

ILLUSTRATION BY - JAMES A. DAVIS III

TASTE

An Erotic Fantasy Series

Book I

By B. Sharise Moore

www.blaqmermaidpress.com • www.myspace.com/tastefantasyseries

Illustrations by James A. Davis III

Cover design by Tifany Jones for Zoe Lifestyle Co.

Cover Photograph by Raymond Henderson

Male Cover Model Marquette Shumate
For booking, email: marquette@dcemail.com

Headshot by Kuroji Ntu

Edited by Nathalie Legerwood

Layout/Design by Uraeus

Library of Congress Cataloguing-in-Publication Data

Moore, B. Sharise
    Taste: An Erotic Fantasy Series/ B. Sharise Moore-- 1st ed.
p. cm.

ISBN 978-1-60585-198-3

1. Fantasy--Fiction.   2. Erotica--Fiction.

First Edition: August 2008

Blaqmermaid Press

ACKNOWLEDGEMENTS

I must begin by thanking the Creator who has blessed me abundantly and those closest to this project: my mother and uncles for their unwavering support, my cousin Lynn for never ceasing to believe in my abilities, Osa, for reading the manuscript in its infant stages and encouraging me wholeheartedly, John for believing in me more than I ever believed in myself, Phil, the original inspiration for General Quince, Sonya Renee, the most talented sista on the planet, for her kudos and constructive critiques, and my editor Nathalie for her dedication, patience, and valuable insight. Abundant thanks to my layout/design editor Uraeus, my illustrator James "Jai" Davis III, my photographer Raymond Henderson, my cover and website designer Tifany Jones, and my cover model Marquette Shumate (rip the runway Quette!). To the authors who have inspired me over the years: Octavia E. Butler, Toni Morrison, L.A. Banks, Ntozake Shange, Sonya Sanchez, Tyehimba Jess, Victor Hernandez Cruz, Larry Neal, and J.K. Rowling. To Makeda, Doughboy, Simone, Zaz, Mieaha, Isaac, Hamilton, Kuroji, Baye, Damon, DuRon, Imara, Ahree, Richelle, Oshun, Shamel, Devan, Cody, 13, Kanikki, Auntie Suzanne, Lady Sunshine, Patty, Jay, Chance Hall, Michaelangelo 1906, and the countless Myspace friends who provided their kind words, constructive criticism, and/or marketing advice. To Milton Davis, Ronald T. Jones, Valjeanne Jeffers and everyone on www.BlackScienceFictionSociety. com, it's been a pleasure sharing and building creatively with you. Science Fiction and Fantasy Writers of Color UNITE! Thank you all!

The Island of Ido

TASTE

An Erotic Fantasy Series

BOOK I

CONTENTS

PROLOGUE

Beneath a sweltering noonday sun, the prickling sensation in her fingertips began to spread. Profuse sweating and violent hallucinations followed when the world around her swirled in the purplish haze of a narcotic high. Time slid to a sluggish halt the moment she closed her eyes, helplessly watching the blinding blue dance with screaming red behind her eyelids. Phase One of the shape-shift brought about a hurt so intense that all thought quickly became a dizzying distortion of memory. Painless movement was no longer an option. The splintering feel of tiny sand granules beneath her skin was an extrasensory nightmare. Simple breathing became a labor all its own; yet still she prepared for the inevitable wave of agony. The tortured moan never received the opportunity to escape her lips. A blistering surge below her navel descended through her large fin etched with thick, overlapping golden scales. She attempted to steady her shallow breaths when an oddly pitched tone joined the ringing in her ears. A horrid visual affirmed what she'd already known; she was ripping in two. White heat coursed through her thinly stretched veins while layers of skin pushed out of the scales in droves only to absorb them again and finally diffuse into dark brown pigment. Muscle enveloped itself over the soft cartilage now hardening into bone as joints slid and popped in place with an unknown precision.

Eyes closed tightly; no energy remained to watch the remainder of her transformation. She gagged on the acidic bile coating her tongue and attempted to home in on the song in the distance. Mental strength prevailed as her erratic breaths matched the melodious tune, riding it peacefully like the wind. Slowly her body's temperature lowered, stabilized, and cooled. Strands of wet hair clung to her cheeks, ears, and forehead, partially obstructing her view of the sea nearby. She fought to open her eyes. The familiar, five-foot wide golden-scaled fin was gone and a foreign pair of legs and feet had taken its place. Carefully, she turned her head, weakly lifting it just centimeters from the sunbathed beach. Peering cautiously into the blinding sunlight, she observed the countless bodies lying in recovery on the white sand. Clarity slowly penetrated her hazy thoughts; and from the looks of it, the others were just as out of sorts as she. Lying back down with a soft thud, she drifted. It was time to heal.

Part One
Of Things Forbidden

1

INCIDENT IN VINE CITY

It was early evening. The sunset wrapped its rays around a group of anxious women, their ebony, coffee, and chestnut hues blurred with the golden rays seeping through the translucent clouds above. Vine City, coveted for its unique beauty, brimmed with a mischievous allure while the waters of the Mer Sea lightly kissed the surrounding shore. From above, the small metropolis was a gathering of peaks stabbing unapologetically at the sky in declaration of its grandeur. The city's structures were sturdy and twisted like emerald webs forming triangular tents on the sand. The focus this evening; however, was the twenty-foot high canopy set closest to the sea enclosing one hundred male and female Youth inside.

Onya inhaled deeply before she and the others stepped onto an elevated platform beneath the canopy. The warmth of the sunlit planks beneath her feet triggered some calm amidst her pre-Rite jitters. She breathed out hard, her nerves like wet noodles sliding from a heaping spoon. Aware of the importance of first impressions, she pondered what awaited them on the opposite side of the large partition directly in front of her. The possibility of a thousand disapproving eyes, open and unimpressed flooded her mind. Tiny beads of perspiration gathered at her temples as she stood with the others, waiting for the vibrating gong that would determine the rest of their lives.

"Ready?" asked an upbeat voice at her side. "It's now or never… and you know what they say," the woman said with a playful nudge. "This is the hardest part anyway."

"I hope so Lyn." Onya sighed vehemently, raked her fingers through her long locs, and turned to face her longtime friend. "Before you know it, we'll be Elders ourselves."

"Yeah, but I plan on *really* enjoying the time leading up to that!" she responded slyly. Onya shook her head in agreement as her best friend added a facetious wink, tossed a few small, reddish brown braids over her bare shoulder, and adjusted her mask.

Lyn wasn't the only one looking forward to the onset of Taste, a cornerstone of Ido tradition for centuries, and here they were, teetering on the precipice of its arrival. Savoring the final moments of adolescence, Onya shut her eyes and allowed her memory to drift back to her upbringing in Nu.

The females and males were immediately separated after birth in preparation for the Mer to human transformation at age seven. Then, at opposite ends of the village, the Youth raised themselves. At age twenty-one, the sexes were intimately reintroduced during the sacred Warming Ceremony, a self-pleasuring gathering held two days before the sacred Rites of Taste.

It seemed it was only yesterday that she and her tandem of playmates had explored the endless beaches of coastline just outside the village. Stubborn shellfish, slippery emerald weeds, and the roaring surf had all been integral parts of their playground while the girls discovered the beauty of their surroundings. The corners of Onya's mouth upturned into a nostalgic smile as her memory jogged toward some of their interesting escapades on the outskirts of the dangerous jungles of Three Wood. Even then they had shown no fear. The daughter of perhaps the most prominent Ido Generals of all time, Onya had always been looked upon as a leader. Many assumed the trait had been embedded in her genes and it was certainly no surprise when she, along with close friends Eesha and Lyn, had been voted one of the three Generals of the female Youth. Together they formed a triad of feminine strength, cultivated intellect, and military expertise.

Like their male counterparts, the female Youth were trained in the Ido martial art of Bgongo as well as in the mastery of weaponry. The thick, solid muscles surrounded by less than twelve percent body fat were living proof of the grueling sessions she'd endured. Eyeno and Dame had been the Elder gurus in the martial arts back then and they'd trained the Youth well. The intermittent spells of guidance provided by the Enlightened Ones insured their self-sufficiency at an early age. Along with her Bgongo lessons, she fondly recalled the lectures introducing concepts of Enlightenment, Respect, and Mental Endurance afforded them by the Mer Ancestors and their visiting parents, now Elders residing in the Enlightened Lands. It was understood that Enlightenment was their ultimate goal, and Taste was the path they were required to travel in order to attain it.

Allowing the memories of her childhood to wash away, Onya breathed in deeply, glanced at her glistening mahogany skin one last time, and prepared for womanhood. Jaw set in a rigid line, she carefully gathered her fraying nerves and mentally stitched them into a solid seam. A shrill gong caused her pulse to quicken as she pulled a blue, beaded mask over her eyes. It was official. The ceremony had begun.

All at once the drumming took on a rich staccato. Obediently, the women's hips swayed in unison with the djembe. One by one they snaked around the tall divider and into the open space on the platform. In no time, the looming spectators in their wake released a collective breath of approval. On cue, the rhythm accelerated as the women began a sensually charged dance. Their torsos and extremities dipped inside the rhythm effortlessly, sliding through each individual tone like a smooth word oozing from the tongue.

Aside from the custom-made turquoise and silver jewelry, intricately beaded masks, matching waist-beads, and assorted pairs of calf-high vine boots (heeled shoes made from intersecting patterns of dyed vine), the female Youth were completely naked, their exposed breasts gleaming with scented Raha oil, a sweet perfume extracted from the trees of Three Wood. Each woman wore their tresses in a single braid to the middle of the spine, partially covering the large ceremonial tattoo etched between her shoulder blades. Much of the ceremony's allure involved pinpointing a potential preferred partner based upon initial impressions. Though the women made the final choice, it was an unspoken rule that the man they'd chosen would have to be in agreement.

Loose limbs displayed their flexibility, swinging, curling, and sashaying in time with the pulsing tune while the women swayed and looped their bodies in patient, fluid motions. As if under the influence of some preordained spell, the hands of time bent passively inside the canopy. Onya felt the moisture releasing gradually from her pores, her heartbeat mirroring the seductive rhythm. The quickness of her pulse carried her on an excited whim as she wound around the perimeter of the stage, eyes closed. A dull crescendo guided them into a single line in front of their audience, a throng of Ido males totally nude aside from the ceremonial chains around their necks and a beaded cloth sac enclosing their maleness. Onya noted that most of the sacs were now nearly bursting at the seams. She smiled inwardly with smug approval, her own concentration quickly shifting to arousal as they boldly approached the climactic finale.

Though nearly naked on an elevated platform in front of 50 pairs of eyes, Onya felt her inhibitions melting away like a single ice cube left in the blistering sunshine. Before her stood an endless field of broad shoulders, pulsing biceps, and glistening abdomens in every shade of brown imaginable.

Warm rays of goldenrod and tangerine drenched their skin, allowing hues ranging from hazelnut to midnight shimmer with a sun kissed sheen. It took everything in her not to stop short and gawk at the possibilities. Never before had she witnessed such unscathed beauty. Quietly, her eyes scoured the fine musculature and tapered waistlines that seemed to be sculpted from stone. Her nostrils flared gently while she attempted to inhale their collective strength through her nose and taste their anticipation on the tip of her tongue. Mesmerized, she wound her body in wide circles before lowering her gaze to the multitude of bulging silk sacs girding the males' heaving organs. The beat slowed. Simultaneously, they turned their backs to the audience, their round buttocks gleaming in the light of the setting sun. One by one, the women arched forward and stretched each hand to the platform below.

Peering through her open thighs into the crowd behind her, Onya gradually rose to her full height in time with the others. In unison, they turned forward, slowly, sensually. Falling to her knees, she caressed her thighs with intensity before lifting her fingers to the neatly trimmed V just below her waist beads. Careful to evoke the correct visual, the women threw their heads back as one. The djembes embraced a slow syncopation while they parted their moistened lips, gently rubbing the enlarged center peeking through a delta of fertile ground. Immediately, the males revealed rock hard shafts of all shades and sizes. Some stood erect at beautifully odd angles while others hung handsomely to mid-thigh. A minute few nearly kissed the knee. Instantly, they began stroking their hardened members in rhythmic time with the accompanying drums.

Enticed, the women responded accordingly. Onya drew her hands above her waist, locating a pair of erect nipples attached to a set of soft, small breasts. She held them delicately in her palms and caressed the stiff flesh in small semicircles while swinging her wide hips and ample buttocks boldly from side to side. Little by little, she felt a fierce confidence rising from within as she exhaled all that was feminine, sexy, and assertive.

Carefully she lifted her gaze and, within seconds, stood face to face with one of the most handsome men she'd ever seen. Her lashes fluttered as she attempted to mask her surprise. It was only a matter of time before the totality of his presence swallowed her whole. Mahogany skin reminiscent of royalty and stature set off perfectly sculpted features while a groomed mustache lined a set of full lips curved in an aroused smile. Glistening droplets of sweat gathered in the grooves of the eight ebony cinder blocks of his abdomen before sliding toward his narrow waist and thick, muscle-laden thighs. Noticing her sudden preoccupation, he paused and winked, a twinkle of interest glittering in the center of his deep brown eyes.

Tallish with short, dark hair thick with defining waves, the roiling fire in his gaze penetrated all of her defenses. The two exchanged an intense stare as he ran his tongue across his top lip with a deliberate passion. Onya felt her heartbeat skip while a brazen desire spread through her like a boundless combustible flame. With every fiber of her being, she wanted this man to want her. Never before had she witnessed such an epitome of perfection until now. In an instant, all thought evaporated into steam.

Suddenly gathering herself and taking care not to lose her concentration, she held his piercing gaze as it saturated her thrusting hips. In the meantime, she pulsated in time with the hypnotic drumming, moving as if she were in a trance-like state. She stretched her arms overhead and closed her eyes, an imprint of his profile tattooed beneath her eyelids. A broad smile spread across his face. Overcome with awe, she wondered if she'd ever experience anything more pleasurable than this moment. Their eyes locked again while her wandering index finger traveled back to her enlarged bud. His eyes followed obediently as if he were willing, no, *daring* her to climax. After a slight quiver, a tiny moan of exhilaration escaped from her mouth as she prepared to explode.

"Stop! I said stop!"

The dancing and drumming came to an awkward, screeching halt. Arms flailed and legs landed awkwardly on the wooden planks while heads swiveled wildly in the direction of the commotion. A few feet from where she stood, a strange man climbed through the large, door-like opening in the canopy of vines. His appearance was unlike any she'd ever seen. A hooded cloak concealed his entire body aside from the tangled mane framing his thin face. Hastily, the women covered their nude bodies as the men formed a protective barrier around them. In surprised confusion, they turned their attention toward the prominent Ido Elder at the stranger's side. According to tradition, interrupting the Warming Ceremony was forbidden, and allowing a foreigner in their midst was an unforgivable abomination. An angry hush fell over them as the Elder strode forward. Onya looked on in absolute shock. The man venturing to the center of the crowd was Dame, head of the Elder Ido Clan, and her father.

2

THE GUIDE

Vye had only been submerged for a few seconds and already Dame believed. Her appearance was almost angelic as the thin rays of morning shone through the crystal clear waters and zigzagged playfully across her golden skin. He'd always admired her courage, her ability to fight. They'd shared a mutual respect over the years while noticing one another from afar and recently they'd formed a friendship he sensed would flourish under the new Faith.

Nearly twenty seconds had passed, nevertheless, The Guide held her down firmly. Fully comprehending her need to be "cleansed", she did not struggle. The white cloth she wore billowed underwater, dancing like a large jellyfish swimming casually with its school. Moments later, her eyes opened and three large bubbles escaped from her nose. He released her as she emerged to the surface with a soft splash. The witnesses bowed their heads in silent prayer.

The Elder General glanced back at the vacated pyramid of vines before looking up in the direction of the salmon streaked sky. The weather today was tricky, unpredictable, and though clouds were absent, a light rain fell into the Mer Sea. This would not have been strange aside from the fact that it didn't rain on Ido except in the confines of the Rain Caves near the island's central core. Plant life found nourishment from plentiful underground lakes and streams while the various living creatures remained wholly dependent upon the Shine River, which, like a menacing blade, sliced the island in half.

There was something about the baptism, or *Wave's* ambiance that made Dame's otherwise machismo demeanor more subdued. He struggled to shield his eyes from the splatter of seawater as another believer plunged below the pristine waters. His eyes burned as he licked the salt from his lips. He turned and waded a short distance away from the shallow pool he and the other Elders were standing in, allowing his eyes to rest a bit and his lungs to fill with fresh air.

The seriousness of yesterday's decision weighed heavily on his heart and mind. Fairness had always been a major priority since he'd assumed the responsibility of General of the male Youth while at Nu and head of the Elder Clan since crossing into the Enlightened Lands. He recalled how ferocious his spirit had once been. Quick to anger and slow to compromise, he'd stolen respect rather than earned it. Dame was as impulsive as he was intimidating and standing at nearly seven feet, many joked that his massive biceps and muscular torso had been sculpted from the solid rock of Triple Peak in the Western territories.

Shamefully, he recalled how he'd enjoyed Taste twenty years before. Extremely attractive and gifted with charm, it had been easy for him to over indulge in the activities of the flesh for a large portion of his life. Not to mention, securing Imar, the most beautiful Ido woman at the time as his preferred partner had been the ultimate final frontier. Their union bore a daughter they named Onya who was as strong-willed as she was beautiful. He couldn't complain, however; she'd gotten the traits earnestly. He remembered her birth vividly. She'd entered the world fin first and swishing, a fighter from the start. He wondered what she was thinking after yesterday's jarring events. She could not have been happy. He'd seen the white flames of rebellion in her eyes after the interruption and his short speech. But surely she would see and accept The One Faith once she was exposed to The Guide, he was sure of it.

The stranger had appeared suddenly and without warning one day. Had he not been accompanied by Ankh, the leader of the Sphinx healers and longtime Elder ally, they may have been more skeptical. Speculation regarding his identity was immediate. It was apparent that he was not a member of the Ido clan or The Painted Folk, though he walked upright and held other human-like characteristics. The intrigue surrounding his origins along with the habit of covering himself from head to toe heightened their curiosities. Some suspected he was a leper. Others thought him to be an albino or a diseased outcast from another realm. Soon they began to address him as The Guide, a deformed messenger from another land who could perform faith based miracles in front of their very eyes.

Though forms of sorcery and magic were common on the island, only the seldom seen Djinn and Mer Ancestors held the ability to conjure in its purest form. Even the infinitely wise and immortal Painted Folk were held to certain limitations. Though the Ido were given the gift of transformation, their ability to shape-shift was beyond their control, occurring only at three specific intervals; first in the womb, then at age seven, and finally upon death. The Guide referred to his own abilities as miracles gifted him by an entity he called The One, an omnipresent God with a distinct wrath far greater than their Ancestors and an affinity for love spanning the length of the horizon.

The Guide's message had penetrated Dame's own hollow shell like a poison arrow piercing the heart of a worthy adversary and there was no turning back. Change is good, necessary, he told himself fervently. After witnessing the sheer power of the stranger along with his message, the Elders were convinced of the need for change. The final decision to abolish Taste, he was certain, had been the correct one. Still he wondered about the backlash. Would the Youth resist? Surely they would. How much time would pass before they took action? Should the Elder Army strike first? It would be an unorthodox move, yet a necessary one in order to ensure the spread of the Faith. They would all believe in the end.

He turned once more toward the gathering. The Guide was now opening the tattered scroll he'd conjured from a handful of glittering sand. He read carefully as he held it up to the light, ensuring his audience's comprehension of the sacred text. His voice shook with force and authority, yet somehow managed to lack intimidation. He was easy to listen to and even easier to trust. There had been a quiet confidence about him that Dame had respected since his arrival. He wasn't an overly assertive man, but the strength of his beliefs made him appear larger than life. The message he brought included the importance of moral discipline and the weakness of the flesh. The assembled believers hung on his every word until the last left his lips as he ushered the next devotee into the quiet waters. A massive wave of guilt flooded Dame as he listened from a distance. He was happy for the newfound hope and possibility of forgiveness brought to him by this man. Still unaccustomed to their new permission to show emotion, he swallowed his tears, inhaled deeply, pulled back his massive shoulders, and stood tall. Weeks ago, he'd been living in darkness, oblivious to the damning consequences of his desires and the traditions of his people. Now, he had been given the gift of eternal life, beyond Enlightenment and the confinements of Taste.

Out of the corner of his eye he spied a lurking shadow. Just as he'd expected, the Ancestors were joining the gathering. Swimming toward him was Born, leader of the Mer. Half men/women, half fish, the Mer were deceased Ido who'd passed through Taste, The Enlightened Lands, and the Afterlife. The Mer represented the cyclical existence of the Ido people. Everyone was born Mer before their human transformation and would become Mer again in the Afterlife.

"Is this he? Is this the man they call, The Guide?" asked Born in a thunderous voice as he drifted nearer.

"It is," Dame replied simply, deliberately avoiding the old Mer's eyes.

Born was everything The Guide was not: direct, domineering, and brutally frank. The Ancestors rarely spoke to the living except in the most urgent of situations. Having traveled beyond the boundaries of death, their powers were beyond limitation. Though they rarely exercised the right, an Ancestor could very well dispose of a life without explanation or consequence.

"I see it did not take much for you to turn your back on the ancient customs that were in place before your Ancestors' Ancestors inhabited these lands." He paused as if trying to choose his words correctly. "Tell me, what kind of leader leads his people away from the fabric of tradition and into the clutches of foreign ways? What kind of leader leads his people into an existence of thoughtless sheep?" he hissed in his ear. "Think!"

Slowly, Dame turned to face him with narrowed defiant eyes. The old Mer's broad chest rose and fell rapidly. A thick, white mustache and beard framed a thin line of a mouth, bitter with disappointment, broken as if betrayed. The bushy white eyebrows arced in a menacing frown while his bald head glistened with a slick finish. His skin was the color of cocoa butter and a gleaming blue-black fin of intricate scales where legs should have been bobbed freely in the clear afternoon waters. Close behind him, Dame saw more Ancestors surfacing, observing the confrontation with curiosity; many were lowering their heads in shame.

"I was voted leader of the Elder Clan for a reason," he replied with a defiant sneer. "Therefore, *I* was charged with the duty of leading my people where *I* see fit. We have long been slaves to traditions and customs that have begun to stagnate our kind. Our traditions are perverse, twisted! Change is necessary. The One Faith teaches restraint, The One Faith teaches love--"

Born spat angrily and folded his arms across his chest, interrupting. "You fool. For all of your physical strengths, for all of your military genius, you have no reason. *You are your traditions!* A people must never separate from their culture unless they wish to wither away and die! Mental Endurance. Enlightenment. Respect. These are the pillars of Ido tradition. These are rock solid ideals built for and maintained by the Ido people!" he exclaimed through flared nostrils. "Love is not solid. It can be bent and broken. It can crumble over time. Love cannot be restrained! There is nothing more unbridled or needy; nothing more lacking in discipline than love! With love there is emotion. With emotion there is weakness. We have survived for thousands of years because we respect one another. Respect cannot be shaped and molded into what we want it to be. It is rigid and defined. It is unchanging!" he paused for a moment and glanced at The Guide who was submerging yet another believer into the Mer Sea, then the old Mer's gaze swung back to Dame.

"Look at this!" Born exclaimed, teeth clenched tightly as he shoved an index finger in the air. "Rain! Rain on Ido? The balance is off... unnatural!"

In spite of the intimidating rant, Dame stood his ground. He looked in the direction of Born's angry finger, shaking with rage. "It is symbolic of the change we need---"

"Change is only necessary if its people are threatened by danger," Born cut in, his tone of voice strangely calm. "The Ido are a vibrant folk General, hardly stagnant and lost and perverted and... *twisted*. Do not dilute your people with the foreign faith of a stranger who has yet to prove the worth of his words."

Before Dame could dignify his remarks with a reply, Born descended into the deep with a flip of his massive fin. The others followed quickly behind. Having already been warned of what the Ancestors may say; he pushed Born's accusations to a remote area in the back of his mind. Somehow he felt his instincts had been correct. Slowly, he waded back to the ceremony just as it was signaled that his time had come. He waded toward the slim figure radiating all that was love and light and spiritually prepared himself for what he'd been convinced was right. With a snap of The Guide's long, bony fingers, the light rain sprinkling from above ceased. He held Dame firmly around the waist while he crossed his arms over his chest and closed his eyes.

Soon, Dame thought, I will be cleansed of all wrongdoing. *Change is necessary.*

3

A GATHERING IN NU

Shoulders squared and pulled back with pride, Quince focused on the large, thatch-roofed hut a few yards ahead. The quiet shuffle of feet on hardened dirt was the only sound to penetrate the night. The usual calls of animals hunting and foraging in the distance, was absent. There was an odd echo. It was as if every thing, living or not, was aware that something was amiss. He walked on, eyes squinting through the darkness while a sweaty palm clutched the brilliantly lit torch he drove into the ground like a cane.

"Ido Ido aye!" came a loud, clear voice behind him. *"Aye Ido Ido!"* The crowd answered the call with intensity.

The male Youth marched in single file under the face of the full moon, their bare chests heaving in the glow of the torchlight. They were dressed simply tonight. There were no scented body oils, ceremonial chains, or extravagant silk sacs girding their loins and rightfully so, the collective mood was grave at best. Quince steadied his torch in a mound of dirt just outside the entrance to the main hut and drew the rope on his loose brown pants a bit tighter. One by one, the others filed in, forming a wide, open circle flush with the hut's inner walls. After the last male had entered, Quince sauntered gracefully through the wide entryway and took his place in the circle's center. He greeted the others with a slight bow. With respect, they humbly returned the gesture.

Shoulder to shoulder they stood, the smiles of yesterday had long since faded into uncompromising lines. Quince removed the chew stick from his mouth and stood next to another chisel-featured male whose deep complexion was twin to a clear midnight sky. Maal, one of Quince's closest friends, had a presence that projected confidence and power. Long, neat locs flowed well past his broad shoulders; piercing brown eyes gleamed with anger and frustration. Early on, Maal gained recognition for his military prowess and having studied directly under Dame's tutelage, he'd become a Bgongo master and warrior. On the other hand, Quince was respected for his level-headedness and keen wit in times of need. Together, they were the perfect combination of muscle and mind, and because of this, they'd been elected co-Generals of the male Youth just before their journey to Vine City.

Side by side they stood, gazing out at the others. Smoothing his goatee and mustache with his right index finger and thumb, Quince noted the angry charge permeating the space around them. Uncertainty in their eyes; a hint of worry furrowed their questioning brows. They whispered to one another in uneasy tones as he lifted his hands high in the air, palms facing inward. In an instant, the room went still. Maal took a step forward, raked his fingers through his long locs, and spoke in a deep baritone.

"A time has come that I never thought would have existed, not even in my wildest nightmares." With a grave look, he paused thoughtfully before addressing them again. "We have received word from a reliable source that the stranger we saw in Vine City has succeeded in polluting our Elders." A wave of murmurs spread throughout the well-lit hut like wildfire. Again, Quince signaled for silence.

"They have been poisoned to abandon Taste and the old traditions in favor of a new way of life called The One Faith." Again the room erupted into appalled shouts and protests.

"Does this mean war then?" asked a tall, lighter skinned male in the corner. "If our traditions are being threatened then I would think a war should be waged. The Taste Rites officially begin at dawn. We should go through with them, but prepare for battle after the Rites come to a close." Heads nodded in agreement and the level of noise in the room continued to rise until it reached a deafening roar.

"*Ido Ido aye!*" Quince shouted with raised arms.

"*Aye Ido Ido!*" The men responded as one. Silence returned.

Maal began again. "The men of Ido have long been indulgent of women and pleasure. It is through sex that we communicate and climax spiritually, intellectually. And I have to agree with you brother, war seems to be the only viable option. However, we must not act in haste and first consult the Ancestors. If our needs, our traditions, and the customs that make us uniquely Ido are threatened, we have no choice but to wage war on our Elders, even if they are our flesh and blood, our mothers and fathers." Reluctant sighs and grunts followed.

"What is this One Faith? How is it different from Taste?" asked another.

Maal yielded the floor to Quince who stepped forward to answer.

"The One Faith is the inverse of Taste. It teaches love and marriage, discipline and monogamy." The revelation of his words resulted in a disquieting stir as the dumbfounded crowd attempted to digest what they were hearing.

"This is hypocrisy!" shouted another male with thick, shoulder length braids, his lips quivering in anger. "These are the very ceremonies that led the Elders to the Enlightened Lands. It was they who experienced Taste just twenty years ago, and their Elders before them. At one time, they were Ido Youth themselves!"

Quince fingered his goatee before responding. "Yes, this is why the developments are so disturbing. This stranger must have a foreign power of monumental strength. I did not think our Elders were of a weak mind. But then again, I have been wrong before."

"Who is this stranger and when do they expect us to do away with Taste?" asked another shorter male with a thin mustache. "We have been preparing for as long as we can remember!"

"Just as the Elder General announced at the ceremony, they have demanded that Taste be abolished at once and that we not go on with the first Rite tomorrow. However, as far as the stranger is concerned, I know very little about him. We are thinking of hiring a Diaw Bird to gather as much information---" Again the hut rumbled to life, cutting his reply short.

"The Diaw cannot be trusted. They are soulless troublemakers with their own agendas. Though they can communicate with us, they speak with forked tongues!" yelled two others.

Quince recognized the voices at once, physically identical in nearly every way; the men were his brothers, Dez and El. The three were triplets and he more than understood their frustration. It was a Diaw's superstitious riddle that had nearly caused the Elders to sacrifice the boys when they were born. The Diaw had openly declared multiple births to be an abomination.

"What part would the Djinn play in this? Could they be summoned to help us?"

Maal cleared his throat and let out a weary sigh. "It would be in their best interest to help us as they play a significant role in Taste, but the Djinn are forces with half lives. They are elemental spirits who have no real stake in our affairs. I expect them to remain neutral throughout the conflict."

Suddenly, the hut became engulfed in a fragile silence as the ideas bounced around inside their heads. Wheels were turning, thoughts clicked in place like a fine tuned machine and everyone present was pondering ways to avoid the inevitable.

"Have you considered a Sphinx?" asked El hopefully. A few of the others looked at Quince eagerly.

Quince shook his head. "Though the Sphinx are more levelheaded than the Diaw, they are more concerned with their medicine making and the preservation of their own race than providing us with any information. Let's not forget that they would lean more toward the Elders if there were conflict. They came to Sphinx aid during the Insect War twenty years ago."

"Have you considered a Stripe? At least we can be certain of their loyalty to us," inquired Dez thoughtfully, desperate for an alternative.

"Yes we have. We will meet with the Stripes at Glo City after the first Rite. Though they are our allies, we still must respect their traditions and travel to their territories. Until then we have no other options. For now, the Diaw are our only link to finding out about the stranger and this new---"

"That is not entirely true," interrupted a soft voice from the hut's entrance.

Unexpected surprise washed over the gathering as three women stepped inside. The one who'd spoken stood in the middle. Those at her sides, held their heads high, their bright eyes totally void of fear. Each possessed her own unique beauty, one slim, the other curvaceous, and the last, petite. Dressed in warrior attire, the three women were clothed in dark green halter- tops and matching linen pants. All three were visibly armed. A bronze knobbed mace, heavy bow, and shining broadsword dangled within reach. The woman in the center's long locs flowed over her shoulders to the elbow. The woman at her right wore her tresses piled on top of her head, while the woman on her left donned long, shoulder length braids. Immediately, Quince recognized the woman in the center as the female Youth he'd connected with during the Warming Ceremony. Though short in stature, her energy created a tall and knowing shadow. He breathed in her aura like the aroma of his favorite meal, tasting her potency on the tip of his tongue.

"We understand that it is against tradition to contact you before Taste begins tomorrow," the woman in the center began, "but as the elected Generals of the female Youth, we also recognize that much of our tradition has already been compromised. I am Onya, daughter of Imar. To my right is Eesha, daughter of Sharo and to my left is Lyn, daughter of Deena."

One by one, they bowed to the gathered males. Still in mild shock, Quince and the others returned the respect and introduced themselves accordingly. During the extended flurry of introductions, Quince sucked in Onya's beauty slowly, momentarily dazed by the silhouette of her hips and breasts. He could see her nipples hardening, threatening to tear through the thin fabric covering her upper body. Her scent danced toward his nostrils, threatening to compromise his sanity, as he stood rooted to the ground. In a hasty attempt to mask his intrigue, he cleared his throat loudly and gathered himself.

"Onya, Eesha, Lyn, we respect your presence here tonight and do believe it is necessary." The males in the room nodded in agreement, many of them unable to control their wandering eyes. "What information do you have to share?" Quince asked with gentle curiosity.

She breathed deeply before beginning to speak. "The stranger is not from this time it seems. Some believe he was summoned here through prayer. Still others say he has fallen from the sky as a deformed, albino messenger. It has been reported that he can work miracles without magic and his sorcery is rooted in his faith. He walks on two legs, but is not Ido nor of the Painted tribes. Whatever the case may be, he is of a species we have never encountered."

He sensed her sudden surprise. Her eyes darted around the room as she spoke. Was she attempting to quell the excitement of seeing him again, or was this his imagination? Whatever it was, she was doing a damn good job of rattling him. *What was wrong with him? She was not supposed to be having such a profound effect... and in such dire times!* He shouted at himself silently, alarmed with the way she seemed to call him with her eyes, direct his thoughts, and enter his mind with a mere flutter of her lashes. With a controlled discipline, he shut out his extraneous desires and shifted his concentration back to the dismayed gasps and rising roars of outrage within the hut. The backlash from her speech was instantaneous.

"Sorcery rooted in faith? Impossible! Only the Ancestors possess raw conjuring power!" said one.

"Miracles? To what degree?" Questioned a few others.

Quince held up his hand as silence spread through the hut. Once peace had been restored he motioned for her to continue.

Onya blew out a resigned breath before continuing. "He speaks our language and has been conducting worship services where he spreads his beliefs. He is also performing *Waves* in which those who have accepted his message are submerged in water and exit as cleansed souls."

"Water?" shouted Dez incredulously. "*The Ancestors own the sea!* How is it possible that this foreigner can transcend their power and enter the Mer Sea? I could see him possibly controlling the land, but the Ancestors' powers are limitless in the salt waters surrounding the island!"

Maal's eyes grew wide in alarm while Quince searched Onya's face for a moment. In it, he found a funnel of concern much like his own. Shock had given way to confusion and finally an echoing silence. They all knew the direction in which they were headed. Dread filled the room. Something tugged at his spirit as he continued to lock his eyes with hers. A suffocating stillness lingered.

"I will not ask you to reveal your sources Onya, surely your information is too detailed to be fraudulent," said Maal, splicing the uneasy quiet.

Onya nodded curtly. "We would never bring misinformation to the men we respect so dearly."

Out of the corner of his eye, he saw a slick smile spreading across Maal's lips. It made Quince uneasy as he continued to study her, wordlessly staking his claim for her hand in the forthcoming Rites. Though the males held the luxury of first choice, it was the females who made the final decision. With a subtle blink, he attempted to pull himself back to the pressing matters of war and away from the cosmic pull of her allure. Desperately, he tried to collect himself for fear that the weakness in his knees would expose themselves to all in attendance.

"The Painted Folk also have a stake in these events. They must be notified of what has transpired." Her eyes gripped his physique in a choke hold of a stare. "Have you declared war?" she asked, honing in on Quince's muscular chest.

"We have not yet consulted the Ancestors, this will be done within the hour. However, we would be grateful if the three of you would travel into Three Wood and speak to Gallah. She must be informed of the imminent danger," Quince replied, examining the firmness of her thighs. "After the first Rite we plan to travel to Glo City where a Stripe informant awaits us. We hope to find out more about this foreign messenger from him. By that time, the female Youth will be traveling east for the second Rite, as will we after our meeting. We will handle all matters in your absence."

"Of course." The three women responded with a quick bow before Onya continued on. "We will journey to the jungle while you consult the Mer. The Painted Folk are our allies; we have nothing to fear from them. Let it be known that if it were not for the second Rite, we'd be traveling to the cocooned city at your side," she paused before pulling her shoulders back with pride.

"Understandable General Onya, and as you know, we are due to make the journey to the Oasis one day after your return as it is the only gender separated Rite." Quince found himself wrestling with her magnetic pull again. He fingered the hairs of his goatee, clearly preoccupied.

"The Ido women's expertise in combat is akin to their beauty. We fully understand where your loyalties lie," Maal cut in with a small smile.

Onya nodded affirmatively before continuing. "If there is nothing else then... we declare on behalf of the female Youth that we accept whatever is decided and in turn, pledge our loyalty until we are Ancestors." Her eyes were inviting. It was as if she were declaring her arousal purposely, publicly.

"Your support is accepted and appreciated," Maal replied smoothly.

"The hour is late," cut in Quince, his voice laced with seductive undertones. "Go and prepare for Taste. We will have more dialogue when the time presents itself. We, the male Youth of Ido are here to fight beside you when dangers arise and please you when the hours are at hand. May our pleasures be with you." He sensed her heart flutter as she stared into his welcoming eyes. The perfect purse of her lips like striated clouds drawn on a palette of sky.

"We will meet at dawn. And may our pleasures be with *you* as well," she said coolly before turning to leave, the remaining women in tow. Quince allowed his gaze to follow her round buttocks as she disappeared from the shadows of the flaming torchlight and into the darkness. Snapping abruptly from his reverie, he turned to Maal who was clearly preoccupied with Onya as well. He stroked his chin thoughtfully before turning to the group.

"You will be told of what the Ancestors advise before we set out for the Amber Cliffs at dawn. Prepare for the first Rite and keep your ears open for any news," he declared to the men before their departure. Above the conversation, Maal turned to him and spoke softly.

"Onya," he said with a wink. "I will remember the name and make sure we meet again. I don't know about you, but I am already looking forward to tomorrow."

Quince bristled while the delicate pangs of jealousy meandered through his veins like a slow burn. Gazing toward the hut's entrance, he let out a heavy sigh as his glance slid once again toward Maal. Seeds of confusion began to spread and take root in his mind. There was something about this woman that triggered an internal longing far beyond the physical. Her presence was a magnetic charge still lingering in the humid, night air. Inhaling deeply, he attempted to right himself before their meeting with the Ancestors. What would be; would be, he thought to himself. Tradition had already been altered.

4

THE FIRE AND RAINBOW RITUAL

"They deserve to know Lyn. The Elders' attempt to abolish Taste and the possible civil war affects them as well!" Onya said through clenched teeth.

"Fine, but why do we have to tell them in the dead of night?"

Onya ignored this and continued to carefully pick her way through the outskirts of the dense, dark jungle. Eesha and Lyn followed behind unenthusiastically, watching their steps cautiously, hands glued to their weapons, and listening for danger. The brilliant moon, like a noticeable dimple in the velvet sky, continued to shine, supplying patches of light through the thick canopy of leaves fifty feet above. Nearby, Onya noticed something large scurry up a tree. Its long arms swung from its sides haphazardly. The chestnut colored hair and gangly body could only mean one thing, an Ido monkey, strong, but completely harmless. Under the cover of night, many creatures lingered in the shadows of trees and mossy crevices of earth. With the balance of the island tipped, they would have to be completely on guard.

"Something isn't right. I feel it. The jungle doesn't feel the same *and--*Three Wood, need I remind you, isn't the safest place after---"

Annoyed, she rounded on Lyn, abruptly causing her to stumble backward. "Just be quiet! You heard Quince; we were given an assignment to carry out! Besides, we are all Bgongo masters and Generals! Start acting like it!" Onya reached for the leather sheath on her hip encasing her broadsword. She drew it swiftly while the others gazed at the sharpened blade. The scant moonlight bounced from its steel edge, basking the women in a slender stream of light.

Eesha sighed after dodging out of the way and placed a firm hand on her mace. "The quicker we get this done, the quicker we'll be able to get back to the village, and the quicker we can get to the Amber Cliffs by dawn. Onya, just ignore her and lead us to where we have to go. But, I have to agree with Lyn, this place is starting to get a little scary."

"Starting to get a little scary?" Lyn scoffed sarcastically under her breath with one hand on her bow and the other on the arrows stuffed securely in the deep brown quiver strapped securely to her back. "We're only on a mission in the dead of night to find and deliver messages to some of the most frightening species on the island, *and* the balance is clearly off. I can feel it," she muttered to herself as she crept along carefully.

Onya exhaled heavily and ducked beneath the lowered bough of an enormous Raha tree the size of a medium sized building, its three burnt orange trunks rooted stubbornly in the damp ground. Their nervous breathing sliced the humid air as the slithering sounds of night crept eerily close.

"Misunderstood maybe... but not frightening," countered Onya. "The Painted Folk are our allies. Why be frightened of them?"

"Oh, I don't know... maybe it's the white hair, the painted skin, *the white eyes that seem to look right through you!*" spat Lyn as she nearly stumbled over a bulging, entangled root protruding from a patch of moss.

"Once again... you are an Ido warrior! If you are having a problem--"

"Listen!" Eesha pressed her fingers to her lips and narrowed her eyes. "There's something lurking in the shadows over there," she said in a harsh whisper before motioning ahead of them.

Immediately, the women huddled together, drew their weapons in front of them, and waited. A low hiss slid through the suffocating air, undulating vines, and damp grass. From out of the shadows, slithered an orange snake. The uncoiling of its body seemed endless. As it drew nearer, it raised its head, let out an imminent hiss and revealed a set of sharp fangs slick with dripping, venomous saliva.

"It's an Ero," Onya whispered slowly.

"Viper-anaconda hybrid," Eesha echoed.

"Venomous constrictor. Double threat. Fan out on my cue!"

Onya let out a low whistle. Instantly the three women spread into a battle stance in preparation for a three-pronged offensive. The monster was surrounded on three sides, but slithered up and off the ground, hissing again un-phased. Within seconds, two others joined the fray. One of the creatures was brick red, the other a shade of chartreuse green. The three women eyed the things carefully. The chartreuse snake closest to Lyn had the thickness of one of her thighs. The others were longer, but not nearly as large in diameter.

Carefully, Lyn circled. The creature kept its beady yellow eyes fixed on the mahogany bow set out in front of her, cocked, aimed, and ready.

"On my signal," Lyn said low in her throat. The two women beside her nodded carefully. "Now!" she screeched.

Lyn sent an arrow flying into a nearby tree, causing the snakes to lunge simultaneously. The warriors dodged the initial strike narrowly. Eesha launched her body off the ground at full throttle and swung on a low branch. Onya back flipped toward the thick tree trunk nearest the orange snake and held her blade inches from its large, diamond-shaped head. Carefully, she moved the shining sword from side to side, holding the snake's attention as it hissed loudly. Without warning, she went airborne, tumbling behind its coiled shape and plunged her blade into its body. The thing catapulted from the ground and writhed in spasms of pain, spilling dark blood onto the rain forest floor. Momentarily distracted by their companions' undoing, the remaining snakes halted their attack. Immediately, Lyn sent an arrow flying into the body of the serpent nearest her and Eesha connected her bronze knobbed mace with the remaining snake's midsection, bludgeoning it lifeless. Careful that the danger had passed, Onya inserted her blade into the three creatures a second time, ensuring their safety. The women looked up at one another, chests heaving with uneasy looks plastered on their faces.

"Good work," Onya said, slightly unnerved. "Now... where were we?"

They continued on the path they'd been traveling with their wits about them and weapons drawn. Lyn ceased her nagging, but made it a point to remind everyone that she'd had a feeling something was wrong. Clearly, nature was no longer in sync. Though the jungle had always been dangerous, the creatures *never* attacked humans. The event they'd just experienced was a rare first. The remaining journey was a quiet one. Each of the women seemed to be milling over the "why" of what had just occurred. Somehow the presence of a foreigner on their soil, the snake attack, and the betrayal of their Elders were linked. Even the animals sensed the disharmony. It was all too profound to speak on.

"Shh! Look up ahead. I see a light," Eesha whispered, the stillness evaporating as they turned their attention toward her outstretched arm.

Just ahead stood a clearing flanked by several tall stone pillars. The graceful monuments rose nearly as tall as the nearby trees and were decorated with looping symbols and glyphs. Onya felt her jaw drop in awe as her gaze swallowed the ornately designed ivory-colored pillars that seemed to penetrate the sky. The square clearing in the center was bathed in what looked to be an artificial light. The women huddled closer together and walked on. With each step, they traveled deeper inside the heart of the rain forest. Onya's heart began to pound in spite of herself. The Painted Folk were some of the most peaceful creatures on the entire island. In spite of their gentle nature; however, she also knew there were certain rules to be followed when entering their lands, rules she hoped they'd been abiding by. Carefully, she rubbed the horizontal white chalk line on her forehead, a ritualistic symbol of their coming in respect, peace, and with an important purpose. She quickly scanned Eesha and Lyn, checking one last time that their marks were in tact as well. Clairvoyant and immortal, surely the Painted Folk had already been made aware of their presence. Silently, she hoped she hadn't led her friends into the grips of any unnecessary danger, but she knew Gallah, the Supreme Maiden of the Painted Folk, would find the information she had to share invaluable.

They continued on until the clearing lay a little more than a few feet away. Lyn cursed fervently under her breath while the other women remained alertly on guard.

"Don't get too close," Onya whispered.

"Oh really, and why not? Hell, we've come this far!" Lyn whimpered with sarcasm.

"Will you both please---"

Eesha's earnest plea was interrupted by an earth shattering crash as the ground beneath them trembled violently. Their legs lifted in the air from under them and the three women tumbled to the ground with a hard thud. Scurrying to brush the damp dirt from her backside, Onya rushed to her knees. Her eyes grew large with disbelief. The sight had already transfixed Eesha, while Lyn looked into the eyes of her two friends. Reluctantly, she turned to face the spectacle before them.

Not ten feet away stood at least one hundred figures. The artificial light they'd seen was in fact the rays of the moon reflecting off of a massive, thousand square foot mirror lying on the ground. Before Onya could make a sound, the ground trembled yet again, throwing the kneeling women flat on their backs. Wild with curiosity, Onya quickly obtained her bearings and turned again toward the mysterious gathering. She gestured for them to kneel closer to the ground. At once, she saw what was causing the earth to quake. The flames of a pale pink fire were spewing upward from the center of the mirror like a gigantic fountain. In fact, she would have sworn the pink spray to be water had she not felt the extreme heat and perspiration pouring suddenly from her forehead and nape. A buckling haze encompassed the pink bonfire. Though smoke was absent, sparks flew from its mouth while it crackled and sputtered as if it were gaining momentum.

A large group of hypnotized figures stared at the lapping flames, which now took on the semblance of human hands reaching higher and higher toward the sky. The rainbow pigmentation differed greatly in each of them, as did the oddly unique patterns traced over their bodies. This was the closest she'd ever gotten to them, let alone one of their gatherings. Immediately, she discovered that the females' patterns were delicately curved and their pigments were of pastel pinks, lavenders, and pale green or blue. Meanwhile, the males' patterns were sharp and intersecting and their pigment contained the standard red, blue, and yellow along with white and black. The males were bald while their female counterparts sported white, spiked mohawks. Looking closer now, she also observed the obvious differences between male and female. Without difficulty she located breasts and exposed genitalia.

The fire fountain's height seemed to reach its limit now and one by one, the figures headed inside its flames as if entering a routine morning shower.

"What the---" began Lyn.

"Of course." Onya whispered slowly. "The Rainbow and Fire Ritual."

Eesha and Lyn cut their eyes at her in surprise.

"It's their cleansing Rite before the beginning of Taste," Onya explained. "How much do you know?"

The two women looked back at her with blank expressions. With a deep sigh, Onya pieced together her thoughts before continuing. "The Painted Folk were forced to give up their right to reproduce and copulate. They were the only creatures on the island to give up two human practices. As a result, they received both immortality and infinite wisdom. But just because they'd yielded their right to engage in sexual activity didn't mean their desires ceased. So of course, those wants still needed to be fed." Eesha and Lyn listened intently as they watched the figures bathe inside the fire without injury, their bottom jaws nearly unhinged in shock.

"For decades, this need haunted them. The race became restless, unhappy. Soon it was a common quest for all to find a way to feed their desires without dishonoring their ancient vow. One day, a member of their clan stumbled upon the Ido Youth during the third Rite, which of course, takes place in Three Wood. According to the story, she ran back to their dwellings deep inside the forest and shared what she'd seen. They all rushed to witness the Rite, climbing high in the trees to watch. A self-pleasuring frenzy ensued as they fed from the Ritual's passion and raw energy. The voyeurism and masturbation that takes place once every two decades on that day is now the single source of their content and survival. The cleansing by fire is just a ceremony marking the beginning of their arousal. I suppose it's kind of a twist on our Warming Ceremony."

"That's a helluva twist," remarked Lyn, eyebrows raised. "And how did you come to know all this?"

"I eavesdropped on the Elders when they visited us at Nu," Onya shrugged nonchalantly. "You'd be amazed at what you can pick-up if you just lurk and listen."

Lyn let out a low whistle, sidetracked by the scene before them. "Wow, when you look at them, they are ...beautiful. I mean... once you get over the initial shock of a naked person with rainbow colored skin and colorless eyes."

Onya and Eesha chuckled softly.

"Who found out about the Rite and led the others there anyway?" asked Lyn. "Sounds like a heck of a find."

"Her name was Gallah and she's now their Supreme Maiden, has been for over five hundred years."

As if on cue, the crowd before them parted, revealing a stunningly beautiful woman. A shining silver afro surrounded her pale blue face like a soft, cotton-spun cloud. Royalty simply oozed from her veins. While the others' skin was comprised of several colors, Gallah's was a simple, yet regal pale blue and silver. The colors snaked around her body in broad, alternating ribbons. She was sitting on the shoulders of two red-skinned, broad shouldered men; her delicate palms cradling each of their bald heads. Immediately, Onya noticed her large, firm breasts, also a pale blue, and the silver dollar sized nipples pierced with diamond jewels. Her small waist and wide hips were also apparent as they set her down in front of the fountain of fire. She kissed one of the men who'd carried her before striding elegantly forward. She whisked through the fire at once and appeared on the other side, inches from where the women lay. Immediately, she acknowledged their presence.

"Ido friends, introduce yourselves and tell us why you have come," she commanded as the others gazed in their direction.

Caught off guard, they stood up hastily. Onya cleared her throat and spoke loudly, addressing the entire crowd.

"I am Onya, daughter of Imar. To my right is Eesha; daughter of Sharo and to my left is Lyn, daughter of Deena. We are the Ido Youth's female Generals. We have come because we have valuable information regarding Taste."

There was a slight rumble in the crowd at the mention of the Rites. Gallah snapped her fingers abruptly and silence fell upon the clearing.

"Go on, Onya, daughter of Imar," she said with a tempered curiosity.

"As we speak, the male Youth of Ido are summoning Born."

Again, the Painted Folk whispered anxiously amongst themselves. Gallah peered at the three women, obviously taken aback. "Born, but no one summons the leader of the Mer unless--"

"War. The Youth plan to gain permission to wage a war," Onya cut in.

Gallah looked deeply disturbed and lowered her head slightly before refocusing her attention on the women before her. "Who are they waging war against if I may ask?"

Onya sighed heavily before responding. "Our mothers and fathers. We, the Youth of Ido are planning to wage a civil war against the Elder Ido Clan."

Instantly, unrest began. Cries of *Impossible! It's an atrocity*, and *Never before*, rippled throughout the gathering. Snatches of Folk Language, their native tongue, pierced the air around them. Gallah snapped her fingers again and peace was restored.

"Our Elders have been poisoned, brain washed by a conjuring foreigner." Onya pressed on quickly as the stymied rage within her returned while she recanted the unfortunate events of the past few days. "He calls himself The Guide and brings with him a new religion called The One Faith. This religion teaches love, discipline, restraint, and monogamy. But above all else, the religion and its followers are intent upon abolishing Taste. They interrupted us during our Warming Ceremony at Vine City. They demanded that we not go on with the first Rite tomorrow or any Rites thereafter."

Gallah held her hand to her heart as the two men who'd carried her rushed to her side. Those in the crowd looked on in disbelief.

"Conjuring power? But only the Mer..." her voice trailed off as she gathered her thoughts and began again. "Taste is essential to our survival Onya, daughter of Imar," Gallah choked aloud. "We are not a warlike group, but we will fight for our survival..." Gallah's white eyes deepened into a dangerously dark shade of gray as she frowned. In an instant she summoned a jeweled dagger with a twisting blade to her open palm. "In spite of our wish to keep to ourselves, we are shrewd warriors." She paused and turned to her followers. In an instant, all were armed and ready, their eyes flickering in the moonlight. "As your allies, what will you have us do?" she asked as she whirled around to face them once again.

"Until we find out what Born decides, we can give you no instructions. We merely ask that you keep your ears and eyes open. You will hear from our male Youth within the coming days. In fact, they are already working with your kin, The Stripes."

The muscular male on her right looked up brightly. "Perhaps this is what we need to make peace!" he said to Gallah as she clutched her sword angrily.

"Yes Ohm, maybe this is what we need to make peace with our kin for leaving the homeland of the trees for the brilliantly lit city in the south."

Onya's gaze swung back and forth between Ohm and Gallah, perplexed.

"There has been squabbling between The Painted Folk and The Stripes though we are the same," she explained with a weary sigh. "Some of us resent their choice to leave the enchanted rain forest. Their relocation diminishes their wisdom and has caused their skin to dull. Because we think collectively, many see it as their diminishing the wisdom of our people as a whole. I can only hope that this will draw my people closer," she replied gently.

Onya shifted her gaze. The woman's glowing beauty was almost overpowering and her sincerity held a magnetism of regal grace. "Thank you for your loyalty in spite of your own issues. It is greatly appreciated."

"Will you be going ahead with the first Rite?"

Onya shook her head affirmatively. "As far as I know, the answer is yes. We were told to prepare for the journey to the Amber Cliffs at dawn."

Gallah looked to be in deep thought as she nodded her head. "Thank you for this information. We will discuss possible courses of action amongst ourselves between now and the time we next meet. A vision bind may be needed to fully understand this foreigner. We will gather information and aid you in all ways possible." Gallah inhaled deeply before addressing them again. "Onya, Eesha, and Lyn, the forest is not safe. I sense great discord within the natural order of things. I will send a guide with you to lead you back to Nu Village."

She bowed majestically before she was lifted onto the shoulders of the men again in a sudden flourish and taken back toward the ever-spewing flames. Lyn gave Onya a shove in response to Gallah's last words. Moments later, a tall, muscular man with red, gold, and black skin strode toward them.

"Oh my goodness---" Eesha gasped, eyeing the thick organ dangling near his thigh. Onya responded with a playful pinch as they followed him back in the direction they'd come.

"They're not frightening at all," smirked Lyn following closely behind their handsome guide.

5

MOONLIT OFFERINGS

"Avoid eye contact *unless* they address you specifically." Quince whispered nervously.

"They... hold on. I thought we would only be speaking with Born!" Maal replied, running his fingers over his locs uneasily.

"You never know, the others may come. I actually expect more of them to gather given the severity of the situation. We're asking for permission to wage a Civil War, Maal. That's a *major* request. It would be something our people have never experienced."

Maal shook his head in agreement and stroked his chin, the automatic ritual he often performed when in deep thought. "What do you think his response will be? You three are the only living Youth to have actually had dialogue with Born before." He looked hopefully in the direction of Dez, El, and Quince.

"That was years ago and we didn't say anything to him. It was just necessary that he see us. Our mother was pleading with the Ancestors to save our lives. We were going to be sacrificed." El responded quietly.

"Murdered. Don't sugar coat it. We were going to be murdered," Dez retorted bitterly.

"We were barely through with our transformations when the Diaw began making their thoughts known about multiple births, especially since it was unheard of on Ido, not to mention it violated the one offspring rule," Quince mused aloud. "The matter was settled when we were brought before Born. But again, we were really young."

"What could mother *possibly* be thinking right now? She's such a strong woman. If anyone should be indebted to Born it's her!" Dez hissed irritably.

"You've got to remember who we're talking about," reasoned Quince as he knelt in the sand. "Dame is their leader. You remember how domineering he is. No one probably wants to even risk the chance of standing up to him. Even if she isn't in agreement with him, she probably feels like she has no choice."

"I've spent hours and hours alone with Dame," Maal cut in. "Elder General. Youth General. Bgongo Guru. Insect War hero. He has a sternness about him, probably the most intimidating person I've ever met... taught me everything I know to be honest. I just can't believe he'd be this gullible."

"If it weren't for Born, *I* wouldn't be here... plain and simple. So I say we place our faith in the wisdom of the Ancestors," Dez spat in disgust and took a seat on a nearby rock. "He knows what's going on. How could he not? Taste was disrupted before it had a chance to officially begin. Several species have been dependent upon these traditions since the beginning of time! How could Dame do this to us? Born will see things our way; he is both reasonable and wise."

Maal nodded and began the silent preparation of the offering. El lit a cluster of incense and placed them in the hollow shell of a large nut filled with blackberries, dried leaves, and an assortment of metal tools. Carefully, he positioned the concoction on a slab of porous bark. Methodically, Maal pushed the offering out to sea, the flame from the incense growing higher as it floated. They knelt, heads bowed, hands clasped together like a group of meditating monks on the cool, white sand. After a few moments, the waters sliced and rippled as if disturbed from a deep slumber.

"Keep your heads bowed until you are addressed," Quince reminded them quietly.

There was a giant splash as a blue-black fin ripped through the dark waters. As quickly as the splash had disrupted the calm of the surrounding beach, stillness returned. Again, the waves began to ebb and flow gently. Under the protruding chin of the shining moon, Born rose from the water, arms outstretched in the direction of the sky above. He opened his dark eyes, located the offering and swam toward it. In a single motion he blew the small flame of the incense as if nurturing it into a magnificent conflagration. Instantly it grew and steadied at a height to his liking, creating a dance of light and shadow over the vast sea in the dead of night. His cream colored skin and distinct facial hair illuminated brilliantly against the brightness of the fire as did the silhouettes of Maal, Quince, Dez, and El still kneeling in the sand. He surveyed the four men some twenty feet in front of him before speaking.

"Come closer," he thundered.

Bumbling nervously, they stood, wading toward Born until the water was waist high. Once in his immediate vicinity, they bowed their heads again.

"Four men. Four incense of Terra Root. Four metal tools. You have prepared a war offering," he said gently.

Taken aback by his tenderness, Maal opened his eyes, but kept his head bowed as Quince had instructed.

"You may raise your heads, respect has been noted and returned." Smoothly the Ancestor bowed in acknowledgment. "I have already spoken with Dame and expected this request would come." His speech was deliberately slow and precise. Maal sensed a solemn undertone. "Who is your elected leader?"

"The Youth have decided to elect two leaders. I am Maal, son of Eyeno."

"And I am Quince, son of Vye."

Born studied the two men intently before yielding a reply. "Ah yes, Vye..." he said while honing in on the triplets. "She pleaded for your lives some fourteen years ago. A most unusual case that was; I recall it as if it were yesterday," he paused. "And so, you wish to wage a civil war in order to preserve Taste?"

It was more of a statement than a question. Unsure of how to respond, the four men nodded gravely, yet without an ounce of indecision.

Born folded his large arms across his chest and turned toward the offering still floating nearby. "Dame is as stubborn as he is strong. Waging war is one thing, but winning is another. In all his haste, Dame is smart. He is first and foremost a warrior and a formidable one at that. He will gather all of his allies and resources in order to defeat you decisively. He will show you no mercy."

With these declarations, the flame seemed to grow larger and burn a bit brighter. In an instant, countless Mer surrounded them. It was like nothing they'd ever witnessed. No fewer than fifty figures rose from the water. There were men as well as women. Scaled fins in a myriad of colors rippled on the surface of the water and reflected against the moonlight. Clusters of wrinkled wisdom gathered at the edges of their mouths and eyes. Moles of experience dotted their drawn skin. They surrounded Born in a large semi-circle and looked about skeptically between Born and the four Ido Youth.

"We will prepare to defend tradition," Maal responded bravely.

"Yes, you will. The Ido ways must be preserved," he said solemnly. "Without Taste there is no Ido. I trust you recognize this otherwise you would not be before us now."

"Yes, you are correct in this assumption," Quince replied.

Born bobbed silently for a moment, his gaze roving among the four men standing in front of him. He toyed with the white hairs in his beard before continuing. "I'd always thought that with age came a certain amount of wisdom. Yet standing in front of me are four Youth who seem to possess more reason than the Elders who were Enlightened twenty one years ago."

Maal's chest swelled with pride as Born's remarks registered in his mind. The mere idea that he'd be able to speak with the Ancestors during his lifetime had never occurred to him and now here he was, standing in awe of the most powerful Ancestor their people had ever seen. "The Oral Rite begins at dawn. Shall we continue?" he asked.

"Oh yes," Born responded swiftly with a raised brow. "To not continue with tradition would be an acknowledgment of its defeat. However, you must realize that resuming Taste is a declaration of war. The Elders will see it as such. But be ever vigilant and cautious. Though I know they will not attack during the Rites themselves, they may choose to do so soon after, when your energies are most depleted. You will need Sphinx remedies to ensure your essence is replenished."

Maal allowed the calm of the sea to consume him while Born's words gradually sunk in. The wise Ancestor was absolutely right. Dame had been his mentor for years and one thing he'd preached incessantly was the importance of the art of surprise. In spite of his arrogance, Dame realized that the Youth were younger and more agile. At this very moment, the General was more than likely trying to anticipate their every move. A preemptive strike after a pleasurable, but very draining, twenty-four hour sexual encounter would be a smart move; right up Dame's devious alley.

Quince let out his breath hard, interrupting the stillness before speaking. "How will we convince them to supply us with remedies? The Sphinx will certainly align themselves with The Elders due to their pact."

Born looked toward the moon thoughtfully before issuing a reply. "The Sphinx cannot deny their medicines to those in need. It is part of the natural order of the island. Each species had to sacrifice something monumental for guaranteed survival on Ido," he looked away suddenly as if an unpleasant memory had struck him. "We were forced to give up our right to act on emotional love. The Painted Folk abandoned their right to engage in intercourse and reproduction, and The Sphinx agreed to heal those in need, no matter who they may be. So you see, they *cannot* deny you treatment. To do so would result in certain exile and perhaps even death. It was a most ancient pact made between the creatures of the island and their former god, Orun," Born explained, his once booming voice now reduced to a raspy whisper. "Now, the hour is growing early," he exclaimed, the bass in his voice suddenly returning. "Already, the moon is tucking herself inside the folds of the dawning sky. Head to the Amber Cliffs and receive and reciprocate your pleasures. It is tradition. It is what Youth is. *It is what we are.*"

With those final words, the flame extinguished and the gathering of Mer Ancestors returned to the depths of the sea with a brisk and powerful splash. Maal shifted his weight, waded back to shore with the others, and sighed. They must prepare for war; the answer had been clear. He gazed into the faces of his three comrades. Nothing needed to be said; their sullen expressions spoke volumes.

"We will tell the others before we set out to the Amber Cliffs," Quince said in a low murmur.

Maal replied only with a slight nod. "Go on back. I will be there shortly."

With Dez in the lead, the triplets began the short trek back to Nu, a walk that could be covered in less than five minutes time. Maal's shoulders slumped as he mentally rewound the events of the last seventy-two hours in his mind. His entire world had been turned on its head in less than four days. The Ido Youth had been forced to mature more quickly than they ever would have imagined. He raked his hands through his hair and stared in the direction of the still floating offering. Now the soft glow of the rising sun cast a faint shadow over the Eastern side of the village where the women resided. Snatches of their pre-Ritual songs could be heard a short distance away.

Soon his thoughts drifted away from the impending civil war and back to the woman called Onya. He could hardly stand the wait. Imagining the touch of her skin, he rubbed his throbbing length and smiled. A faint rustling of the trees startled him. Immediately, he was alert and on guard. Again there was movement and a sweet song approached. It was a woman. He could not afford to be seen. Careful to remain undetected, he crept behind a large rock nearby. The voice continued, louder now. As dawn approached, the color of the sky transformed. Deep charcoal gave way to splinters of gold as the first remnants of sunshine veined, rippling through the sky like a bird hatching from its eggshell prison. Maal knew there wasn't much time before his whereabouts would be exposed by the daylight; so he lurked inconspicuously under the cover of what was left of nightfall.

Slowly, the woman moved into focus. Wearing only a flowing piece of fabric, she knelt in the sand. Maal, his breath caught in his throat, stood rooted in place as she untied the cloth above her shoulder. Gently, it fell to the ground. Gleefully, he observed the perky breasts, curvy hips, and solid thighs basking in the pale light of dawn. Carefully, she stuck a toe in the cool waters before plunging in. He could hardly believe his fortune. The naked woman had just entered their hut hours before. It was Onya.

"Maal, what are you doing? We're leaving soon," hissed Quince in an impatient whisper.

Maal put an index finger to his lips and pointed to the sea. Hunched behind the rock, Quince glanced in the direction of his finger. Surprised, he abruptly looked away.

"We've got to leave. The others are waiting," he whispered shortly.

With a reluctant sigh, Maal nodded and crawled toward a group of trees a short distance away. Hoping she hadn't seen them, Quince followed. Before they were completely out of sight, he sneaked another peak at the nude woman. *Let the Rites of Taste begin,* he sighed to himself before veering onto the rocky path.

6

THE FIRST RITE

Onya lie prostrate beneath the shadow of a massive cloud, waiting. The Amber Cliffs were, in fact, two, steep moss-ridden plateaus. Towering Kywe trees shielded the Cliffs from the sun, while the barks' smooth amber jewels dazzled in green, red, and honey gold. Gently, she rubbed her tense shoulder blades against the cool exterior of a nearby tree, and turned toward Eesha and Lyn who lay only a few feet away.

"What's taking them so long? I know we're all beautiful, but goodness!" Lyn declared under her breath.

Eesha and Onya chuckled softly at their friend's impatience as they turned toward the group of males gathered about fifty feet from where the women were lying in shimmering body oils and jeweled garments. Onya's nerves were jittery as she shifted. Her brassiere, studded with semi precious jewels, clanked softly as she folded her knees toward her chest.

"I've been thinking about this for quite some time," Lyn said before a dramatic pause. "I want Maal. That just needs to be made clear."

Eesha let out a long, low whistle. "He's top notch, as good as it gets... unless you factor in Quince."

Together, the two women glanced at Onya, studying her reaction carefully. She chose not to bite. Though they'd been her close friends for as long as she could remember, she felt the need to keep her infatuation with him quiet. There were few things worse than declaring your interest in someone, only to find that they'd chosen someone else. For a while only the rustling of leaves could be heard along with the nearby chatter of birds. In spite of the awkward pause, Onya held out on any information. Her feelings were hers and hers alone.

"Even if you aren't chosen by the man you want in the first Rite, *you* make the final decision," Eesha said as if reading her friend's intimate thoughts. "*And* even though they have to agree, the men never argue when preferred partners are chosen."

"But I want him to choose *me*," Onya cut in with more emphasis than she would have liked. "I want the interest to be mutual. Who wants to drag a male into the preferred partner Rite?"

Eesha sighed knowingly. "*Everyone wants to be wanted Onya.* I'm only saying that either way you win. The preferred partner Rite is months from now. Stop worrying."

"Well, all I know is Maal had better want me. And as I look around, he'll have a difficult time finding a finer female," Lyn declared with a flip of her braids. "Unless it was one of you," she said quickly, toning down her egoism. "But you two don't count. You're my best friends," she remarked with an off-handed wink.

"We know, we know," Eesha said, rolling her eyes. "I'll take either of Quince's brothers. They're triplets... how can you lose?"

"True, but Dez is a little bit shorter than El and Quince's chin is a little more pronounced than Dez--" Onya began.

"Hmm, looks like *someone's* been thinking on this a little bit more than she's willing to admit!" interrupted Lyn in a slightly playful, slightly accusatory tone. "And how can you even tell Quince and Dez apart? You've only seen them twice!"

Feet away a procession of males moved toward them. Shoulders squared and heads high, they approached with eager eyes and confident smiles. "Shh, they're coming!" Onya warned.

The women quickly spread out and sat up as they approached. One by one, they knelt next to the woman they desired to pleasure for the Rite. Onya held her breath nervously. She spotted Quince in her periphery. Out of the corner of her eye, she saw Eesha smile broadly when Dez knelt beside her and kissed her hand.

Awkwardness set in suddenly. She looked up in surprise. Maal and Quince were now standing shoulder to shoulder, both gazing down at her. It seemed the two men were just as shocked as she. Maal flinched while Quince rolled his shoulders backward. When everything was said and done, it was Maal who blundered and, taking full advantage of his hesitation, Quince knelt quickly at Onya's side. Taken aback, Maal swiftly disguised his disappointment and bowed before Lyn.

"May I?" Quince asked in a deep baritone.

Onya shook her head fervently as he took her hands in his and poured a sensual gaze over her welcoming physique. The sparkle in his eyes flickered into a lasting flame. A smile spread across his lips. He bent over slightly, parted her legs like the blades of a dulled scissor, and ran his tongue along her inner thigh. She shivered a moment, the dark raisins atop her breasts hardening instantly. With ease, she watched him roll them between his thumb and index finger as an extended breath slipped from her lips. Carefully, he laid her flat, lightly kissing her toes, her ankles, her shins, before parting the already moistened lips of her center. He manipulated the hood, rubbing it sensually until it swelled.

Lost in a pleasure-filled whirlwind, she rested her palms on his thick, black waves and guided his head toward her pleasure. Her only thoughts now were of paradise. Every pleasing smell, color, touch, and taste she'd ever experienced ripped through her memory and attached itself like a strong adhesive. What she felt was beyond mere enjoyment; the word simply didn't capture the moment's intensity. Flawlessly, he pinpointed her erogenous zones as if by instinct. They were communicating in a wordless language, an intoxicating blend of utopia and taboo where everything existed on a plane void of inhibition. Had it not been for the raw passion she was feeling, she would have certainly been terrified. The only words she could muster were a few excited yelps while he attended to her like a seasoned artist would a masterpiece. Treating it like a palette of endless color, he lifted his head, purposely locked his eyes with hers, and licked his full lips passionately before again plunging between her thighs.

A panoramic view of heaving breasts, arched spines, and raised legs dotted the horizon as the female Youth willingly received their bliss. Wails of lust echoed from the steep plateau and, as if in recognition of the Rite, the moody clouds overhead parted to reveal a sizzling sun. The boughs of the Kywe trees swayed delicately against the fragrant air while Onya lay on her back, eyes fastened to the pale blue-sky overhead; her thoughts cushioned by the hovering clouds.

Flicking his tongue this way and that, Quince created delicate swirls, pulsing waves, and gentle pressure, all of which sent a prickling sensation to the tips of her fingers and toes. These duties were performed with an ever-intensifying stare. Keenly, he observed the slightest flinch of her forearms, the flutter of her eyelids, the sudden arch of her back, the alternating of clinched fists to open palms scooping small mounds of cool earth. She called out as he lapped up her fragrance like a hungry guest. Now he turned to her pink center, pleasing to all of his senses. With the insertion of his index finger, she observed his maleness lengthen in his pants. She moaned while his outstretched fingers teased her hardened nipples and the others became acquainted with the delicate flesh that seemed to call his name.

As he leaned in further, the trim hairs of his mustache grazed her navel. The hairs stood on the back of her neck. Without warning, the thrusting explorations began while he rubbed her soft bud with his thumb. Instantly, there was a multitudinous wave like the echo of a cymbal reverberating throughout her entire frame. Her body quaked and fell limp. Instinctively, she pushed his head away and pulled her knees together. Panting breathlessly, she lay still. In no hurry at all, he waited patiently, observing the by-products from the extensive spasms he'd caused.

Moments later she pulled herself up and smiled. He winked before she lifted him to his knees, his length rock hard and ready to be pleasured. With the utmost care, she untied the small knot in his lightweight, drawstring pants and pulled them below his muscular thighs. He stood, towering above her now, and removed his pants fully before tossing them aside in a hasty pile. Never before had she seen such an attractive organ. A deep shade of beautiful brown, she found its thickness to be arousing, enticing. The firm head stood strong on the end of its lengthy shaft as it bobbed back and forth, inviting a caress.

She grabbed it aggressively with one hand, introducing it to her moist lips and began by merely flicking her tongue around the underside of the head. She looked up from where she knelt just as he bit his lip, gratified. Then she massaged the large sacs, rolling them between her palm and forefingers, examining the soft, curly hairs and tender stretch of skin on its underside. Removing her other hand from the shaft, she thrust it down the opening of her throat, careful to cover her teeth with the rim of her mouth. He moaned. His eyes rolled so that only the whites were visible and with open palms, he gently grasped two handfuls of her silky, sun-spun locs. Repositioning herself, she reached for the sweaty, solid, ebony cinder blocks that made up his abdomen while he bent over slightly to caress the smooth, round buttocks resting on the backs of her heels.

Tiny beads of sweat dotted her forehead and nape as she continued to slide her tongue about his throbbing member, enveloping her lips tightly around the bottom of the shaft. On the first upstroke, her tongue lingered, dancing around and around the head for playful moments of what seemed to be an eternity. Then, without warning she enveloped her lips tightly around his shaft, down stroke-her tongue became a suctioning funnel of ecstasy. Slowly, he wound his hips in a forward motion, pushing himself further inside the warm crevices of her mouth. The mere satisfaction of his throaty whispers and sharp intakes of breath were a thrill all their own. She picked up the pace. In a blinding blur of lust, she lost herself in the sweetness of the encounter, the soft thrusting, and the slippery sounds of bliss. Before she knew it, he'd lifted her from the ground, lay down on his back and positioned her dripping mound firmly on his face. With an erratic shudder, she slid her pulsating valley over his warm tongue, guiding her hips in a circular motion now, absorbing the fruits of his flawless technique. Mindful not to neglect his pleasure, she leaned forward, taking him between her lips once more as he squeezed her buttocks gently.

Electricity permeated the air as the men and women began to climax, some separately, others as one. Then there was a thunder that only they could hear and in a blur of iridescent delight, tension, and elasticity, Onya and Quince exploded, together. Within minutes, they slid across one another and rested side by side.

"Whew," she murmured on an exhausted breath. "Thank you." Onya continued to pant, while she lay there across his torso, slick with glistening sweat.

Quince pried his eyes open slightly and ran his palms over his face. Carefully he shifted his weight and propped up onto an elbow. "No ...*thank you*," he replied tenderly as he ran an index finger lazily over one of her shimmering thighs. "Maal almost got to you first, good thing I was persistent," he chuckled softly.

Taken aback by the mention of the awkward turn of events, Onya sighed and turned to face him. "I'm glad you were persistent," she said while stroking the dark hairs of his goatee. She blanketed him with a sultry stare. "Besides... Lyn made it clear she wanted Maal and he did a pretty good job of dismissing the whole thing. It certainly looks like she bought it," Onya said with a small smile as she gazed over Quince's shoulder in the direction of their entangled bodies. He cupped her chin in his palm and allowed their eyes to lock before he spoke. His propensity for romantic suspense was truly appreciated.

"So... tell me a little about the woman called Onya." She loved the way he allowed her name to roll over his tongue suggestively, like her name alone emitted a raw and undeniable passion. "Who is she *exactly*?"

She found it difficult to wrestle herself away from his words. His eloquence was unprecedented and her nerves were clearly frayed. "Okay Mister Change the Subject," she chuckled nervously and settled on her elbows. "Onya is whomever she needs to be when the time presents itself," she replied carefully after a deep inhale. "Onya is a shape-shifter and a chameleon; a friend and a General. A warrior and a lover."

Quince fixed his eyes on her longingly, pondering her response. "And what does this particular situation require you to be?"

She couldn't help but allow a small smile to reveal itself through her pursed lips. The gig was up. She could no longer feign the "just going through the ritualistic motions" persona she'd been attempting. The man was suave and the genuine to the bone interest that gleamed in his pupils caused her heart to skip. "This moment," she replied slowly, "requires me to be an artist and a lover, an instrument of pleasure. Intimacy *is* art after all. It falls in line with the teachings of Enlightenment."

Quince's broad smile revealed a set of perfect white teeth as his gaze shifted toward the clouds. "Good answer and right you are."

"And what about you Mr. General? Exactly what makes General Quince tick?" she asked, tilting her head to the side.

"The simple things," he said in a faraway tone while homing in on the horizon. "I enjoy air and earth and water and fire and beauty..." he trailed off as he caressed her cheeks before gently grasping a handful of her hair. Thick locs cascaded over his palm, catching the red rays of the sun until they were gleaming auburn-tinged spirals. The shine of her lips cast a spell on him. No longer able to bear even the slightest distance between them, he leaned in and kissed her deeply, enjoying the sweetness of her lush mouth like a succulent bowl of fresh citrus fruit. "I enjoy you," he said in a seductive growl as they parted.

As the setting sun slowly gathered into an evening haze, they alternated intense conversation with seething pleasure. Talk of the war and Enlightenment; The One Faith, and Taste littered their dialogue as they lay lazily on the cliff side. He kissed her bare shoulders lightly, wondering if he'd ever truly be able to vanquish the smoldering flame she'd lit inside him. Meanwhile, she knew that the dance they'd begun teetered on the precipice of what was forbidden. Unable to pull away though, she thrust her instincts aside and allowed nature to take its lovely and unexpected course.

7

GLO CITY

A flattened cloud tinted a striking orange-red spread itself thinly across the sky. It was early evening and again the genders had separated. With the first Rite behind them and conflict in plain view; the male Youth returned briefly to Nu in order to gather their weaponry in preparation for the possibility of battle. The pleasures they'd experienced the day before notwithstanding; Quince, Maal, and the others were taking heed to Born's advice. The Elders would certainly see their continuance of Taste as a blatant declaration of war and they'd attack when they believed the Youth were most vulnerable.

Quince ran his fingers along the stitching of his slender leather quiver as he packed a thick bundle of handcrafted arrows firmly inside. He'd stitched the quiver by hand when he was a boy. All those years ago, he'd wondered if there would ever be a time to utilize his weapons on such a peaceful island. He sighed heavily at the thoughts of innocence, grateful now that the Elders had the foresight to train them in the mastery of weapons and in the Ido martial arts. The Youth had been preparing for combat since their transformation; it was part of their disciplinary regimen. However, Quince was more concerned with how they'd approach their new and unique enemy. Suddenly, it clearly resonated with him that they'd be fighting their own parents to the death. Both sickened and saddened by the thought, half of him wanted to arrange a meeting with Dame and the other Elders to sort out the matter. However, the painful truth was evident. If Born had been unable to reason with him, a conference surely would not be worth the effort.

He swung a thick bow over his left shoulder blade as Maal stirred slightly in the corner of the hut. His co-General appeared to be in deep thought as he applied a bit of poison to the serrated edges of two long, expertly hewn spears and a broadsword. With one last, longing look at the hut where he'd spent his youth, he headed outside where the others were gathered in a loose huddle, waiting for further direction as to their next course of action. As he gazed out at the concerned and solemn faces; a sinking feeling in his gut told him that life on the island would never be the same.

Heavy footfalls fell in step with his own as he exited the cool room into the blazing heat. A familiar voice rang out behind him before he could advance further into the sunshine.

"How was it?" Dez asked with a sly smile as he wrapped a long arm around his brother's shoulder. Quince responded with a feigned expression of confusion.

"Onya," he prodded. "Come on Quince, ever since the night of the meeting I *knew* she was the one you wanted." El joined the two men as they walked swiftly toward the larger group.

"Oh," Quince said thoughtfully, drifting back to the Oral Rite the day before. "It ... it was good." He said with a vague grin.

Dez stopped short, folded his arms across his broad, bare chest and grinned broadly. "What kind of answer is that? We're triplets, not mind readers! Come on, give us the goods…we're your brothers. If you can't talk to us, who do you have?"

"Leave me out of this one." El said jokingly. "Let the man talk about it when he wants."

Dez waved off El's comment and turned back to Quince. "You know you want to know as bad as I do El," he said with a smirk.

Quince exhaled and let out a long whistle. He literally had to fight to keep his lids from lowering while he recalled the events of the day before. "It was good, *really good*. She was unbelievable. It was better than I'd ever thought--"

"Come on, we need to get going." Maal's voice rang out sharply over the snippets of conversation. Quince felt a pair of eyes boring into the back of his head as he passed. Dez gave Quince a questioning glance.

"We'll talk when we get to camp," Dez whispered, annoyed.

***

Within minutes they were traveling east to the confines of Glo City for a clandestine meeting with a Stripe informant. Glo had been constructed during the Insect War twenty years prior between the Butterfly Dragons, flying miniature lizards with colorful wings, the Sphinx, and the Lena Bugs, palm-sized beetles plentiful in Three Wood. At the time, the wings of the Butterfly Dragons were heavily sought after and used in Sphinx medicine.

In order to save their species, the creatures chose to wage a fierce revolt. Having underestimated the power of the Dragons, the Sphinx turned to the exoskeletons of the Lena Bugs as a replacement medicinal agent. Now facing extinction just as the Butterfly Dragons had, the Lena Bugs chose to align themselves with the Sphinx in order to protect themselves.

The Ido Youth held a vested interest in the war. Without the Sphinx, the island would be without skilled healers to attend to them in case of injury or illness. Led by Dame, the Youth sent forth a well-trained company of warriors. With their aid, the Sphinx survived brutal attacks along the perimeter of the Smoke Desert and Oasis Fall territories. Though the war ended without a clear victory and a treaty of peace was sworn into existence, the Butterfly Dragons designed the cocoon to discourage future attack. It had since been enhanced by the Stripes, deftly astute in architecture and masters of construction. Together they'd created the island's economic center and entertainment hub, rivaled aesthetically only by Vine City.

A thriving city enclosed within an opaque cocoon, Glo received its name from the autonomous laser lights illuminating its ever-present darkness. Glo City was Ido's bustling marketplace and lone red light district where bizarre indulgences could be fed for the right price. Though largely inhabited by the Stripes and Butterfly Dragons, there was a sprinkling of intelligent beasts, mysterious Djinn, and the occasional Sphinx, weary from his or her redundant fact-finding and eager for a good time.

On the city's wooded outskirts, El quietly stoked a crackling fire while Dez slid the evening meal on wooden skewers. The male Youth sat in bunches under the cover of trees, their individual fires casting playful shadows on the leaves as the sun took a final bow before days end.

"It is nearly nightfall," observed Maal between heaping mouthfuls. "When will we be led inside the city?"

There was a noticeable strain in his voice. Sitting with his legs crossed, Quince shifted on the ground. Their tension split the still air down the middle. "At sundown. The Stripe informant, who goes by the name of Well, has agreed to meet us here. Stripes are normally punctual. Gather ten men, we should be going soon."

Maal rose from where he sat and sauntered into the center of camp. Men were laughing and chattering over their feasts of funnel fish, herb, and bread. The succulent smells of spices and slow roasted fish tickled his nostrils pleasingly. It seemed the outcome of the first Rite had raised the men's spirits considerably, even in the midst of an impending war. The conversations subsided once they'd noticed his presence.

He cleared his throat before beginning. "Soon we will be inside the walls of--"

A faint rustling between the nearby trees shifted their attention. Quince straightened his spine and peered over El's shoulder as he tended the fire. Dez hastily placed his half eaten skewer on a leaf and walked briskly to Maal's side. Heads swiveled toward the disturbed branches while blades, bows, spears, and flails were drawn instinctively. An icy silence fell; this was *not* the way a Stripe would enter an Ido camp and they all knew it.

"Declare yourself!" Maal boomed loudly as the males formed ranks around him.

From between two massive trees there was a gurgling sound, soft at first, but growing louder until it erupted into a nonsensical laugh. There was more shuffling when out stepped a bird of nearly 6 feet standing on a pair of thin, spindly legs. Its eyes were large and cross. The long and pronounced beak jutted out from its head in the likeness of a human nose and its feathers lay in distinctive shades of purple. The bird was odd looking, almost laughable, but in a frightening kind of way. At their first sight of it, the men relaxed their weapons as well as their nerves. Slowly, its mouth crumpled into a broad grin.

"Ah, temper, temper. What have you to fear from a Diaw?" Its voice was hard to follow. Like the scratching of fingernails, the uncomfortable pitch sounded as if nature had never meant for it to speak at all. The Diaw blinked slyly, expecting an answer from the men. Receiving none, it marched forward with an awkward bounce, twitching now and again and leading with its beak as most winged creatures do.

"What do you want with us, Diaw?" Dez demanded maliciously, one hand still steadying his blade.

"This Diaw has a name," It said proudly. "I am called Ly and I come to do what Diaw are meant to do, relay messages. I have word from the Stripes," said the bird while grinning widely at Dez.

"Speak your peace; we have no time for games," Maal demanded, stepping between Dez and the large beast.

"Well cannot meet you. In his stead, I will lead you into the city of lights."

Quince approached the tight inner circle now. "This is very unlike the Stripes," he commented uneasily. "They are true to their word always. We were told he would meet us here by nightfall."

Ly attempted to snort impatiently, but the sound that escaped its beak was more like a cross between a cough and a clucking sneeze. "I only know what I am told. I have no knowledge of what words are true and what words are un--"

"You sniveling beast! You know treachery all too well! Your kind invented it!" Dez exclaimed before allowing his gaze to swing angrily between Quince and Maal. "We should enter the city alone and take our chances with what meets us there!" he shouted, lunging his weapon at the throat of the now visibly frightened bird.

"We cannot enter Glo without a guide. Nothing there is as it seems. None of us have ever experienced life inside its walls, Dez! Lower your weapon!" Quince commanded.

Reluctantly he obeyed, but continued to snarl in Ly's direction.

"Enough of this! Take us into the city and to Well," dictated Maal in an annoyed whisper. "Ten of you will enter the city with me. The others will man the camp and keep a lookout for the Elders. El, you are in charge of those staying behind." El nodded obediently and returned to the fire he'd been tending.

Still visibly shaken, the bird dug its yellow claws into the dirt before turning back in the direction it had come. Those chosen to enter the city returned briefly to their individual fires, extinguished the small flames with dirt, and gathered the remainder of their dinner.

With Maal in the lead and Quince bringing up the rear, the men walked carefully among humongous tree trunks and soft, mossy undergrowth. Quince trudged along in deep thought unable to ignore the strangeness of their current situation. Throughout history, the Diaw had never been apt to align themselves with the Stripes and vice versa. Somehow, he couldn't shake the feeling that they were walking into a trap. Cautiously, he ran a palm across his large mahogany bow and glanced at the small unit ahead of him. With a slow exhale he marched behind the others, hoping for the best, but half expecting the worst. It was wartime after all; and treachery was to be expected.

After a short while, they found themselves standing face to face with the entrance to the city. From a distance, its outer shell looked more like a massive, rounded tent than a cocoon. At a closer view, one could make out the overlapping layers and spidery patterns etched throughout like pulsing, bluish veins. The city seemed to be alive, breathing. The main entrance was a wide cut in the side of the cocoon's shell. Two statues flanked each side, one of a Stripe lying lazily on its back, the other, a Butterfly Dragon dressed in a suit of armor, ready for battle. On Ly's cue, they passed through the entrance in pairs.

The lights inside were blinding, flashing diagonally, horizontally, and vertically, but in a fluid pattern that became bearable after a short time. Quince squinted through his surroundings after giving his eyes time to adjust. The buildings, which were made of the same cocoon layering as the city's outer shell, stood on stilts of brilliant light, a staple of Stripe architecture. Hollow tubes connected clusters of buildings to one another in a vast labyrinth. Glo City was a matrix of fast-paced movement; nothing seemed stationary. The "street" they'd been standing on instantly began to move as if they were on a giant conveyor belt. The belts wove throughout the city according to one's destination. There were signs in folk language, the native tongue of the Painted Folk and Stripes, directing visitors to places inside the city. Quince stared for a moment at the soft symbols of curling lines and circles as Dez arrived at his side. Ignorant of the city's unusual make-up, they continued to follow the gangly bird ahead of them.

In his periphery, he could make out a few other Diaw walking through the city, bumbling, giggling, and talking amongst one another and to themselves. A male and female Sphinx huddled outside one of the brilliant crimson tubes. Mischievous smiles spread across their faces as they flicked their tails gingerly. One by one, they disappeared inside the red light and whisked away to the building above. Oddly though, there were no Butterfly dragons in sight. He glanced around quickly; scanning the rainbow-colored skin and signature, white-blond tresses of the Stripes manning their elixir filled carts and luminously lit stores. He couldn't shake the feeling that they were being given sideways glances.

"Take us to Well," Quince commanded as the last of the male Youth entered the city.

Ly bowed his head ever so slightly and led them toward one of the hollow tubes. Awkwardly, he stepped inside.

As Quince followed close behind, he realized that the tube wasn't a tube at all. What he thought to be hollow was in fact, a pillar of emerald green light. In an instant, Ly was swept away to the pulsing green building above their heads. In twos, they followed. Maal stood beside him now, basking in brilliant green. Dez lagged behind to bring up the rear. As they stood there, shoulder-to-shoulder, Quince felt a sudden wave of warmth as a smooth *whoosh* compressed the air around them. The two men were, in fact, being pushed effortlessly off the ground. Forcing his eyes open, he looked down at the others as he ascended, the bottom of his stomach still on the ground below. Before he could so much as blink, they were standing in a dark green foyer large enough for the men to stand in comfortably. Several moments passed before the entire group was transported from below.

In front of them stood a large oak door with an odd, spear-like handle. The air was thin and uninviting as if it were creating some kind of transparent shield of protection from a known intruder. Maal stepped forward to open the door. Instantly, the handle that had once protruded outward sunk inside the oak and politely swung away from them on a hinge. Quince blinked in surprise and looked around at the others. Puzzled expressions lined their faces as they stepped inside cautiously. The large room revealed what looked like a dining area basking in a florescent shade of green similar to the light that had guided them there. The men shuffled inside, anxious to move from the now cramped space in the foyer to the roomier 'restaurant' ahead. There were chairs made of Raha tree bark resting beneath sturdy tables. A bar of some sort, sat against the far wall, high chairs and wooden goblets lie unoccupied. Shining glass bottles containing various colorful liquids stood on the counter, but there was no barman waiting to attend to them. In fact, there were no customers waiting to be served at all. As the last of the men entered, Quince felt the hairs stand on the back of his neck; something was terribly wrong.

"Don't close that---", but his directive was too late. The heavy oaken door closed behind them with an echoing thud and the bright light inside flickered and faded at once. Instinctively, the men drew their weapons and assumed position. No one spoke. It was completely dark aside from the weaving lights shining on the outside of the building's shell. In the inky darkness, their remaining senses would have to serve them well.

Quince moved backward a few paces until he stood shoulder to shoulder with Dez and Maal. He could hear their anxious breathing, the rise and fall of their chests like thunder before a deafening rain. Instinctively, they began forming ranks. The ten men were now flush with the room's circular wall, spreading themselves strategically in preparation for conflict. It was an intelligent tactic. Though they'd been taken by surprise, they would not be surrounded. And then, it happened. The unmistakable sound of an arrow whistled through the air and an insufferable cry rang out. The lights were ablaze again as the combat began.

The wail had come from Dez, a large arrow jutting painfully from his left leg. Bright red blood began to pour, drenching his loose fitting pants. After grabbing his injured thigh, he crumpled to the ground. Quince bent low to shield his wounded brother as he cursed in agony. Bow in hand, he reached into his quiver for an arrow with a fluid motion and released, hitting a dark figure dressed in white sheik-like pants and headgear. However, instead of making contact, the arrow sailed long and the figure disappeared.

"It's a diversion! They're using holograms!" he yelled wildly to the others.

"Oh, but I assure you, I'm quite real!" said a deep voice overhead, lunging the edge of a serrated sword at Quince's exposed chest. Seconds away from death, Quince saw the flat surface of a leather bound shield intercept the weapon before it could make contact. Maal dove between them fiercely. Caught off guard, the Elder recovered from the counterattack a moment too late. Maal swept his legs from beneath him causing the man to land on his back with a sickening crunch.

"We've got to get out of here. Three of us are already---," Maal trailed off, anger flashing in the pupils of his eyes. He gestured toward Dez who convulsed in pain. "Take him to the entrance while the rest of us hold them off. We'll form a barrier," he said through clenched teeth while surveying the ensuing battle around them.

"Okay," Quince shouted. Maal had just saved his life. His unspeakable appreciation had been communicated through his humble expression. He knew that this was no time for sappy regards. Maal stood up, brandishing a blade in front of him. Skillfully, he grappled with two more Elders, one who turned out to be a hologram. The lights were flashing madly as Quince attempted to lift his brother from the floor. Recognizing their exposed vulnerability, an Elder ran toward them, the loose fabric of his garments clinging to an injured and bleeding calf. Dez screamed in fury from the floor and lifted himself momentarily on one knee. Quince reached for another arrow as Dez drove the sword he still held in his right hand into the man's chest. The Elder's bloodthirsty expression slackened as he fell forward onto the ground. With a lighting quick release, Quince managed to thwart another's progress by sinking an arrow in his abdomen. He sputtered and fell inches from their crouching position.

As quickly as he could manage, Quince headed toward the door, Dez wounded and woozy as he carried his weight. Dez did his best to help their movement by hopping on his good leg toward the entrance a few feet away but his eyes were beginning to roll backward as his complexion grayed. The symptoms could only mean one thing; he'd been poisoned. There were only a few of them left and the holograms continued to confuse and muddle their bearings. The great oak door had already been forced open by one of the Youth as they backed into the green light transporting them back to ground level. They all managed to crowd inside the tube of light at once and were whisked away in seconds. As soon as their feet touched ground, carrying the wounded and dead on their shoulders, the unit broke into a fierce counter productive run along the conveyor belt toward the entrance of the city. Bloody, wounded, and panting furiously, the men were met with surprised stares as they ran through huddled creatures and throngs of Stripes. Maal, the last to exit the tunnel of light, ran to their aid. Together, he and Quince lifted Dez, balancing his weight equally on their shoulders as he grimaced.

"He needs to see Ankh," Maal said gruffly, looking over his shoulder for enemy pursuit. "Once we gather everyone back at camp, we'll head to the Falls." Quince nodded in agreement. As he peered down at his brother, he fought back rage. Again, Dez yelled out in gut wrenching pain.

8

COURTING VYE

There were songs in the air surrounding the gentle slopes of vivid green. The Tremor Hills housed its own choir of clouds; a harmony existed among the birds and the trees hummed in echoing content. All obstacles seemed to melt and dissipate into nothing when within their reach. Wrapped in white cloth from head to toe, Vye knelt under the broad umbrella-like branches of a Weeping tree in vigilant prayer and meditation.

In her mind, she visualized the size of a tiny ding seed. According to The Guide, the very hills she sat on could shift if her thoughts were truly pure. This kind of faith was new to her. No ancestral offerings were needed. Sacrifices in exchange for atonement were unnecessary and considered pagan. Still, she found the old Ido customs familiar while these new beliefs seemed so alien that they were almost discouraging.

For instance, she thought she'd had faith that the Youth would accept their demands, yet this belief proved futile. Yet again, she had faith that the differences between Youth and Elder would not culminate into a Civil War, but here they were readying themselves for conflict. Opening her eyes to the sprawling sky, she thought of her sons: strong, handsome, charming, intelligent. True enough, she hadn't raised them. None of the Ido Elders had a hand in rearing their own children. But when she visited, she saw combustible life in their eyes. Quince, born first, was the levelheaded leader. He was truly an old soul, an Ancestor held hostage in the body of a child. Dez, on the other hand, was the joker, the squeaky wheel who'd always made his opinions known, the charismatic charmer and hothead. Then there was El, the youngest of her nearly identical sons. Born three hours after the first two, El was a quiet storm, the first to be underestimated or even dismissed, but the least likely to be crossed ever again.

One by one she pictured them as she had seen them last. El was the tallest; his lean physique accentuated by his smile, welcoming and kind. Quince always looked to be contemplating the fate of the world, even when nothing was awry. He was muscular and strong, the most handsome of the three. Physically, Dez was a combination of his brothers. He was the same height as Quince, but a bit stockier. Where were they right now? Surely, they were preparing for war as Dame had been. She bristled angrily at the thought. Under the new faith, the Elder women were forbidden to engage in combat. The new decree was a hard sell to everyone, especially Eyeno, the female Bgongo guru and former General of the female Ido Youth. In the end however, the female Elders felt it best not to participate. No parent should look forward to opposing his or her own offspring in war. The price was too high.

In spite of the strict upbringing forbidding her to express emotion, she was frightened to know of what Dame was capable. Having lived during the times of the Insect Wars, she'd seen his imposing will at full throttle. She closed her eyes tighter, praying harder, as if the tightening of the eyelids and the clenching of teeth somehow affected the outcome of her prayers. She meditated vehemently on the safety of her children and hoped with every fiber of her being that they would see the light of The Guide.

On that fateful day when it had been suggested they be sacrificed, she recalled her tearful pleas to Born on their behalf. Darm, her preferred partner and the boys' father, had long since perished in the Insect Wars. She recalled standing before the powerful merman alone and clearly distraught. Mercifully, he had obliged her request and for that very reason, she was one of the last to convert completely. Naturally, she'd needed more convincing than the others had. There was a certain loyalty she had to Born and still there were times when she questioned her decision to leave the traditions of old behind.

"I thought you'd be here."

Startled, she opened her eyes and peered up at the shadow before her. His shoulders were so broad; the sprawling hills were concealed behind him. A delicate smile spread across his lips. He was an incredible sight to behold. Though his presence was whole enough to cause a shiver, the new faith had calmed his spirit, made him gentler, more approachable, and likable even.

"Dame. What brings you here this evening?" she said with a small smile.

"You," he said simply, studying her expression with interest. There was something hidden behind his back. She jerked her body around to steel a peek.

He let go of an easy laugh. "Just ask, Vye. If you want to know what I have behind my back, just ask." He shook his head as he set a large basket and a bouquet of fresh cut Amethyst grass at her side. "May I?" he asked before taking a seat beside her.

Breathtaking and rare, Amethyst grass were clusters of gemstones grown on long, flowered stems and found only in the eastern parts of the island. They were most plentiful in the Keep Grasslands and Oasis Falls. She'd developed an affinity for the bouquets during one of the Rites to Taste. Shades of purple were calming to the spirit and she'd been pleased to know that purple was one of the colors worn consistently by members of the Faith. In fact, The Guide had anointed them all with amethyst and obsidian anklets after the completion of their waves.

"How did you know?" whispered Vye, still ogling the sparkling stones in shades ranging from pale lavender to deep indigo.

"I have my ways," he remarked with a hint of mystery. She rolled her eyes impatiently until he surrendered his source. "Okay, okay," he chuckled. "Actually I just asked Eyeno, she knows you better than anyone."

"Thank you. That was...thoughtful of you," she replied, still admiring the bouquet. "Very thoughtful."

Nodding slightly, he bent toward the basket, lugged it forward, pulled out a thick blanket, and spread it on the ground next to them. "Let's sit on this. We should eat. The sun will set within the hour and we still have to get back to Vine City."

"What's in the basket?" she asked curiously, enjoying the show and tell he'd gone to the trouble of planning.

He winked. "Why don't you open it and see?"

Excitedly, she obliged. Inside was an assortment of breads and cheeses along with fresh fruits packed in individual wooden bowls. Dame pulled out a bowl and motioned for her to do the same. For a few silent moments they enjoyed the flavors, delicate, savory, and sweet. Vye could not recall a time when she'd had fresher fruit since her own childhood. She tilted her head backward toward the dimming sky and breathed in the aroma of the fresh bread.

"We have to be the example Vye," Dame blurted out suddenly.

Clearly caught off guard, she gave him an awkward glance before responding. "The example for what Dame?"

He exhaled through his nose before taking one of her hands in his, moved in closer and planted a kiss on her lips. *"We have to be the example,"* he repeated in a low, intense whisper, his dark eyes twinkling.

She savored the kiss. Though brief, it had been heavy, rich with meaning and simmering with intent. She looked away, embarrassed of what The Guide would think. The discomfort that followed was thicker than falling molasses. She rocked forward, clutching her knees to her chest and thought about the emotions she would have been shunned for feeling under the old ways. Then there came a wave of relief. A large part of her was thankful for the ability to truly feel at last. It was strange though, like an intrusive rush of cold air or an unexpected splash of water. Suddenly, she wondered with guilt as to what rules this kiss; this small token of affection, had broken.

"He knows, don't worry," Dame said softly, reading her mind. "I've told him about the respect we shared in the past. I also informed him about Darm and Imar's deaths and their decent into the realm of the Ancestors. He gives us his blessing. We would be the example and everyone else will follow. Besides, there's no harm in an innocent kiss," he paused to look at her a moment, holding her hostage with his stare.

Vye fumbled with her words nervously and looked around, searching for answers. There were none. Though unsure of how she truly felt; she knew coupling with Dame would be the right thing to do for the Faith. Confusion plagued her mind like a nagging cough before the onset of sickness.

"Things won't ever be the same again Vye...you know that, right?"

Instantly, she was snatched from the nervous energy clogging her mind and yanked back into the moment. Dame's statement had been layered. The One Faith of course, brought with it a dizzying amount of change. There were still things she was unaware of; there seemed to be something new to learn with each passing day. But it wasn't the religion he was speaking of and she knew it. A civil war was unprecedented on the island. They were embarking upon uncharted territory.

She wiped her mouth with a damp cloth before speaking. "I was just thinking about...my sons," she said finally. "I was wondering if..."

He held her close and kissed her forehead gently, all the while his heart thumped loudly in his chest. "Vye, they have declared war--"

"But we never received official word from them. They never said they *wouldn't* accept the Faith---" she cut in, raising her head from his muscular chest to meet a pair of serious eyes.

"Vye," he interrupted. "They went ahead with the first Rite. You and I both know that is a blatant declaration of ---"

"War," she said with him. The breeze picked up, causing the tall tree overhead to sway. She looked away, her expression worried and torn.

"They've also asked for permission from the Ancestors."

"And Born granted it?" she asked with shock.

"Apparently yes, but what would you expect from him? The Ancestors and Taste are one and the same. Why would you expect them to discourage a war that seeks to preserve the old traditions?" he asked firmly.

"The Born I know is merciful. He is wise and ---"

"The Born you know is now obsolete. The One Faith has no room for Born unless he converts. He is a pagan god that we were wrong for elevating to power. We were wrong for revering the Ancestors Vye!"

She shook her head in reluctant opposition. There was so much she still hadn't bought into, so much she was reluctant to accept. "The Ancestors are revered because of their raw conjuring abilities, and still, those abilities were earned. They have passed through Youth, Enlightenment, and the Afterlife. Power is their reward. The Ido reward their Ancestors in our culture. They protect us and because of that they deserve our respect," she stated in an angry rebuttal.

Dame shot her a stony glare and made sure their eyes were locked and leveled before he spoke. "The Ancestors are false idols, Vye," he said in a harsh whisper. "They are pagan gods and goddesses. We now have in our midst a man whose conjuring power remains rooted in his faith. His powers rival those of Born and all of the Mer. His message is love and if we only believe, we can make that same ascension, perform the same miracles... *without* the perversions of Taste!"

Maneuvering away from his grasp, Vye sat up and pulled her knees back to her chest. "We can agree to disagree on that fact... but what about my sons Dame? What about all of our children? They have no wartime experience. I saw you during The Insect Wars." Her voice grew louder, creating an echo in the deserted distance. "I know the warrior you are. Lives will be lost. *My sons lives may be lost!*"

"Are you forgetting that my daughter is also a part of this so called Youth Cause?" he replied haughtily.

She cut her eyes at him sharply, her tone strained. "You have informants! What else do you know? How are Quince, Dez, and El? Have you attacked them yet? I want to know Dame! I want to know!"

He pulled her flailing arms closer to him, wanting to avoid the inevitable but knowing he could not. "Yes, we launched a surprise attack yesterday in Glo City," he said finally in muffled tones. "We had losses as did they. The Youth lost three: Dion, son of Sinaa, Tor, son of Bria, and Sheek, son of Livia."

"Their poor mothers." She spoke through gulps and varied breaths, but her expression remained stern. "My sons are alright Dame?"

Dame sighed like a man with an unbelievable burden to bear. Her breathing faltered as her stomach sunk to her knees. She knew. Her cheeks flushed. She felt faint. It was all she could do not to scream at the top of her lungs, not to lose control as she sat safely under a weeping tree in the Tremor Hills when she should have been protecting her sons.

"It's Dez isn't it? It's Dez!" Her voice rang out among the hills, scattering the chirping birds, disturbing the choir of clouds. Dame could do nothing but hold her as she cried out in pain.

"They are moving toward the Smoke Desert now. He needs Sphinx medicine," he said quietly, unable to meet her eyes. "Vye, this is the nature of war. We must trust in The One. The Guide says we should lay all of our troubles down."

With a wave of her hand, she dismissed his words and buried her face deep inside her hands. He held her as she moaned, still unwilling to allow the tears to fall.

"I can only hope that The One is just. I can only pray for that," she said softly on a quivering breath as the sun set ominously behind the swaying trees.

9

THE SECOND RITE

Finally, the air was changing. Two hours ago the humidity had been stifling. Bits of clothing clung to their skin and tempers had begun to flare from the obvious discomfort. The trek through Three Wood was filled with biting insects and their movement was hindered significantly due to the heat. Though the thick canopy above shielded them from direct rays of sunshine, it also trapped in moisture like a closed lid on a giant container. Now they welcomed the arid dryness as their sleek wooden boats sliced eastward through the crisp waters of The Shine River.

The fifty women traveled comfortably in ten slender canoes. At nearly fifty feet across, the river was large enough to hold four side by side. However, they chose to make the voyage in five rows of two as a safety precaution. A barren desert immersed in smoke loomed ahead while the bountiful greenery of the Keep Grasslands sloped downward onto the riverbank on their immediate left. Though picturesque, it would not be an easy journey. They were moving upstream, against the stubborn current and toward the mouth of the Falls. They knew; however, that this was the only logical way to enter the Sphinx Territories. A journey on foot through the desert was a dangerous and tedious one taken only if no other option was available.

Onya along with Eesha, Lyn and the other women, continued to row methodically, digging their colorful oars deep into the crystal clear water. Between heaves Onya took a moment to wipe the sweat from her brow and gazed pensively into the river. Funnel fish, named for their delicate shape, coiled fins, and iridescent color, zipped through a labyrinth of brilliantly colored weeds and fresh water coral jutting from the riverbed below. Spring abounded and she watched closely as the fish headed upstream to spawn in warmer waters. She found it quite interesting the way their voyage was much like the Youth's journey to Taste. Rituals were to be honored, not abandoned, and the fish were living proof, no matter how different they were anatomically.

A mixture of anger and shame ransacked her mind as she thought of her father. Though he hadn't made the decision on his own, in her mind he was fully responsible for the precarious situation in which her people now found themselves. Remembering vividly his heavy hand and domineering personality, she wondered who among the Elders was strong enough to resist him if there was any dissent. The truth was there probably weren't any at all. Frustrated, she shook her head, tightened her grasp on the oars and continued to row.

"Crazy isn't it?" asked one of the female warriors seated directly next to her. "And for all of this to happen on *our* watch…"

Onya lowered her chin and shook her head. "It's embarrassing… knowing that my father, *the* Elder General Dame, the greatest warrior in Ido history, is partly to blame for all of this. I'd always been so proud of him, proud to be his daughter--" she trailed off, fixating her eyes on the lush green trees lining the riverbank. It was important for her to appear strong and unmoved no matter how she really felt. The fact remained that she was one of their leaders and if they couldn't seek reassurance from her, then who? It was a domino effect. Eesha and Lyn were only as strong as she was. They operated as a singular unit with a common purpose. Several pairs of eyes bored into her back as she adjusted her body language. Her warriors needed her to be a rock and crumbling under pressure was not an option.

"Whatever it is…. we will get to the bottom of it or we will fight. We are Bgongo masters and outstanding warriors. We've been trained well." Immediately, the tense mood lifted a bit; a perfect time to change the subject. "What do you think tradition has in store for us once we get to the Oasis?"

Lore, the woman who'd spoken up before was the first to answer, her golden triceps gleaming with beads of sweat as she pushed and pulled methodically. "Maybe something to reinforce the ideals of feminine strength while at the same time stressing the importance of sensuality," she offered.

"Perhaps. Especially since, the males won't be there," remarked another near the stern of the boat.

"Might even involve the Djinn," Lore mused aloud. "*Now that would be very interesting.*" Onya raised her eyebrows while the others laughed. "I mean seriously Onya… can you imagine? Seduction by a Djinn?" She threw her head back and feigned a dramatic swoon. The laughter on the vessel echoed through the crisp air, causing birds to squawk and flee from their perches.

"Hey! No laughing allowed," joked Lyn as her vessel of inquisitive warriors careened ahead. Onya stuck her tongue out playfully and turned back to her giggling crew.

"You know now that you mention it that may not be so far-fetched Lore. I'm just not so excited about their mind locks," replied Daye, one of the warriors seated directly across from Onya. "You know they have to enter your mind to seduce you. Sex is 90 percent mental, 10 percent physical and all of them don't exactly have the best intentions."

"They wouldn't dare defy Born or Taste. The Djinn and the Ancestors have always worked in tandem," countered Onya as the rest of the female Youth nodded in agreement.

Lore took a moment to throw a thick braid over her shoulder and grinned. "Well if that's what we're in for, let's quit talking and get rowing!"

Onya let go of a small smile and shifted her gaze forward. After a few silent moments, she permitted her thoughts to drift to Quince. In spite of the very real and very imminent opportunity of a Djinn seduction, she couldn't help but look forward to the third Rite. All else paled in comparison to another interaction with him, no matter how brief. Still, shying away from the possibility that anything more than a powerful attraction existed between them was the correct thing to do. But she could still feel the remnants of electricity pulsing through her body from his touch. His kiss was a cloak of addiction, his scent a savory taboo. When her thoughts suddenly involved wondering if he was thinking of her, she quickly gathered herself, pushed them to the back of her mind, and half-heartedly prayed they'd teeter and fall from a dangerous edge. A shrill whistle interrupted her reverie as she glanced questioningly toward one of the nearby canoes.

"How much longer?" Lyn shouted, temporarily massaging her lean, aching biceps.

"About half an hour, so you may as well deal with it like the rest of us," Eesha shouted back in exhaustion. Lyn groaned loudly, but picked up the slack as the muscles in her arms visibly contracted and expanded with each pull.

They drifted now into the eerie mist of the Smoke Desert. Wisps of smoke engulfed the boats and riverbanks mercilessly, obstructing their view on all sides. Onya felt her skin crawl as the wide ribbons of smoke wove in and out of the vicinity like ghostly hands. This was a prime opportunity for attack. Attentively, she reached for the blade beneath her seat. She gave a shrill whistle of warning signaling for the others to be on guard and, hand on the spear in the leather holster wrapped around her thigh; she felt the minute particles of anxiety beginning to rise. Just then, an excited shout grasped her attention.

"I hear the Falls! We're almost there!"

Hopeful, Onya squinted through the layers of smoke and observed it dissipating some twenty feet ahead. Within minutes, she could hear its' monstrous pounding. Almost immediately the smoke parted like a grand, pale curtain to reveal the breathtaking brilliance of the Oasis Falls.

Fifty feet in front of them stood a tall, continuous chunk of rock. Though the overwhelming structure lacked enough height to be considered a mountain, it provided powerful, cliff-spilling waters that tumbled into the Shine river. The Oasis Falls housed a bustling city enveloped in the arms of two vertical rainbows. Meanwhile, the rock formed a barrier of protection from the drastic drop to the jagged coastline of the sea hidden on the other side.

Where there were breaks in the water falling over the rock face, Onya could make out the robust activity of the Sphinx. The Oasis and surrounding desert had been their home for centuries and they'd adjusted perfectly. As their boats drew closer, she saw several tiers of stairs and slanted walkways enclosed within tubes of glass disappearing and reappearing from the pounding water and towering palm trees extending from the cliffs. Caves and other smaller nooks were also sealed off with transparent glass for residences and other rooms of shelter.

Following her lead, the boats coasted toward a gentle curve to the right where the Falls tapered into a wide, shallow pool. They continued to row against the current until they came upon a large, well-hidden cave. Onya and the women on her boat threw themselves over the side and into the warm, calf-high water before pulling their lightweight canoes onto the sand. With little difficulty they anchored securely to a sturdy rock. The water was shallow here and the sunlight basked the hidden cave in an orange glow. Once docked, they perched on nearby rocks, or simply sat back and allowed the beauty of the oasis to wash over them.

After a much-needed break and some light conversation, the women stared at one another, awkwardly anticipating what would come. Onya looked around nervously as the women began to peel off their drenched wrap skirts and lay either completely nude or topless near the shallow pool. Onya followed suit, her mind wandering away from the present as she untied the yellow fabric gathered just above her shoulder.

Just after she'd settled on a damp rock, the wind came. It began as a breeze, airy and welcome, lifting the long, dark locs from her neck while a cool splash cascaded over one of her bare shoulders. Her eyes lowered steadily when an exhilarating spray began dousing her nude form in playful stints. The hidden cove filled with sighs and giggles as the others allowed themselves to drop their guard and relax.

"I told you it would be them," said Lore with a wink as she waded nearby, her pendulous, golden breasts skimming the surface of the pool.

A light brush against her cheek caused her eyes to flutter and open wide. The breeze had morphed into a growing whirlpool. Effortlessly it rose from the azure water and took shape. Looming above her now was a transparent, liquid funnel. Taken aback, she inched slowly across the flat surface of the stone, eyes squinting in disbelief at the majestic beauty of the Djinn.

Your desires are mine to fulfill. Allow me, General Onya, to become whatever you wish.

The voice she'd heard was inside her head. Gradually, she sat up on her elbows, not allowing her eyes to leave the funnel in front of her. *Quince.* The thought had emerged in an instant and before she could ponder her next move, the liquid mass gained density and took the shape of a man. Broad ebony shoulders and a muscular torso tapered into a small waist and strong tree-trunk thighs. Full-lips lined by a neatly trimmed goatee and mustache slowly formed on a face all too familiar. Beside herself with awe, Onya reached out to touch it.

The Djinn instantly liquefied and again became an ever-turning whirlpool. *You make the request. I control the fantasy, understood?*

Onya nodded fervently as her jaw went slack. Again the Djinn took Quince's shape and hovered above her nude and dripping frame. She watched closely as its ebony skin and flawless features slipped in and out of its liquid form like a shimmering, rotating mirage.

Permission to please?

Onya nodded affirmatively, utterly amazed at how it had managed to expertly mirror Quince's mellow timbre.

Her spine arched instinctively while it blanketed her and began bestowing airy kisses everywhere at once. A slight force led her arms above her head and crossed her wrists as her eyes slid shut. The touch of fine, damp silk looped around her ankles and toes before climbing toward her abdomen in a ribbon-like fashion while she lay there. Droplets of what felt like warm honey began to fill her navel until it swelled into a pool on her stomach. A cool wash of air skidded across her torso, causing the delicate folds of her nipples to harden into pebbles.

I see you are enjoying yourself. It whispered sensually while nibbling her earlobe.

Onya released a sharp intake of breath when her legs spread slightly and a delicate spiral of mist engulfed her pulsing valley. Her eyes fluttered open as she jerked forward beneath the pull of a powerful erotic surge. Muscular arms held her close while she stared into a pair of incandescent eyes struggling with the threat of climax. The Djinn's touch was a winding ribbon of chiffon, applying bits of tender suction in places no human hands could possibly reach.

The waves around them rose and fell in delicate crests and the hidden cave became a blur of hips and breasts, shouts and giggles while the shrieks culminated into an echoing rhapsody.

Cool sprays of water danced across her heaving breasts and she braced herself for what was to come. The Djinn smiled broadly and cupped the lobes of her bottom with both hands before angling itself beneath her. In an instant, it dissolved into mist and undulated around her curves while massaging droplets of burning kisses into her exposed skin.

Onya let go of a small yelp when it assumed human form again and prepared for the smooth parting of her thighs. Again, she found her eyes closed tightly while it entered her mind, thirsty for mental foreplay.

I can be him...do what he does...only better. Tell me how to please you.

She clenched her fists and attempted to hold onto the slippery rock beneath her. Its form was a cool satin whisper cloaking her sex. *Please* was the only coherent word she could muster under such circumstances. Temporarily undone with pleasure, she whimpered in a low murmur when her body heaved forward yet again. Dissolving first into a crystal stream, the Djinn encircled her hips, its touch like the kiss of a rich rainbow between her thighs. Then it quickly became second skin, enveloping her in an airy lattice-like bubble. The liquid-spun lattice clung to her desperately before warming and becoming droplets of sugar-cubed ice.

She licked the sugary residue from her lips as the cubes melted into the pool, gathered and returned to human form in a fluid instant. A tiny transparent globe spun in its hands as it loomed overhead. Her eyes remained focused on the tiny globe as it revolved on an imaginary axis at an unbelievable speed. Enjoying her satisfaction, he watched her closely as he lowered it toward her protruding center. Immediately, the heat from its topspin engulfed the folds of her valley, stealing her breath. Seeing specks of stars behind the brilliant blue light of her eyelids, her body erupted into multitudinous spasms. With a sudden splash, she found herself drenched by a steady stream of water from above. Breathless, she lay down with a small thud and swallowed hard.

Anytime you need me, echoed the sexy baritone. *Anytime.*

10

OLD WOUNDS

Quince's anger steadily increased with each of his brother's labored breaths. He looked around at those in his company. Several among them were wounded; three had lost their lives. The fury of their return from Glo City several days ago caused immediate alarm. After a proper send off of their dead, they hastily gathered their belongings, vacated the premises, and traveled at breakneck speed toward the difficult northeastern trail leading to the Smoke Desert. No one spoke after all had been explained, from their entrance into the city to the surprise attack once inside. Instead they allowed their rage to simmer into a boil, concentrating on mourning those who'd fallen and attending to those in need. Tradition had been greatly compromised and sooner or later they would have to discuss their options.

Once inside the desert, Quince felt the barren terrain nibbling at his will. Several of the others commented on a "depressing bite" in the air that seemed to feast on what was left of their already frayed nerves. The slightest rustle of the wind resulted in raised weapons, alert and readied for action. For this reason, they barely spoke, but rested often. The emptiness of the land was draining, clearly lacking in vibrancy and life. Dry heat and arid air sparked flames where there should not have been, causing them to use their drinking water to put out dangerous fires. Their food and water rations were now running almost as low as their spirits.

The uneven earth beneath them gave way to long, spidery cracks thinly stretched into deep caverns below. It was from these openings that the smoke drifted upward and out. It was as if they were standing on an over-sized stove, waiting to be cooked or eaten alive by either gloom or time. Days had passed them by, but as to exactly how many, no one knew for sure. Hours blurred into misshapen blobs of misery that held neither seconds nor minutes. Their sense of time was moot in the barren wasteland and they longed desperately for a break in the hopelessness. At this point, any living sound was welcome.

Normally, the trek on foot through the desert would take a maximum of three days, but the injured men slowed their pace to a crawl. Dez's condition in particular, was growing worse. The night before, he had begun to mutter to himself in hallucinatory fits. He lay helpless on a makeshift stretcher made of tree branches and loose fabric. Quince and El refused to leave his side. More and more he was confined to a deep, deathlike sleep, only to awaken in violent sweats when prodded to be sure he hadn't passed into the Afterlife. They'd managed to remove all but the poisonous arrowhead from his injured leg. Before leaving camp, El collected roots of Gye, Jah, and Calla in order to create a soothing paste for the wound. Though it did not heal, it seemed to subside his pain and momentarily halt the poison from spreading.

"Do you think he'll make it?" El whispered quietly while gazing at Dez as he slept by their side. They had stopped to rest and eat a quick meal. Quince looked up, startled by the break in silence.

"He has to, I can't imagine him not being here."

"I wonder what mother would do if she were here," El stated solemnly.

"She'd do exactly what we're doing now," Quince replied.

"They are our mothers and fathers, yet they've waged war. Is it *possible* that they still care about us at all?"

Quince thought for a moment, his gaze roving toward the crackling fire before them. "They are under the thumb of a foreigner and a foolishly headstrong leader. I can't bring myself to believe that all of our Elders are in this willingly. They are afraid to speak up, frightened of disagreeing."

El seemed to think for a moment before nodding in agreement. Carefully, he unwrapped the fabric clinging to Dez's thigh and cleaned the three-inch wide, grayish-green wound. The bleeding had stopped, but the surrounding flesh had become swollen, hard, and discolored. Gently, he dabbed an ample amount of fresh balm on an oblong leaf, applied it to the thigh and wrapped it tightly again. Dez was breathing shallowly now to Quince's relief. He wasn't sure how many of the deep sleeps he could endure without resisting the urge to shake his brother awake again.

"How is he?" Maal asked as he stood over them with a sullen expression.

"About as well as can be expected," El replied.

Quince cleared his throat, needing some kind of distraction from the gloom. "How long until we reach the Falls?"

"This place erases all concept of time," he said peering through the floating strips of smoke. "I can gather though that we must be at least within five miles. I saw a bird gliding in the distance not too long ago, so we must at least be on the perimeter. Nothing can survive here."

He knelt next to the two brothers as they picked over their food and straightened or rearranged their ailing brother's blankets compulsively. Maal laid a hand on Quince's shoulder before speaking again. "Dez is brave. He will fight." Quince responded with a slight nod and covered Dez in a wide red blanket to protect him from the sun's blistering rays.

"Because of the wounded, we have no choice but to forgo the second Rite. The balance has shifted. Three have died. Three of the female Youth will be without preferred partners." Quince said quietly. "Is their anything written on the sacred scrolls that can tell us what to do?"

Maal's reply was slow and thoughtful. "No. We are in a unique situation. Civil War has always been an unthinkable phenomenon. Tradition has been in place so long, no one expected there to be a question of establishing something different. The best solution is to allow the three women to forge with three established couples."

"Yes, that would be logical, but what about the offspring rule? After conception, six Ido children will be born with siblings. From here on, the balance will be tipped. The number of males and females will be uneven."

Maal sighed slowly as he pondered Quince's words. His co-General was absolutely correct. The premature deaths of three of their men before they'd impregnated their preferred partners provided an exorbitant problem. "The Ancestors must be consulted after we tend to our wounded." He said motioning toward Dez. Sensing Quince's uneasiness, he clasped his shoulder firmly. "We will deal. We are strong and there will be solutions available. We cannot lose hope." With this, Maal rose and returned to the center of camp. "Let's go!" he shouted to the others as they gathered their things in preparation to move.

Quince and El balanced the stretcher between them while everyone aided in carrying their belongings. They walked at a slow, but steady pace in the sweltering heat. On two different occasions they stopped for a brief but necessary rest. Within the hour, they heard the pounding of the Falls. Instantaneously, the smoke dispersed and they stepped across the barren threshold into a soothing, warm pool.

At first sight of the Oasis, they erupted in cheers and shouts of relief. Maal warned them to hold down their celebratory outbursts, but could barely contain his own hoot of happiness once the tropical plants and churning waters stood in plain view. In the distance, Quince could see the city perched within the jagged rock as hope returned gradually.

"It isn't necessary for us all to approach Ankh," said Maal, interrupting Quince's thoughts. "The three of us will take Dez to him and I will leave Clay in charge." He motioned toward El. "I know he'd want to go."

Quince nodded and turned to address the men. This time they prepared for attack and set up a perimeter. Several men were sent to survey the area for signs of the enemy, while others set out for fresh water, fruit, and other necessities from the nearby trees. Maal noted detailed descriptions of the men's injuries while El figured out what root medicines to inquire about. Once all the assignments had been delegated to those staying behind, the four men set out to find Ankh, the Sphinx's most learned healer, scientist, and leader.

Quince held his breath and hoped against all odds that his brother's health would be restored quickly and without incident. Perhaps their greatest asset was their knowledge of the ancient pact amongst the island's creatures. Born's voice echoed inside his head as he drifted back to the fateful night they'd asked permission to wage war. *The Sphinx cannot deny their medicines to those in need. It is part of the natural order of the island.* Quince reckoned that in all of the Sphinx's egoism, they'd probably assume that this was not common knowledge, especially among the Ido Youth. This bit of information could certainly be used in their favor. He tried to feel more confident knowing that they possibly held a bargaining chip, but none of them had ever dealt with a Sphinx directly and he himself had only seen one from a distance.

According to legend, they were brilliant creatures whose knowledge was only exceeded by the Painted Folk of Three Wood. Even still, their craftiness in the sciences was unmatched. Their medical genius was proven with their recent strides in genetic mutation. Other focuses of Sphinx study included the strengthening of their own weak immune systems, the development of cures for existing ailments, and the discovery of natural remedies that prolonged life. They'd also been known for their cunning deception, one-sided loyalty, and narcissism. Quince vaguely recalled overhearing one of the Elders comparing the Sphinx with the Zo, dangerous leopards residing within the Rain Caves. After all, they'd been solely responsible for the island's only recorded war since the beginning of time. The three of them would have to be on their toes to grapple with these bizarre creatures. After a long glance at his injured brother, he knew he was ready.

"Remember, they cannot refuse us medicine," he said while lifting the heavy stretcher for what he hoped would be the last time.

"Right. It's funny, but I have a gut feeling this isn't going to be a cake walk," El replied as he balanced half the weight of the stretcher on his shoulder.

"As long as we keep our wits about us, we'll get out of this thing alive.

The only thing I'm concerned about is the fact that they are allies of the Elders," Maal said as they sloshed through the ankle deep water.

"If they're as self-absorbed as everyone says, they may not know or care about what's going on," El responded.

"Trust me. Dame has surely covered all of his bases by now. They know," Quince replied confidently.

"I agree," added Maal. "There is no way this war is being hushed up. Dame is too skilled a warrior for that."

Quince took notice of the sealed compartments within the rock face and could not help but stare with awe as the water pounded between the crevices. Maal pointed toward a flight of stairs not far from them and headed in their direction. Before they could climb a single step, they were halted by one of the city's guards. Maal stepped back, clearly flustered by the intimidating sight.

Possessing the head and torso of a human and the lower body of a lion, the Sphinx were quite large and imposing at close range. Before them stood a male whose complexion was similar to Maal's, dark and clear. His kinky hair was braided in cornrows that fell below his shoulders and the thick coat of black fur covering his lower body gleamed in the light of the sunset behind them.

"It is obvious that you are in need of medicine. Who are you?" he asked in a thick foreign accent as his deep brown eyes swept over the three able bodied men and the stretcher holding a sleeping Dez. They made their introductions as he stared at them, expressionless. He did not introduce himself but gave a kind of approving grunt and stepped toward Dez. Quince lifted the blanket and allowed him to look at his wounded thigh. He put his nose to the wound and recoiled quickly before glancing at them with what looked to be genuine concern.

"A most severe case, I will take you to Ankh at once. The stairs are only for human visitors," he nodded toward the steps behind him before glancing downward at his black paws. "Our kind use the flattened walkways and from the looks of that stretcher, you would be wise to do the same. Follow me."

Gracefully, he leapt into the warm water and directed them through a series of well-hidden caves before turning into a rounded glass tube. Inside the tube was a paved walkway. The men followed the Sphinx inside and stopped abruptly. Quince and El lowered Dez carefully to the ground and waited. Once he'd seen that they'd gained their footing, he placed his paw on a small indentation in the corner and they began to move. Taken by surprise, Quince and Maal stumbled a little before taking hold of the railings on either side.

The pavement moved slowly through the large glass tube on a steady incline. Quince turned to look as they moved further inside the cliff and behind the powerful Falls. Elaborate hieroglyphs had been hand painted on the cliff's walls and ceilings chronicling Sphinx history and creation. The water washed over the glass freely as the continuous pounding died down. The several-inch thick glass drowned out the water's roar, which would certainly be deafening at such a close range. El and Maal leaned closer to the glass as they watched the eastern portion of the island unfold before their eyes. To their left, they could see the steaming Smoke Desert, while on their right lie the brilliant green of the Keep Grasslands. The Diaw birds were grazing in flocks, their indigo feathers blending perfectly with the patches of amethyst grass dotting the plains. The Shine River sliced the land in two like a thin, silver spear.

"We also need replenishing herbs and healing roots for more of our wounded," Quince said, remembering Maal's list. Maal immediately handed the list to El who began reading aloud the injuries and recommended roots. The Sphinx nodded quickly as El completed the list.

"I am sure that can be arranged."

Quince shifted his gaze to the opposite side of the tube where he noticed large gaps in the rock interior showing other rooms also enclosed in glass. A large room filled with square glass tanks filled to the brim with water slowly met his eyes. It was an odd looking place loaded with what looked like security bars and chains. As they moved along, Quince saw a Diaw bird being led into one of the humongous tanks, his beak clamped shut as he squirmed under the arm of a Sphinx. The view was obstructed now as the walkway continued to move steadily upward.

"Is there something wrong?" The Sphinx asked when Quince's eyes narrowed. Startled, he looked up at the large creature. "Your gaze indicates you disapprove of our penal system. However, you must agree that transgressors should be punished for their crimes. I think I forgot to add, I am Heru," the creature said while looking down at Dez.

Surprised by this sudden act of courtesy, Maal and El nodded, but remained enthralled with the images outside. Quince thought back to what he'd seen moments ago. Of course he believed in punishment for crimes, but something about the concept of a liquid jail cell seemed excessively cruel.

As they traveled deeper inside the rock, a halogen light ignited, keeping them from total darkness. Quince thought he'd heard screams or shrieks of pain from a remote area inside the cliffs, but dismissed it when the others made no comment. The walkway slowed to a stop as they neared a stone wall. Heru pressed his paw on another indentation and instantly the wall parted to reveal what looked to be the bustling downtown area of a city.

There were Sphinx everywhere. Men and women darted this way and that, all with some place important to go, or so it looked from the way they weaved around one another hurriedly. Quince and El balanced the stretcher once again on their shoulders and followed Heru's lead. Quince was utterly amazed with the differences among the Sphinx. Though they all had the obvious human head and torso and lion's lower body, their facial features, skin color, and hair texture varied drastically. He noticed a woman not far from where they walked who was as pale as Heru was dark. Her short, blond hair was tucked neatly behind her ears. Yet another green-eyed Sphinx with olive skin and oily hair examined them critically. He acknowledged Heru's presence and introduced himself as Tehuti before continuing on his way. Their eyes were brown, blue, green, and hazel. Their hairstyles ranged from long and straight to thick and curly, or short and wavy.

"This way. We are nearly there."

Heru led the gaping men into another cave. As they squeezed into its cramped quarters, a sheet of glass sealed them inside and they began to rise upward. After a brief moment, they stopped. When the rock wall on the other side opened, it revealed a vast scientific laboratory. Pristine and white, the air inside the room smelled completely sterile. As he stepped inside the lab, Quince observed that they were inside a dome shaped bubble. Water soaked glass surrounded them entirely. Nothing ceased upon their entrance, though their presence was recognized at once. Countless Sphinx outfitted in white lab coats peered inside microscopes and liquid filled beakers as odd-looking machines pumped and rattled along with the pounding falls in the background.

Lining the back wall were several clear, water-filled tanks holding odd looking creatures. One of the tanks held a small, gray fish with the tusks and ears of an elephant. Next to it swam a creature that looked to be a mixture between an alligator and a crab with a blue shell. In a tank of greenish liquid, swam two blue, leg-less frogs. A sharp squeal and a low, rumbling roar caught his attention. Feet away, large bars revealed three openings in the curved wall. In the central cage, standing the length of the room was a giraffe with what looked to be a human head. On its right was a gorilla with human limbs. Nearest him, lay a gray leopard with the fins of a seal. Several lab coated Sphinx stood near the cage poking and prodding at the beasts with stethoscopes, needles, and other medical instruments as they grunted and growled in annoyance. Confused and slightly unnerved by the sight, Quince turned back to Heru while a long white sheet was hastily spread over the tanks by several of the Sphinx scientists.

An older male approached them. Quince knew at once it was Ankh. His bushy hair was graying at the roots and a pair of small black spectacles hung from a chain around his neck. His coloring was a light brown, the color of butterscotch. The man's features were large and dominant; his look, ill tempered and dubious. Immediately, he motioned for them to lower the stretcher to the floor. He threw back the blankets with his front paw and proceeded to remove the bandage covering Dez's wound.

"Who concocted this paste?" he asked after pressing his broad nose to the sticky leaf. The Sphinx's accent was heavy and unidentifiable, yet easy to understand as the words he spoke rolled over his tongue with ease.

"I did." El began. "I thought the Gye mixture would absorb some of the poison --"

Ankh waved him off with a grunt. "Place him over there. He is nearly dead," he replied flatly.

Startled by this frank declaration, Quince and El quickly lifted Dez from the stretcher and laid him on a sterilized table. His body fell limp. Quince's heart thumped hard in his chest. The three of them exchanged worried looks as they glanced down at Dez. His grayish complexion seemed to be even more apparent under the bright lights of the operating table. Then, an eerie silence fell and all eyes seemed to turn in their direction. Ankh was preparing to speak into some sort of megaphone.

"We will be performing a rare Scarab transplant," he boomed loudly. "All apprentices are asked to gather around sector six. This will be a jewel to observe."

Quince bristled in response to what he'd heard. His brother's operation was going to be used as an object for field study! However, noting Ankh's rush to begin, he chose not to address what he'd considered to be a gesture of blatant disrespect. Within seconds, it seemed the entire lab had descended upon the small operating table.

"Come and sit." said Heru.

Reluctantly, Quince, Maal, and El left Dez's side and sat nervously on a low bench in the corner of the room. Heru placed a medium sized bag made of animal skins in Quince's lap. "Here are the roots you've asked for. The one you call El will be familiar with their uses and more than able to tell them apart. He seems knowledgeable in root working." Quince nodded, before placing his head in his hands.

Meanwhile, Ankh was providing a detailed explanation for each tiny incision. His harsh voice boomed throughout the laboratory as the crowd around the table grew dense.

"The Elder poison has been advancing for seven days," he was saying.

Seven days! They'd been wandering through the desert for that length of time! The three men exchanged worried glances.

"The cells are attacking one another vigorously. The object of the Scarab transplant is to provide enough glucose serum to the wound in order to offset the warring enzymes. Then we will insert the poison-eating insect and close him up. His body temperature has lowered drastically. If the serum does not work, the leg must be amputated, or worse..." Ankh trailed off.

With this last statement, the group of male Youth lowered their heads in Ancestral prayer. It didn't take long for the surgeons to prepare. Sterilized instruments were gathered and

set on a metal tray and those directly involved applied plastic gloves and hurriedly pushed masks over their mouths and noses. Things seemed to go smoothly until Ankh began yelling.

"The glucose serum needs a key! His cells have lost the necessary enzymes for proper decryption. Glucose serum now! Glucose serum now, or we'll have to amputate! We may lose him!"

Silence returned abruptly after the outburst. Quince and the others listened closely, praying for a miracle. They could not bear to hear each minute detail of the surgery.

"Steady...steady. Is he stabilized? Good. I need the scalpel, Ra... now! Make a small incision along the anterior tissues. Ignore the abductor brevis and locate the abductor magnus. Steady... steady! Scissors. Knife. Perfect. Luckily the enemy agent entered through the fatty tissues of the thigh. The poison has been feasting on the tissues, which we can re-grow easily. They are mere lipid molecules packaged with the occasional amino acid building blocks to add the necessary rigidity. Good. It looks as if the poison hasn't yet reached the primary muscles. Insert the scarab. Syringe. Steady... now. Good. Apply thirty CC's of pressure. Good. Wonderful. Another twenty CC's. Stitch it up. Close it."

As quickly as it had begun, it was over. The room erupted in applause and the crowd around the table dispersed, congratulating Ankh as they went. The men could not believe it had been this easy. Wary of their good fortune, Quince rose to his feet and looked in Heru's direction. After he gestured that it was okay for them to approach the operating table, they proceeded with caution. Ankh gazed at him from over his specs.

"The healing is immediate. He should awaken in ---"

"Where the hell am I?" Groggily, Dez lifted his head from the table. Quince and the others smiled broadly as Ankh traipsed away unnoticed while the Ido Youth conversed happily.

"Is it done?" Heru asked quietly.

Ankh nodded. "Indeed. Operation Scarab transplant was a 100% success."

11

THE UNEXPECTED SERMON

Dame received the news within the hour from an Elder messenger. Wholly satisfied with the results, he folded his hands behind his back and grinned smugly. For years, the Sphinx remained dedicated to insect research. Their mating cycles, habits, and exoskeletons were at the core of Sphinx experimentation. After decades of pondering ways to chart a patient's progress throughout the vast island, considering the fact that few creatures would willingly remain in close proximity to the Sphinx territories after treatment, Ankh discovered the value of insect pheromones. Soon, they'd mastered the process of using the insects' own natural mating lure to their advantage as their pheromones could be used as a simple monitoring tool that would reveal information about the success or failure of surgeries and their various effects on different creatures.

Now, Dame found himself benefiting from the technique. The exact location could be pinpointed within a plus or minus of one-degree longitude or latitude, thus Dame would always be privy to the exact location of the Youth as they moved about the island. It had been more difficult than they'd thought to compromise the Stripes at Glo in order to carry out the surprise attack. Now, they were no longer dependent upon old war tactics, the new system was nearly foolproof.

According to Ankh's information, the men were still on the outskirts of the Falls. He guessed they'd take the Shine River westward toward Three Wood for the upcoming third Rite. That would be the easier journey. Pleased with the new developments, he smiled inwardly and glanced toward Vye. He couldn't help but feel a bit of guilt. But his tactics were necessary, he reiterated to himself. If the Youth would not obey and convert to the new faith, they would perish at the hands of the Elders and answer to the One. He planted a small kiss on her forehead as they parted to prepare for the midnight services to be held that evening. Victory, he thought, was just around the corner.

***

There was standing room only inside the crowded One Temple. The new wooden pews cushioned with pillows wrapped in majestic purple cloths emitted a soft polished finish in the torch lit dome. The high ceiling gave off a royal air and the flames from the candles quavered in the breeze from the open windows. The soft moonlight doused its circular sanctuary delicately while tall shadows crept up the sides of the walls. He'd helped to build everything himself, from the ground up. Piles of burgundy-tinged wood were chopped and carved into a massive, five roomed structure. The entire Elder Clan of nearly one hundred men and women squeezed inside its doors for a midnight vigil and sermon.

Dame looked around eagerly at all who'd gathered, his chest rising with immense pride. He was amazed at how quickly they'd come to dedicate their lives to The One Faith. Now, in a time of tragedy, they were doing exactly as their new religion had taught them; gathering together in fellowship to celebrate the lives of the first casualties of their cause. There was a hushed chatter amongst the parishioners filing inside and comforting one another as they took seats on the long benches. Many dabbed at swollen eyes and tear stained cheeks. Emotionally, he was torn. A seasoned General, he knew death was the fraternal twin to war. However, he gained a certain solace with the understanding that their Afterlives would be much different than those who'd passed on in shadow, ignorant of the One Faith's beliefs. The brave warriors who'd lost their lives at the battle of Glo City had attempted to spread a faith of love and discipline. Now, they would be more than just powerful Ancestors confined to the surrounding seas. They would be given the handsome reward of joining with The One who'd created them all.

Dame sat in a wooden chair on the raised platform facing the entranceway. Beside him sat another slightly larger chair reserved for The Guide. He smiled to himself in anticipation, wondering what the night's message would bring in these difficult times. Like a small child discovering the primary uses of its limbs, he waited, eager to learn. There was a hush over the crowd signaling that the time had come. The late stragglers rushed to take their seats as The Guide strolled confidently down the center aisle, his deep purple cloak billowing behind him. He held some tattered, off-white

     B. Sharise Moore

scrolls in his right hand and a thick black book in the other. They would not have to wait much longer.

"My fellow believers," he began before reaching the podium reserved for his midnight sermon. "I greet you in the name of the One who knows, sees, hears, and creates. We are, because He is."

Dame sat up in his chair uneasily, noting the new subtle pronoun choice. He located Vye in the crowd, beautiful as always, seated on one of the benches near the back with her good friend Eyeno and a few of the other Elder women. He caught her eye just as she acknowledged him with a small smile. Straightening in his chair, he turned his attention back to The Guide.

"Three among us have perished, but their souls are free now," he continued. "I am confident that The One is comforting them in His bosom as we mourn their deaths. But let us remember their lives, their decision to accept a new faith void of the old pagan ways and celebrate that decision. Before their deaths, they chose to turn their backs on perversion in favor of the righteousness you yourselves have chosen."

They nodded, trying to gain some kind of comfort from his words. The entire concept of death had been reinvented under The One Faith. It was obvious from the furrowed brows and sidelong glances that they were listening intently, trying to make sense of things. According to the old ways, death had been easier to accept knowing that those who'd passed on would become Mer Ancestors. However, The Guide was now making it clear that those who'd died would not be visible ever again. Toying with the new concept in his mind, Dame found this to be an unexpected emotional blow. Instantly, he felt deflated. He hadn't realized that he would never be able to communicate with his three comrades again. And even though the Ancestors rarely fraternized with the living anyway, they often found solace in knowing their exact whereabouts. Erruk was a very real and tangible city in the waters of the deep. He was suddenly solemn, now realizing how much there was to learn. The church remained silent as the worshipers clung to The Guide's every word.

"I have chosen to specifically address the women of the faith tonight. As both mothers and women, you are fully responsible for your children and you must take an active part in raising them." There was a faint rumble of discussion after these remarks. Dismissively, The Guide waited for silence to restore itself before continuing. "Furthermore, women are the epitome of femininity: delicate, tender, gentle. They must be loved and respected by the husbands who have chosen them. But women must remember that the man is the head of the home. It is your duty to stand by his side during each and every endeavor, as a faithful mate must. It is his job and his alone to make all major decisions. Your duty is to supply a support system while raising his children. I implore you all to think more about family and its importance in our faith--"

Most of them were no longer listening to the sermon. The women were either shifting uncomfortably in their seats or shooting looks of dismay in the direction of their male counterparts. Dame could feel the mounting unrest. Suddenly, the energy of the room had shifted from sorrow and loss to questioning anger. He had to admit that he too was taken aback by the implications. The Ido women had always been headstrong and very accustomed to heading their own lives. Their former society had been one of gender equality and balance. Subservience would certainly be a bitter pill for them to swallow.

Immediately, his eyes searched for Vye, and not a moment too soon. She stood up proudly, her countenance a sheet of seething rage and moved toward the building's exit. There was a surprised hush as Eyeno followed her lead. In seconds, a handful more of the female Elders walked out. Seemingly oblivious to this defiant act, The Guide simply bowed his head and began to pray. While those remaining were engrossed in prayer, Dame left his chair and walked swiftly down a side aisle to the exit. Outside, the moon was covered in a halo of clouds as the women huddled together quietly. Quickly, he approached.

"What are you doing?"

They continued their conversation in hushed voices. Dame could hear the rising tension in the tight circle. Eyeno turned to face him; her sneer rigid with anger.

"We're starting to believe we've possibly made an error in judgment. This isn't what we thought we were signing up for Dame. It's one thing to want to impart discipline, but it's obvious he means to extinguish our culture entirely. Women can no longer yield weapons and fight. Husbands choose their wives, women are suddenly subservient-- our dead will not become Ancestors, it's just too much--" she spluttered in amazement while Vye placed an arm around her shuddering shoulders.

Dame interrupted abruptly. "You must have faith! The Guide is merely the messenger! He should not be blamed for the harsh realities of the message! If you had more faith---"

"Don't you dare speak to us about faith!" spat Vye through clenched teeth as she whirled around to face him. "Faith has our sons under your thumb! Faith has us praying to who knows what that they are alive and safe! And who ever heard of assigning the Creator of all things a gender?

This merely falls in line with his declaration of female inferiority. Quite convenient!"

Dame shot back, enraged. "How dare you question---"

"I will question whomever and whatever I please, especially if I feel I've been misled. Questioning is what intelligent people do, Dame! It is the unintelligent who follow blindly."

"Faith is the substance of things hoped for and we believe by faith, not by sight! Need I remind you all of that?" he asked the five women standing before him. "I beg you to remember how you felt the day you exited those waters. How did you feel once your spirit was cleansed?" He paused as they continued to stare, desperate for answers, searching to find some iota of truth behind his eyes.

"Life is not without hardships and obstacles. The Guide never promised us perfect lives after we'd converted. He only promised that we'd be free of the hellfire, exempt from the judgment! And let's not forget the endless possibilities. Under the old ways, we were not permitted to love. I must admit that since I've had the chance to taste its sweet sweet nectar, I cannot imagine going without for the rest of my days." He looked deeply into Vye's eyes with this last statement.

A slight breeze blew the women's white dresses as they stood together, clearly a united front. Dame desperately hoped that they would not lose sight of everything The Guide had done to save their blackened souls. Eyeno turned to Vye and they nodded together, wordlessly acknowledging that they'd concede this specific battle. One by one they returned to the service. Vye was the last to be alone with him. Pulling her toward his chest, he stroked her forehead delicately before speaking in a voice just above a whisper.

"I need you beside me Vye. I can't imagine you leaving..." She released their long embrace to look up at his handsome face just as his bottom lip began to tremble. "I--I love you Vye. I want you to be my wife."

Half expecting those very words, she stared at him a moment before slowly nodding her head yes. Dame embraced her tightly and lifted her from the ground. In his heart, he believed in The Guide and his message, but even more so, he believed in love. Looking down at his wife to be, he counted his blessings as they held one another beneath the darkening clouds. Silently he thanked The One for change.

12

GALLAH'S TALE

"Make sure the spiral is *just* right. I really want to make an impression," the woman said in a muffled whisper, her face buried deep inside the pillow below her.

Eesha rolled her eyes knowingly and sighed. "We all do sis, we all do. Just relax. You know I always aim to please."

It was a humid summer evening and the ornately decorated hut she shared with Onya and Lyn was nearly packed to capacity. Nevertheless, she had no complaints. In exchange for her services, she'd received everything from elegant clothing and elaborate handmade jewelry to mouthwatering meals. Realizing that the sun had set just moments ago, she picked up her pace. Though she hadn't quite finished with the forty-nine clients she'd been tending to since their arrival from the Falls, she knew it came with the territory of being named the village Awo. The time crunch hadn't been foreign either; she'd also been solely responsible for the design of their ceremonial tattoos during the Warming Ceremony. With the use of several brushes and a complex combination of semi-permanent, oil-based dyes, she carefully decorated their glistening bodies with a beautiful creation. Eesha prided herself on making certain that each design was unique and eye-catching in its own way. She enjoyed both the craft as well as its benefits and as she'd told the woman lying beneath her, she aimed to please all of her clients.

Intrigued, Onya stood over her shoulder and watched as her friend created delicate swirls and shapes in an array of color and breathtaking detail. Methodically, she dabbed her brush into a striking bluish-green mixture and applied it to the woman's glistening skin with precision. An elegant cluster of butterflies now spiraled from the top of the woman's spine to the small of her back, and continued around her waist to the middle of her left thigh.

"Do you need anything? New brushes, more dye?" Onya asked, eager to help.

Eesha wiped the perspiration from her forehead with the back of her hand and looked up a moment. "Come here," she said motioning for Onya to turn around. Quickly, she examined Onya's tattoo of a silver vine winding diagonally from her left shoulder to just below her right hip where it wound around her right leg. Several ancient Ido symbols were painted a bright pink and placed at random on the vine like leaves. Carefully, she tapped the tattoo lightly with her thumb. "I need for you to sit outside in the breeze. You won't dry if you stick around in here. And you're in my way!" she winked jokingly.

Onya smiled in agreement and rose from her kneeling position. All around them women were chatting nervously about the forthcoming Rite or commenting on one another's finished tattoos. Onya smiled to herself as she walked through the crowd toward the entrance. She would be in Quince's presence in a matter of a few short hours and her nerves were completely on end. It had seemed so long ago since they'd last seen one another. The third Rite had always been a mystery and instead of their being informed as to exactly what it entailed, they were more or less given a specific destination and told when to arrive.

Once she'd stepped beyond the hut's threshold, she walked several paces and turned toward the sea. East Nu, the portion of the village housing the Ido women, had a breathtaking view of the ocean. As she glanced past several more thatched roofs, she could have sworn she'd seen a giant black fin poking through the delicate waves. With the sun now tucked away and the curtains of evening drawn, the sky had taken on a mystic orange glow. She sighed to herself and thought longingly of the pleasures she'd soon be receiving. Before she could settle into a peaceful thought, Lyn nearly knocked her over as she ran full speed around the perimeter of another hut.

"Sorry Onya," she said gathering her breath and regaining her balance. Onya could see and sense the unbridled fear in her eyes. Immediately, her blood turned cold.

"What's wrong Lyn? What happened?"

Refusing to answer, she reluctantly motioned for her to return to the hut. Onya nodded and followed close behind. Once inside, Lyn called for everyone's attention. Based on the solemn looks on their faces, the women knew the matter was a serious one. Eesha looked up from her bent position while the woman she'd been working on lifted her head and turned toward the frightened pair.

"They were attacked," Lyn said weakly. "Apparently, they were taken by surprise while they were in Glo City. The Elders somehow overtook some of The Stripes and used a Diaw to lure them into one of the buildings. The fighting began once they were inside."

After a few brief seconds of shock, the hut brimmed with concerned chatter. Determined to restore order, Onya held up her hand. Reluctantly, the women became quiet again. Slowly she turned to Lyn, who stood in the middle of the hut, distraught.

"Were there any--- deaths?"

Lyn lowered her eyelids before slowly nodding her head. "Several were injured and yes, three of them... died."

Onya felt her stomach flip queasily while the other women looked on in horror.

"Who were the men who ---" began one of the seated women.

"I don't have any names." Lyn interrupted. "All I know is they took all the injured to the Oasis Falls about a week ago for treatment."

Onya's eyes grew wide. "Were they possibly there at the same time---"

Again, Lyn interrupted with haste. "No. They arrived the day after we'd already left. They had to take the long way... through the Smoke Desert."

The small hut boiled over with comments and questions. For a few moments, she watched Lyn struggle to answer them all to the best of her ability. Gripping her side in agony, Onya realized her need to be alone. She walked briskly toward the entrance, not caring where her two feet took her. The thought of *any* of the Youth perishing was unimaginable. Then the idea hit her like a heavy brick, Quince. *Could he have been one of the three who'd lost their lives?* It was certainly possible. As their male co-General, he would have been heavily involved, if not on the front lines. Her heart sank as she neared the village perimeter. She was unable to bear the notion of losing him and the mere realization that this was even a possibility sickened her. The fear of the unknown was numbing. She pictured her father the last time she'd seen him. The once domineering man she'd recalled since childhood now seemed weak and easily led. The blood drained from her cheeks. Desperately she tried to understand why Dame had caused such unrest. Had he considered the repercussions? She picked her brain until it felt raw. No one had the answers to any of her questions.

Stunned and grief stricken, she stumbled toward a large gap in the three-pronged trunk of a nearby Raha tree and settled there, dazed and oblivious to the sounds of ensuing night. With her head cradled in her hands and her eyes closed tightly, the grisly images of war smashed into her skull. In her mind's eye, fallen men lay in pools of crimson. She saw herself stepping through twisted metal, broken weapons, and debris until she saw Quince's slack expression gaze up from her in a puddle of red-tinged mud. The agony of the image caused her to shiver. She brought her knees to her chin and beckoned for the sobs to escape, but they refused to fall. Instead, a few stuttering breaths exited her lips along with a silent prayer to the Ancestors. How could they allow this to happen?

Just beyond earshot lurked a large jungle cat. Its slanted eyes glowed gold in the night as it trekked lithely along the forest floor. Carefully, it honed in on the figure seated just feet away. Dinner seemed to have fallen from the sky! *She is off limits.* A tinkling voice floated into the leopard's ears as it made its way toward the disoriented human. *She is one of ours.* It stopped abruptly, confused and accustomed to the hunt. Something was wrong. Occupied now by its long, silver whiskers, the leopard decisively turned away from the unsuspecting woman lying exposed in the darkness. The gray cat bounded away in retreat, wanting nothing of a standoff with the Supreme Maiden of the Painted Folk.

"Onya, daughter of Imar."

Startled, Onya looked up. No one was in her immediate view as she rose to her feet, withdrew her blade, and assumed a battle stance.

"Look up and stand down," commanded the voice again.

Wanting desperately to postpone what might meet her gaze, Onya cautiously lifted her gaze skyward. Immediately, her muscles relaxed. Perched on one of the tree's massive branches stood Gallah, alone. Before Onya could respond, she jumped lithely from the tree limbs and landed directly in front of her. Gallah's blue and silver skin took on a mysterious allure under the night sky. A set of perky breasts stared at her sumptuously while the sparkling nipple rings shone in the moonlight. Onya looked at her questioningly. She hadn't recalled The Painted Folk casually conversing with the Ido for any reason.

"Why do you insist on visiting Three Wood during these dangerous times?" she laughed, attempting to ease the tension between them. Carefully, she took a seat next to Onya before placing a hand gently on her knee. "You are upset. Share with me what causes you distress."

Onya sighed deeply before blurting out the news of the battle at Glo City and the deaths of three Ido males. Crossing her legs, Gallah's brows knitted uneasily. Once Onya had stopped speaking, she responded gently.

"This is the nature of war. Did you not expect that people would die?" she inquired, her eyes soft and searching as she glanced at Onya.

Onya looked at the ground and shut her eyes. She felt like a child. Gallah was correct. She and the others hadn't realistically dealt with the fact that things on the island had drastically changed. War and death went hand in hand. They were all guilty of not preparing for the inevitable.

"Quince... it's just so difficult not knowing if I will see him tomorrow or not. I was looking forward to sharing..." she trailed off as Gallah's gaze intensified.

"Who is this Quince of whom you speak... not the co-General of the male Youth?" she asked, perplexed.

Onya understood her blunder immediately. She was showing signs of emotion. Clearly, she had developed feelings for Quince in their three short meetings. However, this was the first time she'd freely admitted this to herself or anyone else.

Gallah sighed heavily before placing a hand on Onya's shoulder. "Sometimes I wonder which one of us gave up the most," she mused aloud. Onya responded with a confused stare. "You know the story, of course, of my people and yours." Gallah continued. "We were forced to give up sexual intercourse and the ability to reproduce, but in turn were granted clairvoyance and immortality. Meanwhile, as the legend goes, your people were granted a dual existence, the right to walk the land as humans do for a time and exist in Mer form until the age of seven and after death. Somewhere along the line though, your people were made to sacrifice love." She looked toward the canopy above as if pondering something heavy. "Journey with me. I will show you," Gallah said taking Onya's hands in hers.

Onya pulled herself together emotionally in preparation for the vision bind. Aware of the Painted Folk's clairvoyance, she stared at The Supreme Maiden in reverent awe. Vision binds were sacred journeys practiced only among the Painted Folk. Gallah's eyes flashed a bit of sapphire blue. While bearing witness to the event, Onya became aware that she was the first Ido ever invited to participate in the process.

"We share a common bond and I consider you both friend and ally," Gallah said softly, reading Onya's thoughts. "The vision bind may supply a bit of the insight you seek. Breathe in deep and never let go of my hands while we are bound."

Onya nodded and grabbed hold of Gallah's hands. Immediately, a tingling sensation ricocheted through her fingers and palms before traveling the length of her forearms. Onya felt the instantaneous droplets of perspiration gathering around her temples and exhaled deeply.

"That's right," Gallah coached. "Breathe deeply and watch. Though you have not yet received Enlightenment, I can aid you in opening your crown chakra."

Behind her eyelids, Onya observed a black and white vision slowly coming into focus, its edges fuzzed and wavy.

"Open yourself to truth," Gallah coaxed soothingly. *"Relax and breathe."*

Onya did what she was told, allowing her muscles to relax and her breaths to circulate in delicate spirals. In seconds, her senses piqued. A three-dimensional image presented itself clearly and in brilliant color. Before her stood the vast Three Wood rain forest just before nightfall. Suddenly, the vision blurred as if it were skipping ahead to a more important scene. Then, her senses slammed into the sights and sounds of pure, adrenaline-filled ecstasy. Nude bodies dangled from tree limbs. Legs and arms curled around one another as pleasure pants and aroused fits rode the wind. She was bearing witness to one of the ancient Taste Rites. As for when it had taken place, she could not tell. Without warning, the vision veered toward a shapely figure lurking high above the action on one of the tree limbs. Instantly, Onya recognized the woman as a slightly less regal looking Gallah. She lithely descended several tiers of limbs and settled on a branch above one of the Ido couples. Just then, more Painted Folk followed until the trees were overrun with white tufts of hair and vibrant color.

Nearly lost inside the beauty of the vision, Onya inhaled deeply and homed in on Gallah and the red-skinned man now at her side. Onya recognized him as Ohm from the Fire and Rainbow Ceremony. When Gallah turned to face him, Onya felt a jolt of desire travel toward her now pulsing bud. Ohm and Gallah's eyes locked as they exchanged a knowing smile. Onya exhaled heavily, recognizing the glance she'd shared with Quince after the first Rite. Tidal waves of happiness and love spilled over her, washing her soul with patience and trust. Gallah wasn't just sharing with her the history of her treasured find all those years ago or the looping thrills of pleasure; she was sharing with her the raw emotion behind erotic love. Then, the techno-color image in front of her eyes faded into a blue haze almost as quickly as it had come. She sighed heavily when Gallah released her hands.

Onya inhaled slowly before opening her eyes. The journey had been indescribable. Gallah sat across from her still, allowing her to slowly purge the intensity of the emotion transfer. Though she wore a small smile, Onya sensed a lingering sadness underneath.

"It is difficult for both of us Onya, daughter of Imar. While your kind can share in the pleasure and closeness of intimacy, you are forbidden to love. And while The Painted Folk can indeed love without shame or criticism, we can never share in the closeness or intimacy that love demands." She paused for what seemed like a long time. "The transfer was not totally foreign. You love him, don't you?"

Onya wiped haphazardly at the fresh tears now rolling toward her chin. It was the first time she'd cried. Though there was relief in finally being able to release, she could not bring herself to meet Gallah's eyes.

"It is ok", the Supreme Maiden said reassuringly. "I am not of your kind; I pass no judgment. But I do not envy your situation. Ohm and I share a similar love that you are building with General Quince. He is my reflection, sensing my pain, fears and needs. He shares my goals and an unconditional love for our people. He is truly the ideal. We have the freedom to live forever and know one another's thoughts, but we will never experience each other in the way that the Ido are allowed during Taste."

Onya pondered Gallah's words before replying. "The civil war is challenging all allowances now Gallah. If my father and the Elder army have their way, Taste will be no more. Maybe the old ways need to be modified, just a bit," she suggested quietly.

"Then that makes you no better than the Elders," Gallah commented quickly. "We cannot bend some portions of tradition to fit our own selfish desires. Our universe gives and takes. It is a gift in and of itself that we have lives to live at all. Our survival depends wholly upon our honoring the old ways. The balance of giving and receiving should not be disturbed. I pray though, that your love is in good health. Whether your feelings are forbidden or not, no one deserves to lose the one who makes them whole."

Onya nodded slowly as Gallah wiped away the tears from her cheek. Somehow, she felt at peace.

"It is late. I will lead you back to Nu."

The two women walked slowly side by side through the thick jungle. Silence was the third companion as they each processed what the other had shared.

13

A SACRED UNION

Compulsively, Vye twisted the long brown locs between her fingers. To say that she was nervous would have been an understatement. All around her, last minute preparations were being made throughout the temple. Overwhelmed, she watched as glittering candles were strung across the vestibule, special carpets were unfurled down the three aisles, and clusters of amethyst grass and other flowers were bundled and strewn in corners. The room, in all of its splendor, began closing in on her like a suffocating, wooden mass. She located the closed door at the back of the temple and immediately jogged toward it. After entering the small room, she eyed a glittering white gown with an amethyst studded neckline hanging in the corner. Alone now, she let go of a deep, heartfelt sigh. Soon, she would be married to the man she had grown to love under a new faith that actually permitted it, but things seemed to be moving too quickly. She needed to breathe.

On the one hand, she was ecstatic to be given the opportunity to embrace her emotions. However, the fate of so many subsequent events hung in the balance because of the trade off. There was the ever-threatening welfare of her three sons to think of as well as the fate of the entire Ido clan. How would they survive this war?

Her head was throbbing. Being made into an example, a prototype of what marriage stood for seemed suddenly overwhelming. Together, she and Dame would be expected to cohabit, an unheard of phenomenon before the arrival of The Guide and the Elder's acceptance of The One Faith. Bit by bit she felt the doubt creeping inside her like a formidable enemy poised behind a set of shabby doors. She needed to be alone because suddenly, she wasn't sure she'd made the right decision at all.

"Having second thoughts?" asked a voice near the door.

Vye wheeled around to face a dark skinned woman with lengthy lashes framing a pair of intense, almond shaped eyes. Once the Ido Youth's female General and standing at just over six feet, Eyeno was the most physically intimidating of all the female Elders. She carried her height with an abundance of grace however, and shied away from any unnecessary attention. Though her presence rarely allowed her to fade into the background, a nonjudgmental demeanor provided her with the label of village nurturer and confidante. Eyeno had been Vye's best friend for as long as she could remember. They'd gossiped and grown from girls to women and delivered their sons simultaneously. It also pleased her to know that Maal and Quince had developed a firm and lasting friendship much like their own.

"Vye, I'm going to ask you again...are you having second thoughts about this?"

"No. I was just thinking about some things, that's all," she responded non-convincingly.

Eyeno strode briskly to where her best friend stood in the middle of the small, circular room and embraced her lovingly.

"Vye, this is me you're talking to. We've known each other for nearly all of our lives. It's okay to shed this strong facade you've got going on. There's no one else in the room but us. Come on, spit it out."

"Fine," she declared while sinking in a nearby chair. "I don't know about this," she blurted out quickly. "I care for Dame; you know that. He's different from the way he was before. He's gentler, kinder. He's always been extremely handsome and now I actually *love* him. But I'm nervous. Marriage is new. It's different from what our kind is accustomed to. I'm just starting to wonder if this really fits us. You heard The Guide the other night! The gender roles will change and I don't care how big Dame is, you know I have a *serious* problem with playing a subservient role in our relationship!"

Eyeno was silent for a while, thinking of the proper way to respond. Behind the door, they could hear the preparations increasing rapidly. A loud crash followed by a comical howl eased the tension in the room a bit as the two women broke into hysterics. They grabbed at their sides as tears ran down their cheeks uncontrollably.

Once the rumbling hoots subsided Eyeno took her by the hands and spoke seriously. "Vye, most of us are more unsure than we're letting on. I feel the same as you do. Ido women have always been on equal footing with men. These new roles will be difficult for us all, including the men. They aren't all that comfortable with this new phenomenon. But no one has the guts to defy your future husband."

Vye shrugged her shoulders and chewed nervously on the fingernails of her right hand. "This war is getting to me too. It's real Eyeno, people have already died and more will follow."

She nodded in agreement. "You're right. I was thinking about it on the way over here. Let's be honest, we were excited about the faith because it would give us the opportunity to love and having already gone through Taste, The One Faith doesn't seem as restricting to us as it does to the Youth. Truthfully, if I were in their position, I'd probably rebel too." Vye directed her gaze toward a nearby open window. "I just pray our sons make it through this in one piece. In fact, I thought of Maal this morning. He reminds me a lot of Dame actually; they share the same physique and hot headedness. You know it was Dame who taught him Bgongo personally. He saw some of himself in him at a very early age." Eyeno paused thoughtfully. "I just hope the master and student won't have to meet in battle. Did you know Maal and Quince were voted leaders of the Cause?" she asked proudly.

Vye grinned brightly. "No! Wow, our sons are growing to be such good men." She turned from the sunny window and raised her eyebrows suspiciously. "How are you getting all of these inside tidbits of information?" Eyeno blushed heavily and covered her face with her hands. "Does this have anything to do with Chi? I saw the two of you talking yesterday after service."

Eyeno nodded and smiled girlishly. "Chi has accepted the responsibility to become Dame's first commanding officer, so he shares things with me here and there. It's kind of natural I guess. He's Maal's father anyway and One forgive me, but I remember how great he was during Taste... so, I'm hoping we may be next in line. He's pretty dedicated to the faith. Dame seems to have most of the men on his side."

Vye rose from her seat and strode toward the breathtaking gown. She took in a large gulp of air before exhaling slowly. The soft fabric slid between her fingers as she turned toward her friend. "Help me get this on. I have to become Dame's wife soon," she said with a sudden resurgence in confidence.

***

The journey down the aisle of forever was longer than she'd thought. On her left and right, the Elders rose to acknowledge her entrance. Friends and fellow warriors greeted her with genuine smiles as she began the long walk toward her husband to be. A flicker of light had gone off in her brain after she'd spoken with Eyeno before the ceremony, though she'd chosen not to share her plan. Perhaps she was the key, the ex-factor! What if she could stop the civil war? The mere thought of her strategies broadened her smile. Her stomach did several flip-flops as she gazed up and into Dame's smiling eyes. Everything was more beautiful than she'd imagined. The fabric of her dress felt softer than the fluffiest cloud. The scent of fresh flowers and perfume filled the air. She couldn't remember him ever looking more handsome, or feeling more loved. The tug of war inside her had finally given way to a clear winner. She had chosen to marry the man who she'd grown to adore in spite of their differences.

He handled her left wrist delicately before placing the coveted deep violet and silver ring on her finger. The setting beheld five amethyst stones varying in size, shade, and shape. The central stone was a large marquise and the surrounding smaller stones on each side were pear and pillow cut. Lovingly, he slid the ring on her finger while she smiled broadly and fought off a sudden surge of lightheadedness. Eyeno handed Vye Dame's ring now. She peered down at it proudly. Its setting consisted of a row of alternating obsidian and amethyst stones set in a silver band. She slid the ring over the knuckle of his fourth finger and sighed. In a few short moments, she would be venturing into un-chartered waters and suddenly, all doubts erased, she felt more than capable of handling it.

"Do you Vye take Dame to be your lawfully wedded husband, to have and to hold, for richer or for poorer, in sickness and in health, until death do you part?"

Vye smiled confidently as her mind wandered. She'd temper this man or die trying. Yes, she loved this man; but she also had an ulterior motive... saving the lives of her sons and the entire Ido clan. As she searched Dames genuine, watery eyes, she fought back a tiny surge of guilt. What she was doing was for the good of them all and eventually, he'd understand. "I do."

14

THE THIRD RITE

Blindfolded, naked, and visibly anxious; the women stumbled through the dense forest into a small clearing during the early evening hours of the following day. A near silence fell with the exception of a few distant growls as darkness set in comfortably for the night. The air was heavy with moisture aside from the slight breeze barely blowing inside Three Wood's leafy green walls. To his immediate right, Quince saw Dez's mouth crumple into a broad grin from out of the corner of his eye. Though his injured leg remained bandaged, he seemed to be managing just fine as far as Quince could tell. Maal stood proudly on his left with El by his side. The male Youth smiled to themselves and each other as the final light from the darkening sunset poked through the giant umbrella of trees.

The female Youth were told very little about the third Rite. They were simply left an anonymous message instructing them to gather at the edge of Three Wood during the earlier portion of evening after which they were to immediately blindfold themselves. Then they would be led inside the forest's perimeter by a member of the male Youth. The women stood before them with their backs turned. When they were instructed to face them, the men began a swift walk toward the woman with whom he desired to give and receive pleasure.

Quince identified Onya with little difficulty and smiled in approval. Her ceremonial markings were absolutely breathtaking. The mere sight of her caused his heart to slam against his chest in anticipation. With imminent danger at bay for the time being, he was free to think of the electricity of her touch and the sheer power behind her kiss without interruption. A rising flame within burned for her presence, demanded her to be near. No matter how forbidden his emotions were, she eased his intensity without effort which, truth be told, was no easy task.

Suddenly, tiny blue lights illuminated the clearing revealing hundreds of elaborate tree houses made of solid silver. The residences were of a variety of shapes and sizes and situated in nooks between the enormous burnt orange limbs of the massive three-pronged trunks of the surrounding Raha trees. Quince did a sudden double take as he noticed that some of the trees were hollowed out and streaming with mini-waterfalls, their pure waters aglow with color and tinkling like a relaxing song.

A rustling in the canopy above signaled the arrival of the Painted Folk. Gracefully, the rainbow-skinned people swung from limb to limb, eager to watch the sight before them unfold and hope to be asked for inclusion, though their activity could only be minimal. Quince was momentarily struck by their awkward and unorthodox beauty. He admired the winding colors and bright white tufts of hair that stood unapologetically on the women's heads. The male members of The Painted Folk stared intently at the female Youth with just as much anticipation as he.

Tearing his attention away from the new arrivals, he turned back to Onya. There she stood, trembling. Why was she nervous? After what they'd shared on the Amber Cliffs, pre-Rite jitters were unnecessary. Surely she knew he'd choose her again. Carefully, the men began to untie their blindfolds. Determined to take a different approach, Quince swung her around and pressed his lips lightly against hers before he did the honors. She let out a quick gasp as the cloth drifted to the ground. When their eyes met for the first time in weeks, he witnessed the muscles in her face relax in relief as she threw her hands around his neck.

"I'm so glad you're alive!" she whispered in his ear, relieved.

Quince gave her a puzzling glance before speaking. "Yes, but how did you know--"

In the distance, they could hear the identifiable moans. The women who hadn't been as lucky as she had were now without a pleasure mate. As was decided, it was up to another previously formed couple to accept one of the women into their partnerships. Because of the three Ido deaths, three men would be responsible for two women. Their world was swiftly changing around them. The balance had shifted and a representative would need to consult the Ancestors again soon.

Onya and Quince exchanged a knowing glance before she buried her face deep in his chest, finding solace in his arms. She did not want to waste a single second with mundane conversation. Swiftly, she put an index finger to his lips and gathered his entire body in a warm embrace. Quince responded immediately by lifting her clean off the ground for a moment and leading her toward a vacant patch of ground nearby. Before they could reach their destination; however, a woman with pale blue and silver skin swung from a nearby limb and landed softly in their path. Shoulders pulled back and head held high, she stood in front of them gallantly. Quince nearly lost himself in her pearl-white eyes before landing a sweeping gaze over her inviting physique. Her full breasts were accentuated by sapphire nipple rings connected to an elegant double silver chain. The woman's navel was also pierced with a large sapphire stud and joined with a larger chain that hung loosely over her wide hips. She pointed above their heads. Yards away hung a thick, winding branch. Wide enough to hold several people, it dipped close to the ground and twisted upward for as far as the eye could see.

"Gallah?" Quince asked, slightly unsure.

She nodded her head affirmatively and offered them both a reassuring smile.

"I choose the two of you as my Rite partners," she said softly. "Come."

Quince began to follow at once while Onya lagged behind. Sensing her insecurity, he turned back while Gallah waited patiently.

"The third Rite is a threesome Onya. Gallah will participate in our pleasure...well, not wholly, their kind is not permitted to engage in intercourse. However, she is allowed to explore our bodies through touch and vice versa."

She nodded slowly before acknowledging the Supreme Maiden with a curt nod.

"Onya, daughter of Imar. We meet again. Your markings are exquisite."

Onya managed a small smile, but in her shock, still seemed unable to speak. Quince could feel her disappointment hardening like a scab over an open sore. She'd hoped that they would be able to experience one another alone. However, tradition must be followed down to the very last detail, as they both knew. He quickly rounded on Onya and kissed her deeply before running his mouth along the sides of her neck and palming her breasts with his hands. Her eyes melted and she relaxed her rigid stance in an instant.

"I'm ok Quince," she said in a low whisper. "We will enjoy ourselves no matter what the stipulations are." Quince winked at her slyly before turning back to Gallah who was now walking briskly toward the trunk of the massive tree.

The three of them climbed to the limb above with ease. There were plenty of sizable grooves in the smooth, burnt orange bark for them to keep their footing. Once they reached the heavy branch, Quince watched as the women lay down on a glittering piece of fabric covering the bare limb. He wandered closer and stepped on the odd looking blanket. It was unbelievably soft to the touch. Cool and soothing, it almost felt as if it were made of a foreign fluid. The material sunk inside the spaces between his toes and gave easily when he stepped forward. Colorful bottles and burning incense were arranged neatly in the surprisingly sprawling space creating a beautiful ambiance of relaxation and comfort. Behind them stood a solid silver structure that was far greater in beauty and size from a closer view.

"My humble abode," Gallah said dramatically, gesturing toward the tree house.

"Wow," Quince managed, mouth agape.

"We are masters of architecture," she added with surging pride. "Its actual size is misleading. There are twenty rooms inside the Maiden Cove, but one would never know at first glance." Both Onya and Quince gazed at the gleaming oval structure, which looked to hold two rooms at best. "But enough chitchat, we will experience the Rite in the open evening air where our moans can mingle with the others. Our experience in the pleasures of others is just as important to us as our own. Now, kneel in front of her," Gallah dictated as she turned Onya on her stomach.

Obediently, he kneeled in front of Onya and watched as Gallah straddled her from behind. She poured the contents of a bottle of clear liquid into her open palms and rubbed them together. Quince watched with growing anticipation as Gallah began to massage the base of Onya's neck, back, and forearms methodically. From below, Onya released an exhilarated sigh.

He noticed Gallah's gaze shift from his muscular torso to the thick organ jutting from beneath his ornately decorated loincloth. Attentively, he rubbed its head directly against Onya's soft lips. Excitedly, she took it in her mouth and began rotating the shaft on her tongue with care. He closed his eyes, absorbing the warm jets of surging pleasure and leaned slightly forward. He took a moment to squeeze Gallah's breasts, rubbing the stiff flesh with his fingers until she threw her head back in delight. She continued to knead Onya's back with her thumbs before sliding backward in order to tend to her buttocks and thighs. Onya's body was now glistening with the sweet scent of mint oil and her ceremonial tattoo sparkled beneath the soft silver hue of night.

Below him, Onya forced his length farther down her throat as she flicked her tongue on the underside of its head while massaging his large sacs in a counterclockwise direction. Quince leaned closer to Gallah and managed to place one of her large silver dollar-sized pebbles in his mouth. Her skin tasted as if it were dusted with honey and nectar as it hardened instantly. When he glanced beneath him, he saw her insert a finger into Onya's moist vagina. Barely able to control himself, he took the other and rolled his tongue around the sapphire studs, silver chain, and stiff flesh. Gallah shivered in ecstasy and let out a high-pitched scream before sliding back onto the tree limb from her straddling position.

Still preoccupied with Quince, Onya removed the throbbing organ from her mouth and rose to her knees. Lightly, she ran her tongue up the middle of his chest and around the strong muscles of his abdomen while manipulating his member in her right hand. Wanting desperately to reciprocate the pleasure she was bestowing upon him, he laid her carefully on her back and opened her deep brown thighs. Meanwhile, Gallah lay down at Onya's side and took one of her heaving breasts in her mouth as she began to rub her own pulsing mound with a seductive fierceness.

Quince bent toward the pink opening and wrapped his lips around Onya's moistened flesh. Her juices were buttery and warm as he drove his tongue into her tight center and sucked lightly. He watched her eyes grow wide and her lashes flutter a bit while Gallah rubbed her index finger along her delicate curves, pleasuring herself. Eagerly, Onya inserted her finger inside Gallah's moist center and reached for one of her large sapphire studded breasts. She sucked and caressed as they moaned together in a fruitful bliss.

The trees around them swayed as if they were enclosed within a fluffy cloud of unbridled lust. Tiny silver lights cast silhouettes over the gathering of arched backs, bare thighs, and incoherent shouts. He'd waited long enough. The building suspense had become unbearable. He had to enter her body completely. Slowly, he sat up and licked his lips, still admiring the two women groping at one another beneath him. Gallah's silver afro dangled dangerously over the far edge of the tree limb along with Onya's left arm as they tangled themselves in an asymmetrical blur of arms, legs, and desire. Anxiously, he untied his loincloth and tossed it haphazardly near the burning incense and pleasured himself while the two women observed. He bent forward to give her pulsing center one last lick. Again, she groaned happily. Back on his knees, he playfully tapped the throbbing head of his penis against her pulsing bud before sinking it inside. The blood began to rush to his brain as he pushed himself deeper inside her soft valley. She gathered her knees together and he felt the moist flesh squeeze tighter around his shaft. Her jaw was slack now while she took in deep breaths. She stared up at him with a concentrated glare. Their eyes locked as Gallah's large breasts bounced along with their hypnotic rhythm. He pulled Gallah up to a seated position and guided her free hand to Onya's protruding center. Thrilled with the sensuality of their actions, Onya shivered uncontrollably while Quince ventured deeper inside and Gallah pleasured her bulging hot button.

Quince grabbed hold of her ankles now and pulled her legs from a bent knee position into a right angle as he pumped. His thighs smacked her buttocks continuously and she begged for him to quicken the pace. He could feel every inch of her now while his heart fluttered weakly. The warmth of her walls provided a moist cushion as he delved deeper into what he swore was heaven. He found himself tasting her toes, ankles, and the soles of her feet as she contracted her muscles rapidly causing a rippling wave of slick enjoyment.

Feeling the sudden urge to climax, he pulled out quickly and circled her breasts with his tongue. Gently, he sucked at the nape of her neck and whispered how much she meant to him. Moments later, she took the initiative to lie him on his back. She kissed his thighs softly before mounting his thick rod. Gallah happily licked her nipples while Onya slid her pleasing mound back and forth over his throbbing member. She lifted from her knees and secured her feet below her and began a swift bounce as he cried out before returning to her knees again. Squeezing her cheeks together with intense pressure, he lifted her off of him and back onto her knees. Then, he climbed over her arched back and entered from behind. The soft slap of her buttocks against his abdomen caused an unspeakable thrill to rise from the depths of his loins. Varying his rhythm, he began to wind his hips as her cries echoed along with the others in the distance. All around them bodies either dangled dangerously over branches or were pushed firmly against the smooth bark of the Raha trees. She threw her weight back at him until they perfected a calculated beat of sound and satisfaction. He reached below her and grabbed both of her wrists while her chin dug deeper into the blanket below. He thrust her upward and held her wrists securely behind her back as he guided himself further into her heavenly abyss. The thrust began gently then forcefully until she demanded more.

Gallah was now hovering above them, pleasuring herself with one hand and holding onto another higher limb with the other. Her climax was imminent; and nearly capsized by the moment at hand, Quince observed the two women in his wake in absolute bewilderment. Gallah threw her head back among the low hanging branches and arched backward, her moans at a fever pitch. The silver and blue pigment of her skin burned brighter as if it were set ablaze by some means of sorcery. Her eyes flickered from sapphire to gold before finally smoldering a smoky gray. From where he knelt, Quince could see the shimmering outline of her aura wrapped tightly around her profile. She swallowed before letting out a heavy sigh. Then, ample breasts shimmering with minuscule beads of sweat, she let out a smile of gratitude, mouthed the words thank you, and gracefully leapt out of sight in search of her next climactic adventure.

Before Quince could right himself, the lights began to blur into odd-looking circles and squares. Onya's inner walls were now expanding and contracting rapidly while Quince delved deeper and secured her wrists behind her. Finally, she gave a violent jolt just as a bolt of shuddering lightning shot through his lower body. He felt like he'd just traveled among the stars, been introduced to the moon. Utterly exhilarated, his nerves tingled wildly while his blood struggled to slow its passage between vessels and veins. After the lightning, came a thunderous groan as he climaxed. He flinched before letting out a shrill sound of finality. He continued to hold her as they attempted to gather their breath. Excessive droplets of sweat dampened their bodies as they held one another passionately. He pushed aside the long locs from her ears and kissed her lobes.

"I know what I feel is forbidden, but I cannot live without you. I don't want to try."

She grabbed his face with the palm of her hand and pulled it toward her own before responding, "I don't want you to."

15

DAME'S ULTIMATUM

It was high noon over the shimmering green of the Keep Grasslands when Dame wiped the dripping sweat from his brow with the back of his hand. Bleary-eyed, he looked in the direction of the sun. A buckling haze surrounded the orange sphere as it radiated smothering heat on his exhausted platoon. They'd been attempting drills since the early morning hours and now even he thought it might be wise to cease their practice session in lieu of the extreme heat.

Twenty years removed from his initial experience as the Youth General in the Insect War, he felt the fatigue creeping into his twitching musculature as he threw yet another mid-range kick in the direction of his sparring partner. Though he was in remarkable shape at forty-two years old, he recognized that there were just some things he couldn't do as quickly anymore. He hadn't lost his fierceness, nor his heart, that was something that had very little to do with physicality. However, he noticed that he'd become at least a half step slower here or there and a similar notion seemed to be occurring to the others as they glanced toward him wearily between flying kicks and short jabs. The fact remained that they were now middle-aged men preparing for a younger, quicker, more agile enemy. In all of his stubbornness, Dame liked their chances. He stepped a few feet backward and signaled to his partner before turning to the others.

"All right men, let's call it a day!" he shouted shrilly.

Many of the men hunched over in relief, gripping at their burning sides or taut calf muscles with discomfort. The absolute depletion of energy and fluids from their bodies revealed itself on their pain stricken faces. Dame reached toward the short grass and grabbed hold of the leather bound canteen of water at his feet. After taking a few large, refreshing gulps, he poured the rest of the cool contents over his sweltering body and waited for his heartbeat to normalize.

Admittedly, he'd forgotten the mental and physical intensity of the Bgongo martial arts and immediately feared he'd pushed his men too hard.

As he looked around him, most had retreated into the shaded areas provided by the wide leaved Glick trees dotting the grasslands while others drank thirstily from their containers. Some still remained hunched over gasping for air.

"Now that.... is what I call... a workout!" heaved Chi as he slowly made his way toward Dame.

While adequately quenching his thirst, Dame thought in amazement about how much the faith had altered his life. He smiled at his first lieutenant general and good male friend, the first he'd ever had in his life. The tall man with toffee skin now standing in front of him had been one of his chief rivals just before they'd set out for Taste as Youths. This rivalry was due largely to their mutual attraction to Imar. In fact, they would have fought to the death had she not intervened and gently informed Chi that she'd chosen Dame as her preferred partner. Thinking back to that very day, he wondered if Imar had chosen him because she truly desired him or to save Chi's life. Somehow he thought the latter to be correct.

"I hope I didn't work you all too hard," he said, his breathing still staggering in shallow pants. "I just want us to be ready. We aren't twenty-one any more."

Chi took a gulp from his own canteen and squinted through the blinding rays.

"That's for sure... but what we lack in age, we more than make up for in experience. No matter how long ago The Insect War was, we all remember. They've never seen war before so how can they have a clue as to how to win one? Born can offer advice, but he cannot fight for them. His days of walking on land as a man are long gone. He wields no power on our battlefield."

"Good point, which is why I'm going to give them one last chance."

"One last chance for what?" asked Chi as he poured the remainder of the water across the breadth of his shoulder blades.

"I think we should allow them one last chance to convert. I am now married to a woman with three sons I may meet in battle," he responded thoughtfully. "There isn't a day that goes by that she doesn't worry or show concern for their safety. Not only that, who will my daughter have if the male Youth are killed? Who will our sons have if our daughters are killed? They will fight as well. Ido women are proud and headstrong. I'm thinking of my line here. It must continue. Therefore, it's only fair that we provide them with another chance. If they defy us again they will be dealt with, but I will be able to rest better knowing that they were at least given the opportunity to have a change of heart."

Chi stroked his dark beard calmly. "I agree. Though I must say, they held their own in Glo. I was there to see it."

"Yes," replied Dame reluctantly. "I expected more casualties on their side and less on ours. Instead, the results were even. They've been trained well."

"They were trained by us."

"Indeed."

"How does Vye feel about this? Her son is one of their co-Generals. And as you know, my son Maal is the other."

Dame sighed and turned toward his friend. "Vye is back and forth. There are days when she is undoubtedly dedicated to the Elder Clan and there are moments when she speaks of loyalty to Born because of his sparing her sons' lives all those years ago."

"Hmmm, my doubts about the Faith have passed, but fighting them has been another story. There really is no preparation for the possibility of having to take the life of your own flesh and blood," he paused for an extended inhalation of breath. "My heartbeat quickened when I met Maal in battle that day. I remember the awkwardness of the moment. My military garb kept me hidden, but the feeling after seeing him was a cross between pride and fury. He handles the broadsword ferociously... nearly severed my head from my neck twice."

Dame nodded. "Maal is a fighter, a natural warrior. I saw some of myself in him. That is why I trained him personally when he was a child."

"Let us hope that you did not train him too well," Chi replied with a hint of bitterness. "There are still some nights when I pray for his well-being. It is only natural for one to wish a long and healthy life for their child. But the Youth are wrong and if they must pay the price, then so be it. When will you be sending this message and by what means?"

"Soon. Ly the Diaw is on his way as we speak. I have already given him directions to leave the message in the hands of my daughter."

***

Onya quickly scanned the tattered scroll under the light of a nearby torch. It was in the dead of night when she emerged shrouded in a hooded cloak on the marked path separating the Eastern and Western sides of Nu. She'd been summoned from her sleep by a sharp and unexpected rapping outside of her hut. The messenger was a Diaw. Quickly, she dressed and exited. Now it stood over her, ogling her every move. She would not speak to it though, for fear of a response from its oddly pitched voice.

The message, though warped, was perfectly clear in its meaning; *Convert or suffer the consequences.* Her father's looping script was harsh and intimidating, even from the page. She had to get the message to Quince.

The male Youth must be made aware of the ultimatum. Carefully, she thought back to her decision to interrupt their meeting after The Warming Ceremony in order to share what she'd learned regarding The Guide. It seemed that this bit of information was also worthy of defying tradition once again. The female Youth were not scheduled to see the males for another few weeks, during the coveted fourth Rite. Despite the possible ramifications, it took less than a second to make up her mind. She nodded slightly to the bird, dismissing him at once. He bounced away in the opposite direction as she headed toward the entrance of West Nu and the hut Quince shared with his brothers. As she quietly approached, she noticed two guards flanking either side of the arced entrance.

"I must see Quince, the co-General of the male Youth at once," she said firmly.

"General, you are aware that we should not have interaction between Rites. It is against tradition--"

"Formalities and protocol were thrown out of the window long ago. In case you haven't realized, we are at war," she replied sternly. "I have with me a message from the Elder General Dame. I need to speak with the General at once!" she exclaimed pulling the scroll from beneath her cloak.

He eyed the papyrus suspiciously before signaling to the other guard. After the two armed men looked it over; the guard she'd initially spoken to motioned for her to follow him inside the village. Onya did so silently. The area was well lit by flame burning torches beside the huts' entrances. After a short distance, the guard signaled for her to wait beside the larger one she, Eesha, and Lyn entered that night over three months ago. She paced for a few moments before Quince appeared. Immediately, the guard disappeared from sight.

"Onya, what is the matter?" he said rushing to her side in surprise. "What brings you here and at this time of night?"

"I have a message... from my father," she whispered gruffly. "Is there a place we can go where we won't be overheard?"

Quince shook his head and motioned for her to follow him. Together, they continued through another cluster of huts and finally down a winding path that looked to lead eastward toward the women's side of the village. She watched as the wide leaved palms thinned in front of them. Soon, the crashing of waves could be heard nearby. He grabbed her wrist lightly and guided her over a few small, but precarious dunes toward two large rocks. A slight breeze whipped her cloak against her body. Nearly overheated, she removed its hood as they sat on the rock's smooth surface. With care, she removed the scroll from beneath her arm and handed it to Quince. He unfurled it at once and began to read.

Youth of Ido,

Though we know you question our reasoning, please understand that as Elders of this Clan, we have your best interest in mind. War is not our intention. It is love that we plan to spread. The ways of The Guide are pure and in a short period he has revealed to us truths that one can only imagine to gather in a lifetime. The One Faith teaches honor and order. It has also opened our hearts to love. With this faith, you will be allowed to love whomever you please and live out your days knowing your souls have truly been cleansed. You will be free from judgment for eternity. I charge you to accept these new ways. Change is necessary for all things at a given time. Divorce yourselves from the heathen ways to which we once adhered, I beg of you. It is through love that war and loss of life can be avoided. If we are not informed of your conversion within one week, we will assume you desire to meet us in war. Choose carefully for we will fight to the death.

The Elder Clan c/o The Elder General Dame

Only the waves slapping gently against the beach could be heard for several moments after Quince's intense gaze fled the page and took root out to sea. Silently Onya examined the soft flare of his nostrils while pondering their next move.

"I suppose I should inform the others of this message, though I'm sure it will not make a difference in our approach. If anything, your father is fanning the flames of our anger."

"I'm so sorry," she replied, looking down, embarrassment flushing her cheeks.

Quince turned to face her and took her hands in his. "There is nothing for you to be sorry about Onya. You are clearly not your father." There, in the moonlight, she allowed her eyes to meet the intense pupils cradled inside his soft, brown irises. A caring smile supplied her with reassurance. "You have remained dedicated to Taste and tradition. It is not your fault that our Elders have been poisoned," he paused a moment before continuing. "You know your father Onya. Did he ever at any time seem easily led or gullible? I only know him as the fearless hero of the Insect War."

Onya sat thoughtfully for a moment. "No, I don't recall. This is why this seems so unusual. My father was always criticized for being inflexible. He never conceded once his mind was made up, which I guess makes sense now. His mind is made up about this new faith and he's not looking back.

He's consistent."

Quince turned toward the sea again. His next words were barely above a whisper. "Do you think they could have been brainwashed? Could it be possible? Look at the facts," he said hurriedly while counting on his fingers. "Taste has been in place for centuries. It's just difficult for me to accept that one man can come in and persuade an entire group of *Enlightened* Elders to follow him within days. It just doesn't make sense."

Onya settled her chin in her palm as she thought. Quince was right on target. The Ido Elders weren't just some random, easily led species; they'd participated in decades of lessons on Mental Strength. "How could they have been brainwashed Quince? By what means?"

Quince exhaled forcefully. "I don't know, but I certainly intend to find out... and hopefully, before any more blood is shed." He turned to Onya and placed a hand on the side of her face. They sat for what seemed like hours before the silence broke.

"Freedom to love..." Onya began before leaning back and allowing her thoughts to drift. "What do you think that would be like?"

Quince exhaled a long breath before answering. "I don't know."

"We wouldn't have to sneak around. Think about it Quince, we'd be able to do what we wanted without judgment, without living a lie!"

Quince was slow to respond, his eyes centered on the sway of the waves. "Yes, but not this way Onya. As Generals, we have taken oaths to protect our people. Part of that protection involves ensuring that the Rituals survive. Who are we without Taste?"

Onya did not answer. After several moments, she blurted out the first words to enter her mind. "What's your favorite color?" The question occurred to her almost out of nowhere, yet it seemed appropriate to ask. She genuinely wanted to know. She genuinely wanted to know *him*.

"Green," he said with a perplexed grin. "And yours?"

"Would you believe me if I said the same?" she answered, fluttering her long lashes.

He smiled toothily before responding. "Given the connection we share, I wouldn't be surprised if we shared a lot more similarities."

"Oh you really think so?" she said slyly rubbing the soft hairs on his chin. "Well then, you must love Funnel fish roasted slowly in herbs as well as the sound of the waves pounding on the beach just before the sun goes down," she paused, studying his reaction eagerly. "I love to watch the trees blow in the breeze and sometimes I write poetry," she concluded shyly.

"I can honestly say I love all of those things along with a few others," he paused, giving his reply ample thought. "I enjoy Bgongo; not because we were required to learn it, but because I can truly see the beauty in its movement." His eyes twinkled with interest. "I remember learning it as a child. I wasn't the natural that Maal was, he was so gifted your father took him under his wing and trained him. But I remember what a challenge it was to learn. I practiced the cadences well into the night for several years. In fact, I still do some days. Stringing my bow also calms me when I'm unnerved."

A broad grin formed on her face as she rambled on. "The bow is ok I suppose, but I prefer my blade. The bow is Lyn's expertise. Eesha prefers the mace." Quince nodded, obviously impressed, but not surprised. The Ido women were fierce fighters. They'd been trained as such. "I was taught by Maal's mother Eyeno. She was our Bgongo guru. She was hard on us, but it paid off. We are disciplined women." Her voice trailed off with the last statement. Could she really consider herself disciplined? After all, she'd broken tradition. Against all things sacred, *she'd fallen in love.*

Sensing her internal battle, he gazed in her eyes a moment before speaking again. "I don't know if I've ever shared with you how beautiful you are," he whispered before kissing her hand.

A smile spread across her lips. "And I don't think I've ever shared with you how handsome you are," she commented back.

He moved closer. "I think I knew I loved you when our eyes met during the Warming Ceremony," he added as he drew her near. "It was more than seeing you naked. There were fifty naked women on that platform. It was in the way you moved. You had a confident innocence that not only aroused me; it made me want to know you far beyond Taste. It was always more than just becoming your pleasure mate Onya. I knew I wanted to be your preferred partner from the moment I saw you."

Seconds passed before she chose to respond. "At first, I merely wanted you to want me physically. I have to admit that. I think the infatuation transformed when Eesha, Lyn, and I interrupted your meeting. I had no idea that you were the co-General of the Cause. But seeing you dictate with kindness and lead with such humility made me want to learn from you. I admired you. I still do."

"Love at second sight... okay I guess I can take that," he said playfully before kissing her deeply. Slowly, he lifted her garments, running a hand gracefully up her inner thigh. It wasn't long before they found themselves lying on the beach, their silhouettes intertwining effortlessly in rays of moonlight. Soft moans were engulfed by far off shadows as they twisted into bends and curves of courageous lovemaking. The fact that a union outside of the Rites was forbidden did not seem to cross either of their minds. Instead, they were pulled inside a gripping sphere of passion of which only they were aware.

***

In the shadows of the rocks and palms, there lurked a figure. He made no sound as he watched the two lovers enjoying one another under an unassuming blanket of night sky. The dark pupils of his eyes flickered with the rage of betrayal.

How can we fight to save a tradition we so easily bend? They are no better than Dame and our enemies, the muscular Youth thought to himself in wild surprise. As co-leader of the Youth Cause, Maal had a serious decision to make. Their behavior was cause for major disciplinary action and should be brought before the entire group. He weighed his options with disappointment. With their people already unraveling at the seams, he feared that this would certainly be a fatal blow to the Cause. Hastily, he finished sharpening his trusty broad spear, returned it to its leather sheath across his shoulder blade, and quietly backed away.

16

THE YOUTH COUNCIL

Ankh's head jerked upward in anticipation when a remote sound in the distance piqued his interest. The Sphinx leader had managed to keep one eye on the opening in the rock wall for the last hour, but found it difficult to fight off an onslaught of anxiety while the Falls gently pounded the outside of the dome-shaped glass. A midnight glow from an orange moon reflected through the blurred sheets of water as he waited. Alone inside the laboratory, and with little left to do, he again went over his practiced spiel step by step.

The last few months had been uncomfortably stressful at best. The initial reports regarding the Youth's successes in the surprise attack at Glo City had been alarming. According to his sources, they'd far exceeded expectations in battle. Dame had nearly guaranteed an Elder victory, but surprisingly, they'd come up with an even amount of losses. He'd met four of the men now and their skills both impressed and concerned him. It was only a matter of time before the bug would be found and the Sphinx people would be exposed. Now that he was aware of their headiness in wartime situations, he found himself disconcerted in spite of Dame's promised protection. His people could ill afford a war with the invigorated and agile Ido Youth.

Ankh's gaze slipped impatiently toward the liquid filled tanks lining the walls. Some of the mutated creatures slept, while others continued to adapt to their new existences. *Never!* He would *not* allow their medical advances to be thwarted by a group of hyper-sexualized Youth! His people were so close to achieving the goal that had been in the works for centuries. Ankh sighed heavily as he envisioned a speck of light at the end of a very long tunnel. Without a doubt, he was looking forward to reaping the benefits that came with leading the charge.

Momentarily distracted; he glanced at the data from the pheromone readings of the scarab. According to one of his lead scientists, The Youth hadn't moved from the twenty-one degree longitude, forty-six degree latitude coordinate of West Nu Village in some time. His shoulders relaxed instantly. With this news, Dame would certainly be pleased and his pleasure, no matter how short-lived, was all he hoped for at the moment. In a short while, he would have to commit one of the most brazen acts of dishonesty ever seen on the shores of Ido. He understood that it was necessary; however, and prepared himself once again to sell the blatant lie.

The pristinely pressed white lab coat swished about as he trotted toward the well-hidden door in the wall, muttering to himself. His nervous tension was spiking. The carrier should have been here! The time they'd agreed upon had long since come and gone. Suddenly, all sorts of possible debacles and mishaps littered his mind.

Could he have been found out? Impossible! He whispered to himself and dismissed the idea immediately. He'd covered and recovered his tracks flawlessly. Drops of perspiration began to gather at his graying temples; he could barely stomach the anticipation. Panic was clearly setting in.

Just then, the invisible opening in the solid rock face rose swiftly from the polished glass floor, revealing a man of medium build dressed in what Ankh had come to identify as the traditional garb of The One Faith. Accompanied by his loyal underling, Heru; the carrier approached briskly.

"What is the reason for the delay? Are you certain you were not followed here?" asked the Sphinx in a gruff voice.

"That is precisely the reason for the delay. I took care not to be followed."

Ankh scanned the Elder standing before him and looked questioningly toward Heru.

"He was not." Heru replied at once. "I had the perimeter scanned thoroughly both before and directly after his arrival. In addition, there are round-the-clock lookouts stationed at each corner of the Oasis."

The old Sphinx grunted in approval. Heru was perhaps his most trusted friend. He'd never failed him before and Ankh had become accustomed to his excellent work ethic and zero tolerance for failure. The Elder responded with a swift nod and held out an empty hand. Ankh peered at the man through his small, circular spectacles as if scanning him one last time for any sign of deceit or foul play. Satisfied with his findings, he traipsed toward a large, locked cabinet. Methodically, he placed a large brown paw on an indentation on the cabinet's hinge and a slight click sounded as its heavy door popped open. A single item lay inside. Ankh proceeded to gather a small pouch made of animal skins and with a fluid motion, tossed it in the direction of the Elder messenger who caught it deftly with one hand.

The man squinted his eyes as he peeked inside. "Is this all of it? Dame led me to believe there would be much more," he asked while examining the bag's contents.

"It will be enough. Be sure to inform your people that its sweetness is deceiving. An overdose could cause multiple births, triplets, quadruplets, quintuplets and the like. The amount in the pouch should be a large enough dosage for forty-nine women. Ovulation will increase up to fifty percent after the initial dosage. Conception *will* occur and quickly. You have traveled a great distance. You are welcome to stay behind in the Oasis quarters for the night until daybreak."

The Elder initiated a low bow but respectfully declined. "I have been given an assignment to carry-out. The herb is expected by daybreak. I must take my leave."

"Very well then. Please tell General Dame I give my regards." Again the man gave a polite bow before securing the sac in an invisible pocket beneath his white tunic and hurried back the way he'd come with Heru following after him. Alone again now, the Sphinx leader sighed. "The question is not whether they will conceive," he said aloud. "But *what* they will conceive in time..."

***

"You have all heard Dame's ultimatum. The Elders have made their demands clear. We have discussed a plan in which one of us will be sent off on a covert mission, alone. The man who has agreed to do this is El." Maal nodded toward El, who proudly acknowledged his dedication.

After a one-minute, incomplete briefing, Quince knew he was against the strategy. Foolhardy and dangerous, the plan had all the makings of a complete under analysis of the problem at hand. Hurriedly, he scoped out the reaction of the others in his wake. Every brow seemed knitted in contemplation as Maal gestured emphatically. Still, Quince managed to swallow his words while his thoughts raced at sonic speed. It had always been his style to listen before speaking in haste, one of the very reasons he'd been voted co-General in the first place.

"It will be necessary for El to travel dangerously close to the Elder territories and allow himself to be captured. He will then assume the identity of Quince and convince Dame that the Youth have decided to surrender. As you know, only a General can offer surrender and we need both of our real Generals here with us at all times," Maal rattled off. "Upon his capture, he will gather valuable information. Dame will of course inquire about when the Cause will surrender as an entire group. I studied under the man; he *will* require the presence of all of us before he truly takes the bait. He is too savvy *not* to make such a demand. El will disclose that we are awaiting word from him. Dame will provide him with an Elder messenger. After we receive the message, a small group of us will travel to the location he provides for us. Then, an attack will begin. All those in favor of the mission, please respond by saying I. All those who oppose, respond by---"

"I don't like it," Quince cut in finally. "I disagree with offering one another up as bait with the hope that things will work in our favor. There are two many variables, two many things must go smoothly for the strategy to be effective."

Maal rolled his shoulders backward before meeting his co-General's questioning stare. "We are the only variables here and I trust our warriors. We have been trained to endure without folding. Our lessons have prepared--"

"The Elders are behaving as though they are without conscience. There has to be another way. We *must* examine other alternatives. Never were we trained for civil war Maal. The factors are volatile; any outcome is unpredictable. To approach this without thorough analysis would be unwise," Quince interrupted hastily before continuing his anxious plea. "Our Elders have been poisoned! Let's take this week to investigate other options. We can set up a team to infiltrate The Enlightened Lands and find out more about The Guide. Then we can try and determine what methods he may be using to control them. A *team* would be most wise, no one should be sent on a mission alone during these---"

Maal's only response was to signal for silence. Angrily, he turned to face his life-long friend. "Need I remind you that the Elders aimed to kill us the day they attacked at Glo City? Have you forgotten that it was they who disrupted The Warming Ceremony, which I might add, is an abomination? Need I also remind you that three of us lost their lives and others were seriously wounded in battle? Your brother has already agreed to the mission. He knows of its dangers. Part of being a warrior in the Youth Cause is putting yourself in danger!"

Quince met Maal's ferocious stare and scanned the area. Many of the men were throwing him sidelong glances of disappointment. Two of those men were his brothers, Dez and El.

"We have already gained permission to fight Quince; it has been sanctioned by the Ancestors." Maal continued on. "Are you actually suggesting that we pull back from our original plans and abandon the protection of tradition in favor of a hunch?"

Quince swallowed his pride before relinquishing a reply. "I am aware of the precarious situation we are all in; however, we have been given a week--"

Again, he was interrupted. "Are you now suggesting that we comply with their demands? You can't possibly think---"

It was Quince's turn to interrupt now, his cheeks growing hot with frustration. "I am only providing reason in a time of rash behavior! I believe our Elders have been brainwashed. As to how this has been done, I am uncertain. However, it is in our best interest to at least follow up on this theory. Perhaps we can save lives as well as save our people, *Youth and Elders alike!*"

The circle buzzed with conversation. Their stares slid from Maal and Quince to one another. For the first time, they were clearly divided, which Quince regretted wholeheartedly. However, he could not ignore his gut feeling that The Guide was playing the part of a puppeteer whose purse strings beheld more than just a promising new religion.

"Does this call for a council?" Maal questioned as the voices died down.

Quince ran his fingers over his thick waves and slowly nodded. "Perhaps that is the only way the matter will be settled."

"Indeed," Maal quipped ardently. "A messenger must be sent to the female Youth. They must take part in the proceedings as well."

The open air around them was still as the shocked Youth searched one another for answers. Their Generals had always been on one accord. Things had taken a dreadful turn for the worst.

"We will break and organize our cases," Maal stated without bothering to mask his disappointment. "In one hour we will reconvene for the first council of the Youth Cause," he declared when some of the men retreated from the circle to talk among themselves and others stayed behind to assemble the required long, wooden benches. Quince stood alone, pondering.

Never in his lifetime had a council been necessary. Carefully, his mind traveled back to one of their many lessons on the pillars of Ido culture. He visualized himself seated on the beach with his legs crossed as the Elders strode before them, lecturing. Glyphs and symbols were introduced and drawn in the sand or on stripped logs. Soon after, the teachings were to be memorized verbatim. To his knowledge, a council was called whenever parties could not agree on a given issue. During the exercises, each side was given the opportunity to further explain their case while an impartial or undecided Youth served as a presiding judge. At the close of the council, an anonymous vote was taken. A two-thirds majority was required in order to arrive at a clear decision. There were no appeals. After the process was seen through to its end, the argument was never mentioned again and the clan continued on as was determined by the decision.

Out of the corner of his eye, he saw his brothers huddled together, refusing to meet his gaze as he peered in their direction. Solemnly, he understood their position. Dez had been on the receiving end of a poison arrow that had nearly cost him his life. Most of the Youth were seeing red by now and their only thoughts were of avenging those who'd perished or had been wounded. Carefully though he rearranged his plan in his head and prepared to present a compelling case. He was more than convinced that an assumed surrender followed by an attack was not the answer.

After a quarter of an hour had passed, the women began filing into the central meeting place. Led by their three Generals, they took their seats in an orderly fashion, expressions of confusion lining their faces. Onya was careful to avoid his eyes as she strode past. For this Quince was thankful. It was important for them to downplay their feelings for one another while in public. It was only by grace that their own forbidden acts were not the subject of the council's vote.

The benches had been aligned in the formation of an inverted pyramid with an aisle dividing it into two sides, one for the males and the other for the females. Clay, a lean Youth with a bronze complexion, short locs and a protruding brow had been chosen as their impartial judge. With a serious sweeping gaze, he took his seat on a high stool in front of the Cause members. A hushed silence fell over the gathering as the last of the Youth organized themselves and Maal and Quince sauntered toward opposite sides. Clay was positioned between them. Wasting no time, he brought the first ever Youth Council to order.

Confidently, Maal strode forward and took his place in the center of the space. "We are a proud people with a rich culture and a wholesome tradition. Months ago that culture, those traditions that we hold so dear, were violated and defaced by a group of its own members," he said with ample conviction. "Our Warming Ceremony was interrupted and we were disgraced by a foreign religious zealot and the leader of the Elder Ido Clan. Three of us were lost during a surprise battle at Glo City and others received wounds that were near fatal." Maal paused dramatically to gesture in Dez's direction. "I propose that we attack the Elders when they least expect it. Our dead, who have now drifted into the realm of the Ancestors, deserve to be avenged and our traditions protected. We will gather our resources responsibly and seek out our enemies. Coordinates will be scouted and considered while preparations are made. One of our own, he said while motioning in El's direction, has volunteered to infiltrate the Elder territories, take on the assumed identity of General Quince, feign our surrender, and gather the facts necessary to guarantee a victory. We must prepare for the imminence of an all out war," he ceased with a graceful flourish before yielding the floor to Quince who began to walk forward. Ever mindful of the ninety-six pairs of eyes on him, Quince cleared his throat before beginning.

"Taste is as dear to me as it is to all of you. Since our transformation fourteen years ago, we have been preparing for the sacred Rites. We have all looked forward to them for as long as we can remember and those traditions are certainly worth fighting for. However, we owe it to all of our people to battle wit against brawn. I am sure that no one here is wholly convinced that our Elders have been willingly converted." He paused and glanced at his audience thoughtfully. When his eyes locked with Onya's, he immediately felt the warmth of her support and continued.

"It is apparent that they have been led through other means. As far as what those means are, I am unsure, however, we owe it to ourselves to find out and possibly undo the damage that has already been done and avoid more. Let's cut off the head of this festering beast that calls himself, The Guide. Let's infiltrate their temple and prayer services and find what mysticism or outside element he has used to turn our mothers and fathers against their children and their culture. Let's use our heads in this matter and defend ourselves only if necessary. Sending one another on suicide missions is not the answer. *Together* we must find other alternatives that can save lives. If we attack... then we are no better than they." Quince clasped his hands together, signaling an end to his argument. He couldn't read the reactions on the faces of his peers. There was nothing left to do now but hope for the very best.

Clay cleared his throat. "Please be mindful of both arguments presented today. It is up to you to decide our fate to the best of your abilities. The parchment beneath your benches should be used to tally your votes. Please write yea if you wish to go forward with an attack," he said as he gestured toward Maal. "Or nay if you wish to investigate other options," he said before motioning in Quince's direction.

The scratching sounds of chalk on parchment permeated the open space. The generals at odds avoided one another's eyes. A medium sized wicker basket passed through the neat rows, collecting each ballot. Quince ignored his sweaty palms and scribbled the word nay on his own small piece of parchment. Soon, the baskets were filled and brought to Clay for counting.

Two Cause members, one male and one female, rose to count the votes. Quince inhaled deeply. There were five yeas before the first nay arose, followed by another. He mopped the sweat from his brow with the palm of his hands as Clay continued. "Yea, yea, yea, yea, yea..." Soon, he'd begun to drown it all out. His defeat was imminent. Shoulders slumped; Quince struggled to save face while honorably acknowledging the inevitable.

"That's ninety-five votes yea to two votes nay. The Youth will go on with the covert mission and organize an attack on the Elder Clan within the coming weeks."

With that, the group rose from their seats and quietly scattered elsewhere. Among them, his brothers still managed to avoid his gaze. Quince held back a bit, his heart heavy with disappointment. After visibly sweeping the area, he noticed that Maal had remained behind, his large frame looming in a nearby corner. Not wanting to create an unnecessary schism within the Cause, Quince trudged toward his friend and offered his hand.

Maal scowled at the peace offering. "I never thought I'd have to question your dedication to this Cause and to Taste," he declared, his words like daggers. Quince's defeated visage managed to stretch into a confused frown, but before he could defend himself, Maal shot back. "I saw you last night with her. Intercourse outside of the Rites is completely forbidden!" his co-General seethed. "How long have you been bending tradition to suit your own selfish wants?"

"What--"

"Are you suggesting that we hold back on our attack because Dame is her father?" Dame rattled on.

"How can you possib--" Again, Quince's efforts to defend himself proved futile.

Eyes fixed in a piercing glare, Maal backed away slowly. "I question your ability to lead and make decisions that will benefit us all. You disappoint me!"

As the clouds gathered in the distance, Quince watched his friend thunder away, the nettled energy of his outburst charging after him in a static clump. He slouched forward. Mentally exhausted, he rested his palms on his knees and looked around in disbelief. In the now vacant space of his home and village, he recognized that for the first time in his short life, he felt completely ostracized and alone.

17

ANCESTORS' BROOD

"You're forbidding us to respond to their offerings? Why?" exclaimed the mermaid seated at his right hand, her massive burgundy fin thrashing about in a fit of frantic motion. "Shutting them out is not the answer! The island is in complete crisis!"

"Since when have we ever meddled in the affairs of the living this often? Already I've had dialogue on two different occasions. That is more than I've had in the past five centuries," replied Born settling in a large blue, spongy chair. Not to be dissuaded, the Merwoman in his wake continued her infuriated rant.

"Not only has Taste been heavily compromised, but now, due to the deaths of the Youth, the balance has been thrown off. Death is inevitable Born! As much as I hate to say it, more will follow. The war is literally threatening the race!"

Fateem had been one of Born's closest friends and confidantes since their time as Youth and Elders centuries ago on Ido. It hadn't taken long for her to choose him as her preferred partner during the Fourth Rite. The rest had been history, so to speak. Together they conceived a daughter, Rya, and lived out their lives and Afterlives as close associates. She had always managed to restore peace where there was none with her natural knack for nurturing and calming the afflicted. Aside from her valuable insight and sharp wit, this was probably the main reason he'd kept so close to her even after their experiences at Taste. It also didn't hurt that she remained one of the most beautiful women he'd ever laid his eyes on.

Fateem was an entity of softness and curves, seven hundred and seventy years later. Men desired her, women desired *to be her*, and after nearly eight centuries, this still proved true. He watched while she swam in frustrated circles, wordlessly inspecting her smooth, toffee complexion and the curly, dark brown afro softened at the temples by streaks of gray. Her physique had thickened over the years, but in a way that added to her attractiveness. His eyes grazed the V shaped cleavage spilling over the golden clam shell brassier cupping her ample breasts. Indeed, she was beauty personified.

"This dilemma is far greater than the Insect War twenty years ago begun by the Sphinx. It's bigger than the woman who came to you twenty years ago begging mercy for her triplets. At least they were born to the same parents!" she exclaimed. "We now have to worry about the half brothers and sisters the newly formed unions will create. How can we separate the sexes at birth as we have before? They will be unaware of their blood relations... and that would cause utter chaos. We do not mix blood. We cannot allow incest to disrupt the lineage of the Ido people!"

Born formed a tent with his index fingers and thumbs and exhaled. The bubbles released from his mouth and ascended upward. "Fateem, I know and I too am fearful for us... but what advice can I provide? We must remain impartial in the matter. I have no idea what to tell them. Taste must be preserved. I cannot tell them not to fight. They are our only hope at this point. The fate of the Ido now rests on their shoulders."

"Did you do all you could to convince Dame of his ill-advised decisions? Are you sure of it?" she countered fiercely.

"Of course I did. I made a point of discussing his errant ways... his break with tradition... his breach with what is expected of an Ido General."

"Fine. But we cannot possibly claim to be impartial now. We granted them a request for war. To turn our backs on them now would be absolutely irresponsible, not to mention unforgivable!"

"Our backs would not be turned," replied the Merman calmly, his even tone a sharp contrast to her angst. "We must take into account what is at stake here. The ancient laws do not forbid us to remain neutral. There is a place for everything and everything must stay in its place. Our unnecessary involvement would tip that balance."

"*Unnecessary!*" she retorted hotly. "I'd hardly call us taking part in a civil war to preserve our culture and tradition *unnecessary*! I am not questioning your judgment Born, but remaining neutral may not be what is best for our people," she pleaded.

Born placed his large index fingers at his temples and began to apply a gentle massage. "Have you heard how they handled themselves at Glo City? They were ambushed and managed to hold their own," he said meeting her eyes. "They've been trained well, Fateem. Have you thought that they may see our involvement as a symbol of our lack of belief in their abilities?" he asked softly.

"No I hadn't thought of it that way," she said, retreating a bit. "I'm just concerned Born. The very thought that our traditions may be exterminated is--"

Born placed the pad of one of his fingers on her lips as he looked intently into her gray eyes. "Don't say it," he whispered. "Taste isn't something we do, Taste is something we *are*. It breathes with us. It is a living organism that we have nurtured for nearly one thousand years. That being said, we must have faith that the power of Taste will manifest within our Youth. It certainly did so during their first battle. Do you understand?" he asked before placing some distance between himself and the beautiful Merwoman. She nodded abruptly before lowering her head in concern.

"I do," she answered.

"I need to sort out my thoughts. Our people are experiencing grave dangers," he said with his back toward her. He turned in time to see the burgundy flash of her fin rounding a corner at the far end of the room.

After releasing a long, hard sigh, he glided swiftly toward one of the windows of the breathtaking palace he called home. Outside of the oval shaped window, the underwater metropolis of Erruk sprawled before him. Having helped to build the city with his bare hands; its infinitesimal beauty made him proud. He stared down at the colorful rooftops of daring yellow, soft green, and shocking red carved from the coral reefs and anemones rooted to the sea floor. Though threatened, life among them had not ceased. The Ancestors were tending to their daily duties as usual.

Yet still, Fateem's points echoed in his mind. He hadn't really thought about the Youth

feeling betrayed if the Ancestors did not step in. Though they were physically limited to the sea, it was widely believed that the scope of their powers traveled well beyond those parameters. Until now, Born had done a decent job of ebbing his own fears. The Ancestors *owned* the sea, so how had this foreigner compromised their sorcery to even walk in it? The breech hadn't occurred to the others yet, but he'd been worried since he'd first laid eyes on the stranger as he conjured boldly, as he performed baptisms in the Mer Sea... the home of the mighty Living Dead! There existed only a few others who held the answers to his questions. Soon, he would set out for a face-to-face meeting with an old ally. With only the gentle sway of the current to comfort him, he wondered how much his forthcoming decisions would cost both he and his people.

18

CLAWS IN THE DARK

By now, Quince had become accustomed to spending time alone. He'd been all but outcast by his male counterparts since the infamous council ten days ago. He was sure the lone nay vote had come from Onya, though he hadn't had any communication with her since their subtle exchanges during council. Since then, the Youth Cause had asserted themselves as a very united front in spite of their co-General's difference in opinion and anyone who stood in the way of that unity was kept at arm's reach. Since the vote, they'd avoided him in nearly all aspects of village life.

On the gleaming beach, by the light of the rising sun, he practiced the accuracy of his archery along with the strict Bgongo cadences that would aid in their defeat of the Elders. It had been made unequivocally clear that he was not wholly welcome in the en masse training sessions held in the center of the village. However, no matter how much he was against their decision, he was prepared to defend himself, the Youth, and the Rites of Taste. It was a must that he train. So, he took it upon himself to make headway alone.

The shining white granules of sand warmed between his toes while the temperature climbed. He let another high kick fly as the perspiration trickled down his temples, between the solid blocks of his tightly packed abdomen, and finally toward his muscular thighs. His breathing gave way to short pants as he leaned against a nearby rock. Suddenly, his thoughts shifted to images of Onya and their unexpected night together. Loving her had been easy, and if pressured, denying those feelings would be difficult. He realized this after Maal's poignant accusations after council. Though it was understood that what they felt was forbidden; they'd never discussed ways of hiding their feelings for one another should others begin to question, a gross oversight on both of their parts. In fact, given their limited time together, they'd barely had the opportunity to discuss anything at length.

Now, Maal was completely in the know and this, coupled with his anger with him over the war strategy, made Quince wonder exactly how long he would or could keep the burning secret to himself. Of course it was well within his right to bring the matter before the other members of the Cause immediately. Somehow though, he believed Maal would harbor the secret for as long as he possibly could, thinking the infatuation would pass. His co-General wasn't much for words; he more or less expected Quince to redeem himself in some form after realizing his mistake. These expectations were simply understood; actual dictation was unnecessary. Little did Maal know, Quince's feelings weren't fleeting. They were real and permanent. He shook his head in frustration as her image reappeared in his mind and wondered how long they could continue the charade. At this point, their only saving grace was the fact that Maal's case, should he decide to create one, would be easily dismissed. How can one prove two people are in love? True, they'd engaged in intercourse outside the confines of the Rites, but other than that there existed no concrete evidence.

Dripping with sweat, he headed back to the village for the final meeting before their journey to Ido City in the northwestern territories for the Fourth Rite. He gave the bright orange disk in the sky a final once over before turning toward the winding path. When he returned, the men had already begun to prepare for their voyage. The pace was slow but steady as they talked in small groups, sharpened their weaponry, sparred in pairs, or bundled clothing and other necessities in sacks. Avoiding all eyes, he wandered toward the hut he shared with his brothers, wishing it empty. For once, he just wanted to bask in some peace and quiet before the long trek to the north. Though shady glances and awkward hellos had become the norm; he'd never become accustomed to them. In their world, Respect reigned supreme. Hell, he had a right mind to bring all of them up on charges of defying the pillars of tradition.

Exhausted and in no mood for confrontation, he sauntered through the entrance of the hut, only to unintentionally interrupt one of Dez's spirited tall tales. The roaring laughter ceased abruptly upon his arrival giving way to an uncomfortable silence.

"Don't mind me. Please continue on with the story," Quince shot coldly to the two men in the room. Being ignored was getting the best of him.

Immediately, the two brothers busied themselves with other things and took great pains to avoid all contact, not matter how minute, with Quince. Unexpectedly, after a still ten minutes, Dez's pain stricken voice pierced the quiet room.

"I was almost killed," he began slowly. "I almost died! Why wouldn't you want to avenge that man?"

Quince was taken aback by the question. Having barely uttered a word to anyone in ten whole days, he struggled with a response as the words clogged his throat. "Is that what you really think Dez? I never left your side from the time that arrow pierced your thigh to the moment we placed you on the operating table in the Sphinx laboratory," he answered, his voice quavering with hurt.

Dez looked away quickly, unable to meet his brother's eyes. "I know you never left my side. I would have never left *your* side. We're blood. This is what we're supposed to do, just like we're supposed to seek revenge on those who wrong us swiftly *and* mercilessly."

Quince strode to a sack in the corner and retrieved his quiver and arrows. Not wanting to indulge in the conversation, he began to pay needless attention to the thick strings of his bow. "Well, you all have gotten what you wanted anyway," he shrugged dismissively. "We had a council and I was outvoted. We're going ahead with the mission. We're going to attack."

Quince gave them his back to consider and attended to his pile of belongings. Uncomfortable still, he grabbed hold of his things and turned toward the entrance. He didn't feel like answering any questions. It was obvious that everyone seemed to be overlooking the big picture. His suggestions were not the quick fix of a bloody battle, but a possible solution for the whole. Being misunderstood and misinterpreted were new to the quick-witted warrior admired for his headiness.

"It's more than that Quince. I understand that you want to see how more bloodshed can be avoided, but we should have done that from the very beginning instead of preparing that offering and asking the Ancestors for permission to wage war," blurted Dez as he blocked the entryway. "Not only that, *we were attacked first!* The rules of engagement were followed to a tee."

For the first time in a long time, Quince looked in his brother's face. The fiery pupils mixed with a hint of disappointment crumbled his strong facade. In all of his twenty-one years, Dez had never allowed anyone the luxury of seeing him this vulnerable. Quince didn't know what to feel. They stood there staring at one another in silence before El joined them.

El met Quince's eyes now and spoke. "We'd do it for you, man. You're our brother! The Youth are all we've got. Our mother has blindly joined the Faith. Our father is an Ancestor. We're all we've got," he whispered again. Dez's lip began to tremble as he fought back angry tears.

Quince lowered his chin to his chest before relinquishing a reply. "You know I'd do anything for you Dez... and you El! It's not a matter of killing arbitrarily. It's about saving our people. If we lose this war... forget *Taste*, there may not be anymore *us* to be sure it continues!" Quince retorted. "Have you thought about that? Have you actually sat down to think there may not be anymore Ido as we've known it?"

"That's why we have to fight!" boomed a voice standing just outside. "We're way past talking and investigating and putting together exploratory committees," barked Maal flatly. "Now either you're with us or against us. There is no lukewarm in this matter. I don't want any warrior fighting halfheartedly in battle. We need to know you have our backs."

Quince whirled around to face the powerful figure in the doorway that had once been his confidante. *How could they possibly be questioning his allegiance to them?* Hadn't he proven over the years that he didn't waver when it came to what was important? Didn't they know who he was? Suddenly, he realized the men in front of him looked like strangers, though two of them were his spitting image. He kept his cool in spite of their unwarranted accusations, but realized how much he didn't deserve this. "I never thought I'd have to explain myself to the three men who know me nearly as well as themselves," he drew his shoulders back proudly before continuing. "I am dedicated to the Cause. For you to question this, solely because I suggested an alternative to your plan is hurtful to say the least. I deal in black and white, not gray. I feel I have proven this as your co-General." He then turned toward El and looked him squarely in the eyes. "When are you set to begin the mission? As you all know I haven't been attending the meetings. I didn't feel welcome there."

Dez and El lowered their eyes while Maal stood tall, jaw locked in defiance. El then held his brother's gaze before responding. "I will leave just after the fourth Rite. The plan is to skirt the outer walls of Ido city near Triple Peak. We've received information suggesting Elder activity in these areas. Apparently, the Elder Army often trains there. The Painted Folk have located them from their houses in the trees."

Quince shook his head thoughtfully. "Have you told Sunni?"

El sighed heavily at the mention of his pleasure mate and soon to be preferred partner. "We were able to speak after council. She is aware that I will not be attending Taste, however, she will be expecting by the time the fourth Rite comes to a close. We just won't share the experience of Enlightenment together..." he trailed off.

Quince looked at his brother sympathetically and attempted to change the subject. "I am pleased to hear that we have close allies. The Painted Folk are a force to be reckoned with. We should consider ourselves most fortunate to have their allegiance."

"They have a stake in this too. The Rites are necessary to their survival as a people. The extinction of Taste brings about the extinction of The Painted Folk. The outcome of the war is crucial to the balance of the island," said Maal. "We will leave for Ido City within the hour."

"Good," Quince replied shortly.

***

They decided to take a northwesterly route to the underground city of the north. This way, they could bypass the dense foliage of Three Wood and cross the Shine River at its most shallow point in the west. After this, they'd continue on past the Rain Caves, the notorious Sinking Sands, and finally enter through the Northern Arc into Ido City. The march was long and tedious, but far different from their draining voyage into the Smoke Desert. Old wounds had long since healed and the journey passed quickly and without any unexpected incidents.

It was early evening on the sixth day after the journey began before Quince could comfortably stretch his long, muscular arms behind his head and concentrate on the light of the crackling fire next to him. The burning embers were now ascending into a beautiful mauve-colored sky. The tension between he and the members of the Cause had eased considerably since the confrontation in the hut, and for this he was particularly grateful.

The imposing east wall surrounding Ido City could be easily identified from where they'd decided to set up camp for the evening. Maal, El and a small group set off to check the surrounding perimeter for enemy presence while Dez expertly seasoned the fish and vegetables for their evening meal. As they settled in the picturesque grasses one-quarter mile west of the Rain Caves, Quince allowed his thoughts to drift to more pleasant subjects. A vivid image of Onya floated toward his mind as he lay back on his forearms comfortably, eyes fixed fondly on the full moon. A large part of him longed for the scent of her. He pondered both her thoughts and whereabouts as the succulent aroma of herbs and spices tip-toed beneath his nostrils, teasing his sense of smell. Quince filled his lungs with crisp evening air and hoped he'd been occupying her thoughts as well. Since their initial meeting, the only thing that had monopolized his brain waves more than the war had been Onya. Unknowingly, his lips gradually bent into a soft smile. Dez looked up from the crackling fire with a raised eyebrow and questioning stare.

"What's the smile for?" he asked, stifling a deep chuckle as he stoked the vegetables carefully.

"Just... looking forward to the next Rite," Quince remarked, sidestepping the question purposely.

Dez homed in on his brother's easygoing smile and pressed the envelope a bit more. "You know you never did fill me in on how things went down with Onya. You feel a connection with her, don't you?"

Quince sat up abruptly, drawing his knees to his chest. Gently, he summoned the ability to calm himself. There was no way he had been on to them. But what if he'd figured it all out? *What if he'd figured them out?* Dez was as strong-willed as Maal when it came to laying down the laws of the land in spite of his surface silliness. Just relax, Quince told himself before exhaling slowly. He doesn't have a clue. Keep your cool. "We're supposed to feel connected to our pleasure mates. Otherwise, the Rites would be futile," he said a bit more defensively than he would have liked.

Dez responded by raising one of his brows. "Just a question Quince, calm down."

Sensing the sudden discomfort in the air, Quince snagged the opportunity to divert his brother's attention back to himself. "So... how have things been? You have two pleasure mates now on account of Dion's death," he said as his voice dropped to an empathetic octave. "How is Eesha adjusting to the addition of Lore?"

Dez stroked his chin pensively. "Eesha is a beautiful woman and she's been wonderful. She's accepted Lore in every way during the Rites. I can honestly say that I enjoy them both. But I hope we are within our limits, Quince. We haven't located any scrolls telling us what we're supposed to do in this case."

"That's because we've never had a civil war before. Nothing would be in existence to dictate our next move." Quince straightened his posture and reached for a grilled skewer. His brothers were outstanding chefs, where he'd found it difficult to make even pre-prepared food edible. Carefully, he brought the succulent meal to his lips and bit in, savoring the flavor for a few seconds. "Damn," he whispered. Dez responded with a knowing grin. "Scrolls or no scrolls, Maal and I decided to proceed with common sense," he said, picking up where he'd left off. "Procreation is necessary. The women of Ido must give birth to a child. If the women who had the misfortune of losing their preferred partners don't join with another couple, how will they become pregnant? We also haven't received word from the Ancestors. They have been unresponsive to Maal's offerings."

Dez whistled in slow disbelief. "I never thought Born would have abandoned us, especially when we needed him most. He is the father of this island, our eldest male Ancestor. He claims to live and breathe Taste. This just doesn't make sense Quince."

"Don't look at it as abandonment Dez. Remember, the Ancestors rarely have human contact. Only extreme circumstances call for their intervention--"

"And an Ido civil war isn't extreme enough? We're killing each other out here Quince! This is self-inflicted genocide! Mother against daughter, father against son! You know this is a lot for me to admit. Good ole hand-to-hand combat is almost as good as intercourse as far as I'm concerned. But listen, we're literally killing ourselves. How did it come to this?"

Quince could barely muster a response as his shoulders dropped. "Not sure. It all happened so quickly." His brother's observations were right on target. They needed the advice of the Ancestors and he'd also become wary of their silence; but as their leader, he couldn't allow the others to see his concern. He and Maal would decide what was best for the group.

The two men sighed as the night sounds intensified. Dez concentrated on the crackling fire in front of them, while Quince pondered on the Ancestors. In just a matter of moments, the energy had changed. Usually they'd all look to Dez to produce a joke or some laughter if need be. Quickly, he thought of a welcome topic to lighten the mood.

"What do you think the last Rite will be like?" he asked, grabbing Dez's attention immediately.

"I don't know. The first few Rites were so amazing; I can't imagine anything topping it. The first time I'd ever seen the pyramids was when we left the Falls. They made me shudder just looking at them from a distance to be honest. No one is allowed to reveal what goes on inside anyway."

Quince nodded in agreement. "True. I just know I'm looking forward to whatever it is. Something that's been honored for centuries certainly can't be a let down." He sighed to himself and focused on a makeshift visual of the final Rite. There were two more installments of Taste to encounter before their journey into Elderhood. He could barely contain himself as his heart pounded in his chest.

A sudden rustling sound from the low brush startled the two men as quiet set in. They exchanged a knowing glance before instinctively securing their weapons. Quince put a firm handle on his bow and removed the leather shield strapped across his shoulder blades. With a calculated stare, he slid his wrist into the shield's leather cuff. The two men crouched low along with the others in their company and covered one another's backs in pairs. A familiar high-pitched whistle in the vicinity sounded as the gathered Youth dropped into ranks. The two brothers turned impetuously in the direction of the familiar signal. As the figure moved closer, Quince noticed his swollen and bleeding lip. He looked as if he'd been rolling around in the mud and his left arm was bleeding profusely. The staggering figure's familiar face crept into his line of vision. El was out of sorts and soaked to the bone.

"The caves...ambush...we're fighting...for our lives... over there," he wheezed in a throaty whisper while advancing toward them. Quince immediately looked eastward. From where they were gathered, he could make out the sudden flashes of lightening briefly illuminating the foreboding caves. On his left, Dez had already begun to tend to El, utilizing the piece of fabric sheathing his sword as a tourniquet for his brother's wound. He grimaced in pain as Dez applied the necessary pressure.

Quince's pupils twinkled with fury as he mentally digested their plight. How were they tracking their whereabouts? Was there a spy lurking in the camp? *There couldn't be!* Slowly, he gazed between his pain stricken brother and the rocks in the distance. The anger inside him boiled slowly as the rest of their company gathered around. All thoughts of peace and alternative solutions for the conflict escaped him as visions of an exposed Maal and several others embroiled in a fierce battle ran through his mind's eye. He gripped his bow in quiet rage and without taking the time to formulate a concrete plan of action, Quince made for the caves, his long legs in full stride within seconds.

Minutes later, the entire male Youth Cause found themselves skirting the jagged rocks jutting from the outside of the chamber. Quince positioned his body as flat as he was able and scaled the raggedy gray rock wall. He could hear the echoing of thunder as they moved quickly and cautiously toward the entrance of one of the subterranean clusters.

Liquid slid down his back while rainwater from the caves above soaked the rock's outer surfaces. The men formed a line behind him and crept along quietly. Quince poked his head around the entrance as thunder echoed throughout the vast space. Swiftly, he pulled his bow from beneath his arm and stole around the corner. One by one, the men stole inside the stormy cave. Quince strained to see through the steady sheets of precipitation as he grasped several arrows from the quiver strapped to his back. Poised for attack, the men took hold of their weapons and continued behind him.

"Remember the Zo," hissed Dez through clenched teeth. "They may be an even more formidable enemy than the Elders. Aim for the jugular if you encounter one, it's their most vulnerable area. They are blind but they can hear and smell everything." None of the members of the Cause had ever come into contact with the dangerous leopards and Quince prayed silently to himself that they'd be spared the opportunity.

The men moved swiftly through the swirling rains, parting the sullen dimness in half. Inside, a faint violet light peeked through the blackness. Quince found himself welcoming the frequent bolts of lightening as they provided sudden bursts of light to better guide their way. Ahead, there were loud groans and sounds of a struggle. Alert, the Youth continued on soundlessly, weapons drawn and ready to strike as they traveled deeper into the forlorn Rain Caves.

Just then, a sudden flash of light revealed a pair of Elders running toward them in mid-stride. Their silhouettes appeared almost surreal and the first instances of fighting began. Dez was the first to draw blood, applying deep gashes to the lower legs of his adversary. The Elder stumbled to the ground in surprise. Through the blinding buckets of water, blood spilled on the cave bottom, creating currents of burgundy and brown. Several more Elders appeared, outfitted in their signature white tunics. Quince took cover behind a thick stalagmite before releasing a barrage of arrows in their direction. He stood, chest heaving, with his back flush with the jagged rock. The slick mixture of gravel, sand, and stone beneath his heels covered his toes in a slippery, sharpened mush that made it difficult to move about with ease.

A flurry of arrows zipped through the air in deadly retaliation. Carefully, he slid downward into a crouching position and peeked around the side of a huge rock. The fray was in full swing now as he caught sight of his brother Dez and Youth member Clay in an intense sword fight with two Elders. Back to back, they maneuvered expertly in calculated circles. Broadswords and battle axes sliced through the air with inconceivable accuracy. When a bolt of lightening brightened the space again, Quince glimpsed yet another sword aiming for Clay. Without thinking, he reached inside his quiver. In a fluid motion, he released three arrows, wounding the unnoticed warrior from where he sat in the shadows.

A sudden crackle catapulted his thoughts toward his next move. A few feet from where he lay hiding, someone headed in his direction. He squinted to make out the profile before recognizing the long locs and brawny build. Maal was limping badly. Quince whistled shrilly from where he sat. Maal lifted his head, peering anxiously through the pounding rainwater for the source of the sound. Quince took a firm hold of his bow before running swiftly toward him.

"I gotcha," he said while gathering his weight under one arm. "How did they find us? You don't think there's a spy do you?"

"I don't know Quince, but there are a lot of them. This isn't a coincidence. We've been compromised somehow," he said bitterly. "We tried to hold them off. We tried!" he said, his voice noticeably strained.

"I know you did. El made it back to camp. He's safe. Almost the entire Cause is here." He made an about face back to his hiding place in the shadows. "Stay here." Quince could see the anger in Maal's eyes. He was a warrior who wanted desperately to fight and it was killing him to be unable to do so. Finally, Maal gave a defeated wave after grimacing in pain. Quince lowered his eyes to the deep and very visible gash in his left leg.

"There were about fifty or so of them. El and I took out ten. I'm not sure how we're doing right now, but given our numbers, I'd say there are probably at least twenty of them still roaming."

Quince nodded and turned to set out from behind the massive rock. Before leaving his co-General and friend, he turned back. "I'll be back for you. You know that."

Maal doubled over in pain again before nodding. "Go. They need you."

Quince turned obediently on his heels and headed around the corner. The soaking rain had slackened, though it still fell steady. He dipped around the stalagmites and stalactites with care, feeling like he was inside the mouth of a sharp-toothed beast rather than an actual cave. Suddenly, thunder shook the space as he spied the blade of a short spear hurling toward his exposed abdomen. It took him half a second to respond. The stiff leather shield met the shining silver with a thump as his attacker emerged from the shadows. Unable to unleash his arrows in time, he used the bow as a weapon, driving the tip and upper limb into the man's exposed forehead, drawing blood. The Elder crumpled instantly and fell to the ground. An onslaught of footsteps caught his attention as he turned. Urgently, a mixture of unharmed and injured Youth and Elders raced frantically toward the mouth of the Cave.

"The Zo... they're coming--- run---"

Immediately, Quince back peddled and fled with the others. Dodging the treacherous boulders in his path, he struggled to maintain his footing in the deepening mud-rock consistency of the cave floor. As he looked to his left and right, he noticed the Elders running alongside the Youth, desperate for an escape. Racing wildly, something clicked inside his mind. "Maal!" he shouted aloud. He was nearing the place he'd left him behind. Skidding off course, he burst between the two giant stalagmites. The space was empty. He looked around wildly for his friend. The only things in his periphery were the shouts of terror and white tunics in the lavender shadows.

"Quince, we've got to go," shouted a shrill voice he recognized as his brother Dez. "They're coming. They've already killed some people."

"Maal... I left him right here. Where's Maal?" Quince yelled, his voice cracking in terror.

Before he could think or reason, the unmistakable roar of a large cat echoed through the cavern. Unsure of what to do, he bolted toward the entrance, hoping against all odds that Maal had already exited in haste. As he ran, wind gusts and warm water funneled in blurred circles. His heart pounded inside his chest as the men ran for their lives. Out of the corner of his eye, he glimpsed a flash of electric blue. The sleek body of a cat bounded in his periphery. Its massive head beheld two large, unseeing eyes. Long, white whiskers framed a giant mouth bearing rows upon rows of bloody, jagged teeth. However, the most frightening part of the Zo's anatomy was the eight-inch claws protruding from its paws. Quince fought back the fear brewing within him as the possibility of death resonated in his spirit. In a flash of frightening thought, he envisioned himself lying in a growing pool of his own blood. Never before had death seemed such a certainty.

Meanwhile, the leopard leaped beside him, keeping pace, its eyes like white beams shining through the dimness. It let go of a ferocious growl and hurdled a sturdy boulder. Quince could see the entrance looming as he sprinted. He dove for it face first just as an otherworldly pain gripped him. Hot blood trickled down his shoulder, mixing with the rainwater and dirt kicked up from the muddy floor. The leopard's claws gouged a five-pronged gash running the length of his shoulder to lower back. Heartbeat racing and resisting the urge to vomit, he scooped fresh dirt into his fingernails before glancing back toward the caves. A pack of ten Zo stood snarling at the entrance, bearing their teeth in warning. They did not follow, however, and soon disappeared inside the lightning streaked darkness.

"Come on. I know you're hurt, but we've got to keep fighting," said Clay limping toward him. Quince nodded and looked around, ignoring the alternating jolts of dull and sharp pain maneuvering through his body. Sure enough, now that the animal threat was gone, the Elders and Youth were renewing the me lee in the open air. Pure adrenaline kicked in as he stood tall and ran to the defense of a Youth who'd been surrounded by two Elders. His pulse quickened frantically; it was Maal. Quince removed a short spear from the holster tied around his lower calf and hurled it forward, catching one of the enemies between the shoulder blades. He fell to his knees, dead. Unfortunately, Maal was still in trouble. Quince reached inside his quiver for fresh arrows just as the Elder standing over Maal raised his weapon, poised for a kill. He let the arrows fly just as the heavy weapon connected with Maal's right shoulder. The arrows penetrated the man's chest and he fell to the ground.

Quince dashed to Maal's side in time to notice the remaining white tunics retreating to the north. The brush was littered with bodies as he lifted Maal to his feet, steadying him. Groggily, he looked at Quince, his face distorted in pain.

"I think-- we got--- the best of them," he said attempting to stumble forward. Quince nodded, his own pain showing itself as Maal inadvertently brushed a hand across his wounded back. They sidestepped the wounded Elder as a slight breeze blew, rustling the short grasses beneath their feet.

Maal stopped abruptly and looked at the white headdress, now blown slightly aside by the wind. He squinted and looked down. Focusing on the fallen Elder, Quince immediately felt his heart drop to his knees. The man lying on the ground was Chi, Maal's father.

Wounded, but not dead, he glowered at his son before speaking. "Dame trained you well," he said, his voice strained. "But you will die if you do not accept the faith," he continued through a bloody cough. "My soul has been cleansed. I can die knowing I will be with The One. What can you say of your own death, my son? Where will you spend eternity?" And with that, his eyes fluttered once and he was gone.

Maal stood expressionless. He merely urged Quince forward and turned his gaze toward the body-ridden trail ahead. "Let's get back," he murmured. "Thank you. I should have never doubted your loyalty… or your friendship." Quince nodded as they headed slowly back to camp.

19

MOTHER NATURE'S GAME

The swirling breeze caused the dark-colored garment to flap wildly against her protruding stomach as she stole through the night. Panting slightly, Vye vaguely took notice of the gleam from the bluish moon hovering above her as she ran. *I'm almost there. The others have to know what's going on.* As it was, the women had begun to question their bizarre symptoms. In spite of their age, things seemed odd. Eyeno was the first to take notice and comment on the strangeness of it all, but it had taken Vye some time to accept the inevitable and whom the discovery could possibly implicate. It was clear that after her marriage to Dame, she'd become clouded, distant, and defensive toward matters regarding both her husband and the faith. That is, until now.

She struggled to forgive herself for not trusting her initial instincts. Vividly she recalled the pangs of doubt and the constant uneasiness careening through her spirit. Angrily, she thought back to the night of Dame's proposal. Then, more than ever, she'd become weary of The Guide. There seemed to be subliminal messages between his phrases that night along with the outright sexist sermon he'd delivered. The idea of living in a patriarchal society had been disturbing and unnatural to her. *She should have trusted her gut then!*

They'd agreed to meet on the Tremor Hills beneath a cluster of trees in the wee hours of the morning. This way, they'd be afforded a bit of privacy. Even with the men away at battle they couldn't take any chances. Vye gathered her ankle length skirt above her knees as she made her way up the steep hillside. How was she going to present herself, *reinvent herself?* It was important that she be seen as one of them again. She was just as angry, shocked, and afraid as they were! Had Dame known and given his stamp of approval? Was this possible? Would he knowingly sanction the end of his own race? Not wanting to believe her husband would willingly agree to the extinction of his own people, she pushed the thoughts from her mind and persevered through the night. She shook her head wearily before locating a group of seated women in her sights. The area was packed, and from the looks of things, she was the last to arrive.

Vye entered the conclave expecting an awkward reception. Though once looked upon as a strong and worthy leader among the female Elders, her position had unexpectedly diminished after the marriage. Because of her husband's status of near royalty, Vye was now considered an outsider and suspected of being a possible informant. Therefore, the sidelong glances and intense glares followed her always. This didn't bother her, until they began to come from her best friend. It was because of Eyeno's sudden withdrawal that she'd chosen to come up for air and see the elephant standing in the room. She valued both her opinions and her friendship.

Vye took a seat in the shadows just as Eyeno stepped forward. "I have called this meeting in order to share some disturbing news." The women shifted as the wind whipped through the night. There was a chill in the air. Vye noted it as an unfavorable sign and clutched her robe tighter.

"Many of us have taken note that ours are not normal pregnancies." The group of women nodded affirmatively, rubbing their round stomachs or sighing heavily. "All of us have delivered before and *never* have we experienced the symptoms we've reported in recent weeks," she trailed off for a moment choosing her words carefully. "The Ido birth Mer who take human form after the seventh year. The Ido pregnancy lasts only five weeks," she paused. "All of us are now nearing our third month of the pregnancy cycle. There is one among us who has developed a theory to explain this. I have heard it and am convinced of its validity... Vye."

There was a small stir as Eyeno yielded the center of the conclave. Vye hoisted herself from her comfortable seated position, stepped forward, and gazed around the group slowly before speaking. The grim expressions were noticeable in the bluish glow. Suddenly, the accusatory and distrusting glances bothered her. These were women with whom she had once shared secrets and ambitions and gossip. These were her former friends. She swallowed hard before beginning her speech.

"I have reason to believe that the herbs we were given to reverse our ability to conceive were tainted." A quiet hush fell over the gathering as the wind whistled through the trees. The women were waiting for the other shoe to fall. They'd already suspected foul play and this declaration was nothing new. "It allowed us to conceive, yes, but I don't believe we have conceived Ido children. There is a strong likelihood that the babies we birth may not be Mer."

She shut her eyes, waiting for an onslaught of questions. A trembling voice broke the silence.

"How did you come to this conclusion?" asked a thin woman in a frightened tone.

Vye looked down at the ground a moment before answering. "It is the only logical conclusion we can come to. Our lengthened pregnancy, the kicking in our wombs... we are carrying human children. The Ido race as we know it will be permanently changed." she said gravely.

"How can we trust you, Vye?" shot a short woman in anger. "What do you have to gain by revealing this?"

"Did your husband have anything to do with this? Was he aware?" echoed another.

Vye felt her cheeks growing hot with anger and embarrassment. This was foreign territory for her. She was accustomed to being well liked and respected by the other women in the clan. Now the tables had turned. She couldn't blame their accusations; however, it wasn't as if they were unwarranted. Just after her own marriage ceremony, a rash of others followed, leaving no singles in the Elder Clan in a month's time. In that period, Vye had become someone else. She'd taken the responsibility of being an example as one half of the island's first legitimate couple very seriously, too seriously according to some. She'd also been the one who'd presented the women with the herbs, assuring them of their safety and effectiveness. She had been the first to ingest the herbs, so they certainly couldn't accuse her of intentionally poisoning them. However, they had a right to their suspicions. She'd failed them and the reality of that struck her like a one ton brick.

"I don't fault you all for questioning me," she began slowly. "I realize that because I allowed myself to be alienated, you no longer feel I'm one of you. I can almost assure you though, that my husband had and has no knowledge of the tainted herbs. He has wholeheartedly accepted and dedicated himself to the faith, yes, but he would not sacrifice the Ido race," she said trying to mask her own reservations about the statement she'd made.

"Have you confronted Dame with your theory? Is he aware of what's going on?" Eyeno asked.

"No. As you know, the men have gone off to battle and I did not formulate the theory until well after they'd gone. I also wanted to talk to you all before I took any other steps. I will only reveal this to Dame if it is agreed upon by the entire group."

There was a surprised stir among the gathering before Eyeno spoke. "Vye, I forgive your transgressions, but I am a bit confused with your course of action. If you truly believe, as you stated that Dame had absolutely nothing to do with this, why not tell him? He of all people would have the best chance of getting to the bottom of this. Are you certain of your husband's lack of involvement? Can you guarantee that he had no knowledge of this?" Eyeno asked firmly.

Vye lowered her head. There was no way she could answer her friend's direct question falsely. She fought back an onslaught of tears as she stood before them. "I cannot," she said humbly. "I can only hope against all hope that he had no knowledge," she replied, gathering herself and attempting to stand tall.

"What about the Sphinx? They were the suppliers of the tainted Osu herbs. Perhaps we should be asking what they had to gain by providing us with a tainted product." Silently, she thanked her friend for veering the discussion in another direction.

"What do they have to gain?" someone inquired from the shadows.

Eyeno furrowed her brow in deep thought. "What *don't* they have to gain? Let's be mindful of the Sphinx and their actions throughout our long history. Our males had to come to their aid during The Insect War, our *only* recorded war before the current one. We must keep in mind that that conflict began because of their greed, obsession, and insecurities. They also make it no secret that they could care less about the affairs of others. They have always been a self-absorbed and self-serving bunch. Aside from their medical geniuses, they are a relatively weak race, genetically. They'd have much to gain if the Ido were completely wiped out," she said very matter-of-factly. "And as peaceful as the Stripes and Painted Folk are, they'd rule the entire island."

"So what are we going to do about this? Do we have our children? Do we abort them? Even though my child may live the life of a human, I still think he or she deserves to live!" said a woman directly across from Eyeno.

"I agree," said the woman next to her. "Aborting my child is not an option."

"I'm not so sure," blurted out another. "We were impregnated under false pretenses. We were convinced to birth more children as a means of spreading the faith and creating the first legitimate families on the island. I'm unsure if I want to bring a child into a world under these circumstances," she said angrily. "How do we go about raising a human child? The entire parenting process will be both different and difficult. These children will never be Mer. How will we manage?"

Eyeno raised her hand to signal silence. The chatter was doing nothing to resolve their current plight. She spoke hesitantly with a mild twinkle in her eye. "I think we've overlooked someone," she said slowly.

"The Guide," Vye whispered in unison with Eyeno.

"How can we be certain this wasn't his plan throughout? He could have converted us, formed an alliance with the Sphinx, and finally devised a foolproof plan to be sure our traditions died... literally. Abolishing Taste could have only been a mere smokescreen, a diversion, the tip of an even larger iceberg," added Eyeno simply.

There was a chilled silence under the trees. It was clear that no one wanted to believe they'd all been fools in accepting the words of a foreigner in exchange for their rich and sustaining culture.

"If this is the case... then what do you suggest we do?" asked one of the women.

"There is only one logical answer. We need word from our Ancestors. I say we go to Born," said a tall woman leaning against one of the trees.

"Born is even more powerful than Dame! He would resent our groveling back to Taste and tradition after declaring war and blindly accepting The One Faith. He'd destroy us!" exclaimed another.

"What about Fateem? If we prepare the proper offering, we may be able to return to his good graces through her. She is the mediator and his feminine equal. Fateem would know we had no choice in this matter. Dame is our leader! How could we possibly have gone against him?"

"There is no winning over Born. He is an all powerful Ancestor."

"But he must be told of the trickery! He must know about the plot to extinguish the Ido as we know it!"

"Look, we need to find out the facts. There is still too much speculation for us to take action. Some of us are speaking of terminating our pregnancies, returning to the old traditions, and abandoning the vows we took. We need cold, hard facts before any decisions are made!" shouted a voice nearest to Vye.

"I agree," Eyeno replied, her stern tone quieting the discussion. "But how do we get those facts? Who will be responsible for—"

Vye didn't give her a chance to finish. She knew she needed to redeem herself. "I will," she said without hesitation. "I am the only one here who has the access, an alibi, and the wherewithal. I can try and retrieve the total truth from Dame and The Guide. I will begin the moment the men return from battle. This must be done as soon as possible."

A sudden surge of pride flowed throughout her extremities. She knew she was doing the right thing. It was almost as if she felt the hearts around her softening. They were more than aware of what she was volunteering to take on. Dame was formidable to say the least. No one dared to question or defy him, secretly or in the open.

"Thank you Vye," Eyeno said, touching her arm affectionately. "Since you are volunteering yourself, we must provide you with support. You will have all the resources you need to make your cover airtight. Concealing our motives will be difficult. We've got to prepare. We will meet again in one week. By then, you should have collected some information that will aid us in deciding where to go from here."

Just then, the pounding of footsteps could be heard nearby startling the conclave. Within seconds, a small woman bounded into the middle of the gathering.

"It looks as if the Elders have lost the battle...there are many dead," she said between heaves. Then she turned to Eyeno and spoke in a small voice just above a whisper. "Chi," she stammered, " is among those who have perished."

Part Two
Vengeance Rising

1

THE LEGEND OF IDO CITY

In the beginning of time, Ido was a part of a much larger land mass. As most legends go, the land was abundant in beauty and overrun with natural resources. The grasses were green with an unspeakable essence of life and the creatures lived in a perfected bliss unimaginable to anyone who'd experienced the strains of stress. Over time though, the Ido people became tempted by greed and inebriated with power. In short, they began to desire more though they clearly had more than enough. It was only a matter of time before they became disobedient to their sun god, Orun. As punishment, It bestowed famine and drought upon the land and for decades the people struggled to eat, drink, and survive.

As the drought wore on, some developed a skin resistance to Orun's abrasive rays while others took to shape-shifting as a means of survival. The island's original species soon evolved into three. Decades passed and finally, the Orun sent constant rains to the land for an entire century, purging the island of the arid air, struggle, and strife. After the rains dried up, Orun swore to never again wash the land with rain. Instead, It provided the people with nourishing underwater springs and a river of fresh water named the Shine after Its own magnificent rays.

The few who'd survived both the drought and the Hundred Year Rains remembered the wrath of their god and for another century lived in peace, grateful for their god's mercy. One of the newly evolved species, The Painted Folk, drifted to the moisture rich jungles at the island's center while the shape-shifting Sphinx migrated toward the Oasis Falls in the east. The new generation of Ido chose to settle on the southernmost tip of the island, but soon grew restless and bored with their daily lives. They were an antsy folk who longed to explore beyond the island's limits. Because of the sea surrounding the island, they begged for fins. *How wonderful it would be to swim among the creatures of the sea and experience life in the deep, they wondered?* Orun's closest friend, Afe, a Djinn spirit incarnated as the Wind, warned Orun against spoiling the undeserving Ido. Afe was certain it would create conflict and breed ungratefulness in the very near future. Unable to be swayed, the benevolent Orun ignored the warnings of Afe and granted the people gills and fins. As a result, their friendship became strained and Afe grew to resent its former friend's loose leash on the Ido people.

For one hundred years, they lived as Mermaids and Mermen, exploring the vast oceans created from the rains given to them as relief from drought one century ago. After some time, they became restless again and longed to return to land. Exploring the sea alone had become too confining.

One day, a mischievous and charismatic Ido Youth called Born challenged Orun to a race from one side of the world to the other. Intrigued by the challenge and certain of Its own victory, Orun accepted. The Youth insisted that a wager be set to raise the stakes. If Orun won the race, the Ido would live human lives and would only be permitted to walk on land. However, if the Youth was victorious, the Ido would be granted a duel existence as both Mer and human. Seeing this as a fair exchange, Orun agreed.

There was much chatter and speculation among the Ido until finally, the day of the race arrived. The Ido along with The Painted Folk and Sphinx came out to witness the legendary race. They gathered near the beach just before sunrise. Orun hung lazily in the east at daybreak; certain that there would be no way the Youth could defeat It in a race around the world in less than twenty-four hours. Soon, the signal was given, and the race began.

At its onset, Orun continued a steady pace. Overconfident in Its chances, It saw no need to come up with a strategy for victory. The Youth, who had had the foresight to plan ahead, began to put his strategy in place. Bobbing freely in the waters, he looked up to the skies. Meanwhile, Orun became intrigued and nestled between a few clouds to watch. Suddenly, the clouds began to gather and darken, blocking It's view. Then, Afe began to respond. It ripped and rolled and coiled before funneling downward toward earth. A giant whirlpool was now forming in the sea. The wind cleanly parted the waters and began to drill effortlessly until it reached the earth's core.

Though the Youth failed to win the race, Orun awarded the Ido a dual existence due to Born's tremendous bravery. Unfortunately though, Orun required that the Ido forfeit their right to act upon their love for one another, lest they be punished and judged accordingly. Appalled with the decision, The Painted Folk challenged Orun to a similar race. They too failed, and because they'd dared to challenge; they were forced to give up their rights to copulate and reproduce. For years, The Painted Folk suffered until Orun recognized Its harshness and granted them immortality and infinite wisdom in exchange.

The Sphinx, who hadn't taken a genuine interest in the outcome of either challenge, began to plot and plan for their own rule with the Ido and Painted Folk weakened severely by their punishments. Finally, they presented Orun with a final challenge. Because of their scientific genius, the Sphinx were nearly victorious. Though outraged by their defiance, Orun decided to reward their near victory with a more lenient punishment. The Sphinx' immune systems were weakened and they were required to aid those in need at all times. Their innate talent for healing became their burden to bear. Thus a natural order was created and defying it came with a price.

The mark where the legendary race began was commemorated Ido City, the official site of the fourth Rite of Taste. To this day, the massive funnel remains, spiraling into the ocean where the Ancestors of the Mer City of Erruk continue to reside. By right, Born was their leader, an architect of history, and upon his death, the most powerful Ancestor of all time.

2

THE FOURTH RITE

"It is forbidden to love you. We cannot continue on this way."

The words spilled from Onya's lips before she'd had the chance to think them over. She stopped herself abruptly; surprised at what she'd said and instantly regretted it. Quince's only response was a pained expression. He turned away, his jaw set tightly as his visage contorted with a mixture of embarrassment and rejection. Onya continued to stroke the firm biceps in spite of his effort to withdraw from her touch.

She had been overjoyed to set her eyes on him from the moment the men descended down the massive spiral stairs and into the city, but the conversation could no longer be avoided. They needed to clear the air. As it was, strict laws prohibited them from seeing one another as regularly as they would have liked. Their once a month visits were reserved for carrying out the specifics of the Rites, not speaking earnestly and openly about their blatant disrespect and disregard for tradition.

Onya sighed heavily before speaking again, choosing the correct words when addressing the topic was essential. She maneuvered her body so that she stood directly in front of him and placed a hand on his shoulder. "How can we possibly lead the Youth if we are unable to abide by the laws we seek to defend? Hasn't this crossed your mind Quince? We don't just enjoy each other physically, we are in *love!*"

"You cannot speak those words out loud!" He said with an imminent hiss, placing an index finger on her lips. He looked throughout the cavern nervously, trying to discern if they'd been overheard. "Do you really think I haven't thought of this? Of course it is a struggle to live as a hypocrite," he said in a strained whisper. "I am co-General of the male Youth! It is painful to know that I have been guilty of treason since I first laid my eyes on you! If you do not feel the same, deny it now!"

"I can't deny the way my heart smiles with every thought of you," she replied hotly.

Quince met her piercing glare and refused to back down. "Well then, what do you suggest?" Onya stood silent, searching for a viable reply. "Should we share our plight with the others and risk being outcasts or should we continue lurking in the shadows?" Again, he did not wait for a response and rambled on. "Though the shadows are not ideal; there we can at least satisfy our love. There are several preferred partners who remained close friends after Taste. Born and Fateem are two I can think of off the top of my head. My mother and father were very close until his death during the Insect--"

Onya couldn't allow him to skirt the subject any longer. *"They were not in love Quince!* What we feel for one another is different and wonderful and *forbidden!"* She exclaimed through clenched teeth. Frustrated, she wandered through the entranceway of the small cove they'd been standing in and onto its sturdy, wrap around landing. She couldn't remember a time when she'd felt more lost and alone. Here she was experiencing one of the most thrilling emotions she'd ever encountered, yet she'd had no one to tell. She tilted her head upward. Above them a full, pearl moon was shining, its light glinting off the obsidian deposits sprinkled abundantly throughout the exposed earth of the underground city. Sadly, she looked over the railing and down into the black abyss. She longed to share her feelings with her close friends, yet she knew she would be unable to voice the severity of her indiscretions to them or anyone aside from Quince. When she wasn't worried about Quince's safety, she was tiptoeing around questions about him. The other bulk of time was spent eating, sleeping, and being angry with her father.

Echoes of moaning sobs met her ears as more women learned of their dead would-be mates. The stresses of the war were multiplying. The balance was again shifting. Tonight, of all nights should be reserved for two people. Again, more women would be venturing to other couples and requesting a shared partnership. Eesha had been one of those women. She no longer had Dez to herself. When she'd asked her friend about the arrangement, she merely shrugged it off. Onya tried her best to disguise the shock when she'd revealed that she'd be willing to do anything for the Cause. Eesha had merely described the situation as being bigger than her and saw accepting Lore as a part of her duty. Jealousy and envy hadn't seemed to remotely cross her mind. But then again, she wasn't in love. As her heartbeat quickened, Onya could only pray that they would not be approached. She could not bear to share him with anyone. He was hers and hers alone.

While continuing to stare over the railing, she noted the panoramic view of the underground city. Ido city was situated within the ridges of a giant funnel. From where she stood, the countless caves lining the inside of the funnel and the circular staircase of sturdy granite stairs descended down its middle for as far as the eye could see. Burgundy earth shimmered with the glint of shining black minerals and the rock stairs continued to spiral downward into a dark abyss with alternating landings connecting the ridges. From the echoing moans and sighs, she deduced that many of the others had already begun the Fourth Rite. Silhouettes danced behind the shadows and the air felt thick and heavy. For now though, she dismissed it. They were at a dangerous crossroads that could no longer be treated casually.

Tradition required the female Youth to select the cave whose scent called to them just before the four-day long Preferred Partner Rite. A specific Ancestor assigned to protect the union of a particular couple had already blessed each nook. It was highly important for the female Youth to prepare offerings, fast, and pray so that the correct lair would be revealed to them once they'd entered the city. Each female would then select a theme that they felt would best fit their preferred partner. She turned back to the nook she'd designed to please him. Its entrance had been strewn with curtains of iridescent beads while the cave's interior was decorated in shades of green and brown. Emerald mats covered the earthen floor along with large sage pillows to ensure comfort. Peppermint incense further accentuated the crispness of the inlet and giant shells were added to simulate an oasis or soothing beach. The added flowers and leaves provided a more natural effect. It hadn't been difficult to choose a theme after their intimate conversation on the beach. The lair would be used not only as a sanctuary to provide pleasure, but to propose partnerhood to the male of their choosing. Partnerhood linked the two parties indefinitely as they would now work toward conceiving a child together. One hundred percent of the time, Merchildren were conceived during the fourth Rite. For this reason, next to Taste, it was considered the most monumental Rite of them all.

"I don't want to argue Onya. It is unfair to both of us to spend time doing that." She could feel the warmth of his body behind her. The hairs on her neck stood up as he rubbed his unshaven chin against her cheek.

She grabbed his hand and whirled around to face him. "I know, but when will we be able to discuss--"

His kiss put a cease to her questioning. "Later," he said in a calm voice just above a whisper. "It will all work itself out. We have other things to tend to in the meantime." Carefully, he wrapped his hands around her waist and stood back to inspect her. "I'm not sure who is more talented... Eesha or the Ancestors who ensured your conception."

Onya blushed and stood back proudly to show off her beautifully handcrafted outfit, a sheer body stocking that began above her breasts and cut off just above the knee. The stocking was covered with large, bronze leaves and sparkling stones twinkling in the moonlight. Quince allowed his gaze to travel from her silver painted toes to the single stone studding her forehead. Her long locs were pulled up in a ponytail that fell in soft ringlets to her shoulders; she was breathtaking.

"Don't you have something to ask me?" He said slyly as his chew stick rolled over his tongue.

Onya smiled coyly and bowed. "After you," she said gracefully as he sauntered toward the cozy nook. She watched the shining muscles in his back hungrily as he walked through the entrance and took a seat on one of the large pillows. She reached for a basket of finger foods nestled in the corner and located a striking, red cherry. Meeting his eyes, she removed the stem carefully and placed the succulent fruit on his tongue. He bit in slowly, savoring the sweetness and appreciating the pampering. The contents of the basket slowly disappeared as they enjoyed the exotic breads, cheeses, nuts, and fruits inside.

"Come." Her words were soft and simple as she beckoned him toward a corner. There, slightly concealed against the earthen wall sat a large, freestanding bronze tub filled with water. Delicate flower petals floated on the water's surface and rising wisps of steam hovered above its rim. Quince stared longingly at the heated liquid while the aroma from the bath salts settled inside his flaring nostrils. Onya studied his reaction and carefully untied the drawstring in his pants. Without a sound, they dropped to the floor in a silken puddle around his ankles. He tested the steaming water with a finger before stepping inside. She watched his eyes flutter, then close before he settled in.

"Why don't you join me?" he asked when she knelt beside him. He reached over and twirled a few of her locs between his long, thick fingers. "There's certainly room for two."

Onya smiled. "This night is about you. I bathed earlier. Just enjoy the bath salts, they should relax you." Their eyes locked again as she stood and pulled the body stocking below her breasts slowly. He reached upward and massaged her stiff nipples between the pads of his thumb and index fingers. She sighed heavily, returned to her knees next to the tub and proceeded to run her fingers through his thick, dark waves. "Will you be my preferred partner?" she asked lazily while outlining his mustache and goatee with her pinky.

Quince drew his hands behind his head and shut his eyes. "Of course, my love." He drew her face closer before planting a deep kiss on her lips.

She stood back to study him again before reaching for a small bowl at her heals. She submerged an index finger into the contents of hot, golden honey and placed it inside his mouth. He sucked on her finger, twirling his tongue around her nail and down the knuckle without relinquishing an intense stare. Finally, he released her finger. They kissed again, his saliva carrying a certain sweetness. Upon the release of the kiss, she allowed her lips to venture to his ear lobes and down the nape of his neck. Next, she turned to his Adam's apple. With her free hands, she located his shoulders and moved behind him so that she was in a position to deliver a massage. Carefully, she ran her palms across his pectoral muscles before returning to his shoulder blades and upper back. He sighed softly as she continued to lick and nudge the back of his neck and shoulders.

The warm water threatened to slosh over the side of the tub as he stood up, no longer willing or able to control his urge to join with her. Her ravenous gaze blanketed his dripping body while he reached for the soft, fluffy towel nearby. After drying off hurriedly, he pulled her warm body toward him. Wrapped in one another's arms, they immediately began to explore. She grazed the muscles of his abdomen, chest, and back before finally resting her hands on his firm buttocks. He lifted her from the ground and carried her toward the green pillows piled high in the corner. She tightened her embrace and applied hot kisses to his chin, the heat rippled through him, searing his groin, steeping his seed.

She didn't want him to take charge now; that had been the norm since the initial Rite. Now she desired to unleash the boiling want stalling between her thighs. She would make love to him on her terms and hers alone, relinquishing control to no one tonight, not even her preferred partner. As he laid her down and commenced to part her thighs, she leaned forward, preventing him from doing so. He gave her a questioning glance as she reached around him for the container of honey. She beckoned for him to stand as she located his hard member now dangling in front of her. She smiled deviously before dipping his thick shaft in the bowl. He exhaled slowly as she pulled it from the sticky contents. His hardening shaft now glistened with a gleam of sugary gold. She gazed at it hungrily before maneuvering him so that he stood directly above her. Onya leaned back on her elbows, tilted her head back and took him in her mouth. His strong legs trembled as he enjoyed her lips engulfing him wholly.

The flame from the bronze torchlight flickered in the still passion. Echoed moans now catapulted throughout the underground city. Onya shut her eyes and inhaled. The air was pungent with the smells of peppermint and sex. The scent was so strong, she felt she could taste its flavor and add its potency to a delicious meal. She took him in further now until he could be felt in the back of her throat. Carefully, she loosened her suction as his eyes fluttered. His limbs were buckling now, threatening to collapse from the enjoyment of it all. She licked the underside of his shaft clean before inserting his thickness between her lips again. All the honey gone, she licked her lips slowly as they locked eyes.

Wanting desperately to be enveloped by her essence, he quickly fell to his knees and sampled the fleshy folds at the apex of her thighs. She sighed and squirmed as his warm breath danced over her tender skin. From there he flattened his tongue over her hardened nipples and licked downward until he reached her navel. Quince hovered there for a moment, lifting himself on his forearms. She relaxed beneath him as they nudged one another delicately. Her thighs began to tingle as she spread them open from beneath his weight. Without a hand to guide it, his maleness meandered toward her soft opening and thrust inside. Brewing beneath her pelvis was a climactic wave. She lay there, panting helplessly while he initiated the intimate dance of female and male. The once airy ambiance was now heavy and torrid. It covered them like a blanket of molasses as they tumbled over one another in a lust-filled power struggle she was all too determined to win.

She climbed playfully on top of him now, allowed him to enter her, and contracted her walls without warning. He drew his breath in surprise before letting go of a tiny smile and a wink that reassured her of his approval. They commenced a slow winding motion, their hearts beating like a unified bass line beneath a fast paced tune. In Onya's mind, she was a headstrong eighth note pounding away the harmony of their love and he a stern metronome, keeping both time and measure. Together they were the sounds of love washing over the cave walls, bellowing out emotion and wonder and inevitability. Because their mouths were forbidden to speak the words, their bodies took up the slack. Grinding out need; undulating underneath completion, gripping tightly the handles of loyalty and respect and comprehension. His powerful thrusts interrupted her brief spasms as she shook while straddling. She grabbed hold of his taut forearms as he pounded upward and in. The steady force was like an exponentially charged vibration. There was a rippling crest followed by an expected violent shudder as he held her upright, watching her glistening breasts rise and fall. The medium sized buttons stood out boldly as he reached for them, twirling them under his tongue, nibbling just a bit. Not wanting to relinquish her power, she rolled her hips forward and slid further down his member, just before he squinted and burst waterfalls inside. They laughed at their labored breathing now, chuckling at how worked up they were after not seeing one another in weeks. She draped her body over his and focused on the lone flame in the corner. After some time, he reached for her face and traced her jaw-line with his index finger.

"Tired?" he huffed softly in her ear. Onya lifted her head just enough to capture his gaze.

"Never."

3

AN ASSUMED IDENTITY

"I can honestly say that if it weren't for your brother... I'd be dead. He saved my life."

It was in the early parts of evening as the sun sunk quickly in the sky. Maal and El walked briskly against a howling wind on the outskirts of Ido City. Their loose fitting clothing pressed tightly against their muscular bodies as if it were running away from the swirling winds. On occasion, they would walk in reverse to avoid the dust kicking up in their eyes from the dry brush underfoot. The wind was like an invisible hand, preventing progress across the brittle and dry terrain.

The pain of losing his father had long since subsided, though he was barely affected in the first place. Maal had come to this conclusion just after his father's eyes glazed over and the wind had blown his headdress aside for those last, difficult words. The fact of the matter was, he only felt something because he thought he should. To put it plainly, Dame had always been more of a father figure than Chi could ever have been. Dame had been the best and brightest, the strongest and most powerful. Even at a young age, Maal had seen his own father as nothing more than a bumbling underling, forever shy of the mark of greatness.

Though their parents were minimally active in their lives, the Ido Youth never ceased to look forward to their visits. Parents were only meant for conception. They were the vehicles through which the race continued, nothing more and nothing less. The memories of seeing his mother were fresh in his mind as he smiled to himself. He was her spitting image; from the smooth, midnight skin to the tall and intimidating build. Meanwhile, his private Bgongo lessons with Dame stood out as well. It was the first time it had actually occurred to him how torn he was. On the one hand, Maal was as cutthroat and rigid as the mentor who'd trained him and taken a special interest in his budding abilities. On the other, he was not looking forward to the inevitable: killing or being killed by the one man he once respected so much.

"Quince is loyal. I have never really doubted that part of his character. He is my brother, always the levelheaded one. Always the one conversing inside his own head."

The two men paused uncomfortably as they trekked along through the dry dirt and low grasses. It seemed neither wanted to be the first to discredit their good friend and leader. Maal found himself in un-chartered territory. Never before had he had the feeling of walking on eggshells with one of the triplets. He stole a glance at El from out of the corner of his eye as he focused on the Southern Arc in the distance in front of them. The sunlight reflected the shining archway in a brilliant beam. Temporarily blinded, the two men used their forearms to shield their eyes and continued.

"He may have faltered when it comes to judgment lately. What do you think?" Maal asked, forthright.

Maal sensed El cringe at the thought of having to answer honestly. On the one hand, he seemed just as concerned with his brother's actions. However, he still did not seem comfortable with engaging in any gossip about him. Blood had always been thicker than water as far as the triplets were concerned. This was well known among the members of the Cause. As the only Ido on the island with any knowledge of a sibling bond, Maal was certain there were some walls he would never be able to break down. He sighed to himself, half wanting to rescind his inquiry. However, their identicalness was a key to a victory for the Youth Cause. Why not exploit it, use it to their advantage?

El sighed, noticeably torn. Maal responded with a reassuring hand on his shoulder. "In what ways has my brother's judgment wavered as of late? Explain."

Maal stopped short and turned to face his friend. He exhaled heavily and walked a short distance ahead of El in the direction of a nearby cluster of Baobab trees jutting awkwardly from the brush. Once they'd settled in the crevices of its hollow trunk, Maal grabbed his canteen, took a swig and spoke.

"I cannot discuss the views which led to our first-ever council months ago. Tradition forbids me to do so." El nodded in agreement before locating his own flask and throwing back its contents. Maal couldn't help but feel his discomfort.

"I saw something that I have chosen not to speak on until now." He paused and focused his stare upon the large brown bird that had settled on the branch just above his head. "I witnessed your brother in acts that have violated Taste," he blurted out finally.

El responded with a confused glance. Rolling the bottle lightly between his palms, he fixated his gaze on the nearby arc. "What exactly was this so-called event that you witnessed? What are the specifics?" he asked cautiously, almost as if he was'nt too eager to know.

Maal shifted in his seat uncomfortably before beginning again. "Of course you recall the day we received the message from General Dame." El nodded slowly. "The ultimatum was delivered to him by Onya, daughter of Dame. I was sharpening my sword beach side when I saw them having sex outside of the confines of the Rites of Taste."

El's eyes grew as large as saucers and began a series of flustered questions. "Are you certain it was Quince? How dark was it? Why didn't you bring this to the attention of the Cause during council?" El sputtered in shock.

The co-General of the Youth Cause lowered his head between his knees and breathed hard. "The last thing the Youth need is to be in discord. Our people are already engaged in a civil war with our Elders! The members of the Cause can ill afford to be fighting one another during such a delicate time. Quince is an asset to us. He is one of our best warriors otherwise he would not have been voted co-General. He is well respected by us all."

El leaned back on the trunk of the tree thoughtfully. Daylight had been almost fully extinguished now as the clouds skidded around the rim of the descending sun. The two men sat in silence as the birds chirped and pecked in the brush. Weasels and foxes also scampered about, scurrying toward their burrows for shelter. The winds swirled in a calming howl before El rose to his feet.

"But why?" He questioned in a low whisper. "Quince is a fierce proponent of Taste! Why would he risk tradition? Why would he---"

"I have reason to believe that Onya and Quince are...in love." Maal said matter-of-factly.

El spun around to face him, his eyes wide with disbelief. In spite of his surprise though, he spoke evenly. "What? But we are forbidden to love. It is part of the ancient pact. To declare love for another carries with it a sentence of sure exile, perhaps even death. Does *he* know that you suspect this? Have you openly accused him of the crime?"

Maal nodded affirmatively. "Yes. I confronted him about it just after the votes were tallied and read during council. I told him exactly what I've just shared with you."

"And his answer?"

He shrugged. "I was so angry and disappointed; I did not allow him to explain himself. After all, what is there to explain? How can anyone rationally defy tradition?"

"My brother is my blood and my reflection; however, if he is guilty of what you say; then both he and General Onya are no better than the Elders at this point." El's response was short, his voice strained as the words left his lips. "I do believe that you made the right decision in not informing the entire group. The Ido people are already suffering enough. Now is not the time for dissension. But in the meantime, what do you plan on doing?"

Maal rocked slowly backward on the trunk, his speech slow and deliberate. "I believe we should bring both Quince and Onya before Council after Taste. Until then, the two of us will remain the only male Youth in the know. However, we should hope that they are careful with their feelings for one another. The Elders could easily exploit this situation. Dame is as mentally cunning as he is physically strong."

El nodded swiftly. "Do you think one of us should inform him that discreetness should be key? If they are truly in love as you say, the Fourth Rite may have led to a strengthening of their connection. Surely he has agreed to become her preferred partner."

"With you setting out for the mission, the person to confront him would have to be me. I am undecided on the matter though. It is delicate and must be handled accordingly. The one thing we can count on however is that your brother is bright. I have no doubt that he is probably struggling with this just as much as we are. I'm just having difficulty forgiving him for such carelessness, especially now. I just sense somehow that the less he knows we know the better off we are." His voice trailed off while he mulled the situation over in his mind. They were skating on thin ice. Things were becoming more complex by the day. "Are you ready to begin the mission?"

"Yes," El replied with assurance.

"You will not be able to experience the final Rite," Maal said hesitantly. "We appreciate this great sacrifice."

El looked away momentarily. "If I don't go ahead with the mission, there may not be any more Rites to experience ever again, for generations. I will sacrifice the final Rite in exchange for peace of mind and an end to the war. My preferred partner understands and thinks me courageous because of it."

Maal gazed at him in admiration before clasping him on the shoulder. "Go now. Everyone is aware of the plan. We will wait for word from you through the Elder messenger."

The two men exchanged a strong embrace before they parted. Darkness gathered in the open space surrounding them. Maal watched from a distance as El veered south and skirted the outer wall of Ido City. He shut his eyes when he'd finally disappeared from view and said a silent prayer to the Ancestors, hoping desperately that he'd made the right decision as co-General of the Cause and that El would remain safe.

4

ATOP TRIPLE PEAK

Creator of all things great and small, aid me in this time of need. I am in need of Your blessings, Your healing, and Your guidance. Your faithful and humble servant, The Guide, has led me to You. In a short time, he has shown me the error of my ways as a lustful, power-drunk, soulless creature; unfit to kneel before You now. I am unworthy of Your blessings, but knowing Your mercy and Your love and Your generosity; I come to ask You to heal my wounds.

I am suffering with despair after the loss of what quickly became my only male friend and confidante. Though I know he is in Your bosom now, resting safely; I am saddened by his loss to our movement. Chi was a skilled and honest man who took stock in the things I said without so much as a sidelong glance or a question. Without him, I feel weakened, unsupported. With this recent loss, I wonder if my men will be able to remain comfortable with my leadership. I wonder if our women will remain dedicated to You and the Faith. I am frightened that they may begin to doubt. Their respect and support means much to me as I see this through. I no longer desire to rule by the means of terror or intimidation. I want my men to follow my lead because they are confidant in Dame, the General, not Dame the bully.

I am at a crossroads during what should be a happy time. I have pleased You with a marriage to a beautiful and wonderful woman. Together, we have conceived a child whose birth has revealed itself already as different than any other. You know the source within all things and I wholeheartedly trust in You and Your infinite wisdom. I beg of You to continue to guide me. I am already aware that the heathen Youth should be defeated and shown the way toward light. I need the strength to carry out my duty to be sure the One Faith is spread throughout the island to all creatures. In the name of the Faith, the One, and The Guide.

Dame rose from his kneeling position with a heavy heart. He glanced toward the bed where Vye lay sleeping on her side, her light gown rustling slightly as the night wind entered their hut. Her large stomach bulged from beneath the soft sheets as he climbed in beside her. He could hear her soft exhales as he positioned himself comfortably. Right now he needed something to hold, something tangible and loving. He slid closer to her, basking in the warmth of her body heat.

It was the first time in his life he'd felt any real confusion. Any ideas of how to respond to their most recent loss were magnified and blurred inside his mind any time he tried to ponder them. He needed clarity and his only option was to wait for the kind of clairvoyance he knew his God would provide. He turned toward the circular window aglow with soft blue moonlight and shut his eyes to wounded pride, worry, pain, and hurt. The throbbing sensation at his temples became a strobe light of color behind his eyelids. He had much to do in the coming weeks, but the day would soon come when the Youth would fall. He was sure of it.

***

From atop the summit of Triple Peak, the island seemed small enough to clutch, grab, and possess without difficulty. *If only things were that simple.* Dame balled his hands into fists as his bulging muscles twitched slightly in dismay. He'd approached the war hoping it would be both swift and just. However, he'd greatly underestimated the Youth. He'd been both blind and hasty. He had trained them, did he really expect them to roll over and die?

The air atop the island's highest pinnacle was thin and wispy. He watched intently as the sun settled high in the sky as if it were to be praised and worshiped. It then occurred to him that the Sun had indeed been his Ancestors' first god. He shook his head shamefully at the thought of their shortcomings, their blind and willing perversion. It was no wonder they'd been kept in darkness for such a long time. The Ido people should have gathered that the Sun had been fallible when Born nearly defeated it during their legendary race against time.

Dame began to massage his temples while practicing a circular breathing technique to relieve his lightheadedness. Turning eastward, he centered his gaze on the three pyramids of Taste. An omnipresent rainbow sliced through the central pyramid's peak and disappeared inside the gargantuan marble structure. Umbrella-shaped treetops from the jungles of Three Wood formed a protective barrier on the pyramid's south side as did the sparkling Shine River knifing through the relic like a winding, silver tongue finding its home in the mouth of the Oasis Falls. From where he stood, the rock orifice in the west resembled an enormous spigot spilling tons of water onto a bed of quiet sand. When he shifted his body northward, he quickly located the dizzying funnel of the underground city dredged inside the sparkling red earth. Northwest of Ido City, clusters of intersecting green vines crept upward into domes and pyramids from the shores of the Mer Sea. He inhaled deeply again. Vince City was where it had all begun. Turning south now, he honed in on the smooth golden stairs of The Amber Cliffs, the cluster of huts that made up the Youth Village of Nu as well as the old Butterfly Dragon stronghold, Glo City.

It was rare that he had the time to admire his surroundings, even if it was under such bleak circumstances. He smiled to himself and pondered over the sheer beauty of the island. All of this had been created by the One, the Father of the Faith. Only a God with an awesome power and insight such as His could be responsible for such a creation.

"General, the forces have assembled. They are awaiting your direction."

Dame snapped to attention and turned toward his new lieutenant general. Trapped inside his reverie, he hadn't heard the approaching footsteps. He fought back a sense of saddened resentment as he guided a hostile stare in the direction of the trembling man kneeling before him. Second-guessing his sentiments, he softened a bit. They'd lost more than just first lieutenant Chi during the Battle at Rain Cave. In fact, he'd lost several of his first rate warriors to either the agile combat of the enemy or the Zo predators inside the caves. It wasn't this man's fault that he'd ascended the ranks so quickly. It was simply the luck of the draw. He glanced down again at the unassertive man in his wake. How could he possibly aid in leading the Elder Clan to victory? The anger returned almost as quickly as it had dissipated.

"I am a man of the Faith as you are," Dame conceded with forced gentility. "Fear not me, a man who has no power to judge. Instead, I implore you to fear the One who holds dominion over your soul." The man appeared to straighten and stand taller before cautiously meeting the General's eyes. He could have sworn he saw a flicker of defiance in the black pupils.

"Forgive me General. I am now serving as your right hand in Chi's stead. I am nervous and eager to take on the duties our fallen brethren bestowed upon the Clan."

Dame gave the man a sweeping gaze again before applying a hand on his shoulder. "Lieutenant Ka, I will never ask more of you than you can give." He paused before rolling his neck and shoulders backward. A strong crack of bone gave way to a satisfied sigh. Dame shut his eyes tightly and exhaled sharply before continuing. "Therefore, I will never expect you to be Chi. He was an honorable man, deserving of the utmost respect. I trust though, that you will indeed pick up where he left off. Possessing the heart and soul of a warrior is all I ask of you."

The man nodded meekly and stared at the sheer girth of Dame's arm span. Although the faith had certainly softened him, Ka recalled the days of old. During the Insect Wars, Dame had been a merciless warrior. Had he not been, they would have more than likely been defeated. The General cleared his throat loudly to recapture the lieutenant's wandering attention. Ka responded with a nervous jump and reconnected his gaze with Dame's flaming pupils.

"Gather them here at the summit. I have prepared an address designed to invigorate and inspire our men. There is room enough inside the cove for a meeting," he said gesturing toward the open space behind him.

Ka nodded and reached for the hollow horn slung over his shoulder and blew it twice. Dame pulled his shoulders back and retreated into the wide inlet at the pinnacle of Triple Peak. Bowing his head once again in silent prayer, he prepared to greet his men with an inspired tone of hope and fearlessness. Confusion set in once again as he began to second-guess his decision of a hard day of training in the island's cruel mountainous terrain. The very last thing he needed was the attempt of a coup.

One by one the men filed through the entrance, seating themselves in the empty spaces on the cave floor. Their bodies were visibly scarred from the last battle and their foreheads were streaked with sweat. Dame searched each one of their faces. Behind their eyes he located hopelessness, despondency, anger, and doubt. The energy level was lower than he'd expected *and* feared. He took a seat in front of them in a large wooden chair and formed a canopy with his fingers as he contemplated his words carefully.

"There are no words that can subside loss. It is my belief that the only solvent for emotional pain is time." He watched as their eyes lowered and heads slowly nodded in agreement. "However, we must press on toward the mark of the high calling. Defeating the Ido Youth remains the principle goal and attaining it is still very possible. Many in our ranks have been lost. As a result, several of you have been catapulted to positions you have little experience in." Sighing heavily, he searched the faces before him for some kind of spark. He needed someone to look like they still believed in their cause!

"We will work together to learn our new jobs. We cannot lie down." The cave remained silent save for a few exhausted sighs. Dame leaned back in his chair. Everyone was restless and distraught. "We should attack again after the final Rite of Taste. Their energies will be depleted and we will have the upper hand. A victory then would be almost certain."

A large scuffle just outside the entrance of the inlet caused the men to turn their attention away from Dame's speech. He rose from his seat and peered over the heads of the others and into the sunlight. In stumbled three Elders. Confined by rope and struggling within its entanglements stood a lean, handsome figure covered in gravel and dirt, his arms and legs sporting fresh scrapes and dark red bruises. The three men led the figure through the parting sea of seated Elders until they met Dame whose dismal frown instantly spread into a satisfied grin. He motioned for the men to unhand the prisoner who then fell to the floor with a thump, face down in the dirt. Dame knelt next to him, forced the man to meet his eyes, chuckled softly, and tilted his chin upward.

"Who are you?" Dame hissed.

The figure stubbornly refused to reply. Instead, he continued his incessant heavy breathing while lying face down in the dirt. Dame tightened the ropes binding his wrists and turned him on his back. From above, he looked down at the furrowed brow and angry scowl. The jaw line and bronze skin rang eerily familiar. He studied the prisoner's features closely before throwing his head back with a hearty chuckle. The man was Vye's son; there could be no denying it. Immediately, he looked out at the eager faces crowded around the captured man and ceased his maddening cackle in time to spit out an inspired hoot.

"Men, our luck has finally changed. We have here with us one of the high ranking members of the Youth Cause!" Instantly, the space erupted in an array of shouts and audible prayers. "Where was he found? Was he alone?" Dame asked with an excited growl.

One of the three warriors stepped forward proudly before answering in a confident tone. "We heard a noise on the mountainside just before the horn was blown. We'd recently completed our sparring practice, and though exhausted, we thought it would be wise to investigate." Dame noted how the Elder had emphasized the word exhaustion. Perhaps he had overexerted them. For that he was sorry, but this new discovery took precedence over their complaints of unfair treatment.

Unable to contain his enthusiasm, another of the captors stepped forward, interrupting. "He wasn't difficult to catch General; it seemed he was being pursued by another larger animal and had run into hiding."

Dame circled the man, refusing to break the icy stare boring into the prisoner's eyes. "Did you mean to be caught? State your name at once! Is this some kind of trick? Answer me now boy!"

The questions and commands were thrown in the prisoner's direction like rapid fire. El waited for the space to become silent before he spat on the ground next to him and spoke. "I am Quince, co-General of the Youth Cause. I have come in peace and offer our surrender," he lied.

To this, Dame released a sarcastic cackle. "What do you take me for, a fool?" he said under his breath while pacing the floor and glaring at the prisoner as if he were nothing more than a foul stench in the air. "The Youth beat us soundly during the last battle. They have no reason to surrender to the Elders. How dare you insult the intelligence of--"

"Though we won the battle, we still lost several lives and wish for no more blood to be shed. We are still one. We are Ido and the Elders are our mothers and fathers!" El replied convincingly.

After this, the Elders seemed to soften a little. El smiled inwardly, noting their naiveté. However, he was resigned to keep his visage as stoic as possible. He refused to blow his cover at a time like this. The Cause was counting on him.

"We will dedicate our lives to your faith at once," he added.

Dame kicked the man swiftly in the ribs as El doubled over in surprise. The unexpected blow sent a bellowing groan echoing throughout the cave. He wheezed and squinted in pain.

"What did you say your name was Youth?" Dame said forcefully, still pacing around the man in tight circles.

El drew his knees to his abdomen defensively before responding. "I am Quince, co-General of the Youth--"

It was Dame's turn to interrupt now as he signaled for the man to be lifted from the ground. "You are one of three. You have two other identical siblings. How do I know you are indeed who you say you are?"

The prisoner's face remained stony. Refusing to relinquish the upper hand, he spat the blood from his bleeding lip on the floor and yielded no reply.

"Very well then, we shall take you to my wife! She can and *will* distinguish!"

El's eyes grew wide, momentarily shocked by Dame's declaration. Sensing his confusion, the General leaned close to his ear and whispered lightly.

"Ah yes, you aren't aware," he said with a sinister grin. "Quince, Dez, El... whomever you are, it doesn't matter. I am now committed to your mother. We are the first sanctioned Ido couple. I am her husband."

5

THE LEGITIMATE SON

At daybreak, a cacophony of shrieks covered the sullen beach like a smothering tent. Blood red clouds congregated near the rising sun before giving way to a massive sheet of gold streaked gray. The brooding sky was an omen of what the day would bring. Warm air peppered with the putrid smells of blood, pain, and sweat lingered like an unwanted visitor determined to wear out its welcome. Vye tilted her head skyward and squinted against the thin beams of light breaking through the clouds above. At the onset of the birth pains, no one quite knew what to expect. They'd all conceived around the same time; of this much they were aware. So, they took to their own instincts and at the sound of the first labor pain, gathered on the banks of the Mer Sea just as they'd done during the births of their firstborn children.

Nearly twenty-two years ago, she'd delivered three sons from her womb, something completely unheard of on the island and she recalled it as if it were yesterday. Quince came first, followed by Dez. El had decided to take his time; hours passed before he entered the realm of the living. He'd always been quite a bit more patient than the other two. Vye fondly attributed this to his birth and it turned out to be one of his best characteristics.

Her thoughts returned to the present as another angry spasm funneled below her navel and descended through her right thigh. She bit down hard on the mint stick she'd been given to relieve her anguish; but the creatures they would be delivering were human and beyond any Ido's common knowledge. During their first births, they'd been assisted by the female Ancestors, who acting as midwives, guided them through the birthing process with ease. But, having defied them by accepting The One Faith, the women didn't feel comfortable seeking their aid. Though their new beliefs had been visibly shaken due to recent events, they'd decided not to seek out Born or Fateem. They would see this thing through on their own.

Just then, a splintering pain crept up her lower back. Weary with distress, Vye resisted the irresistible urge to bare down and lowered her hands into the waist high water. Carefully, she massaged her protruding stomach with one hand and dug her nails into the thick, wet sand with the other. She felt round and awkward, like she'd swallowed a large, pulsing melon that breathed, kicked, and pushed on her insides at will. Its position had become tricky as a small kick pounded beneath her ribcage.

Teeth clenched, she turned to gaze eastward. The Elder women were side by side, each in different stages of their deliveries. To her immediate right, Eyeno let out a bellowing wail as tears began streaming down her cheeks. Vye found her hand in the calm, morning tide and rubbed it reassuringly. Soon they'd all linked arms, forming a long human chain as the tide ebbed and flowed soothingly.

She realized suddenly, that many of these women were not only wailing from physical pain, but from emotional distresses as well. Many had been lost in the recent battle and again, Vye found herself to be extremely fortunate; her husband would be returning home to her soon. No matter how much she'd begun to doubt his judgment, she loved him. He couldn't have knowingly been responsible for this! Dame was a shrewd man, but he was also fair. She stole another glance at Eyeno from out of the corner of her eye, her cheeks glossy with fresh tears. Helplessly, she continued to stroke her hand as she stood doubled over in agony.

As she neared delivery, short pains commenced at longer intervals; but she continued her circular breathing technique. Vye hadn't recalled this type of pain since her own transformation from Mermaid to human decades ago and the similarities were apparent. Consciously, she wiped the sweat from her brow before grabbing hold of Eyeno's hand again. Her body temperature had risen and the feeling of being ripped in half also returned, yet she now felt the ripping inside her pelvic area, not between her limbs. She shut her eyes and willed herself to concentrate on the top-spinning colors winding beneath her lids. Just then, a sudden shadow and a sizable splash in the distance caused her to open them. She bit down on the root stick hard, snapping it in two. The potent herbs of ginger, thyme, and mint flooded her palate as tears welled in the corners of her eyes. Doubling over abruptly, she hollered, feeling suddenly faint and unable to hold her own weight. Her eyelids fluttered as she struggled to win the war between the orbs of twisting hurt and her body's natural instinct to shut down. The splash returned, closer now. She could feel the comfort of arms cradling her shoulders and pulling her farther out to sea. The subdued sounds of a song floated on a new breeze. Quickly, her eyes flung open.

A cloud of bushy hair blew slightly in the wind like a solid mass of coiling earth, too stubborn to bend against its will and a pair of soft brown eyes accentuated by delicate wrinkles gathered at the corners met her own. It was Fateem. Quickly, she placed the palm of her hand over Vye's forehead causing the pain to slacken considerably. Vye let out an extended breath and gazed eastward again. The female Ancestors had come to them. An Ancestor stood before each woman, aiding her in the birthing process. Some were chanting, others were praying, many were laying hands on the pain stricken women much like the remedy Fateem had just used. She turned back to the old woman and said a silent, thankful prayer. Instantly, her abdomen warmed and released. Fateem laid a palm on Vye's pulsing stomach at the exact moment her vaginal canal began to expand and contract without effort.

"Push... the Merchild is ready to enter our world," said Fateem with a gentle smile.

The surrounding calm was eradicated almost as quickly as it had come. The Ancestors believed the women would be delivering Mer children. Vye's eyes grew wide with fear as Fateem continued to stroke her belly. Suddenly ashamed, she began pushing the woman away, not wanting her to see the human child that would soon be exiting her womb. Fateem looked up questioningly.

"You...you don't understand. The herbs we took were tainted. These won't be Mer children. Please forgive us--" Vye babbled profusely as her concentration broke. A series of sharp pains returned, this time ricocheting throughout her entire lower body. She struggled to contain the urge to gag and dry heaved.

Alarmed and confused, Fateem mumbled an incantation under her breath and placed her index fingers on Vye's temples. An instant numbness consumed her as her sense of reality blurred into an abyss of swirling, circular lines. Weightless now, she felt herself falling through endless sheets of time and space. For the first time in what seemed like a long time, she felt safe, calm, and virtually trauma free. She breathed a pleasant scent through her nose and allowed herself to relax. There was a call in the distance, to which she was reluctant to answer. The voices became gradually louder though as she lounged in the soft space void of suffering and confusion. *We need you Vye. We need you to come back to us. We need you.* Unable to ignore the desperate pleas any longer, she reluctantly crossed the blurred threshold in front of her, catapulting back into the conscious realm. The sound of a powerful suction filled her ears as she returned to the present, her head spinning in psychedelic circles. The nerve endings in her limbs panged with electric energy while she struggled to regain consciousness. Infantile wails permeated her senses, instinctively she felt drawn to them. The pupils in her eyes dilated as two blurred forms slowly moved into focus. She was lying on the beach, granules of sand stuck uncomfortably in her back and forearms. Her lower torso and legs were still immersed in the water. She shifted slightly and stirred.

After blinking back the tears resulting from the noontime sun, she identified the floating forms bobbing in front of her. Both Born and Fateem were staring down at her, their expressions grim. Vye shook off the grogginess and attempted to sit up higher.

"Where's my child?" she asked softly before fully opening her eyes.

Fateem sighed and motioned toward the cloth wrapped bundle in her arms. "A boy," Fateem said with a gentle murmur. "It is a boy."

Sure enough, the male child had toes, two feet, and a dangling pair of pudgy brown legs. Immediately, Vye reached for his sleeping form, gently kissed the soft forehead and pulled him toward her breast where he latched on aggressively.

"Why didn't you come to us? Why didn't you tell us what had happened?" Fateem inquired after the tender moment had passed.

"We weren't sure," Vye said while gasping for air. "We knew you would be angry with us for accepting The One Faith. We didn't think you'd come to our aid."

Born stroked his chin and tilted his head back. He wore an expression that was a cross between ferocious anger and a deepening sadness. Fateem lowered her chin and looked into the distance. She rested an arm lightly on Born's broad shoulder before turning once again to Vye. "Are you strong enough to speak? Are you able to tell us exactly what transpired since the sacred unions of the Elders?"

Vye nodded weakly, pulled her upper body into a seated position, and swallowed hard before beginning. "The Guide recommended that we bear children after taking our vows. Then, he claimed, we would be ordained as the first legitimate families of the island." She paused to gaze down the coastline. Next to her, dozens of women were either dozing restfully or nestling their newborn children to their breasts. Every child appeared human from where she sat. She sighed heavily before continuing on.

"Of course, nature wouldn't allow us to conceive on our own. We were all well past our child bearing years. So, Dame enlisted the help of the Sphinx healers. Ankh provided us all with an herb that could aid in our conception. The results were immediate, but after the normal five-week term, we were still growing larger--"

"What was the name of the herb?" interrupted Born.

"I believe it was the Osun herb and I soon suspected that they'd been tainted, though there was no way to be sure. Dame's assessment of the matter was that everything would be different since our part with the old ways, just as our dead would no longer become Ancestors. I wasn't convinced. Eyeno called a meeting of the Elder women after I'd come to her with my theory that we were carrying human children," her speech slowed deliberately as she chose her next words carefully. "I wonder if it was their wish to eradicate the Ido as we know it."

"They?" questioned Fateem suspiciously.

"Either The Guide or The Sphinx. The idea of our conceiving again was introduced by The Guide. The Sphinx provided the means. Somewhere in there things got muddled," Vye said quietly. She'd mulled it over in her mind a million times already and still no clarity was brought to the forefront.

Born's eyes flickered with contained rage. "The healers will pay. They have broken the ancient pact of the island. They must be driven away." He said in a violent hiss. "Rejoin us Vye. You must help the Youth defeat Dame and the Elder Clan. I remember you. You are a woman of great strength and pride. Once upon a time, you asked me to spare the lives of your sons," he trailed off purposely as she looked away. Born was right, she owed him, *and owed him she did indeed!* Luckily though, her decision had already been made.

"I have already dedicated myself to the Separatist movement. I've agreed to be the female Elders' spy. No one else has the direct access to the high level information I could gain. As wife of the Elder General, I have more access than anyone. Right now, I am angry with the Sphinx and possibly The Guide, but I cannot agree to totally defy my husband until I have more proof. I have developed a bond with him. I…love him," her voice shook with this last declaration and her gaze drifted out to sea, unable to meet the Ancestors' piercing eyes.

Both Born and Fateem exhaled slowly as Vye turned back to the stirring child. She stroked his hair carefully. "I would never have agreed to abort the child though. He is a part of me and his father, regardless of his total human form," she said quietly, reading their expressions.

"There is more," Born said stiffly. "More that may change your mind about your… husband." With this, she looked up, her interest piqued. "The Youth have developed a plan utilizing your sons' likenesses as an asset." Instantly, her body stiffened. She did not like the sound of what she was hearing at all. "El agreed to assume the identity of Quince in order to simulate surrender, which you know can only be offered by an elected General," Born continued. "Upon capture, he was to gather information and convince Dame that the Youth were prepared to accept The One Faith. Then, the Youth will be informed of El's location through an Elder Messenger. The entire Cause will then plan to meet Dame at that time and attack."

"Has he been captured?" Vye asked, her voice shaking. "Has El allowed himself to be captured yet?"

"Yes, yesterday evening. Dame is traveling here. He doesn't know if he should believe El's story *or* his identity. He is aware of your triplet sons and he expects you to identify him properly."

"Have they hurt him? Is he in one piece?"

Almost unwilling to answer her, Born sighed and relinquished the inevitable. "He has been beaten, but he will live. You must go along with the ruse. It is crucial that their plan works."

Vye shook her head in agreement and peered into the innocent face of her newborn son. He gurgled softly before latching onto her breast again. "I will do all that I can to be sure my sons are victorious. The old ways must be restored."

***

Born kept his gaze plastered on the grand, tangerine colored castle ahead of him while slicing through the coral reefs and sea life. Fateem could barely keep up as he propelled himself forward.

"Perhaps ignoring their offerings wasn't the correct decision after all?" she said with a hint of sarcasm.

Born barely acknowledged the comment, continued around one of the castle's large pillars. "It's now a matter of what we're going to do," he said upon coming to a complete stop near the elaborate entrance.

"We fight," Fateem said simply. "It's just that simple. The plan was... *is* to annihilate us. *Human children?*" she declared in disbelief. "I never would have thought the threat against us would be this great. I really didn't. Perhaps it was a bit of arrogance," she said with a disbelieving shrug. "We've never been challenged before and in such a unique set of circumstances-- " she crossed her arms over her chest and swam to Born's side, searching his face with concern. What she saw was alarming; the usual confidant smile was absent now as he slowly turned to face her, his jaw pulsing in anger.

"We fight and we win," he said simply before swimming away. Coral, plants, and other sea creatures whizzed by in a blur. He turned a sharp corner leading east. Afe was the only other entity that would have the answer to their impossible dilemma. The trick was finding it and coaxing it into discussion before it was too late.

6

PLEASURE'S EVE

Flaming embers from the fires rose, floated, and finally fell within the wide circle they'd formed a few feet from the pyramids of Taste. By nightfall, the male Youth had arranged several three-foot bonfires in a circular formation just under the massive trees of Three Wood. Tradition called for the everlasting flames to be stoked and prepared on Pleasure's Eve, the last formal ceremony before the fifth and final Rite of Taste. Shining in every color of the spectrum, the everlasting flames were created from a wood and clay combination gathered from the caves of Ido City. An obvious ode to the omnipresent rainbow shining through the central pyramid, the flames also symbolized the forces of nature joining together for an apex of pleasure. If they could somehow win the war, it would be the island's last set of Rituals for another two decades.

Maal stood anxiously among the trees, sweat from the roiling heat drenching his upper body. Gingerly, he wiped his brow and looked out among the waiting women. Once he located Lyn, his member took on a mind of its own and lengthened beneath his lightweight pants. Her brown skin took on a mahogany hue in the steamy haze. More than her petite frame and their uncanny sexual compatibility, Lyn possessed a feistiness that drove him completely crazy. She was a challenge in every facet of their relationship: in the bedroom, during casual conversation, and in serious chats about war, tradition, and the new faith that now threatened their people.

Maal smiled inwardly before leaning against the massive trunk of a nearby Raha tree. Their experience during the fourth Rite had been an infinitesimal high that neither one of them wanted to abandon. Now his preferred partner, he'd captured a piece of her that he'd always hold dear. Uncomfortably, he sorted through other memories, including his initial attraction to Onya. Not wanting to embarrass Lyn, he wondered if she'd ever sensed his halfhearted approach early on. He certainly hoped not, but the honest man dwelling within would not allow him to keep it from her. However, he knew that timing was everything and he truly enjoyed her companionship. The bottom line was, he'd have to play his cards right in order to keep her interest after the Rites. He envisioned their union to be much like that of Born and Fateem, the model couple of the island. They'd successfully governed the Mer realm side by side for centuries.

Again he drifted back to the first Rite on the Amber Cliffs. It had taken no time at all for him to warm up to her. He began to look forward to their intimacy. In spite of this, there were some things he could not deny; Onya was a beautiful woman with an intoxicating physique. Deep down though, he was happy the rules of fate had taken over. He was truly grateful that Quince had had the foresight to take advantage of his own hesitations. The woman he was meant to be with was seated ten feet away and waiting patiently for the main event to begin.

"We're on in a few. Are you ready?"

Maal turned to face Dez's wide grin and couldn't help but let out a small chuckle. Dez had always been the life of the party, no matter what imminent danger lie waiting in the shadows. Sometimes criticized for his flippancy, Maal could only find admiration for his longtime friend. Dez had always been a formidable warrior, one of the best they had and as long as he handled his business during battle, he had no problem whatsoever with his insatiable appetite for pleasure and fun.

"Yes, I'm ready," Maal answered with a cool smile.

Dez slapped him hard on the back and looked out at the seated women before them, salivating and rubbing his palms together eagerly. "Well then, it's up to you and Quince to start the show. You two are the co-Generals."

Immediately, Maal felt his energy level dip. For just those moments he'd managed to forget the tension between he and Quince. Things hadn't been the same since he'd confronted him regarding his love affair with Onya. The truth was they'd been walking on eggshells since. Though Quince had saved his life, he couldn't bring himself to forgive his carelessness. Behaving recklessly was not a trait of a good leader. Although the other members of the Cause had patched things up with their co-General, he still had an ax to grind. There was something else he'd seen in his eyes that day. For the first time in their lives, Maal had sensed the fear and hurt he'd been feeling. Though the others were unaware, by confronting his longtime friend, he had done exactly what he'd sought to avoid; the Cause was fractured. Even if it wasn't visible on the surface, they were fighting amongst themselves.

"I spoke to him this morning. I think he's finally coming to grips with the decision." Dez replied, reading his thoughts. "No one twisted El's arm. He was just as much of an architect of the plan as the rest of us. El is dedicated to Taste. That is what Quince should recognize. He has to get over everything else and move on. What's done is done. I just hope El can get to the bottom of how they've been tracking our every move, among other things."

Maal nodded, allowing Dez to believe that El's mission was the real source of his worries. "That is one of the major aims of the mission and I don't doubt his abilities. On the flip side though, The Cause can ill afford any dissension, no matter how small." Maal replied softly as Dez passed him a small container. Eyes fixed on a smiling Onya in the crowd; he rubbed his hands together and began to anoint his body with the fragrant oil.

Images of she and Quince on the beach, blatantly disregarding the sanctity of tradition resonated through him. He attempted to quell the rising anger as he stood staring into space, transfixed by the memory. His closest friend had disappointed him and he had no idea when he'd be able to openly forgive such reckless behavior. Quince's level-headedness was perhaps the singular reason he'd been voted in as co-General. Had this been revealed to him earlier, he'd have sworn the teller to be mad.

"Trust me, I didn't want to see El go either, but he volunteered himself. I wish he were here experiencing the—"

A throat-clearing cough interrupted Dez mid-sentence. The two men looked up at once, abandoning their conversation.

"There is no need to worry. I've managed to move past the particulars of Operation: Assumed Identity."

Dez yielded a cautious smile and leaned toward his bother to initiate a sincere hug. Quince obliged before holding out a hand to Maal who gripped it firmly before leaning into another quick embrace.

"If you love her, you are no better than the Elders," Maal fired just out of earshot.

Quince retracted at once, shot Maal a stony glare, and sauntered away from the group. Satisfied that he'd triggered the right response, Maal stole another glance in Lyn's direction and immediately pushed everything else from his mind. He turned abruptly and waved his hand in the direction of the waiting men. There was no need to leave them waiting any longer.

"Alright men, Pleasure's Eve has officially begun!"

***

The moment they'd emerged from the shadows of the Raha trees, the heat intensified tenfold. Torch in hand, Maal felt the perspiration accumulating above his upper lip and wiped it away with the back of his hand. Tension gathered in the back of his neck as he rolled his head around its socket methodically to try and relax. He swung a few of his long locs over his shoulder blade before inhaling deeply. His heart palpitated ferociously as the crowd of heaving chests and muscular bodies descended upon the sacred circle of bonfires. He and Quince led the way, their cries at full strength along with the deep timbre of the drums in the background. Maal's pulse quickened with excitement as he threw himself inside the moment. As one, they began a series of high kicks and powerful thrusts in time with the djembe. Flexing muscles and shimmering limbs dove inside a wild, pulsing rhythm. The uninhibited mood of the ceremony heightened his senses. The graininess of the dirt sticking to his heels as the pads of his feet pounded the ground mercilessly, the collective breath of his audience; he could feel it all leaking through his pores with a climactic rush. The salty taste of his own sweat led him to lick his lips as he caught a glimpse of Lyn in his periphery.

Subtle bolts of electricity shot through his being as their eyes locked. A sphere of pure masculine adrenaline, he sauntered forward, reached for her, placed an index finger lightly on her chin and tilted it upward. Lyn's nonverbal reply was a flippant smirk. It was as if she were daring him to cause her even the slightest bit of arousal. Maal allowed the corners of his mouth to slide into a seductive grin and backed away slowly in time with the hypnotic beat. Out of the corner of his eye, he observed Quince and Onya in a tender exchange. As reckless as they were, Maal still remained thankful that no one besides he, El, and the parties involved were aware of the chicanery. The Cause could not afford the disruption.

Suddenly, silence permeated the space, abruptly shattering the incumbent sounds like expansive panes of glass. The men stood frozen now, their chests heaving against the moisture filled air. Maal's nostrils flared as he prepared for the main event, running it over in his mind several times before Quince gave the signal for them to begin. A bellowing shout and the clamor of shakers andclavescaused them to turn on their heels with military precision. Quickly they partnered off and began a swift Bgongo kata. Maal wound his waist and lower body in smooth circles as he approached Quince methodically. His visage held a cold stare, vacant of the memories of a lifelong friendship. Eagerly, Maal pulled his long locs into a tight band

and returned the challenging glare before they began the complex Bgongo cadences within the fire lit circle.

Carefully, the two men squared off, the muscles in their exposed torsos twitching in heightened anticipation. A steady tempo permeated the air and Maal felt his shoulders and head bobbing in time with the hypnotic beat. In his peripheral vision, he thought he saw the women honing in on them, sensing some animosity. Alertly, he pasted a false smirk on his face that he hoped would camouflage the obvious. Aware of the many eyes scouring them, Quince followed suit. Maal nodded in his former friend's direction and launched his body into a flawless handstand. Quince mirrored him expertly. Moments passed as the two men walked the sacred circle's perimeter on their hands, their bodies arched in perfect ninety degree angles from the dirt floor. Maal's long locs dusted the ground as he held his stance before springing lithely into a backward roll. Quince responded with a flurry of one-handed cartwheels, which he spun in a tight circle around Maal who was now positioned in the center of the bonfires. Maal responded with three lightning quick no-handed back flips causing the crowd to hold their breath in awe as their male Generals went at it, Ido martial arts style.

The pulse of the djembes slowed a bit while Quince and Maal fell back into ground sweeps. Quince found the rhythm easily and swung the balls of his feet outward in slow circular motions. They alternated precision jumps and sweeps for a few moments until Quince broke into a few impressive airborne tumbles. Out of the corner of his eye, he caught sight of Onya beaming. Next to her sat Lyn keenly observing his every move. Maal let a high kick fly, which his co-General dodged easily and returned the favor. The precision of their bobbing and weaving movements was beautiful to watch, their slick bodies like twin knives slicing through the heavy, humid air. Bending backward, Maal dipped his muscled back and shoulders low to the ground, avoiding one of Quince's midrange kicks. Again the crowd breathed as one while watching the awesome martial arts display before them.

Inhaling deeply, Quince collected himself in preparation for the dramatic finale. Unexpectedly, the rhythm of the djembes quickened, ricocheting through the atmosphere with ease, as did the remaining male Youth standing at the circle's edge. Quince and Maal were joined once again by their male counterparts. Sweat laden bodies hurled through the air, tumbling, kicking, flipping, and flying about like an expertly choreographed circus act. One with the beat now, Maal felt the fast paced rhythm creep inside his spine as he bounced in time with its magnetic pulse. Dancing was as automatic as breathing to the Ido. It was the expressive beats of the djembe and conga that drove even their military style. The pulse of the drum was the heart of their cadence. The claves and shakers were rivers of life giving blood. Bgongo was an equally yoked marriage of discipline and rhythm that had been productive for nearly one thousand of years.

Maal tightened his hands into fists one last time as he shot through the air like a loose cannon. Landing on his feet with a soft thud, he knelt to the ground on one knee in unison with the other male Youth. When the beat slowed to a stop and the men turned to face their preferred partners, chests heaving, the female Youth responded with nods of admiration, appreciation and pride for what they'd witnessed. Pleasure's Eve had been a complete success.

Maal exhaled his breath slowly, relaxed, and pulled Lyn into his intense stare. Her approval of the show was no secret. He welcomed her pensive gaze as she surveyed the breadth of his shoulders and massive pectoral muscles. Adjusting his pants as he stood, he felt a swelling between his thighs that could hardly be ignored. It amazed him how quickly she caught on to exactly what turned him on. For some time he did not speak, and in the meantime, she feigned casual conversation with some of the other female Youth. She lured him with her apparent disinterest, which he knew she wouldn't be able to keep up for long. Soon, the preferred partners would drift into the pyramids where the final Rite of Taste would begin.

"Ready for the Final Rite?" he asked in a sensual growl. She leaned into him, causing her chin to gently graze his damp shoulder. He observed her breathing him in slowly, his pungent pheromones causing the dampness between her thighs to accumulate.

"Perhaps," she replied wryly. He bent over, grabbed her delicately by the wrists and ushered her to her feet now as the male and female Youth began to mix and mingle inside the circle.

Leaning in closer, he buried his face in her hair and inhaled. Her scent caused an intoxicating wave of desire to filter through his pores. In his eyes, she was sensual music and cataclysmic color. He felt his pulse quicken before glancing toward the pyramids. Midnight could not come quick enough.

"There is dissension between you and Quince. I sense it."

Completely off guard and tongue-tied, he swiveled her around to face him. The high canopy of trees above cast a shadow over her face. Almost at once, he became stoic, his gentle caress edgy and hard. They hadn't covered up their duress as well as he'd thought. Still, he granted her no reply. Something tugged at his heartstrings as he dropped his embrace and backed away slightly.

The Cause was comprised of both sexes and their roles were equal and free of sexist labels. The female Youth were just as battle savvy and strategically keen as their male counterparts. The only reason they had not fought was because the time hadn't presented itself. However, it was common knowledge that they were more than capable of doing so. His heart suddenly heavy, he exhaled forcefully while looking in her eyes. This was one of the women who dared defy tradition by entering their hut to inform them of information regarding The Guide. She, along with Onya and Eesha, had braved the perils of Three Wood in order to contact Gallah and The Painted Folk. She was, after all, one of the three Generals of the female Youth and their ranks were comparable in duty. His gut told him she'd had a right to know. In fact, *all* of the women had a right to know. Onya and Quince were treading through dangerous waters. They should be judged wholly and without hesitation. The Youth needed to deal with the transgressions of their leaders in order to unite them. Taste had been violated.

"Tell me. I have the right to know if we are in crisis."

Flustered, he sighed heavily and led her away from the proximity of the others and into a vacant space under a looming tree. The reflection of the still burning flames of the bonfires flickered in the pupils of her eyes as he sat next to her.

"Tradition has been breached... by one of our own." The words rushed from his mouth like water over the side of a sizable cliff. She reacted with a blank, silent stare.

"What...who?" she said, the marks of utter confusion and disbelief wrinkling her brow.

"This may be difficult to hear---"

"Just tell me," she said sternly. She held up her hand as a way of signaling that she did not want to be patronized.

"Onya and Quince."

"Eesha and I suspected this. We just didn't want to believe it was true." Her demeanor was sullen now. Shocked by her statement, he stared at her, hard. "There was something between them, even on the night after the Warming Ceremony. There was something there. After Lore joined Dez and Eesha, Onya asked if Eesha was jealous. Completely out of the ordinary! Why would she be? The Ido traditions are governed by respect!" The two of them sat quietly for a moment before Lyn continued, sorting out clues, piecing together the puzzle bit by bit while she spoke. "She barely talks about him. If one of us brings him up, her entire body language changes. *We knew it,*" she continued uneasily. Maal could tell she didn't want to be right about one of her closest friends and confidantes. Lines of hurt and disappointment etched across her face. "What are we going to do about it?"

Maal's response was decisive. "They have to be brought before council."

"How can you prove two people are in love? There is no hard evidence in existence to do that," she chimed in doubtfully.

"But there is a technicality," his breath was heavy again. Suddenly it felt as if he had the weight of the entire island to bear on his shoulders. He chose his words carefully before continuing. "I saw them having sex outside the confines of the Rites."

A look of shock settled itself inside her delicate features. "What? When?"

"The night she delivered the ultimatum," he responded. Lyn remained quiet, her eyes now searching the soft ground for an explanation. "That alone should be enough to come up with a guilty verdict."

"That would mean you'd have to testify... against your co-General and best friend." she replied, just above a whisper.

"You and Eesha would also have to reveal what you know. Friends and Generals aside, they have broken the ancient pact. I've been suffering with this for months now. He knows that I know. I confronted him with it. You and El are the only other Youth who are aware. I suggest we keep it that way until we decide what to do, *after* Taste."

Lyn nodded in agreement. Again, the two were quiet. "Both you and Quince were drawn to her. You wanted her didn't you?"

A piercing gaze met him as he stared, not knowing what to say. He knew he'd have to reveal some things to her, but he never counted on it being on anyone else's terms but his own. "Choosing you was the best thing I could ever have done. You were the woman I was meant to be paired with."

Silence enveloped the space for several seconds as the sounds of the forest were amplified around them. In the distance, the hooting of night owls and the shrieks of other creatures rode the wind. Maal could have sworn he heard the slither of a snake across a bulging branch. Her slow response was deafening. Realizing her strong will, Maal sucked in his breath and waited.

"You aren't being direct."

"Yes, I desired Onya initially. But fate would have it that I did not act quickly enough and the Ancestors saw to it that I was paired correctly. This union was *meant*," he said with as much sincerity as he could muster. The lingering heat caused the perspiration to begin again. His nerves were rattling behind the inquiry.

"I see."

Maal swallowed hard. He'd had every intention of being honest, but knowing the particulars of his feelings was quite unnecessary. "What I *wanted* months ago is unimportant. You are my preferred partner. I am pleased with our connection. It is you that I desire." He reached out for her and tilted her chin upward to meet his lips.

"You are right." She allowed her lips to meet his, but there was something stony about the kiss she planted that alarmed him. "After all, love is forbidden. All that matters is that I desire you as well, which I most certainly do." Lyn said flatly while reaching for the maleness settled between his thighs. "The inseparable bond of pleasure and respect is what makes us uniquely Ido. Unlike Onya, I do not allow myself to love, but I do allow myself to be pleasured. I understand what you once desired, but I am all too *pleased* with what you desire now." He noted her deliberate use of the word and looked down at the ground, unable to meet the intensity of her stare. Immediately, he felt himself lengthen inside her palm. She lowered her chin so that her lips grazed his jaw before traveling the length of his jugular. Maal felt his breath release in short, lustful pants.

"I plan to enjoy you tonight and pleasure you more than you ever thought imaginable," she murmured in a small whisper.

Before he could respond, the resounding blare of a horn alerted them both to the circle of fire. A processional formed instantaneously as the Youth began to make their way toward the giant marble pyramids, the colors from the ever-present rainbow reflected on the face of the moon. The Final Rite was upon them.

7

TASTE

Faint beams of moonlight illuminated the gray marble pyramids inside a silver fog as Onya walked forward with Quince at her side. While gazing upward, she took notice of the pyramid's peak where the moonlight and rainbow blurred to become one shining beam of kaleidoscopic color. The heat from the fires coupled with the humidity from the forest made the night air thick and cumbersome. Not an inkling of a breeze blew through the air as the leafy branches stood stoic in the night, barely acknowledging the life running through their rigid green veins. Onya continued to walk toward the small opening in the large structure. Her shorter strides struggled to keep pace with the longer, more gallant steps of her male partner. The closer they got, the larger the hole became, a hypnotic humming sound buzzing from within.

Anxiously, the Youth gathered around the entranceway into the central pyramid. Onya focused on the gleaming vertical rainbow in the sky. Its colors were now darkening in hue. Blues were becoming purple, orange became red and green deepened in shade. Transfixed by the sight, she barely noticed the marble door sliding aside from its invisible hinge to reveal a blinding blast of light in the wake of the onlookers outside. While shielding her eyes, she could feel the strong pectoral muscles of Quince's broad chest pressing against her back. He took hold of her soft shoulders and guided her closer to the light, his shallow breaths tickling the tender skin just below her nape. Unable to suppress a smile, she stood on her toes, reached up and grabbed hold of his neck. Tilting her chin upward, she accepted the kiss he placed on her forehead.

After a light shove, Onya stepped inside, those who remained followed close behind, temporarily blinded by the massive wash of light. Squinting through the overwhelming glare, she began to make out the dulled shapes and colors in front of her. Quince's hold on her shoulders tightened cautiously as he too attempted to make out their surroundings. A gentle click stirred her concentration. The large marble door sealed just as quickly as it had opened moments ago. They would now be free to venture throughout the interconnected pyramids and pleasure themselves and their partners for twenty-four erotic hours. Onya's heart pounded in her chest eagerly. The other couples were now organizing themselves in a neat row as their blurred vision adjusted to the dimness inside. Slowly, the shrouded darkness began to lift giving way to a delicate bluish light.

Carefully, she took a small step forward; her senses registered the soft moss beneath her bare feet giving way to planks of sturdy redwood. Tinkling sounds of running water flooded her ears with a delicate whoosh. Her eyes suddenly adjusted to the solid silver trees lining the banks of the crystal clear waters of the Shine. Funnel fish swam about happily, their iridescent forms sparkling against the glint of the moonlit rainbow. Grasses softer than feathers slid between her toes as she journeyed from the shining planks of redwood to the running river. They were in a pleasure filled garden filled with baskets of succulent fruit, sweet scented flowers and eccentric trees. The blue-black leaves of the Fulani trees bowed on the banks of the Shine as if stopping for a drink on a lazy afternoon while the square flowered Ono stood rigid and proud, its lean, fire red branches reaching toward the pyramid's apex. Drapes of lush green vines dripping with precious jewels crisscrossed the structure's marble sides. Excitedly, she turned to her left where she located the next pyramid in the distance. Its inner room shone gold while the pyramid to her right held a deep reddish hue. With each pyramid featuring a different cultural theme, she could hardly wait to experience them all. Silenced by the breathtaking view before her, Onya barely noticed Quince's hand as it slid across her bare stomach. Pleasantly overwhelmed, she let go of a high-pitched giggle before turning toward him.

"This… is pure paradise," she cooed longingly in his ear. She felt his eyes scouring her body like a pirate in search of rumored treasure while his irises, like shimmering topaz spheres danced with a flaming want she'd never seen. Stealing a glance below his navel, she saw the stiffness in his loose-fitting pants and grabbed it roughly while running her tongue suggestively along her top lip. With a wink, she ran playfully toward the clear stream of water winding through the delicate moss on the ground beneath them. No one else existed but the two of them.

"I don't think that's *just* water." Quince whispered in her ear. "Nothing about Taste is what it seems. I have a strong feeling everything will be heightened during the Final Rite."

Onya peered over the side of the riverbank and bravely stuck a toe in. Instantly her body temperature rose. She felt lightheaded and dizzy with satisfaction as its warmth sent an electrifying aphrodisiac shot throughout her extremities. "It's... it's unreal."

Quince reached around her and dipped a single toe in the water. Within seconds he saw stars behind his eyes. Hard and almost inebriated, he stumbled backward in awe, wiping the newly formed beads of sweat from his brow. He didn't speak. There were no words to describe the extent of the pleasure around them. Everything in existence was larger than life. The soft pink petals of the fully bloomed Yenni flowers were large enough to hold several people. The aqua-tinged Kosua sponges lodged in the riverbed were buoyant and welcoming.

"Come here," Onya beckoned with an extended finger while perched in the triangular folds of a floating Inkra lily. After sauntering slowly forward and locking his gaze with hers, he dropped his pants, stood naked in front of her and took her hand, following until the water was waist high. Her bikini top dissolved before them as he coated her hardened nipples with gentle blankets of breath. It was like they were standing in a clear pool of warm pashion tea. Onya lifted her hands from the pool and placed them firmly on his heaving chest. He quivered as his eyes softened into pleasure-induced slits. The moment was too illusory for her to believe, the pleasure nearly intangible. Together, they shuddered in the waist high pool, holding one another, allowing the warm liquid to create a flurry of small simultaneous orgasms during their embrace. They held their breath, locked hands and released, locked hands and released, creating an inebriated cycle all their own. Tenderly, he allowed her midnight hued locs to cascade over his fingertips while he tipped her head backward and moved in for a wandering kiss. Lazily, he traced her features, from the perfectly arced brows to the high cheekbones and delicately curved jaw-line while she returned the favor. Her pinky finger scaled the sharp bridge of his nose, the smooth skin of his partially closed lids and lashes, and the full lips situated beneath a shadow of a mustache. He pecked her closed eyelids, nose, the corners of her mouth, gently brushed her lips with his, and with a regal gesture, kissed her hand.

Staggering now and struggling to maintain his sanity, he lifted his head. There in the ceiling, was the possible explanation for the pleasurable liquid. A luminescent vertical rainbow shone from a small, triangular opening at the pyramid's top directly into the water, thus altering it into its current state. The iridescence of the rainbow's color ran playfully over her skin until her physical frame took on the likeness of a vibrant playground.

Her eyes beheld the mystery before her. The brown of her irises were shining amber, the pupils dilated with intensity. Gently he grabbed hold of her round buttocks and lifted her from the stationary flower and waded through the water until they came to a large canary and salmon colored anemone. Its tentacles pulsed and swayed in the almost nonexistent current, welcoming their company. He laid her down on its surface. Immediately it curled around her body. Her lashes fluttered as she sighed. Awed by the beauty of her lying there, deep brown engulfed by the brilliance of orange, yellow, and pink, he stood back, amazed. The mere sight caused him to shiver as he lengthened. However, he chose to prolong his pleasure and hers for the moment. There were hours of play at their disposal and he was more than ready to enjoy each and every second allotted.

***

Maal breathed in deeply through his nose while surveying her nude, petite frame. The mere sight of her cocoa skin dusted with bits of red-gold and meshing with his own was enough for another climax. Bronze kisses fastened to midnight sighs, that's what they were: a kiss and a sigh, a breath and a shudder sifting through tender grass that was chiffon to the touch. They lay there beneath a plum colored tree with triangular leaves and a pecan trunk, catching a breather from the first hour of Taste's uncanny bliss.

Gently he untangled himself from her lean limbs and rolled onto his stomach. "What if I were to tell you that we can shift again...right now? What would you say?"

Just as the question slipped from his lips, she propped herself up on an elbow and turned to face him, her brows knitted above a wide-eyed, disbelieving stare. "I'd challenge you to remember the facts. I'd remind you of our teachings. The Ido can only shape-shift three times: at birth, at age seven, and right after dea--"

Abruptly, he placed a slender index finger on her lips, quieting the rebuttal.

"And I would tell you that you were wrong. This is Taste...anything is possible," he quipped in a seductive baritone.

Lyn smiled mischievously, tilted her head to one side, and placed her own index finger on the bridge of his nose. The two warriors were eye to eye now, swallowing one another's energy, sensing the unbridled, hot-blooded lust shared between them while their hearts slammed against their chests. "Then show me," she dictated on a breathy whisper as he grabbed her by the wrists, pulled her to her feet, and guided her along the edge of the riverbank.

The opulent golden light of the East pyramid bathed their senses in what could only be described as inexplicable wonderment. He and Lyn remained tongue-tied as they strode along, gawking at the surroundings that had so drastically changed. What was once a lush green garden of ecstasy now receded into a gleaming sugar beach littered with exotic shells. The East pyramid's high, angular walls were void of crisscrossing vines. In their place were nuggets of sparkling gold, smoothed like large, weathered pebbles thousands of years old.

In his periphery, he saw Dez and Clay following his lead, their anxious partners in tow. He'd expected the unexpected the moment the heavy marble door creaked open, but still hadn't banked on the magnitude of the thrilling pleasures he'd be receiving once inside. The soft caress of Lyn's warm breath on his neck instantly eased him into full-fledged arousal. Immediately, he led his preferred partner across the warm white sand to an abandoned nook betwixt three open, over-sized shells. There, the easy current splashed against the sand, creating a shallow pool. The soothing smell of lavender filled the air as tiny gusts of wind whirled about.

Maal took a seat and crossed his legs while Lyn followed suit. "Ready?" he asked in a mysterious tone just above a whisper. Lyn nodded cautiously, not knowing quite what to expect. And then it hit her like a ton of bricks. She slapped herself on the forehead and her mouth upturned into a knowing smile.

"The Djinn," she stated simply.

Maal nodded affirmatively and turned his attention toward a gust of wind dancing over the river. Twisting clockwise and gathering speed just as it had done in the Oasis all those months ago, the rising funnel stood several feet above the river's surface along with several others.

Across from her, Lyn observed Maal's lids slowly lowering as he reached for her hands. While he sat there in a near meditative state, she kept her eyes fastened to the growing funnel now racing toward them. With a decisive splash it rose higher before taking the form of a gorgeous, liquefied woman. Gradually, the droplets gathered into what looked to be ample curves and a low bust line before it spoke.

Come. The voice echoed in their minds before his eyes opened. Slowly he rose from where he sat and soon after, helped Lyn to her feet. Arm in arm, they walked toward the river and entered. Maal felt himself shudder immediately, fought against an instantaneous climax, and pressed on with Lyn following close behind. By the time they'd ventured only a few feet; they were both treading water.

What is it that you wish? cooed the female voice. *Permission to please?*

Maal held up an index finger, signaling for the large, swirling entity to wait. *I have a request unlike any you've ever heard.* He replied telepathically.

The curvaceous Djinn threw her head back in amusement. *I am very old young General. I can hardly think of anything that hasn't been asked of me.*

Maal reached forward to pull Lyn's floating form closer to him and smiled. *Request to be granted the gills and senses of the Mer.*

The Djinn tilted its head to the side and seemed to sigh before responding. *I have to admit young General... that is a request that I did not foresee you asking.* It paused for a moment as if it were pondering its answer. *So be it...*

At once, the Djinn imploded with a giant splash, soaking their upper bodies entirely. Lyn blinked, shivered, and laughed as the sparkling water stimulated her every pore.

Without warning, the Djinn returned to its funnel form, touched down and began to descend, carrying them along with it. Lyn held on to Maal's broad shoulders firmly as they spun inside the circular whirlpool, down, down, down until they were fully submerged and traveling deeper still. When the descent slowed to a halt, her eyes flew open. Slowly, she soaked in the underwater wonderland that lay before her very eyes. Fish and other creatures swam and wriggled about carelessly while the coral clung effortlessly to the wide riverbed just below her toes. Golden-lit prisms from the pyramid above angled their way through the water, slicing it into portions of shimmering light and subtle shadow. A grayish flattened stone jutting from beneath a turquoise and maroon colored reef caught her eye. After she'd wrestled Maal's attention away from their surroundings, she nudged in its direction.

He smiled, his thick locs floating airily behind him. After taking her hand in his he swam forward and settled on his back.

Ready? He asked via telepathy while settling a hand on the raised slits on the sides of her throat.

Resisting the urge to giggle from the tickling sensation, she pushed his hand away playfully while floating above him. *Oh... yeah...* she replied slyly as she stared at the amazing specimen sprawled beneath her. When he pulled her closer, she widened her straddle a bit and stroked the long locs spread beneath his neck and shoulders. He looked like sculpted perfection lying there, the brightness of his smile and the sparkle in his dark eyes drawing her into a vacuum of inhibition. She leaned in closer and applied a sumptuous kiss to his lips as his tender grip on her breasts slipped to her coffee colored hips and settled finally on her firm thighs. *Do you need me to take it easy on you?* She asked with a mischievous grin.

Maal tightened his grip and bit his bottom lip. *There'll be no holding back tonight.*

Nope, not at all. She replied wryly before lowering her lips to the place where his angular jaw line met his neck. He shuddered at the point of contact. The corners of her mouth upturned into a satisfied grin. He found her chin and tipped it gently upward as their lips met. The sensation of the deep kiss along with the dramatic strengthening current was almost too much to bear.

Soon they began an intimate underwater tango of twists and turns. His tender grope against her slow grind became graceful spirals of heat rising to a quiet boil. The expression she wore was one of seamless ecstasy as he gripped the lobes of her buttocks and guided the swell of her hips toward his throbbing length. He threw his head back when her pleasure slick folds sheathed him wholly. Her tender valley sucked him in mercilessly; gripping his member like her very life depended on it. She took full advantage of her underwater mobility and slid forward, causing his eyes to roll back. Her pace began to slowly increase as they floated upward; slivers of shadowed silver settled on his dark skin until it looked as if it had been dusted with diamonds. Losing control, she felt her eyes roll while her shoulder-length braids drifted to and fro, swirling around her delicate features.

Fighting against the natural lift of gravity, he pulled her closer, encasing her between the strength of his muscular thighs. A sudden spike in his heartbeat sent intense messages to his jumbled thoughts. He found himself drunken with stimulation. Her slick skin, the feeling of rising and falling, it was becoming pointless to navigate without the crest of a climax to momentarily release him. His muscles tensed; yet the desire to please and be pleased continued to increase exponentially. Lyn's mouth curled into a broad grin as they dropped again, her petite frame pressed against the hard blocks of his abdomen like a second skin. His large hands traveled up her spine and settled on her shoulders. With unexpected force, he thrust his hips upward. The pulsing of her jaw and the arch of her brows communicated her pleasure.

Maal felt his body contract and relax with the magnitude of a small earthquake. Together, they writhed and twisted, swirled and twitched while each and every one of their nerve endings caught fire in a domino effect. Lyn forced herself to release the pulsing shudder between her thighs and allowed it to rise to her chest until it rippled outward through her fingertips and toes. Her body responded in erratic spasms as her arousal took on the characteristics of a dizzying high that shortened her breath and quickened her pulse to an erratic blur. His answer was a series of syncopated thrusts until their sex became undulating passion. The pulsing in Maal's loins was a reverberating flame burning through the secrets of his soul to the very top of his crown. Visibly spent, Maal relaxed his thighs and propelled himself upward, pulling her with him. When they broke through the water's surface, all they could do was shudder and smile in exhaustion. Taste was truly a marathon unlike any other.

***

"Isn't it surreal?" asked Onya in a tiny whisper as she surveyed the ambiance.

"Your reflection," responded Quince as he lightly kissed her ankles and ran his full lips up the instep of her foot before wrapping his warm tongue around her toes.

"You know I'm sensitive," she giggled before jerking her leg back.

His response was a wry smile as he waded toward her and dropped to his knees. The arousal was imminent as more of his body became submerged. His limbs tingled. The hairs on his neck stood on end. Still gripping his lengthy organ, he allowed his tongue to caress the thick brown legs positioned lazily over the side of the giant anemone. His hands found themselves cupping her buttocks firmly as he pulled her closer, mouth open and tongue ready to taste love's epiphany.

It didn't take long for him to latch onto her supple flesh. It had become so easy to lose himself in the moistness of her folds. Her scent was cologne for the psyche. Wafts of it reached his nose and lingered. It was so thick; he thought he could taste it on his tongue. Reaching for her breasts, his hands brushed against the anemone and he shuddered yet again. She tilted her head back lazily, enjoying the titillation from his tongue and hands as well as the added pleasures from the pulsing flower. Theirs was a natural ecstasy she'd never forget. Together they coasted downstream as the river grew so deep, his toes failed to touch its sandy bottom. She floated along on a dream while he tread water.

Unable to resist his need to enter her, he took hold of her hips and firmly anchored himself so his muscular form was suspended above her. She clamped her palms onto the softness of the anemone below and readied herself for him. The searing intensity of the penetration made her gasp. She pulled him closer, nestling her forefingers deep into the small of his back. The taut skin refused to give against the pads of her fingers so she commenced a striking massage of nail tips lightly tracing skin. Heat circulated through her pelvis like a whirling cyclone, touching down on each erogenous zone with the precision of a spirit made machine. Instinctively, he knew her well, knew when she'd shriek, when she'd yelp, knew every inch of her that made her soft and inviting and woman. Emphatically he called out her name, *Onya!* The erotic play continued for hours until their pores were drained by their combined efforts. Refusing to yield a second for rest, she mounted him skillfully while he called out beneath the floating greenish haze. Then, he entered her from the rear. No one else existed as he guided the round lobes of her behind, the sound of her buttocks slapping against his pelvis like a wild rhythm accentuated by invigorating pleas and pants.

The rim of her femininity swelled around his member as he dug deeper, mining for the precious indentations that would trigger her climax. At this moment in time, the only thing he needed in life was her satisfaction. The short gasps and flailing arms gave him a direct buzz. Thundering currents echoed through his scrotum and shaft repeatedly. His head now nudging against one of her thick, moistened walls drove her eyes to cross as she began to instinctively fight the pleasure. He would not allow her to resist. His own lids lowered to a half closed position as he concentrated on the spaces he hadn't explored and the crevices not yet grazed. Moving in slow, counterclockwise circles now, he brought her arms above her head and clutched her wrists tightly with his left hand. Her body quaked as he maneuvered in delicate spirals, alternating between deep thrusts and short bursts while anchoring himself on the drifting flower. Her eyes flew open and freestanding tears accumulated in their corners.

Consumed by their lovemaking, the two lovers barely noticed themselves drifting from the Central to the West pyramid. Soft green light was replaced with a red-hot flare, giving the new space devilish warmth. Illustrious gemstones of every shape and size now clung to the steep, high walls arching into a peak. Tall stone pillars carved with hieroglyphs loomed overhead. Heavy slabs of white alabaster rose from the riverbank in large geometric shapes. They too were decorated with shining symbols and precious gems.

Still, the puzzle had not yet been completed. Before leaning in for a deep kiss, he withdrew from her heavenly cove, and climbed down from the floating anemone. Steadying the flower with one arm, Quince reached to the sand below with the other. From the pristine waters he withdrew seven radiating stones: amethyst, sapphire, topaz, emerald, ruby, tourmaline, and diamond, their pure energy and color intensifying in the palm of his hand as if they were among the living. Satisfied with his selection, he straightened her legs so that she lay prostrate. She lay there dazed as he shut her eyes gently with his index fingers.

"Soon, we will no longer be Youth. It is time for us to become Enlightened," he whispered in her ear. She stirred and nodded, opening her eyes just enough to make out his profile in the red haze. In preparation to trigger her seven chakras, he settled the gemstones on different points of her body, one by one. Before he began, he anointed each of the seven channels with a kiss. Quince commenced the ritual by positioning an amethyst at the crown of her head and continuing on to the sapphire just above her brow. She felt a lone current strengthening, snapping in place like ligament to hardened bone. After applying a kiss to her throat, he set the pulsing tourmaline on the soft space below her chin. The emerald was positioned above her heart, between her breasts followed by the topaz just above her navel and the ruby betwixt her thighs. Carefully he maneuvered himself for a final entrance. He entered as she tensed and shuddered. Feeling his veins constrict, he became light headed and applied a few strong thrusts as sound was stolen from her vocal chords. A vacuum of space quelled the sounds surrounding them. They were nearly there. The absolute apex of their sexual experience was upon them. Carefully, he sat the diamond stone between the folds of her vagina, her body quivered as they awaited the unexpected. He submerged himself wholly inside her shaking frame. The moment the stone grazed her bulging clitoris, the diamond along with the other stones dissolved into a glittering colored vapor.

Gradually, he felt his spirit tearing from his physical frame. Like bits of lace gently torn from leather, half of him ascended in a substance lighter than smoke. In awe, he hovered above his nearly limp body, watching the sudden jerks and jolts of what could only be described as the divine taking total control of his extremities. Overcome by the multiple sensations, he floated there for what seemed like an eternity, sensors torn between two selves. Unable to produce a single utterance, he swallowed a moan as his spirit shook and climaxed six feet above his physical form. His spirit shattered at once, colors splintered into blinding prisms, spun in mid air, fizzled into vapor, and drifted back into his pleasure induced form. Once he'd reattached with his spirit, the uncontrollable convulsing that followed caused the anemone to tip. Over they went, saturated fully now by the warm water.

Befuddled and overcome with the aftershocks of climax, he was almost too out of sorts to swim. Fighting against the listlessness, he reached for her and carried her to the mossy banks of the river. She'd lost herself inside his touch. Limbs twisted into a contorted form, they lay there crying and kissing and hugging and caressing one another. Their nude bodies glistening red under the high, triangular roof, Onya lowered her chin from his damp tufts of hair. There was calmness in his smile. An indescribable knowing flowed between them like a covalent bond. It tugged at her heartstrings. He wiped the tears from her cheeks with his fingertips and traced the outline of her jaw. She kissed him deeply and honestly, attempting to channel her love for him through every one of her senses.

"Thank you," he said kissing her hand.

She felt her lids lowering as she sunk lower in his arms. Her soft lips found the firm skin of his chest.

"This---" she murmured.

"Can't be...forbidden." He completed for her as she drifted into the abyss of sleep. Watching the rise and fall of her chest, he wondered if there would ever be a need to dream again.

8

BUGS AND SMOKE

"Be careful, the cut must be precise! He can't lose too much blood!" shouted Quince through the darkness.

A small crowd was gathering quickly around Dez as he lay on his back, eyes squinting from the insufferable pain. His cries in the night had caused a stir in the pyramids. Though the Rite had come to a close and many were sleeping, he'd felt a cramping in his thigh that had caused him to yell. The supernatural pull of the rainbow along with the height of his double climax with both Lore and Eesha had caused an adverse reaction. He awoke in a sweat, clutching his previously injured thigh. Eventually, Quince, Maal and a few others escorted him back to the bonfires.

Upon further analysis, they'd seen a small mass moving under his skin. They speculated at once that he'd been bugged. Without question, it would have to be removed. Though his mind remained cluttered and dazed, he was aware of what was lodged inside him. He dry heaved while watching Maal place the heat from the flame upon his sharpened sword. The thought of being a parasitic host sickened him. Acrid bile rose to his throat as Maal positioned the blade over the throbbing mass. Hot blood drained from his flesh as he yelled, his cries echoing throughout the forest causing carnivorous creatures to growl and feeding birds to scatter, peppering the sky. In seconds, the insect had fallen to the ground covered in blood and bits of pink flesh. Maal immediately doused the wound with water while Eesha applied pressure with the leaves of healing herbs drenched with pungent smelling salves.

Dez balled his hands into fists and pounded them into the soft ground where he lay nearly helpless. A cool cloth met his forehead as his eyes flew open reflexively. Both Eesha and Lore were kneeling beside him now wiping his brow and massaging his temples. Maal doused it with water, cleaning the blood from its surface. Tiny legs wriggled around its bulging, black body as it crawled and wiggled in the dirt. Maal and Quince spoke in hushed tones while Dez lay there straining to hear the conversation.

It was all becoming clear. While performing a seemingly harmless and helpful operation on his injured thigh, Ankh, the lead healer of the Sphinx, had attached a pheromone-tracking insect to his muscle and closed the wound with stitches. His eyes flickered with a rush of anger. He had been the reason they'd been attacked at the Rain Caves. He was the reason the Elders could pinpoint their every move. An overwhelming feeling of griminess washed over him. He felt tainted, spoiled, and used. Not wanting to meet the sorrowful eyes of those in his wake, he chose to shut his own. Only half listening to their hushed conversations of shock and concern for his well being, he thought only of revenge.

The discovery of the "bug" had been a significant find. Because of it, they'd have to approach the war differently and he knew it. Alert would have to be heightened and awareness raised. Vaguely he remembered being advised not to trust the Sphinx. But they'd had no choice. After the battle of Glo City, his injury and the wounds of several others had required Sphinx medicine. Had they *not* gone to the Falls, he would have surely perished. However, the deception haunted him. He would rather have died than become a traitorous tool used by the enemy to gain ground in the war. But why hadn't they seen this coming? Quince had made it plain that the Sphinx would join forces with the Elders because of their not so distant history as allies. Still he blocked it all from his pounding skull: the Civil War, the unexpected pressures of having two preferred partners, the fact that he'd been tracked like some sort of wild beast for scientific study. Obvious anger was quickly replaced with an indescribable bitterness even he hadn't imagined. His temples ached terribly as he fought the urge to allow the anger to overtake him. A conjured image of Dame revealed itself inside his mind and he spat shrewdly in disgust. With every ounce of blood in his veins he hated the man and all he stood for. He was destroying their people single handedly.

"Wrap it up!" Quince fired again.

As he lay there dazed, he felt the pressure of a tight bandage being wrapped around the deep wound in his sore thigh. Un-phased by his own well-being, Dez propped himself up and fought valiantly to disguise an anguished moan.

"Don't." A firm hand landed on his shoulder as he attempted to sit up further. "You need to lie back down and heal."

Dez looked up into the eyes of Eesha. Lore wasn't too far away. They both glanced at him and then back at one another in concern. He hated feeling like a victim. In his mind, his strengths were nearly all he had. They were his talents. The idea of any weakness made his heart ache. So many thoughts consumed him. He wanted to shout at them, needed to be alone. This was no time for pity.

"I am fine," he winced. "I can already feel my strength returning."

Eesha kneeled closer to him so they were at eye level. "Dez, don't be ridiculous. We just opened up your leg. No one needs you to be strong now. Just relax and heal. It will be ---"

"You have no idea," he cut in. "I am a warrior. It is my job to protect you. The Sphinx must pay for this. They *will* pay for this," he said in an angry snarl.

"The female Youth are more than capable of holding their own in battle!" she shot back before softening again. "Right now, you are an injured warrior Dez. You are a liability to us if you try to go after them now. You can barely walk," she said gently.

With that, Dez bounded to his feet, once again straining to disguise the pain. A hush fell over the small gathering as they watched him hop on one leg beneath the looming tree. Complete silence fell aside from the crackling fires in the clearing.

"What we need is revenge! The Cause cannot allow this to happen. The Sphinx must be punished. We should have no mercy. They should be wiped out as a result of their deception!" His heart slammed hard in his chest. The blood rushed to his cheeks, flushing them with ruddiness visible only by the gleam of the moonlight. Quince walked toward him; Maal followed. The two of them approached cautiously, each clasping a hand on his shoulder.

"Look man, we just need to focus on your getting better. El is still out there. We have to wait for word from him. We can't just abandon--"

Dez refused to let Quince finish his statement. "We can split the forces!" he said in a huff. "Half of us can go to the Enlightened Lands, while the other half can go to the Falls. We're right on the river. We can take some canoes downstream and anchor just outside the perimeter of the Desert. Then, some would go northwest and the others due east. All we need is some time to plan!" He exclaimed in a frenzy. The others simply looked on. Maal and Quince exchanged worried glances until Maal cleared his throat.

"Dez, we're just as upset as you are, but the operation to retrieve El in one piece and attack the Elders will take careful planning. We don't even know his location yet. We understand you're upset, but let's think here! We're down in numbers. We've lost some men. The Elders are strong. Let's not forget that. They just managed to lose more men to the Zo than we did while in the caves," he said quietly. "What we need for you to do is lie down. Your brother and I have this under control. The Sphinx will receive their just reward. That is a direct *promise* from me. I believe in vengeance just as much as you."

To this, Dez relaxed his muscles a bit and attempted to sit back down. He didn't reply, but the small group in his wake interpreted his silence as a sign of surrender for the time being. Dez nodded as the two men helped him to a seated position on the ground.

"Maal is right Dez. You know we will fight until the end. All those responsible for our suffering will pay."

Quince was speaking the truth and he knew it. His brother always kept his word. He lowered his head in shame. How could he have forgotten El? Suddenly embarrassed by his own selfish impulsiveness, he breathed in deeply. "Leave me. I need to heal." Maal and Quince looked at him cautiously and nodded. Gathering his thoughts beneath the graying sky, Dez laid his head back on the bundle of blankets left for him as a pillow. As the last of them filtered back toward the pyramids of Taste, he shut his eyes. Not to sleep, but to formulate his plan.

***

In spite of the pain, he walked swiftly. He refused to allow it to hinder him as he traveled, jaw line set and eyes focused squarely on the Falls in the distance. The terrifying sounds of night barely struck a chord in him as he roamed, clutching the broadsword in his right hand and a wide leather shield in his left. Sweat accumulated between his digits while he gripped the heavy handle. The only people who would soon be realizing their fears were his enemies. He'd been the unfortunate victim of a clever ruse and for this they would surely pay. But he had to do it alone. The surefire calls to think more rationally reverberated inside his skull. So many Cause members would have disagreed. Eesha, Lore, *Quince*. Because of this he'd chosen to steal away under the thick cover of night. This way no one could question or attempt to stop him. By morning he'd be long gone. Anger surged inside him like helium in a balloon. *How had they not known? How could they have not suspected? Nothing could have been clearer!*

The cascading rays from the belly of the sky beneath a rising sun caused him to shield his eyes. The trees were thinning now as he left the humid bubble of Three Wood and entered the outskirts of a barren desert wasteland. He'd been walking for hours, yet somehow pure adrenaline kept his mind from focusing on the stress of the bandaged wound. Unconscious during his first journey to the Falls, Dez speculated as to how tedious the trek must have been. The lone difference between their voyage and his own was they'd been traveling northeast and had had no choice but to veer into the Smoke Desert itself. To his advantage, he was already situated near the river and closer to a direct route. If he stayed the current course, he'd avoid the unwelcoming interior along with all the ill feelings it bestowed upon those who dared travel through its territories.

By dusk the following day he surmised that about another half a day's travel stood before him. The small fire he'd prepared burned freely, but now well within the territories of the Smoke Desert, the fire blended with the land. Still though, he felt much like a lame duck marked for capture or kill. He ate hungrily, nearly swallowing the bread, herbs and fish whole from the skewer while turning over the plan in his head anxiously. It was simple. He'd infiltrate the Oasis and kidnap one of the Sphinx underlings. Then, he'd strong arm his way through the city until he met Ankh. Soon, vengeance would be his. Locating the sun tucked between a few stratus clouds low in the sky, he looked over his shoulder and back in the direction he'd come. By now, they'd noticed his absence. More uncomfortable with his loneliness than he was willing to admit, even to himself, he secretly prayed they'd come for him soon.

His stomach growled loudly as he rushed to scarf down the meal. Smoke or no smoke, he wasn't exactly fond of how exposed he was. A mere stone's throw from Sphinx territory, Dez knew the importance of constant vigilance. Still though, eating was required for basic sustenance and responsible for replenishing his waning energy. The food rations stuffed hastily in his lightweight sack the night before were depleted and if he wasn't careful; he would have to hunt for himself. A pang of regret formed in the pit of his abdomen. *Had he really thought this through?* Suddenly he became discouraged with the decision. Needing a short break, he sat down where he was just beyond a few tall reeds protruding from the rushing river and looked at the bandage covering his thigh. The wound serving as a constant reminder, his boiling rage returned. The width of the large blade and the powerful leather shield beside the still crackling fire caught his attention. In a matter of hours, he would be in for the battle of his life.

The next few hours were grueling. The smoke thickened as he struggled to cross the rugged, cracked terrain. Barely able to see his two hands in front of him and fearful of the possibility of veering off course, he kept close to the river where the smoke was least dense. The journey was a difficult one and he'd grossly underestimated its rigor. It was taxing on the body as well as the mind. Paranoia seeped inside his brain as he crept along, low to the ground, sometimes crawling, sometimes walking in a hunched position for miles. And to think, The Cause had braved the actual interior of the Desert. He was sticking to its outskirts. The thought alone of their bravery provided the motivation he needed to continue. To his delight, the short bursts of pain had begun to subside more and more each day. He felt better now than he had two days ago. The only thing that provided hope was what he thought to be the distant echo of a tumultuous waterfall. At this, his ears perked up and he continued on. In intervals, he stopped and started for breaks. However, the wound was still slowing him down. Cursing its hindrance, he knelt at the end of the Shine to refill his flask. He needed to drink.

A small sound nearby put him on full alert. Bent over on all fours, he froze. The handle of the broadsword in his hand became damp with the sweat of an anticipated battle. His senses piqued as every sound became amplified through intense concentration. From out of nowhere the pitter-patter of footfalls drew quickly near. A sharp whizzing sound flew within a millimeter of his left ear. With one, fluid motion he was on his feet and swinging. In the smoky fog he made out the large head of a man with a lion's body armed with a powerful bow. Its shaggy brown coat gave off the scent of burning myrrh. Dez looked up into its face. A pair of intense green eyes gleamed with aggression and short, spiky black hair sprouted from its head. It was olive skinned and muscular, a formidable opponent. The thing crouched on its hind legs and mustered a scowl. Dez steadied himself, ready for engagement. They began to circle one another hostilely, each man refusing to relinquish an inch of ground to the other.

"Why are you here?" The Sphinx questioned gruffly.

"I am an Ido Youth. Can I not travel where I please?" Dez responded with control.

"Then why are your weapons drawn? And why are you alone? It is wartime and The Sphinx must protect their territory from possible enemies," it replied suspiciously.

Dez chuckled low in his throat. "My weapons are drawn because you are obviously on the attack. An arrow whizzed by my ear while my back was turned. I was drinking from the river... and as you have already stated, it is wartime," he added with sarcasm.

Not amused, the Sphinx grunted and lunged, its claws meeting the sturdy leather shield attached to Dez's lower forearm. At the last possible second, Dez threw himself against its weight causing it to fall backward. He made the most of his split second advantage and leaped onto the thing while it snarled beneath him. With uncanny agility it sprung upward, causing Dez to lose his balance and fall backward, his entire upper body landing into the churning waters of the Shine River. He recovered quickly however and in no time returned to his feet, ignoring the throbbing pain in his thigh. Gathering himself once again, he circled the creature and calculated his chances for a successful offensive series. The thing was skilled and its weight would pose a problem. He hadn't accounted for their physicality in his plans. Just then, it pounced on his chest as Dez brought up his sword to the Sphinx's powerful neck. He could see the fright in its eyes as he began to slash away. Bright red blood flew through the misty air, soaking the ground with a splatter of living color. Mid-swing, he heard a shout and a yelp. Everything went black.

***

When he awoke, Dez was only aware of two things: his leg was throbbing and he was soaking wet. Struggling to open his eyes, he found himself sitting in ankle high water and trapped inside a tank of some sort. All around him, Sphinx guards adjusted the shackles of other creatures, checked the water levels, and scribbled notations on writing pads. His feet and hands were shackled. It didn't take long for him to realize he was imprisoned.

To his left stood several Diaw birds with their beaks forced shut by a contraption he'd never seen before. He recognized one of the birds as Ly, their guide into Glo City all those months ago. It was all coming together. Obviously, he'd been of no more use to the Sphinx and jailed due to his knowledge of their ploy against the Youth. The Diaw were known for their loose loyalties. The birds trudged through the rising water in slow motion and swayed with the waves. Their eyes were wide with fright as the levels rose.

Intermingling with the Diaw were several large Ido monkeys with their large arms chained. Three Zo sloshed through the water in anger, their mouths clamped shut and their claws shaved to the paw. Near his head, several butterfly dragons buzzed around noisily. He watched helplessly as they tried to work together to escape. Lifting his head now, he noticed the lid squeezed tightly over the "liquid cell." He stole a glance outside of his own tank and noticed several others standing side by side. All were filled with Stripes chained much like he had been. He recognized them at once. White Mohawks, bald heads and painted bodies that looked as if they'd faded from too much sun. All of them shared the same fate. They too were sealed inside a watery grave.

I know it looks bleak, but you can't give up.

Dez looked up and into the eyes of one of the frantic insects. Its voice resonated a quivering pitch much like a harmonica inside his mind. The lizard-like body hovered in place as it spoke. Greenish-yellow wings flapped madly against sleek, black scales.

Confused, Dez responded mentally. *Why are you here?*

The butterfly dragon hovered closer. *It is the Insect War all over again. We knew this day would come again. We never trusted them. That's why we built the city.* The miniature dragon began to fly in small, frantic circles as it mumbled to itself.

You mean Glo City? But... the peace treaty... Dez sputtered.

They are not to be trusted. They have been capturing us for months. They are obsessive...fearful of extinction and our wings provide a life-giving cure. The insect trailed off and turned back to the others attempting to lift the lid of the container. Upset by their moot efforts, it began flying around haphazardly again.

Are you aware of the Civil War? The Youth have waged war against the Elders.

We are. To be honest, we have no respect for the Ido. Because of your involvement in the previous war, we were nearly defeated. Had you not joined, the Sphinx would have been obliterated. We were in full command until the Ido alliance. But once we caught wind of the Youth's defiance of the Elders who caused us such agony all those years ago, we have come to make a distinction. We respect the Youth for fighting for what they believe to be injustice. It is what any creature would do when or if their culture were threatened. We are being threatened again. They are slaughtering us.

Dez looked at the creature sadly and then up at it's determined brethren trying to lift the sealed lid. He'd blindly walked into a trap. His heart sank in disbelief. All at once, his mind journeyed back to Taste and the other Youth. He'd left behind a battalion of warriors who needed him and two women who were probably carrying his two children. He'd abandoned the effort to rescue his brother. *It seems you have the best chance of any of us to escape.* Dez communicated after a few moments. *If you do, the Youth pledge their aid to you. Find Maal or Quince, the co-Generals of the Youth Cause. They are our only hope.*

The thing looked at him for a long while before acknowledging his remarks with a nod. Dez looked up again at the tiny butterfly dragons pressing their bodies against the unyielding lid. Outside, the Sphinx guards continued their watch while glaring at the mixture of wild animals on display in massive tanks. All the while the water rose from his ankles to his shins. In a short period of time, he'd be in too deep for rescue from anyone.

9

WORDS IN THE DIRT

"Who is he? Which of your sons is this? We need to know *now!*"

Vye looked up as Dame stormed inside the hut where she and her newborn son were eating. Startled by the sudden commotion, the infant let out a stifling wail. Dame moved toward the small bundle cradled in Vye's arms, peeked through the soft folds and grabbed hold of a tiny hand. Immediately, the infant clutched one of his fingers, gurgled and calmed his wails.

"I'm sorry..." Dame stammered. He reached beneath the blanket, locating the pudgy brown legs. Vye studied his reaction to the human child. His expression didn't indicate the surprise she'd been hoping for. It was clear... he'd known. *But, had he approved of the deceitful plan?* She didn't want to believe it. The Ancestors were correct. Dame's alliance with The One Faith had taken precedence over everything. If The Guide had truly sanctioned the tainted herbs as she'd suspected... her concentration broke as he spoke again.

"I'd forgotten--" His words trailed off and he stood back, his gaze still transfixed by the infant in her arms.

"We must decide on a name," Vye replied quietly. Stemming the brewing hatred in her heart for her husband, she inhaled deeply, determined not to blow her own cover. She might be the Cause's only hope.

"Yes, that must be done soon," he said, his tone significantly lower. There was a small disturbance in the crowded doorway where a group of Elder warriors stood with their captive. Vye glanced up. A tall shadow eclipsed by the afternoon sunshine stood stiffly in the doorway. She feigned surprise when El limped inside, chained and bruised. His right eye was blackened, puffy, and closed, but in spite of his haggard appearance, she sensed the pride swelling in his chest. Angered by the sight of her son's injuries, she struggled to hold herself together.

"Well... who is he?" Dame inquired again, the fiery rage returning to his deep tenor.

Vye stood there a moment, unable to speak. She and El locked eyes. The lack of emotion in his icy stare sickened her. He was eyeing her as if he found her despicable. Noting that all eyes were on her now, she pulled her shoulders back strongly and offered a response. "This is Quince... my firstborn and who I am told is the co-General of the so-called Youth Cause," she said, her voice firm and convincing.

She caught a slight twinkle in the eye he could still see out of, but he stood his ground, insubordinate and defiant as ever. The two couldn't have scripted the ruse any better had they spoken about it and planned before hand. El glared in Dame's direction, mocking him for questioning his initial story. From the outside looking in, the lie appeared irrevocably true.

"Very well then. There is cause for celebration. The war is over. The Youth seem to have surrendered and accepted the Faith," Dame replied hesitantly. His eyes swung between Vye and El as if he sensed their deceit. Mentally, she evoked calm to keep the threatening perspiration at bay.

"When will the others join you?"

"They are prepared to come on my command," was El's curt reply to the General. "They will require at least one week's time for travel. However, I must send word that you have accepted our surrender and no more blood will be shed."

"We will send an Elder messenger and meet on the banks of the Mer Sea," Dame said immediately. "Though my wife has confirmed your identity as Quince, co-General of the so-called Youth Cause, I still must remain on guard, especially with the discovery of our little tracking device." El looked on, attempting to mask his confusion about the reference to a tracer.

Dame circled El slowly, trying to intimidate him. "As a fellow warrior, and a skilled one at that, you do understand my reasons for being wary of this sudden change of heart don't you?"

El nodded. "Of course, if I were in your position, I would do the same General." Feeling the urge to push the envelope, he gestured toward the chains binding his wrists. "Are these still necessary?"

Dame eyed El curiously before breaking into a smirk. "If you were in my position would *you* unchain a prisoner of war?"

Realizing he'd pushed his luck, El replied simply. "Understood."

Dame nodded with satisfaction before grabbing Vye by the waist and embracing her happily. "They have seen the light. Our prayers to the One have been answered," he roared. Vye pasted a wide grin on her face and hugged her husband tightly.

"The Guide must be notified. Come!" With a snap of his fingers, the warriors gathered around El and led him back into the brilliant sunshine. With an excited flourish, Dame exited without another word.

***

Barely able to control her nerves, Vye stood in the corner, frazzled. Her eyes roamed from her sleeping child to the moonlit window. Thoughts of El flooded her mind. He was strong and resourceful, but she still worried about him. A meeting would be out of the question. If she prodded Dame as to where they were keeping him, she'd be taking the risk of raising his suspicions. Her husband still remained the merciless warrior of old. If they were found out, she didn't put it past him to kill them both. The treachery of a traitor was unforgivable in his mind. He'd see to it that they'd suffer. Her stomach twisted in somersaulting knots as she paced. Dame was expected home at any moment and she'd be prepared to seduce the necessary secrets out of him. It would be well worth it in the end.

A slight click at the door startled her from her thoughts. Her body jerked into movement as she pretended to tend to the sleeping baby in the corner. In the doorway, Dame wore a broad and endearing smile. He closed it behind him and sauntered closer to where she stood. Suddenly she found her plan muddied and confused. The man in front of her had recently become the love of her life and in spite of herself, in spite of his decisions and beliefs; that love remained alive and well. Still, she recalled El's bruised and battered body and the human child sleeping feet away from where they stood. Sometimes love didn't conquer all. Sometimes love was used to castigate, manipulate, and annihilate. Their love wasn't enough. In fact, had she understood the concept of love correctly; it would not approve of the sweeping actions of Dame or The Guide.

"I thought of you for most of the day," his normally booming voice was just above a whisper now. He took her in his arms. "Thank you for standing by my side. Thank you for being the woman you are." Vye buried her head in his chest and did not reply. "I know it had to have been difficult to see your son that way, but he was an enemy until now. As soon as we see the entire Cause bowed before The One, he will be vindicated and all will be well. You understand how war works?"

The question was a rhetorical one. Begrudgingly she shook her head, anger overpowering love. Without warning, he began to explore her body fervently. His large hands cupped her heavy breasts while he ran the tip of his tongue below her earlobe.

"I want you," she whispered seductively in his ear. Dame exhaled heavily before pulling her toward him. Haphazardly, he pulled the loose fitting clothing from her shoulders and took in every curve, every dimple, every peak and valley until he felt his sex lengthen mightily in his pants.

"The Youth have surrendered. The war is over and I am free to make love to my wife. It is truly a great day."

She yelped quietly when he lifted her from the ground, kissed her hard and lay her down on the mat. He shifted his body so that the brunt of his weight was on the ground and covered her nude body with endless kisses. She sighed from the sheer enjoyment of it all and placed the palms of her hands on his gleaming bald head as he descended lower. Once his full lips reached the folds of her sex, she inhaled sharply. The flatness of his tongue across her pulsing button caused her to cascade instantaneously.

Vye maneuvered her body so that it cloaked his and mounted him. He took her heavy breasts in his mouth, nibbling ever so slightly. Dizzied and pleasure filled, she felt her eyes roll to the back of her head. Carefully, she positioned her button over his thick shaft and slid in continuous circles. A guttural moan of ecstasy escaped from his gaping mouth as she wound her hips in sweeping spirals. A slick wetness covered him now. He begged her to allow him entry with his eyes. She shook her head, losing herself in the moment. The reason for the seduction escaped her when she rose from her knees and moved her hips forward. She positioned her soft delta inches in front of his nose. Eagerly, he grabbed hold of her buttocks and pulled her closer. She shook feverishly while he plunged his tongue deep in her center, exploring her hardening nipples ever so slightly with the pads of his thumbs.

"Let's forget about everything for just these next hours," she whispered hotly in his ear. He moaned before guiding her torso toward his erection. The insertion was powerful and smooth. Her insides constricted around him tightly, the slick walls providing room for a slippery rhythm of movement. His inches sunk deep within her now as he thrust upward, leaving her breathless and begging for more. His lids were low now while he concentrated beneath her, his large hands palming her breasts. She gazed at him, handsome and strong. Her love for him swelled momentarily, but stymied when she remembered the atrocities for which he was responsible.

A sudden fury of pants commenced as she rode him skillfully, turning his will to putty. Sensing that his climax neared, she strategically lifted herself up and beckoned for him to enter from behind. He knelt behind her and penetrated slowly, then quickened his pace until she buried her face in the mat below. The fierce pounding caused her own climax as she shuddered beneath his massive frame. An irregularity in his pace, followed by a violent quake, let her know that he'd reached his peak. Weakly, he returned to her side and kissed her gently. Now was her opportunity. While he lay there, drained and unassuming, she began the barrage of questions. He answered them while they lay there in the shadows, wrapped in one another's arms. All the while, she felt torn. Knowingly, she was abandoning their love in favor of a tradition that forbade its existence.

***

The meeting was risky, yet the separatist movement had to know what she'd learned. Vye listened intently to her surroundings as she walked briskly in the breeze. By now, Dame was sleeping soundly. Even if he awoke, he knew of her tendency to meditate no matter the hour. He'd think nothing of her absence, or so she hoped. The steep hill loomed into view just beyond a short tree stump. The crunch of twigs and leaves under her feet could be heard well through the night. She looked around wildly, watching to see if she were being followed. Several women shrouded in black came into view, their figures bold and frightening under the dim stars. She observed the look of despondency on their faces, but soon became preoccupied with the fact that the crowd had been thinner than before.

"Vye, we don't have much time. Our numbers are smaller than before. Since the Battle at Rain Cave, some have decided to rededicate themselves to the Faith," Eyeno's voice cracked at the mention of the battle. Chi's death had to have been still fresh in her mind. "Many are confused by the recent events. What news do you have to share?"

Vye didn't like the energy in the air. Something was wrong. Everyone looked nervous. She would share what she'd learned and then they would disperse inconspicuously. The sooner they returned to the comfort of their own homes, the better.

"Dame knew that human births would be a possibility, but I am convinced he didn't know of the lengths the Sphinx took to make sure they were made a reality." The women stirred, some looked awe stricken, others cold and unsurprised. "He didn't seem alarmed that we would no longer be born Mer either. He hinted at the fact that this would stunt the growth of the Ancestors. He implied that it was all in line with our beliefs."

Eyeno stood speechless. "I see," she said after a brief moment. "Is there anything else?"

Vye held her tongue for a moment. She couldn't shake the feeling that they were being compromised somehow. To protect the interests of the

Cause she lied by omission. "They used a bug to track the Youth's location and they have captured my son. He is being held prisoner. It appears the Cause has chosen to surrender and accept The Faith."

Eyeno looked away, her face flushed as if she'd just been punched hard in the gut. Vye kept her gaze on the surrounding women cautiously. Meanwhile, Eyeno tried to keep it together. "What should we do then? Do you believe this sudden change of heart? It doesn't seem like our sons to surrender. They had the upper hand in the war."

Vye's gaze pierced her longtime friend's eyes for a long while before she responded. She was trying desperately to communicate her alarm wordlessly. *Something was wrong!*

"I am unsure of their plans," she said vaguely. "However, Dame's knowledge of possible human births and his detachment from our culture is enough for me to flee. The only question is when."

The assault was so swift; Vye hadn't seen it coming. The men attacked with unprecedented accuracy. In seconds, the women had been either bound and gagged or were engaged in battle. Unarmed, Vye struggled with her hooded assailant. In her peripheral vision, she took sight of Eyeno besting her attacker. Gasping for breath, she pulled vehemently at the thick forearm smashed against her throat. She flailed madly, blindly as the world around her shrunk in distortion from green to blue to black. The dizziness soon overcame her; she had failed her people.

***

The fetid smell of rodents and rotting food met her nose as she struggled to sit up woozily. Her head ached and when she raised her bound, swollen hands to her face, she noticed that her jaw was puffy as well. Her eyes opened to a dim light shining through a set of metal bars. The unbearable heat coupled with the stale stench made her gag.

"It's not that bad after a few hours. After a while, you get used to it."

Vye turned toward the familiar voice resonating from the shadows in the cell's corner. The man, chained to the cement wall by his waist, scooted slowly into the light, revealing his identity. It was El. She couldn't have been happier to see him. She attempted to reach for him, needing his embrace. The bruises caused her to groan in agony. Immediately, he crawled to her side.

"Easy now. You've been hurt. I'm here."

Vye nodded, caught her breath, and attempted to sit upright again. "The Ancestors told me about the trick. We have to defeat Dame and The Guide. The Elder women have formed a separatist movement. We've birthed human children. You have a younger brother now. Have they sent a messenger yet?" she blurted in one breath.

Immediately, El put his fingers to his lips. "Shh... the walls have ears," he said with a wave of his hand. Instead he leaned over and began forming looping letters in the dry dirt with his right index finger.

Can you walk? He wrote hurriedly in short hand.

Yes. She wrote back.

Guards changed. Key outside. He gestured toward the key hanging just outside the cell block door. *Must leave now. They don't see you as threat. I cannot go. Will get you out.* He threw her a penetrating gaze now and paused before writing furiously again. Her eyes began to tear. *I can't go mother. Must believe we gave up. See you at Mer Sea.* He reiterated.

Vye nodded and extended her hands. Carefully, he reached for a small blade hidden in the ground under a pile of dirt and cut the ropes binding her feet and hands together. Ignoring the pain, Vye flung her arms around him as the tears streaked her cheeks. He embraced her heartily and whispered in her ear. "Go now!"

Slowly she rose and walked toward the door of the unguarded cell. Her stomach sinking, she watched as he pushed himself back into the shadows. Immediately she squat low to the ground, skirted the cement prison walls, and moved undetected and out of sight.

10

THE BATTLE OF OASIS FALLS

"How long did you say we'd be?" Quince asked while sharpening a spear on a nearby stone.

"I told the messenger seven days. It gives us time to travel to the Falls, collect Dez and take care of business there, then regroup and travel to the Sea."

"What did you say to hold them off?"

"I told them we needed time to gather the women together," Maal replied with a shrug. "It was believable. They realize Taste only ended days ago. It's been tradition to return to Nu in preparation for the journey to The Enlightened Lands. He's been through Taste before. Not only that, it's a full three days nonstop journey on foot to the northern territories alone. With our cavalcade, it would take nearly six. Seven days was more than fair on our behalf."

Quince looked back at the shining blade and angled it against his thumb, drawing a steady stream of blood. Satisfied with its sharpness, he turned to Maal again. "And they have no idea where we are? They are convinced most of us are back at Nu?" he questioned with concern.

Maal shook his head with a fair amount of confidence. "With the bug destroyed, they don't know where we are, or where we are headed. We have seized the upper hand. Once the battle begins, they will be completely surprised."

"How do you think we'll fare against the Sphinx?" Quince shouted over the clank of metal, the shuffling of bags, and the battle cries of the sparring women in a clearing in the distance. "What's your honest prediction?"

"All we can do is hope for the best. The Sphinx are skilled, but lacking in stamina. Luckily we have some unlikely allies that can provide some insight into how they were nearly defeated twenty years ago." Maal looked up at the butterfly dragon hovering above his ear. Its shimmering blue wings were flapping at such a fast pace; it looked as if it were standing still.

"It is to our advantage however that we've been to the Falls before," Quince replied. "Our platoons should plan to rendezvous near the walkway entrance Heru guided us through when we sought medicines for Dez."

"That would be wise."

The entire Youth Cause moved swiftly along the banks of the Shine. It was high noon and the sweltering heat descended upon them like a swarm of angry bees. Swords and spears were sharpened and burnished until they gleamed in the stingy sunlight. Leather shields were repaired for battle and bows were strung and restrung tightly in preparation.

Quince stepped back from his craftsmanship and took a long look at his company. The women were in the tiptop shape he expected and the men wore the stony facades appropriate for wartime. He hoped they'd be in time to collect Dez. He had been concerned with their meager time frame, but now that they'd secured a week to travel and do battle, he could breathe again. Still, he prayed silently to the Ancestors. In order for the war to be won, they had little room for error.

"General Quince, your shield has been repaired."

Quince glanced in the direction of the soft voice floating toward him and smiled broadly. Even covered in sweat and dirt, she was breathtaking. Clothed in the customary moss green Ido female battle gear, she walked toward him with a smile.

"Thank you," he smiled. "Is the female battalion ready? You all have been sparring since dawn."

"As ready as we're going to be," she uttered with confidence.

Maal cleared his throat loudly, breaking up the beginnings of a gushing and *very* forbidden exchange. "Quince can I see you for a moment please?"

Startled, Quince jumped up and obliged Maal's request. The two men walked side by side to a deserted nook in the forest away from curious eyes and listening ears. Once they were well out of earshot he placed a firm hand on his shoulder, his soft expression suddenly turning to ice.

"She should not go," he said shortly.

Quince merely stared and sighed. He took a few moments to rearrange his thought patterns. "She is one of the three Generals of the female Youth. She is vital to the efforts of the Cause, not to mention a formidable warrior. The women would not want to be left out of the battle. Their pregnancies are in their early stages; the merchildren will not suffer in their wombs unless they are killed in battle. On what basis do you make this request?"

Maal was slow to answer. "I fear that she may distract you. I've observed the way the two of you interact." He said gently, easing up a little. "No good could come from her possibly being injured or killed in--"

"Do you really think I'd allow my state of mind to be altered during a battle? You have seen me fight! You are very much aware that, next to you, I am the best warrior we have!" Quince's piercing gaze glittered with indignation."

Maal sighed deeply, knowing where the discussion would lead. "You must be more discreet. If any of the members of the Cause begin to suspect that the two of you are in--"

Quince cut him short before he could complete the accusation. "She is my preferred partner. There is nothing in the law of the land that states we are unable to speak to our preferred partners! We will be fighting side by side in battle soon. I never admitted to loving anyone, if you remember clearly," he shot back defiantly.

Maal glared at him icily. It was the first time Quince had ever challenged him regarding his love for Onya. He stood without speaking for a while, debating his next move. "Are you denying that you love her?"

Quince stepped aside in rage and turned back in the direction in which they had come. Briskly, he began to walk away. "She will go with us and fight. We will be discreet… for the sake of the Cause…" his voice trailed off and he promptly turned on his heels.

***

"Cover me… now!"

Quince found himself whirling around in circles trying to watch his back and those of the Cause members and Butterfly Dragon allies. He bent low to the ground, sloshed through the roaring waterfall, and followed Virgo, the butterfly dragon, Onya, Lyn, and Clay into a nearby cave. The confusion around them was brutal. Powerful bombs fell into the surrounding knee-high water at the base of the rock face causing liquid explosions while arrows whizzed dangerously close. After hours of steady fighting, it finally looked as if they'd managed to penetrate the Sphinx outer line of defense. All around him, the large, shaggy bodies of dead or severely injured Sphinx lie in the red tinged water. As had been discussed, they were to meet Maal and his platoon at the entranceway to the city. Struggling to remember its exact location, Quince breathed deeply in an attempt to block out the chaos around them.

"Hold on, I remember this!" Quince whispered. Carefully, he closed his eyes and willed his memory back to the day Heru had accompanied them through the vast labyrinths of the Oasis Falls. In his mind's eye he saw the four of them inside a round, glass tube. El and Maal were carrying Dez on a makeshift stretcher while Quince stood near a railing. Heru's black paw searched for an indentation in the wall and they'd begun to move. Instantly, his eyes flew open. "Follow me." The others looked at one another in surprise but chose not to question him as they commenced to skirt the close nooks in the belly of the enormous cliff. Every turn seemed to sprout a dead end; twice he was forced to retrace his steps. On alert with their weapons cocked and ready, the foursome followed him silently and obediently.

Just then, he caught sight of the round, glass tube about ten feet away. He motioned for them to crowd onto the cracked, paved walkway partially covered with water. In an unexpected blur, they found themselves in a scuffle.

"Move and she dies!" said a burly, blond haired Sphinx.

Quince whirled around at once. Onya was in the Sphinx's clutches, his sturdy bow smashed against her neck as he held a pointed blade to her cheek. Quince shot a fierce gaze in Onya's direction, communicating with her wordlessly to stay calm. She shook her head slightly and stood rigid in the grip of the powerful beast behind her.

Quince quickly scanned the small group with him. Virgo hovered just above his right ear, while Clay stood frozen on his left. Where was Lyn? Had she joined another group and not told him? His mind was racing with concern now as he projected all his thoughts toward saving Onya's life. They had to make the right moves. Mistakes could not be afforded.

"Drop your weapons… Now!" the beast yelled.

The three comrades dropped their weapons immediately. There was a splash as they dropped in the running water. Then he motioned toward Virgo, who continued to flit about noiselessly. "Him too," he gestured. "Get rid of it dragon if you want her to live!" Virgo dropped a string of tiny grenades from beneath its wings and focused its attention back on Onya and her captor.

"Look…" Quince began in a compromising tone. "All we need to do is think of a way that this can go…"

"*Real smoothly*," shrieked a defiant voice from behind the Sphinx. Suddenly, Onya was released from his grip. Lyn stepped from behind the large creature as its eyes rolled in its head before tipping over with a significant splash. Her bow held high, Lyn winked at them before bending over to pull the bloody arrow from the back of its head.

"Perfect timing huh?" she smiled as the rest of the group exhaled and retrieved their weapons from the sloshing pool.

Onya shot her friend a thankful look before gathering her soaked broadsword. "Couldn't let my best friend die now could I?" Lyn pinched her arm and winked. "Do we know Maal's location?" she asked anxiously.

Quince secured the leather quiver on his back before answering. "The plan was to meet at the entranceway of the city," he said while pointing toward the partially hidden walkway. "However, they may have been forced into the city ahead of time. It is a strong possibility that they've already been here and are expecting us to provide backup."

Quickly, he scoured the surrounding area. A mousy haired Sphinx lay dying near his shin, its' eyelids fluttering rapidly. Quince sidestepped the dying creature and gazed at the wide slit descending from its throat to its navel. Onya and Clay looked away from the grisly sight as Quince continued to stare.

"He's been here already. I recognize his handiwork," he remarked after pushing the limp figure aside with his foot. "Let's move."

The indentation in the wall hadn't been difficult to locate as they rounded the corner. Once it had been depressed, the group began moving at an incline through the rock. All was quiet as they glided along wordlessly, the sounds from the pounding waterfall drowning out the small squeak of the conveyor belt. The dankness of the rock soon gave way to glass. Quince leaned over to get a look at the world outside of them. Gazing through the glass, he saw the tops of trees and the brilliant green of the grasslands. The ferocious battle continued below. Quince recognized a small platoon of female Youth bravely engaged with a group of Sphinx soldiers. He quickly looked away, not wanting to helplessly witness the deaths of any of his warriors. Though they'd been trained well, death was an imminent byproduct of war. All of them would not make it.

Unfortunately though, the others hadn't taken heed. Onya's loud gasp caused him to turn back to the ensuing battle below. He immediately identified two of the women. Eesha and Lore had been surrounded.

"Don't watch!" he commanded. "There is nothing we can do for them up here!"

But he had given his advice too late. All eyes were now transfixed on the scene as it unfolded, closed off and totally out of their reach. The two women were fighting gallantly, side by side. Lore both defended and attacked with her ebony bow. Quince looked on in awe as she squatted low, leaned back on her haunches, and released several arrows expertly. At her side, Eesha landed several hard blows with her mace. Then, in slow motion, something went terribly wrong. More Sphinx warriors began to descend upon the battling tandem. One of the male Sphinx managed to grab Lore by one of her arms. In a swift motion, he jerked her body backward just as one of her arms fell limp. They watched on in horror as the creature swung her around like a rag doll. They could feel the intensity of the battle just like they were there experiencing it themselves. Lore was lying in the water now, totally immobile. Lyn's eyes grew large. They were barely able to contain their gasps. Suddenly, Lore's assailant reached over for a sword someone had dropped in the swirling waterfall. His strong hands grasped its hilt and aimed for Lore's limp body. At the last possible second, Eesha rolled on top of her, attempting to move the injured woman out of the way. What occurred was unthinkable. The small group watched in horror as the Sphinx threw his arms back in calculated laughter and trotted away. Eesha laid there, a broad, shining blade sticking awkwardly from her back. Lore lay beneath her, still.

Their cries stalled and sputtered. No one seemed to have been able to find the voices in their throats. A haunting echo remained for what seemed like hours. Then came the tears, flowing in buckets, pouring down like torrential rain and hail. Quince cradled the two women as they stood, peering through the glass, barely able to stand, eyes wide with disbelief.

"They would want us to go on." Quince murmured, trying to contain his own emotions. Time elapsed slowly and their movement stalled.

A sudden crash disturbed their mourning as Quince glanced up ahead. Quickly, he gathered his wits. They were nearing the very spot where he'd seen the liquid cells during his first visit. Immediately he put an index finger to his lips and signaled for their attention. The glass that had once sealed the rooms from the hollow tunnel had been shattered. Intermittent shouts could be heard echoing from the walls. Lithely, he jumped over the moving railing and into the room now littered with destruction and motioned for the others to do the same.

The room's contents were in total disarray. Dead bodies lie helterskelter amongst massive puddles of water, twisted metal, arrows, abandoned swords, spears, and broken glass. Immediately, he turned his attention toward the broken glass tank. Slowly, they crept closer to the voices now becoming nearer.

"Tell us why!" echoed a male voice vehemently. "Tell us now!"

Quince relaxed his stance and began to jog toward the commotion. The others followed wordlessly, cheeks still streaked with tears but pressing on.

"I don't know! I said... I... don't know!" screamed a second male, his voice terror stricken.

Soon they were in full view of the scene. A group of listless Stripes and Butterfly Dragons looked on, dazed, near one of the large shattered cells as Dez, Maal, and the Sphinx leader loomed into view. Ankh's face had been smashed against a large pillar. He'd been chained to the fixture by his torso and neck. The man's spectacles were cracked and askew and his bushy hair was littered with bits of mud and blood. Standing next to him was Maal, his broadsword drawn and aimed at the struggling Sphinx's temple. Dez looked on, his countenance holding the remnants of unhealthy exhaustion. Upon their entrance, Maal looked up from the captive and smiled immediately at the sight of Lyn. The grin thinned into a line at the sight of Quince and Onya. Quince returned the frigid greeting with a near frown of his own.

In a quick flurry, Dez stepped forward and drew his own sword from the sheath strewn tightly across his back. "Please allow me to do the honors!" he said angrily.

Maal stepped aside as he brought the tip of the powerful blade to Ankh's already swollen cheek and completed a carving motion. A steady stream of blood oozed down the length of the blade while Ankh wrenched in pain.

"I…was working… for Dame," he spat out painfully.

Still unsatisfied with his answer, Dez dug deeper drawing more blood. "And…"

"He said he needed to bug one of you… but we weren't sure how," he stammered.

Dez gave the sniveling man a sinister grin. "Continue!" he demanded with brute force.

"One of our informants overheard your meeting at Nu. We knew the male Youth would be traveling toward Glo City, so we captured a group of high-ranking Stripes and herded them here. The Stripes were needed for two reasons. First of all, we needed the strong to vacate the city. We know their allegiance to the Youth. Secondly, the Elders needed their expertise in hologram and light effects. It was the only way they could effectively trap you once inside the city. We paid the Diaw to lead you into the trap," he sputtered as he spit out blood. "We counted on at least one of you getting injured and needing us for surgery. When you were brought to us, we knew you were the one we'd have to plant the bug in. Our orders were to get one of the triplets if possible. We needed to be able to track the Youth closest to their leaders." Ankh sputtered between exhausted breaths.

Quince continued to take it all in. Though the entire puzzle still had a few large gaps, things were becoming clearer. The faces of the others seemed to brighten as they began to piece together clues based on Ankh's confessions.

                    B. Sharise Moore

Dez retracted his sword, wiped the blood from the blade with a cloth, and returned it to its sheath. "What was in it for you?" he asked quietly.

Ankh continued to breathe heavily, but took his time answering.

"What was in it for you?" he repeated in a shrill tone that echoed throughout the room.

"Survival," the old man replied quietly. "We need to survive."

"I've heard enough," Dez said with a wave of his hand. "Get him out of here!" He snapped his fingers as two Ido Youth unchained the prisoner and led him toward a door in the corner. "Let's get to the root of this. No more questioning the low men on the totem pole," he said while leering after Ankh. "I want Dame."

"No. Don't! We need them alive. I know how you feel, but they need to be alive!" Quince gasped.

Dez wheeled around in time to see Lyn angling her bow in front of her and Onya standing proudly, her fingers gripping a small sword. Lips quivering, their faces remained hard and unapologetic.

Immediately, Quince ran to Onya and placed a firm hand on her shoulder. Her short gasps and blinding tears punctured his spirit as he watched the pain and attempted to quell it. Maal in turn, ran to Lyn, his heavy hand grasping the readied bow aimed for fire.

"We will have our revenge, Onya. *You* will have it," Quince murmured softly in her ear before moving his hand down her arm toward the hilt of the heavy bronze handled sword. Slowly she gave in to his pleas, her arm lowering carefully before the floodgate of tears gave way to incessant sobs. Maal and Dez looked around in bewilderment as did Ankh, whose disposition was a cross between utter fear and outright relief. Not wanting to be the bearer of bad news, Quince looked away from his brother's drained expression.

"What is it?" Dez asked in a shrill voice. "Who…when?"

"Eesha…" Quince croaked with difficulty. "And Lore. Just a few minutes ago, we couldn't help them." Quince sputtered as a pang of guilt echoed through him. "They were together."

Dez wiped his mouth with the back of his hand. His eyes screamed a fury all their own as he crumpled in front of them. The entire room stilled for a few moments while they grieved. Soon though, Dez rose from his kneeling position and exhaled sharply. "We fight. We win. Any other result is unacceptable."

11

HONEY, HERBS, AND MOURNING

There is no easy way to say goodbye to a friend. Knowing that the physical aspect of a person is forever gone was a difficult concept to grasp; even for the Ido whose dead were given the opportunity to live again as Ancestors. The steady hum of insects singing in the trees provided the soundtrack for their mourning. Conversation was nearly nonexistent as they gathered at the mouth of the Shine River below the massive cliff. Onya looked up to the sky for answers and mused in the direction of the structure that had once been the Oasis Falls. The hustle and bustle was no more. Instead, broken glass, errant weapons, twisted, waterlogged corpses, and the stench of day old battle remained. She tread through the drenched debris carefully, sullenly collecting weapons that could possibly be repaired, refurbished, and used in the future. She also had the daunting task of helping to identify more of their dead or seriously wounded. She wrinkled her nose as the putrid smell of flesh and blood combined with the crisp, new air of dawn. It was a day many of her people would not see through the same eyes again.

Her existence suddenly seemed surreal. The watershed began again as the tears welled in the corners of her eyes and streaked the sides of her face. A tiny smile met her lips when she recalled the talent, bravery, and sacrifice of her long time friend. Eesha had been loyal and kind and artistic. One of the last conversations she'd ever had with her was one of the most selfless Onya had ever heard. After Lore had lost her initial pleasure mate to the Battle at Glo City and joined she and Dez, Eesha had never complained. Instead, she'd chosen to welcome the grieving woman and take into account the bigger picture. Eesha had never seen Lore's presence as a hindrance. In the end, she died trying to protect the woman who'd inadvertently disrupted a perfect union. The irony was almost too much to bear.

Dez stood a few feet from her in an obvious daze. She hadn't taken into account that he'd suffered the loss of both of his preferred partners who were without a doubt pregnant with his unborn Merchildren. Quince stood nearby, coaxing him to eat or drink some of the rations he'd pulled from a heavy bag. His eyes held concern. Dez appeared to be totally unresponsive, yet still he offered solace and gentle healing with his presence.

Because of the sound defeat of the Sphinx, they were able to gather their dead without disturbance. They found the bodies floating as they'd last seen them. Lyn commented softly that it had looked as if they'd gone peacefully. To this, Onya offered no reply. Eesha would never stand at her side again and for this, she felt hurt, shortchanged. As she thought to herself, she came to the painful realization that Eesha may have been the one friend she could have disclosed her feelings to and she deeply regretted not doing so. Eesha possessed a level of understanding that Lyn lacked. Where Lyn stood rigid and firm in her beliefs, Eesha had been more likely to entertain an alternative viewpoint. Though she may not agree, she respected differences in opinion like no other.

The ache in her spirit writhed from the loss. Her thoughts seemed to spiral endlessly. The clang of metal nearby brought her unwillingly back to the present. Immediately, she thought of the specific offering she'd have to prepare for Eesha if they ever needed to consult her and smiled.

"Certainly frankincense," she thought aloud. "And possibly peppermint... something blue." Blue had always been her favorite color.

"Who are you talking to?" Lyn asked, puzzled.

Onya looked over at her remaining female friend and smiled. "I was just thinking about the kind of offering we'd use to call Eesha after she crosses into the realm of the Ancestors." Lyn smiled longingly and produced a teary-eyed laugh.

"Something artistic for sure, but Ancestor knows I can't draw!" The two women doubled over in laughter.

"Me neither!" Onya said heartily.

They turned to one another simultaneously and embraced with heavy hearts crying out, asking why, and finally accepting that their dear friend would never walk the island of Ido again.

***

The return voyage to Three Wood was slow and difficult. Onya and Lyn looked to their mates and each other for consolation. After the bodies had been wrapped in enormous Thine leaves, they set off downstream toward the western edge of the Shine in a solemn processional. Ido, Stripes, and Butterfly

Dragons mourned their dead side by side. By the time they'd reached Three Wood, the Painted Folk had joined the morose death march. Gallah led the way, nodding sorrowfully in Onya's direction after she'd noticed Eesha's body among the dead.

The Cause members threw fruit, herbs, and flowers into the river. Sweet elixirs and honey were also poured into the water as it ebbed and flowed in the high noon sky. It was their hope that the Afterlife would bring them sweetness, beauty, and contentment while they dwelled in Erruk and beyond. By the ceremony's end, the Shine looked like a liquid rainbow filled with vivid color and sweet aroma. Lyn and Onya choked back tears as they gazed upon Eesha's floating body wrapped in large, burgundy leaves. She resembled a butterfly engulfed in a wondrous cocoon. Her color was clear and her smile calm as she drifted; bronze mace nestled beneath her elbows. Onya could barely form the words for a proper farewell.

The moment the ceremony came to a close, she felt the urgent need to be alone. It didn't take much for her to escape. Everyone was reeling from the massive amount of loss. No one was speaking, and questioning was very unlikely, so she walked. A clearing further downstream caught her attention. From there, a clear view of Triple Peak stood in the distance to the west and the Amber Cliffs just south of it.

Sudden movement out of the corner of her eye alerted her to lurking danger. Instinctively, she grabbed hold of her sword and braced herself. In a wild flurry of wind, sound, and flailing arms, she found herself surrounded. Ten women jumped from the trees and encircled her on all sides. Their hooded tops shielded their faces and the thin fabric of their pants rustled in the wind. She could only gather that they were members of the Elder Army. One of the women was tall and strikingly familiar. On edge and staring at Onya's raised sword, she carefully stepped forward and spoke. Onya kept her eyes peeled for attack. If they were foolish enough to do so, she'd be prepared to defend herself and take a few lives. No matter what, she'd go down swinging.

"Onya, daughter of Dame and General of the female Youth," the woman began. "We come in---"

Onya's heartbeat quickened and pure, fiery adrenaline took over. Before the woman could finish, she pounced. In a sudden flash of fury she lunged at the seemingly unarmed leader of the group. Eyes wide with surprise, she fell into a backward roll and returned to her feet. The others retrieved various weapons from hidden sheaths in their clothing and stood poised for battle. The woman held up her hand however and signaled for them to back off.

"Put back your weapons," she said sternly. "I can settle this one alone."

In an instant she pulled off her hood, revealing her face. Onya felt the slender fingers of fear clawing away at her confidence. Standing before her was Eyeno, the island's female Bgongo master. Not far behind stood Quince's mother Vye, and Lyn's mother Dina. The two women began to circle one another.

"Put down your weapon… *now,*" Eyeno commanded sharply.

"I am an Ido warrior, and will never surrender to an enemy. *You* taught me that many years ago." Onya replied in a sharp retort.

"I can kill you and I don't want to do that." The woman said with a calm confidence as they continued their war dance.

"You are already killing us. The Elders have chosen to accept a blind faith without reason. My fellow General, a woman I considered a sister died yesterday because of your stupidity," Onya countered. She felt her bottom lip quiver as fresh images of Eesha flashed through her mind.

Startled, Eyeno stood upright and held up her hand. "You don't--"

She could not, would not allow the woman to complete her statement. Something within her snapped as she lunged forward with her sword.

Eyeno dodged her advances expertly, but Onya quickly recovered. Another swing of her blade came within inches of Eyeno's face and before Onya could register the events that had occurred, she'd managed to knock away and capture her sword. Weaponless and panting Onya fell into Bgongo stance. Eyeno obliged and dropped the captured sword with a heavy clang. Onya charged first, sending a flying kick to Eyeno's chest. She missed her mark and hit the dirt hard. Eyeno responded with a swift, sweeping low kick before Onya could regain her footing. Unsettled dirt flew up from the ground and swirled around her as she struggled to stay in the battle. Eyeno relaxed a bit just as Onya landed a circular kick to her gut. The woman doubled over in pain before gathering herself and landing a short, sharp jab to Onya's face. She saw the blood fly as her lip split. Filthy and bleeding, Onya stared at the woman wild-eyed, a look of pure unadulterated hatred etched across her face. Her heart began to thump loudly. She could hear it resonating in her eardrums while her pulse throbbed almost painfully in her veins. She was winded, but still managed to hurl herself head first into the woman's midsection. They wrestled for a moment as Onya felt herself buckling under the woman's strength. In a matter of seconds, she was lying on her stomach and writhing in pain. Her cheek under Eyeno's foot and pressed to the dirt now, she sensed that the end was near.

"Finish it quickly," she whispered as Eyeno released her weight.

She lay there with a prayer in her heart, knowing she'd gone out with a fight. She would be remembered as a loyal protector of Taste. Quince would be broken, but he'd live. They would be better off without their love complicating the quest to end the war and restore tradition. She waited for the final swipe of the blade, expected the whoosh of the sharp steel as it sliced through the air ending her existence as she knew it. Several more moments passed until she dared to peer up from the rain forest floor.

"Get up."

Onya turned a swollen eye upward. Standing above her was Vye, Quince's mother. She could do nothing more than stare, breathless and defeated.

"Where are the Youth?"

"How... do I know... it's not a trick?" she stammered stubbornly.

Vye sighed before placing a hand on her back. "Because she could have... *would* have killed you if we were members of the Elder Army." Carefully, she lifted Onya to her feet and glanced at her stomach.

"Are you with child? I know the Taste Rites have concluded."

"I am," Onya muttered without looking at the woman.

"Well... at least it is a Merchild. You cannot miscarry." Vye stated softly before taking a long pause. "Who is your preferred partner?"

Onya took a long look at the woman before speaking. The striking resemblance to her sons was amazing. Wordlessly, she studied the cheekbones, skin and welcoming eyes. "Your son, Quince."

"Where are they?" Eyeno chimed in, interrupting the bonding session impatiently.

"Just upstream," she said feebly while pointing eastward. "We just let go of our dead. There was a battle at Oasis Falls, many died."

Vye rubbed her back and sighed. Onya was surprised at how much it calmed her.

"Then we go to them." Eyeno said, her tone short. Though she'd been convinced the woman was not an enemy, Onya remained intimidated. A part of her almost felt silly, but she hadn't known that some members of the Elder Clan had decided to break away from Dame and The One Faith.

"We are members of the Separatist Movement," Eyeno said as if reading her mind. "We have seen the error in our ways. Our desire is to restore tradition. We are on the same side. I tried to give you than information before you attacked me."

Onya didn't answer. Instantly, she knew was wrong. She'd tried to speak to her several times and she hadn't allowed it. Her emotions had gotten the best of her. She was lucky to still have her life. On Eyeno's command, the women walked in the direction Onya communicated with a flaming orange backdrop behind them.

12

DISCOVERY AT KEEP

"Do you think the surrender is genuine?" Dame asked, scrambling through the ankle high grasses of Keep.

"We can only be on guard. Trickery is common during war," replied the hooded figure next to him.

"If I may, General," stated the lieutenant in their midst. "Perhaps the Youth were seeking vengeance for the bug. There is a strong possibility that they are not aware that we were the ones who directed Ankh to secure it in one of the males."

Dame nodded while pondering Ka's words. "This is true. I cannot blame them for seeking revenge against The Sphinx for what they believed to be true. As long as they reach us within the seven-day deadline, I will honor their surrender. With their co-General as my prisoner, I hold the ultimate bargaining chip. If anything goes awry, he dies in front of them."

"And your wife..." Ka questioned carefully.

Dame spat angrily. "If she accompanies them, she dies regardless of their surrender. Her deceit is a separate betrayal and I shall treat it as such."

It was a breezy, gray day. The meager sunlight lit the sky only sporadically while the short grasses swayed lazily from side to side. Two entire days had elapsed since the massacre at the Oasis Falls, and Dame was eager for answers. Heartbroken and hardened by Vye's deception, he'd thrown all his efforts into winning the war and caring for Rahm, his newborn son. The three men broke into a light jog when the structure loomed into view. Dame could hardly control his awe as he neared the giant building made of circular panes of glass. From afar, it held the luminescence of an over scaled, sphere-shaped kaleidoscope. It sat there in an open nook, untouched and weighty like a giant glass blown beach ball.

"We discovered it just last night. Over here... come," said Ka, gesturing ahead.

"When was this constructed? I'm sure I've never seen it. I thought I knew this island backward and forward," Dame exclaimed aloud as he paced around its perimeter.

"Perhaps you did not consider that there are other dimensions to recognize such as sideways and long ways and diagonal," called a misty voice from behind him.

"Yes, you are right as always." Dame replied humbly.

"I am but a man and messenger of the One. However, I realize that I remain severely limited due to the flesh surrounding my spirit. You cannot expect to know everything General," the man said gently.

Dame shook his head and turned toward the thin man standing by his side. The Guide stood there, quiet and observing as was his demeanor. His face was covered three quarters of the way by a navy blue hood as was custom. The long robes he wore billowed with the wind. The clinging fabric revealed the totality of his gauntness and reiterated an inferred daintiness and fragility, though he was clearly male.

"You are correct." Dame said after he'd roamed the front of the glass building.

"Pray that the One will humble you. Though you have come a long way, there remains room for growth." He paused, paying close attention to Dame's reaction to his chastisement. "You must remember, that the word faith loosely means to grow."

He nodded obediently, but continued to focus on the building in front of them. "So... this is the Sphinx's playground, huh? A home away from home," Dame mused, half amazed, half disturbed. "When did you find it?"

Lieutenant Ka pulled his shoulders back and saluted him before speaking. Lazily, Dame motioned for him to answer quickly, thus dropping all unnecessary formalities. "During the early morning hours, sir. The covert team you deployed thought it may be easier to enter the Falls from the north rather than directly. That specific route led us through the Keep Grasslands and here."

"I see." Immediately he turned toward The Guide. "The entrance seems sealed. How do you think the Sphinx entered? There has to be a way for us to get inside and gain a clue as to what they were up to."

The Guide put a slender index finger to his chin as if in deep thought. "The Sphinx were obsessed with science, which is loosely governed by mathematics. Judging from the shape of this structure, I'd say that we might need to consider the degrees within a circle," he said scanning the sphere shaped building. "Circles are abundant in nature. Blood, pigment, cells, atoms, are all circular in form."

Dame ran his palms across the colorful glass panes and shut his eyes. Willing himself to concentrate, he honed in on the creature's way of thinking. Hurriedly, he recalled all the conversations he'd had with Ankh. He was brilliant, no doubt; the span of his knowledge only eclipsed by The Painted Folk of Three Wood. His eyes fluttered rapidly and flew open. Of course, a circle contained degrees.

"Is there any pane that looks abnormal to you? Do any of them stand out in any way? I don't mean just in size either. It could be irregularities in shape or color too." he called to his two companions. Both Ka and The Guide began surveying the circular panes intently. Some time elapsed before The Guide called him over to where he stood.

Just as Dame had speculated, there lay a purple, oval shaped pane. Carefully, he placed his hand over it. It grew warm and glowed for a few seconds before anything happened. Quickly, Dame released his hand and stared as a ten-foot high and seven feet wide area of glass sunk inward and shifted to the right revealing a sizable entrance. The three men carefully scanned the inside of the structure for activity before cautiously stepping inside the circular threshold.

The dimness inside occasionally caught fire and lit up the place when a single ray of light hit the colorful panes. Luckily, the day was severely overcast otherwise Dame didn't know how his eyes would have acclimated to the brightness. Several round glass tables were situated throughout the open space. In the center of the tables sat large Petri dishes filled with glimmering jewels ranging from precious diamonds, rubies, and emeralds to semi-precious topaz, garnet, and aquamarine under large bubble-like covers.

"It's a laboratory," Dame mumbled in a hush before taking a look around the place.

"A geological laboratory to be exact." The Guide replied.

Dame continued to scour their surroundings with his eyes as he walked. It looked as if it had recently been used. Not a speck of dust covered the sterilized tables or floors. He took it all in bit by bit. Since his alliance with the Sphinx, he'd never known Ankh to keep anything from him. Part of their pact was to share intelligence that would protect their people. Inwardly, he cursed himself for trusting the deceptive creature. It was not in their blood to be loyal. Seconds later, he retracted his sweeping assumptions. After all, he hadn't shared *every* single Ido secret with him. The hidden laboratory didn't necessarily mean Ankh had been plotting against him. He recalled the Sphinx paranoia over their survival on the island. Nearly every waking moment of the day was spent experimenting through the use of microbiology and genetics to prolong their short life span. Then he saw it, couldn't believe he hadn't seen it before. In the middle of the room was a large table. Again, a Petri dish sat in its center. However, pillars of amethyst stones sat in the middle. Immediately Dame walked toward it, as if it were calling him, drawing him closer. The Guide and his lieutenant were already standing beside it. Ka was looking through a stack of papers he'd found lying nearby.

"What are those?" Dame questioned, motioning to the papers.

"I... I don't think you want to know General." Ka said slowly.

Suddenly overcome with anger, Dame grabbed the papers from his shaking hands.

His eyes focused on the strange markings and diagrams on the papyrus page. He understood nothing but the etching of an Ido's anatomy in the page's center. "What is this?" he asked The Guide.

The Guide stood over him and looked closely. "Hieroglyphics. It is written in hieroglyphics."

"Well, that much I can gather. What does it say?"

The Guide inhaled deeply and turned away. "We have been crossed," he said slowly.

Dame's eyes grew wide. "What? No! How?" he said, the ferocity in his voice becoming more and more distinct.

"Do you know of any of the uses of amethyst?" The Guide asked, his back now turned to the two Elders.

"Yes," Dame shook his head fervently. "We used it during the final Rite of Taste to---" his voice trailed off in embarrassment. Though he was sure The Guide had been made aware of their perversions; he hadn't wanted to admit them aloud.

"Then you are aware of its propensity to affect the crown and brow chakras?"

"Yes, but I was under the impression it was a calming stone. We've collected them for the One Temple. They are draped throughout the entire sanctuary!" he said, flustered.

"Calming yes, the amethyst quartz is a powerful meditation tool, but in the wrong hands..." The Guide didn't finish.

"What are you saying?" Dame asked roughly.

"I'm saying that just as Ankh tainted the herbs. It is quite possible that he did the same with the stones." The Guide pointed upward toward the ceiling. "Stones can be altered with a mixture of chemicals and light. It is very clear that they've been altering these stones."

Dame wrinkled his nose with deepening thought. "Mind control, but why?" I feel no adverse effects of it. If the crystals were indeed altered, they had no effect on us, correct?"

"It seems that we may have been lucky," the hooded figure said slowly while Ka and Dame looked on with concern. "Very lucky."

13

BORN AGAIN

"I do not think you should make the journey with us mother! The stakes are too high!" Dez shot back sternly. "Your treachery and ours will be considered differently. Seeing you will be nothing more than a distraction! I am a General, I can think as he does!"

"I agree with Dez mother," said Quince calmly. "We have to think about El. Without a doubt, Dame will have him tied to a stake with a blade in his chest if we make one wrong move. Your presence and the presence of any of the Elder women would cause catastrophic results."

The council roared to life before Maal held up a tired hand to signal order. The civil war was beginning to take its toll and though they sensed it would soon be over; it didn't soothe things in the least. The surviving members of the Youth Cause and the Separatist Movement, along with The Painted Folk, Stripes, and a hovering swarm of Butterfly Dragons were seated in a clearing inside Three Wood. Two representatives from each group sat in the circle's interior, while the others observed from the perimeter. Brilliantly lit torches illuminated as the factions faced one another, allies and champions of tradition.

The sheen of Gallah's silver afro twinkled along with her eyes as Ohm sat beside her. Virgo, the Butterfly Dragon, Eyeno and Vye, Onya and Lyn, and Maal and Quince completed the inner circle. They were set to leave within the hour, but before then, careful planning amongst them was a must. Nothing could go wrong. They had no room for error and every single creature among them knew it.

"Why don't we follow at a safe distance then? We will not join the battle until well after it has begun," offered Eyeno. "Think of us as reinforcements."

Maal and Quince exchanged glances and appeared to concede. Lyn and Onya did the same. "We can accept that." The circle became enlivened again. Quince held up a hand, restoring order. "But... you *must* remain at a distance. The ruse cannot fall. The surrender must be believable."

"Then it is settled. The Youth Cause will set off in one hour. After another has elapsed, the rest of us will follow," Gallah said. The others nodded in agreement.

"Let's prepare. The end of the war is upon us," said Maal definitively.

***

Darkness was their cover as they walked along solemnly. Occasionally they rested on rocks, beneath trees, and inside secluded coves. Onya and Quince stole glances at one another not knowing if they'd see each other again after the battle. The closer they got to the lapping waves of the Mer Sea, the more intense the air around them became. A striking sliver of burgundy threatened to tear through the sky as the first inkling of daybreak appeared. Minutes later, the sun's rays peeled through the clouds, pushing them aside like an outer layer of unnecessary skin while the wind took to a steady bellow. In the distance, Quince caught sight of the towering pyramids of Vine City just ahead. Slowly, the large gathering of Elders on the beach came into view. They stood in neat ranks with their weapons drawn and ready for whatever may come. A wide wooden platform jutted out just behind their readied warriors. Three men stood atop the platform. A lanky figure dressed in dark colored robes stood between El and Dame. To his relief, his brother looked to be in good health. Quince's stomach tightened with anticipation.

Armed and on edge, the Youth Cause formed a solid line opposite the Elders on the sparkling sand. The crashing waves on the beach were the only sounds permeating the air. Quince noticed that El's wrists had been bound to one of the pillars on the wooden platform. With one final nod, the two male Generals sauntered forward and addressed the Elders standing before them.

"Why are you armed? I was led to believe this was a surrender." The Elder General bellowed from the platform.

"We are armed for the same reason that you are General. There is little trust between us. We are merely acting wisely, as you so humbly taught us all those years ago," challenged Maal.

"Maal… the Youth with the most potential. You reminded me so much of myself as a Youth. I am glad that you have chosen correctly."

"Unbind him!" Quince called out before gesturing toward El. "We have given you what you desire. Our end of the bargain has been fulfilled!"

"Certainly," The Elder General began slyly. "But that will come once we are satisfied with your surrender."

The members of the Cause murmured in low tones while keeping to their stoic stance. Many looked around questioningly while others shrugged or sighed in confusion.

"What more do you require from us?" asked Quince.

The Guide stepped forward slowly before speaking. His voice was like a light echo against the powerful sounds of the sea. "First you must accept the Faith. Bow and kneel please," he commanded. They obeyed with an instant and convincing flourish. "The One is all powerful and all knowing. The One requires obedience and faith in Him."

Quince's mind wandered as the foreigner spoke. How was he going to free El? One wrong movement and he'd die.

"...And in order for us to fulfill His wishes, we must defeat the Ancestors. They are the only obstacles left that stand in the way of our harmonies."

Quince's neck snapped to attention. Defeat the Ancestors. *This hadn't been a part of the bargain!* Still though, he remained quiet, sensing the uneasiness around him. They were growing restless. The pure gall of the man's rhetoric made him want to snap him in two. Obediently, the Cause members remained on their knees.

Maal spoke this time. "We will do anything to make sure our brother is returned to us safely. We recognize our wrongs, our perversions, our over indulgence and offer our souls to the One," he lied with conviction.

Visibly pleased, Dame stepped forward and gestured toward the Elder warriors in front of him. The Elder nearest the sea picked up a rotting log from the ground. Within seconds, he produced two sticks and began rubbing them together to produce flame. Sparks shot into the sky and the smoldering fragrance of incense floating on the breeze met his nose. The man leaned toward the rising tide and sent the burning log into the sea. It floated soundlessly, bobbing along with the soft waves.

They were summoning the Ancestors. They were calling them to war! Quince avoided Maal's astonished gaze and continued his guise of submission.

It all happened in slow motion. The waves stilled then stirred violently. A ferocious splash brought forth a giant, jet-black fin. Born appeared, his broad chest heaving in anger. He was not alone however. Countless colorful scales sliced through the waters as Mer Ancestors surrounded him on all sides. They swam closer to the beach in dismay and bobbed in the heavy current. The merman scoured the sand before him with his dark eyes. If he were surprised at the sight in front of him, he didn't show it. Instead, he focused his attention upon the Elders and the platform in front of him.

"How dare you summon us to witness your foolishness? How dare you demand that your sons and daughters become slaves to a foreign faith?" Born boomed loudly. The fierceness of his voice made many of the Elders and Youth alike shield their ears. "I am Born, leader of the Mer and you have committed an atrocity that will *not* be forgiven," he said as his arms and torso bulked in anger.

The Guide let out a maddening cackle, his once meek demure evaporating like vapor. "You must be destroyed. It is the only way," he shrieked.

Born roared in anger and with a giant flip of his fin sent a powerful rumble through the sea, ripping the earth. Everyone toppled to the ground. Screams and shouts of fear ensued as the fighting began.

"Attack!" screeched Dame from his position on the platform floor.

Quince felt the first arrow whiz past his ear. Instantaneously, he ducked and retrieved his own arrows from his quiver. Jets of light and flame flew above him while the Ancestors aimed fire and brimstone in the direction of the Elder Clan. The ground shook mercilessly beneath them. Quince struggled to hold his footing and settled on striking from a kneeling position on the ground. Distracted by the Ancestor's arsenal, the Elders hardly realized that they were fighting a two front battle. Still though, they were holding their own. Quince saw Clay struggling with an arrow sticking awkwardly from his right bicep as he crawled past in pursuit of El. Still bound, he saw him struggling to break free amid all the commotion. He'd been afforded the greatest diversion he could have imagined.

The moment the tremors ceased, Quince stood carefully. Heavy footfalls fell hard behind him and before he could react, a giant arm groped him in a choke hold. Quince felt his eyes begin to tear as he struggled with the man. They fell to their knees. He bit hard on his forearm and stabbed his thigh with a stray arrow on the ground. With a sickening grunt, the man fell, the hilt of a broadsword inserted into the small of his back. Onya smiled and retracted her sword before moving on to the next adversary. Quince acknowledged her conquest with obeisance and turned to locate El. The platform was vacant now of all three men. He turned wildly and released another flurry of arrows in the direction of Lyn as she grappled bravely with a stocky male Elder.

Quince made a valiant attempt to block out the blinding lights and powerful earthquakes as he tried to locate his brother. Dez and Maal were getting the better of two Elders in his periphery and Onya was covering Vye's back. Quince doubled back to the colorful scene as it unfolded before him. They'd joined the fight. Their allies had made it there soundly. He'd been so caught up with the battle at hand, he'd forgotten about their reinforcements. The Painted Folk were disarming the enemy left and right with their bows. Gallah held a pair of long, thin Ero swords in each of her hands, their winding, snake-like blades gleaming with the crimson color of freshly drawn blood.

He looked up proudly and located El in a fierce battle with the Elder who'd prepared the offering. Completely unarmed, he was now relying on his raw Bgongo skills for protection. Firing arrows here and there to fight off the enemy and cover his allies, he ran to El's aid. When he reached within feet of the two men, he stepped back and fired his arrows with deadly precision. The man stopped short and teetered toward the broken platform, holding on for dear life. El looked around wildly and ran to Quince's side. A broad smile spread gleefully on his face. Quince jogged over to the dead Elder and retrieved a sword from the ground and thrust it in El's quivering hand. They exchanged a knowing glance and then turned to run toward the front lines of the brawl.

From where he stood, Quince could make out Born as he spewed lava and molten rock in the Elders' direction. Behind him, Fateem and the other female Ancestors were summoning Afe, the Djinn incarnated as wind and rain on their assailants. The sky turned dark and lightening struck the wooden platform, sending splinters and pieces of broken wood into the air. Thunder shook the ground again. Quince lost his balance and fell face first onto the warm sand. One of the vine pyramids split apart and fell crashing to the ground on top of several members of the Allied Forces. A chaos like he'd never seen before broke out as warriors began ducking the flying arrows, swinging swords, and heavy pieces of debris.

In his peripheral vision, Quince saw The Guide raising his thin arms to the sky as if conjuring a cloud. A powerful whirlwind took shape and began funneling above him wildly. From beneath the cloak, he saw a tail extend and unfurl. The Guide removed his hood and his face became misshapen and distorted. *The man was transforming in front of them!* The whirlwind above him still spinning, he hunched over with his arms still spread wide. Short tufts of fur peeked from beneath the cloak as he stood up on all fours. He was becoming a Sphinx! A few feet away Quince saw Dez's knees buckle before he fell to the ground hard. Without another thought, he and El ran toward Dez in a mad dash, releasing arrows as they ran.

The scene unfolded in slow motion. Seconds seemed like minutes as Dez's eyes grew wide from where he knelt. He struggled to rise from where he was, pointing frantically; he stumbled forward with his broadsword aimed at something behind him. Quince turned around just in time to witness the unthinkable. A bolt of lightning exploded just beyond El as he ran toward them. Behind him stood Dame, his sword lunging toward El's midsection. Seeing the warning in Dez's eyes, he spun around just as the sword split his torso.

The moment the deed had been done, Dame's eyes flickered from brown to purple and back again. The cyclone was in motion and moving in their direction. Quince's eyes moved from his brother's limp frame to Dame and back to the thing that was The Guide as he let out a gut-wrenching scream of horror. Quince felt a piece of his soul crumble to dust as he fell to his knees shooting arrows blindly into the swirling darkness. Meanwhile, the quick moving cyclone settled itself over Dame's towering frame. An earth-shattering quake tipped the seas as they all became immersed in the fervent current. Larger than life, Dame stood there with his arms outstretched. Quince blinked back tears and glanced back toward where The Guide had been standing. He was gone. The twisting cyclone soon became a purplish funnel glinting against lightening and now whirling rain.

Dame opened his mouth and almost swallowed his tongue whole. An indescribable vacuum sucked at his spirit, tugging mercilessly before it nearly collapsed his eardrums. The force of it all had momentarily suspended sound. Feebly, Quince put his hand to his cheeks. Fresh blood shone on his fingertips. The magnitude of the sound caused his ears to bleed. In an instant, the Ancestors disappeared and the fiery flames were extinguished by the power of the thundering rain.

"Retreat!" Quince screamed, collecting himself. The Elders were gaining power; it was evident. Quickly, he lifted El's body and threw him across his shoulders. In a chaotic mass of wind, rain, and hail they sloshed over the sea soaked beach, gathering as many of their dead as possible. Quince looked back over his shoulder as Dame stood with his arms still outstretched. For miles they ran through the inky blackness unaware of who'd survived and who hadn't. They'd lost the battle and quite possibly, the war.

A faint, glimmering light that could only be seen from the highest peak in the land flickered in the distance. Dusk was upon them as the sun dipped below the horizon. Crumpled lavender clouds spread themselves amply across an invisible line in the sky. A rumbling moan disturbed the pecking birds settled on the branches of wiry, leafless trees. They flew away in a frightened flock, their formation like the swooping hand of God descending upon the dank mountainside. Large beads of perspiration were pouring down her face and cheeks now. She was feverish, panting, and praying for the excruciating pain to stop.

"She needs more water!" shouted Vye through clenched teeth.

"It was all I could find," Quince replied in frustration. "We are in a mountain cave hundreds of feet above sea level. There is no water for miles. I collected as much as I possibly could! The banks of the Shine are too dangerous. If they see me I can be killed!" he said hotly as he paced around the small, humid cove.

"She is birthing a Merchild. She needs water! The child must not come into contact with air if it is to survive." Vye insisted from her spot above the panting woman.

Onya knelt inside a small basin full of thigh high water and held onto its rim with all her might. Her mind was spinning; the colors behind her eyes causing an inebriated blur. She felt drunk; drunk and disoriented. Had she not known exactly what was occurring, she would have sworn she'd been slipped a bad combination of palm wine and tainted herbs. Her knees buckled. The water sloshed, threatened to run over onto the cave floor had Quince not arrived in time to steady the basin. He held her waist loosely and poured a bit more water from his flask into the container.

"Don't," she wheezed. "We will need to drink that... later," she slurred.

"I will find more," he said. "The moment you deliver a healthy Merchild, I will set out for food and water."

She nodded then convulsed. Vye immediately wiped the sweat from her forehead and around the temples and base of her neck. "I'm fine," she stammered, not believing her own words. She felt like death itself was upon her. Her heartbeat was abnormal in her chest. Her nerves were shot.

How was she going to raise a Merchild miles from the sea? The Ancestors had been defeated and both she and Quince were excommunicated. Under the new regime, the mouth of the Shine could only be an option if she were still a member of the Cause. The Senate of Elders had determined that only the territories south of the Shine were fit for the habitation of Ido Youth. What was left of the Separatist Movement spent their days and nights on the run. The Elder controlled Youth camps could not be considered a safe option. The Senate had also declared that the Youth would never be elevated to Elder status due to their deception and decision to revolt.

Her lids half-closed, she peered at Vye as she soaked a small sponge and held it to her forehead. Thankful as she was for her assistance, she couldn't help but feel she'd only come with them out of pity. However, her own predicament wasn't much better. Now on the run from the wrath of Dame for several counts of treason, conspiracy, and murder, she'd chosen to stay with her eldest son and his pregnant preferred partner. In addition to this, Vye had been estranged from her newborn son. This coupled with El's death and their grisly defeat had all but broken her spirit entirely. Since the Youth Council's decision to excommunicate Onya and Quince, she'd done everything in her power to keep busy. Thankful though that the Council had ruled out the sentence of death, she sometimes wondered if their current existence were worse. Still, she knew that Onya needed her and though she had never been a mid-wife, she thought back to the deliveries of her four sons. She hummed the soon to be forgotten healing song of the Ancestors, wiped away Onya's tears, and attempted to fend off her own.

Onya's eyes welled with water when the pain began to swell and spread through her legs and abdomen. Memories of her life sped through her mind in black and white. The pain of her transformation. Flashes from a giggling childhood. The complexity of Bgongo. The firmness of Eyeno's teaching techniques. Awkward adolescence. Uncomfortable maturation. Then the images skyrocketed to the forefront of her mind in vivid color. The preparation for the Warming Ceremony. Locking eyes with Quince for the first time. The first Rite. The possibility that she'd lost him. A disillusioned giggle escaped when she thought of Eesha's art and ultimate sacrifice. She swayed gently, nearly losing balance as she thought of Lyn's betrayal. It had been her vote that had sealed their fate. El's courage and death struck her spirit along with the outcome of the final battle. In actuality, they'd all lost. The reading of the verdict sent shivers down her spine. Their friends had doomed them; her father, now possessed by the spirit of The Guide, had enslaved them.

Unsure of how much more she'd be able to manage, she moaned loudly. Quince grabbed hold of her wrist and stroked it soothingly. He nudged her soaked skin with his chin and whispered encouraging words in her ears.

"Soon. Soon it will all be over," he said quietly. "I love you," he whispered.

Onya gripped the edge of the tub again and groaned. A searing heat shot the length of her navel to her womb, engulfing her pelvic area. She was through wailing, all that was left to do was to breathe, deeply. Quince clutched her by the arms, coaxing her circular breaths. Vye continued to hum.

Outside, the cocks crowed and the creatures growled while the sun set behind a blue tinged glow. Onya gazed into Quince's eyes just before feeling the massive urge to push. Her head snapped back and another surge of pain traveled the length of her entire body. By the bluish light of the cave she wondered if love were really worth it. She wondered also if the feeling alone would be enough. Looking into his eyes, she suddenly doubted that it would.

Onya opened her eyes with a jolt as the rain strengthened on the roof of the main hut in West Nu. The perspiration above her brow glistened in the moonlight. Groggily, she gathered her thoughts, gradually shaking off the vivid nightmare. All around her, many of the remaining Cause members slept. They'd gathered in the village after the battle to regroup. Exhaustion caused them to sleep in shifts while small groups stood guard, readied for the imminent attack they knew would come.

She heard voices nearby as she shifted on the dirt floor. The whispers seemed to intensify now as she turned from her back to her side. There in the darkened corner stood Maal's massive frame along with Lyn, Dez and Quince. From where she lay, she noted the edginess of their body language and stood up groggily. She grimaced and peeked at the deep wound in her upper arm. The bleeding had finally stopped, but the pain still lingered beneath the leaves and pungent salves. As she approached the mild commotion, a spasm of alarm resonated in her spirit.

"They are enslaving the Painted Folk as we speak---" Quince began once she'd reached the gathered Cause members. "They put up a valiant fight, but we've received word that Gallah may have been captured."

Onya lowered her head and sighed. "What's the plan?"

"We're not sure of that just yet," replied Lyn slowly. "Our resources are strained... we lost so many," her voice shook though she appeared determined not to let the tears fall.

"We must continue to fight," interrupted Maal, his tone stony and even. "We must attempt to reach the Ancestors. Perhaps Born---"

"Born is gone! We all saw it with our very eyes. Let's just face the fact that we're on our own," Onya felt her voice crack before folding her arms across her chest.

"We must at least try," Quince said in a low whisper.

"We're heading to the shoreline, have faith in tradition," Dez said softly.

In a quick flourish Maal, Lyn, and Dez exited and she and Quince were left standing in the doorway of the hut. Onya turned to look at Quince, and when their eyes met, she knew at once that they were in for the fight of their lives.